To my wife and son.

And to my old friends who gathered
for a night of tabletops.

The characters and events portrayed in this book are fictitious. Any similarity to real persons, living or dead, is coincidental and not intended by the author.

ISBN-13: 978-0-578-30905-7

Edited by Erika Steeves.
Follow the author at lukeatkinsonwrites.com and on Instagram at @lukeatkinsonwrites.

Acknowledgement

I honor the Indigenous people who inhabited the land where my story takes place, including the Apache, Arapaho, Comanche, Kiowa, Osage and Wichita.

Shikoba's tale inspired by The Buffalo Go, a Kiowa tale recounted by Old Lady Horse in 1960.

CONTENTS

PROLOGUE

After years of robbing, shooting, looting, thieving, lying, cheating, and generally riding in defiance of the law, I'd finally crossed a line and done something that changed my wanted status from 'dead or alive' to just plain 'dead.'

I couldn't escape the publicity. Everywhere I went, there I was, my face posted on the side of some building, my crimes printed in the local newspaper, or folks gossiping about my misdeeds all the way from the church pew to the barstool. Word was the bounty on my head was the highest seen in a good, long while, meaning every two-bit tracker and part-time bounty hunter saw me as their ticket to riches.

I was living at the height of infamy.

Truthfully, I'm somewhat accustomed to being hunted by my fellow man. It goes with the territory of being me, Cal Cooper, a gunslinger operating in the disreputable and unsavory business of social banditry. I suppose I'm somewhat fairly persecuted for my penchant for the occasional illegal caper, but I'm not ashamed of it. In a country full of miscreants manipulating good folks with their 'rules' and 'laws,' being an outlaw was my role in the world and I performed it well. But I was on the run for something far bigger than a stick-up at a bank. This time, I was fleeing for my life, getting as far away as fast as I could with nothing but a fine steed named Buck, my trusty firearm, and a pair of broken shackles still hanging from my wrists. My pursuers weren't the usual foolhardy fellas who happened to see my bounty poster or cowboys plucked from their agrarian lives by the local sheriff. The men hunting me now were trained killers, soldiers skilled in the art of war.

A whole platoon of cavalry dragoons were hot on my heels after I'd broken out of their camp's makeshift brig. I was being unfairly held, and after a scuffle that involved some foul language and the discharge of firearms, I escaped. Less than a day later, the newspapers had a hold of the story and the marshals issued a statement: Bring me in dead, collect your payment, no questions asked.

The dragoons had been on my trail for days now, stalking me through the desert badlands as I escaped north to Utah. False trails and decoys didn't shake them, and covering my tracks didn't seem to do much either. But then again, I knew it wouldn't work. Not while they had a bona fide ranger along with them.

Not the kind of ranger from Texas, but the

kind with a number of supernatural tools at their disposal for hunting down prey.

I'd been awake for two days straight in an effort to stay ahead of my pursuers. Sleep deprivation was settling in, not to mention my existing thirst and hunger. I struggled to keep a grip on the reins as my gelding wobbled through the midnight desert of Arizona. Shadows of tall saguaro cacti danced on the dunes while the flower moon was full and incandescent, and hallucinations took the shape of ghosts from my past, watching me bobble along the trail. Those poor, wretched souls murmured rumors about me as I rode by. Rumors about how I used to ride with a purpose, contributing to the common good, only to become a dishonorable villain and a bully for hire. About how I was responsible for a massacre, running from my past instead of accepting my fate. They were wrong about me. Mostly.

Was I being paranoid? Indulging my imagination and the mirages it created? Perhaps. Given my knowledge of spellcraft, though, I reckoned that I'd been cursed with a hex. Most likely some kind of tracking spell. That was Marney's style, after all. When non-magical folk, like myself, come into contact with hexes and curses, well, the effects can really mess with your mind.

On the fourth day without food and sleep, I yelled at a buzzard for following me. It'd been circling me since dawn, staking its claim on my future corpse. I took out my revolver and aimed it high. Fancied pulling the trigger, too, but decided to save the bullet instead.

"I ain't dead yet, partner," I hollered into the empty wastes.

On day five, grand formations of towering stone replaced the sand and brush I was accustomed to. I was almost there. Two hours after I'd stopped at a spring to fill my canteen and let my horse drink, I came upon a familiar set of arches guarding a valley filled with rust-red boulders. Buck nibbled at the rope I used to tie him to a scraggly tree nearby while I clamored up a pile of boulders. The top rock settled up against the canyon wall, creating a little alcove that had been naturally excavated. The cubby hole was maybe two square feet in diameter. A perfect spot to hide treasure.

My partner and I had covered the hole behind a flat sheet of rock. It tumbled down the slope after I shoved it away, revealing soft soil the color of copper. I cupped my hands and frantically scooped out the dirt until a sharp corner of a metal container pricked my finger. I whooped and hollered as I hoisted my prize, a tin cigar box that held one thousand dollars. My fingers were stained red from the dirt and the trickle of blood, but I was too excited to worry about cleanliness. I found the biggest boulder near me and smashed the lock on the box. The clash of stone and metal echoed off the rocks surrounding me, a dead giveaway of my location to anyone within earshot. Time was too scarce to care about secrecy now. Those calvary boys could be less than a mile away.

The lid to the box bent open wide enough for me to force a few fingers inside. I rummaged around, feeling nothing but cold tin. My heart sank to the bottom of my chest.

It was empty. I stammered out some string of curses and shook the box furiously above my head. My old partner would never double-cross me like this, would she?

I fumed and crunched the box in my grip, then threw it down the slope and watched it roll until it stopped just shy of Buck. As it tumbled, a slip of paper fluttered out, flopping end over end as the wind swept it away.

"Wait!" I yelled, stumbling down the rocks. I tripped and landed hard on my chest, but managed to pluck the envelope from the wind's grasp. I flipped it over and inspected it. A letter and it was addressed to me.

Dear Cal,

I've told you for some time now that we are a dying breed. If we continue down the road we're on, we'll see ourselves hanged in the gallows of some god-awful, backwater town. I'm not willing to go out like that and I can't let you do that to yourself neither.

I bet you're awfully sore at seeing an empty box, but before you get all huffy, know I didn't be-

tray you and steal your share of the loot. I just borrowed it. Don't worry, I'll put it to good use.

If you're reading this, then you must be in some heap of trouble. In lieu of saying 'I told you so,' I offer you shelter in Hexed Springs, a city thirty miles east of the Black Mesa. I've decided I'm going there to start a new life with our money and, God willing, open the saloon I've always dreamed of.

Enclosed is enough cash for a train ticket that will bring you to a station not far from where I'm setting up shop. I know it ain't easy, but it's time to retire from the wicked lives we once lived. Come see me and we'll get you back on your feet.

Your old pal, Clem

True enough, inside the envelope were a few bucks for the train ticket. The flimsy bills crumpled in my grip.

"Dammit all," I hollered back to my horse. "Would you believe it? She's run off with my half of the loot. Five hundred dollars. There's supposed to be at least five hundred dollars in here."

I growled as I dusted myself off and slid down the rocks toward my horse.

"That money could have sent me anywhere in the world," I said, showing Buck the box and the letter. "I could have retired on a beach ten thousand miles away from here, drinking whiskey out of a coconut. Instead, I have an IOU. Think they take IOUs on ocean liners? And of all the no-good places in the world, she's sending me to No Man's Land to get it back. Can you believe the nerve?"

Buck didn't react. He didn't talk much after all.

I'm sure this was Clem's way of saving my skin, something she'd done more than once before, but I would have appreciated to make the decision of turning tail by myself. What was wrong with California? Oregon? Nobody ever wanted to go to No Man's Land.

That is, unless they're seeking refuge from the law, or they were forcibly relocated there by the no-good federal government.

No Man's Land certainly wasn't high on my list of places to hide out. But truth be told, it wasn't a bad idea. Wildfires didn't spread as fast as word of my misdeeds had. Then there was the fact that all manner of armed forces, public and private, were after me.

And once a ranger's on your trail, it ain't easy to shake them off. Especially not Marney. He wouldn't rest until I hanged. I knew how the man thought. After all, I was his apprentice for a time.

I tossed the box over my shoulder and pocketed the cash and letter. If Buck and I rode hard enough, we could make it to the nearest train station by sundown and hopefully keep enough distance between us and the cavalry. It would take a few days by train and on foot to reach Hexed Springs, which should be enough time for any tracking spells to wear off.

Looked like I had little choice in the matter. I was off to lay low in the most untamed, lawless, and paranormal place in America.

CHAPTER ONE

No Man's Land: A vast expanse of open prairie home to myths and legends, liars and thieves, and honest folks scratching out a humble existence on the plains. Some folks call it that because they say it's a wild land that no one can tame. Others say it's just a worthless stretch of land that Texas didn't want and no man needs.

For me, it was a temporary home, somewhere bandits like me could serve time in a self-imposed exile that didn't involve wasting away behind iron bars. Folks here don't worry about the law, for better or for worse, since the territory is unclaimed. Which is good news for me. I can wither away from boredom out here in peace. Beats the alternatives, I suppose.

The sun broke over the flat horizon and washed the earth in orange. Sunrises are impressive out here and I enjoyed it alone, as I had for the last two days. I hadn't seen or heard from another human being since then. It was just me and Buck. And he still didn't talk much.

I could tell Grandmother Earth was going to make me sweat today. It was only fifteen minutes after daybreak and the temperature was already oppressive. Sunlight glinted off the dewy grass and a cicada buzzed away in the distance. My eyes followed a little roadrunner as it darted through the brush, hot on the heels of a black-and-blue skink lizard for its breakfast. The chase made for decent entertainment as I downed the belly wash I called coffee. I'd been unemployed for the past few months, so I made the most out of the few grounds I had left, on account of being broke. As good as I was at scavenging for food, I'd never be able to rustle up coffee in the wilderness. Times like these, I wish I had an ounce of magical talent to conjure a good cup of joe.

I tossed out the coffee dregs from the tin cup and stashed it away in my gunny sack. Last night, I slept under the stars with a coil of rope around me to keep snakes away and a ring of salt to ward off any malevolent spirits. That's a handy trail tip I picked up from my ranger days, back when I was being harassed by a pixie hellbent on stealing my smokes.

Buck finished his breakfast, a fine selection of roughage and grains. Sometimes, he ate better than I did. He was a real bangtail, fiery of spirit and always itching to run, so he let me know how my morning routine was inconveniencing him by snorting and stomping his hooves.

"All right, all right, I'm coming," I said.

I leaned over to pat Buck's thick shoulder, then slung a saddle on his chestnut back, packed up my belongings, and kicked a healthy amount of dirt over the smoldering campfire before letting him loose on the trail.

I was about a full day's ride from Hexed Springs now, working my first honest job since arriving in No Man's Land. Bill Conway, a local rancher, hired me to hunt a monster that roamed this part of the wilderness. Given my skills in gunslinging and the years' worth of training in hunting the extramundane, I reckoned I'd make a decent-enough monster hunter.

About an hour after our morning departure, Buck and I approached a grove of trees at the bottom of a hill that sheltered a small pool of water. I left him to drink while I inspected the watering hole. Recent stormwater had drained down from an arroyo up the hillslope and pooled down in this basin. The creature had been here, just as I suspected. Sets of its footprints were pressed into the mud around the water's edge. Its paws were enormously wide, maybe two-foot across, round in the heel and spreading into four clawed toes. I placed my hand inside the miniature crater it left behind. Even with my fingers spread wide, I barely filled half of the imprint.

My eyes wandered, searching for more clues. The stalks of grass nearby were bent over and smeared like a trail of melted butter, probably from the monster dragging its belly on the ground. Paced out every few feet along the streak were more footprints, which crunched the brush in a sweeping circular motion, a pattern similar to how an alligator walks.

Whatever I was hunting was big. Really big. Big things can be scary but also tend to be slow. And anything slow is an easy target for me and Cloudsplitter, the name a druid from Tennessee had bestowed upon my revolver. As long as I didn't engage with the monster up close, where it was most dangerous, I'd be fine.

I dragged a finger across a slick of mud leading from the water. The sludge was still moist, leaving a fresh trail to explore. I whistled to Buck and he trotted over to me, his chin still dry.

"Water not good enough for you, buddy?" I said, scratching his chin. "You can lead a horse to water, but you can't make it drink. You're a walking stereotype, you know that?"

I gripped the saddle pommel and hoisted myself up, while Buck scrambled up the gentle slope to the hilltop. We were surrounded by native grasses, tall, amber stalks swaying in the wind like water in a stream that had no boundaries. Up ahead a crag of rock jutted diagonally into the sky, hanging over a gravelly trail that curled around its base. It would make a good vantage point for scouting out the monster's path.

I pulled a brass spyglass out of my saddlebags, one of the many tools I use on the trail.

I reckon it's one of the most important instruments I own. When I'm alone in the wilderness, I need to know who or what is out here with me—preferably before it finds me first.

From the top of the rock, I could see for miles. Most of my surroundings were flat, perfect for tracking. I traced my steps from the watering hole and followed the monster's trail as far as I could see, until it bent behind a cluster of blackjack oaks a couple miles ahead.

Noting the path's trajectory, I surveyed the rest of the area with my scope. In the distance were hills and trees and more flat land, a herd of bison here, a rolling tumbleweed there. Nothing else of interest, really. I lazily spun in a circle, nature darting across my vision, until my eyes landed on a black heron perched on a faraway branch.

And I swear it was looking at me.

I don't mean looking in my general direction, but actually aware of me. It clacked its golden beak a few times, spread its wings wide, and turned slowly to match my gaze. I felt like it was staring right into my soul. For a beautiful bird, it sure was creepy. The eeriness of it all sent a chill up my spine.

Buck snorted impatiently as I took my time observing the bird. The idea that I was being studied by a silly bird was ridiculous, and I laughed off my suspicions as I placed the spyglass back in the bag. We headed down the hill toward the monster's trail, galloping to a row of trees that hid a winding path into a grazing valley. Even though I hadn't fired my gun in some time, I was still confident in my gunslinging and monster-hunting and was in no rush to prove myself.

More cicadas joined in on their screeching song. Not even my whistling could drown them out. A hot, dry wind rustled the leaves of the grove as we approached. Buck's ears pricked up and he came to an abrupt stop. He'd heard something I hadn't. I got quiet and listened close to the land around me. Off in the distance came the wails of a heifer in distress, then a deep undulating growl.

I'd found my prey.

I kicked Buck into a hard run. The Morgan horse leaned into the wind, bolting through the trees and into an open patch of grassland. As we made the corner, I could see it—a humongous creature staring down an enraged bull.

Clad in scaly armor, a long, lizardlike creature had its claws dug into the earth and back arched toward the bull. The monster's golden eyes sharply contrasted with its mottled gray skin, which was rough and calloused. It was potbellied and had to have been at least twenty feet long from snout to tail. The closest combination of critters I could compare it to would be if a horned toad mated with an iguana and birthed something hewn from stone.

The black bull challenged the monster, scraping its hoof and scarring the ground beneath it. The rest of his herd swarmed and circled behind him in a frenzy. The bull twisted his head to provoke the monster further, his sharp horns drawing a figure eight in the air, then bucked his back legs and broke off into a dead sprint. The lizard monster clenched its clawed feet into the ground and curled up the front of its body, exposing its fat underbelly. Snout pointed toward the sky, the monster swelled its stomach as it took in a breath, belching out a ball of flame as it crashed back down to the ground. The blast sped across the open field and burst across the bull's face, blinding it. Nearly every cow in the herd was screaming now, even more panicked than before.

Buck stood his ground as the explosion took the bull head on. I could feel the uneasy tension grip his muscles. I had reacted the same way after witnessing my first dragon, or rather a lesser species of one. For all the courage my horse had, he also had the instinct to survive. Buck grunted nervously as the thundering herd took off up the ridge away from us. By now, the bull had broken away, bucking and twisting its body in vain as the fire engulfed his head. In his confusion, he swerved and bore straight toward us. The rest of the herd changed course to follow him, even though it put them within the dragon's reach. They scattered down the hill at full speed, fleeing in terror for their lives.

Buck and I were about to be trapped in a stampede.

Luckily, my horse knew just where to go. Buck careened around a bend near the tree line before the cattle could overtake us. Trees behind our backs, we were safe for a moment, with the cattle between us and the monster. I yanked my revolver from its holster and steadied my aim while balancing on the fidgety horse. I squinted shut my left eye, peered down the barrel, and lined up the sights. My chest inflated with a big, deep breath and my shoulders tensed. I waited for the perfect opportunity to blast the monster, but the herd of frenzied cattle made it nearly impossible to get a clean, lethal shot.

The monster charged into the herd and headbutted a decent-sized cow, sending it flying. It crashed into a group of frightened calves and brayed in fear as the beast bared its teeth. Its tongue hung out, pulsing like a dog panting in the summer shade. Instead of tearing into its meal, its golden eyes shifted to me and my horse. We must have been a more appetizing morsel because it bounded toward us, completely ignoring the helpless heifer struggling to return to her feet.

I was caught off guard by how quick the thing moved. The monster plowed through cows like a steam locomotive cutting through snow. Its hooked claws churned violently through the grassy patch of land, propelling it forward at a great speed, its head and tail held high to balance its hulking frame.

Buck didn't have much time to react as it closed in. We took off in a flash, and it didn't take long for my gelding to create a distance between us and the beast. The rumble of hooves and bellowing cattle faded into the distance. Then a different sound, one that would be awfully familiar to anyone that has spent time on a ranch. That same whooshing sound, the way air whips around a spinning lasso, echoed behind us. Buck lurched forward and screamed, throwing me into the tree line. As I tumbled down into a ravine tucked away behind the trees, I bounced across rough roots and trunks, smacking my head on a clod of clay. I didn't stop until I landed face first in a shin-deep creek of running water.

Water began filling my nostrils and my head buzzed. I couldn't move my limbs. I laid there, panic gripping my burning lungs as water rushed past my ears. With the last of my air, I heaved my torso out of the creek, drawing in a deep breath. As sensation flooded back, all I could do was sit there and listen to the horrors coming from above.

Buck's wailing was silenced by a sickening crunch. My blood froze and my heart plunged into my stomach. I slammed my fists into the water and hollered.

The monster, drawn to my fury, poked its head through the tree line, those long claws curling around the soft clay wall. Its plump, pink tongue lolled out of its mouth as its gluttonous stare poured over me. I reached for my gun and lined up the iron sights over the bumpy scales right in the center of its skull. But I was too shaky to get off a shot. As I fidgeted with my revolver, the monster croaked, cracking loose its fleshy whip with lightning speed. It coiled around my shooting arm, from wrist to elbow, and pulled my arm in the air. I fired and hit nothing but sky. A heartbeat later, it yanked me out of the ravine and dangled me above its blood-stained mouth, the size of a deep cast-iron kettle. The smell of blood and raw meat was so strong I could taste copper, and I nearly vomited.

By now, my options for escaping with my life had dwindled down to next to nothing, and I couldn't stop panicking long enough to make a plan. I tried twisting my free arm to grab the serrated knife I kept on my hip. It took me three tries to grip the rough antler-bone handle. It sang out as I jerked it free and swiped furiously at the dragon's tongue, but all I did was bob up and down like a worm on a hook. The monster, finally done playing with its food, swallowed me whole.

Everything went dark as the monster snapped shut its massive jaws. Warm cheek meat hugged me tight while saliva soaked into my clothes. I couldn't tell which way was up, but I still held onto my weapons. I dragged my blade every which way, flailing my arms until I connected with throat flesh. The monster shrieked and coiled its tongue tighter around me.

I struggled hard and managed to free my shooting arm, but my wrist was turned in such a way that I might end up shooting myself. While I squeezed my hand through a tight gap of cheek and tongue, I saw a light down the monster's throat. It was getting brighter. And hotter.

The soles of my boots were getting toasty, and the smell of burning fur and leather wafted up around me. The putrid aroma belonged to my saddle and the smorgasbord of furry chunks of flesh burning inside the monster's belly.

I was about to be cooked alive.

I growled and worked faster at turning the barrel of my revolver away from my face. Just as my toes began to feel the heat, I got free and aimed at the dragon's now-illuminated uvula. I howled as I fired every last bullet in the chamber, feeling the spray of moist flesh burst around me with each blast. On my final shot, the tongue went slack and the light growing inside the beast dimmed back to darkness.

I blew out a shaky breath as my heart thumped against my ribs. I had survived. Barely.

A death rattle gurgled up from the monster's gut, soured with the smell of burnt hair and boiled blood. I choked back my breakfast as I quickly groped around for a way out. One of the dragon's tusks made for a good hand hold, allowing me to lift myself back out into the sunlight. My clothes were soaked through and slick with slimy saliva. I flung globs of it from my face. My old shirt was charred, and the skin of my forearm was raw from where the creature's tongue had lashed me.

Even though I was still alive, this was no victory. This was a total disaster, a loss by any real ranger's standards.

The dragon had carried me out of the ravine and back into the field near the dead bull. Out of the corner of my eye, I glimpsed Buck's outline laying still on the ground. I couldn't bring myself to look at him. He was a great horse. I didn't want to spoil my memory of him by burning the image of his half-eaten corpse into my mind.

The adrenaline coursing through my veins deepened the hollow cavity growing in my chest. Not only had I lost my fine steed, but I'd lost a friend. And now all my possessions were incinerated in a stew of stomach fluid. No spyglass, no saddle, no canteen, no rope. All I had left were my knife, my gun, and the singed shirt on my back.

I sighed, placed my hands on my hips, and took a good look around. The herd was long gone now, save for a few cattle that had been trampled to death in the stampede. Not far off behind me lay the smoldering corpse of the bull. Smoke still fluttered from its hide. I steeled myself before inspecting the poor animal. The front half was charred and roasted, whereas the back end still had its fur. The Conway brand was burned into its hind flank. It was one of Bill's, all right.

"You better be worth the bounty, you ugly son of a bitch," I growled at the dead monster.

I couldn't just leave the dragon in the wilderness. Scavengers or buzzards might pick it clean before I got the chance to show Bill and collect my due. Without a horse, though, it was going to be awfully hard transporting it.

Wind whipped past me as I gazed into the distance, waiting for a good idea to come to me. A particularly strong gust rushed by, jingling a brass bell tied around the bull's thick neck. I craned my neck and found a thick piece of rope that was, miraculously, only slightly burned by the dragonfire. It was barely long enough for what I needed, but it would do. I tied the length of rope around the monster's hind legs and cinched it up with a rough knot. I kicked it in the head with the last of my energy. That one's for Buck.

Come hell or high water, I was dragging this bastard all the way back to town.

CHAPTER TWO

I crashed through the saloon's swinging double doors looking like a madman, parched and out of breath. My shadow stretched out long and tall before me in the late afternoon sun, reaching all the way to the bartop. A sea of faces cloaked in cigar smoke shot ugly glances my way. I paid them no mind and marched up to the bartender, my spurs jingling with every step, the dragon's carcass slung over my shoulder.

It's not every day that townsfolk around here see a gruesome monster. Most monsters don't wander very close to human civilization, even in No Man's Land. The sight of dead lizard's lifeless body made every last jaw in the place drop. The poker players stopped dealing, the piano man quit mid-chord, and a waitress gasped in fright. A hush fell over the typically lively joint until the familiar, smoky voice of my dear old partner, Clementine McGillicutty, cut through the silence.

"Calamity Cooper, just what the hell is that

thing and why are you dragging it into my saloon?" Clem hollered from behind the bar.

I didn't answer, just gave her a look and a grunt. After a couple days of dragging this heavy load under the sun and across the wilderness, I couldn't think straight and the words wouldn't come to me, anyhow. My clothes were tattered, red dirt covered me head to toe, and cottony foam gathered at the corners of my mouth. I don't know which was more shocking, my raggedy, near-death appearance or the monster I'd just hauled in.

I gestured urgently for a drink as words sputtered through my cracked lips.

"W-w-w," I croaked.

Clem snatched up a silver pitcher and poured me a glass of water. I growled and pushed it aside, reached behind the counter, and yanked out a bottle of brown liquid. She let out an exasperated sigh and rolled her eyes as I downed a gulp.

"Whiskey. I was asking for whiskey," I said after exhaling a quenched sigh of relief. I chased the shot with the glass of water and gave her a look that meant *keep it coming*.

My captive audience was so quiet I reckoned I'd find livelier conversations in an undertaker's parlor. Not even crickets dared to chirp.

"Cornelius, if you ain't playing, I ain't paying," Clem shouted across the room. "And the rest of you, get back to your cups and cards or find a duller place to drink. I don't remember charging admission for you to see a freak show today."

Cornelius, the portly piano man, whipped around anxiously and began tapping out a lively tune, and the drinking crowd of card sharks, diners, and lowlifes hastily issued their apologies to Miss Clementine.

Clem was a tough, no-nonsense gal whose establishment, the Howling Beast Saloon & Inn, had become the finest and most notorious place to wet your whistle in Hexed Springs. Luxurious wasn't a word you'd use to describe much of the town, but Clem's establishment was the closest thing to it. Truth be told, it really was a nice place. A crystal chandelier hung from the ceiling and the walls were lined with a patterned maroon wallpaper. Fine art from our bank heist days adorned the walls. Clem even served her drinks in real glasses, not those crummy tin cups you get in other small-town bars. She maintained an inn upstairs, too. Her rooms were cozy and comfortable, with real feather beds and a chest for safely storing your belongings. Her finest amenity was the washroom, complete with fragrant soaps and claw-foot tubs carved out of real ivory. You could hire one of her pretty girls to scrub you down, among other titillating services, all starting at the cost of a dime.

Clem's heavy pours downstairs gave her saloon the reputation of being the best bang for your buck. Plus, most of the menfolk fancied her, even though she wasn't interested in any of the men in town. Fellas tipped their hats to her, stood when she approached, and dared not tread on her last nerve. I was one of those fellas, too, but I could usually get away with a few antics, on account of our long friendship.

Or what was left of it, after we had a falling out over the money she'd 'borrowed' and couldn't yet repay.

I glanced over tonight's crowd. The regular local barflies—some normal, some paranormal—turned away when I met their eyes. A lot of new faces were gathered around the tables today, probably from the recent influx of new humans moving in. Hexed Springs had become something of a mortal boomtown as of late, displacing a lot of the folks who'd lived here first. I didn't know why the town had become so popular, but I didn't care for these 'settlers' and their disregard for the customs of the West. Neither did the native extramundane, the ones here before the government passed a law forcing the relocation of American Indians and magical species. Clem said many of the elves and other magical folk up and disappeared around the time these changes started happening. No one knows where they went.

The new humans coming in were soft, sometimes obscenely wealthy, and bought up land all around the area. Some of them represented corporations looking to tear up the land for a profit. Folks back east didn't care about the people out here, but they sure loved to read romanticized accounts of the Wild West. As a washed-up outlaw and gunslinger, I felt like someone's travel souvenir, or an animal in a zoo.

My scowl cleared the barstools around me. I wasn't in the mood to entertain questions about my kill, which I made sure everyone in the room understood, so they'd leave me to my whiskey.

Once the saloon had returned to its regular state, Clem shifted her gaze to me, ready to give me an earful.

"Evening, Cal. Haven't seen your face around here for a while. Now that you've quenched your dying thirst, can you tell me what on God's green earth possessed you to drag whatever this nasty-ass thing is across my clean floor?"

"This? I truly have no idea what this is," I said, nodding down at it. "Might be an inferior breed of dragon. All I know is it can breathe fire and use its tongue like a whip. It's been terrorizing Bill Conway's cattle herd, so he hired me to put it down."

Clem scrunched up her face in disbelief and leaned over the bar to get a better look. She grimaced as I pointed out its unsightly features, explaining them to her like a nimrod explaining calculus.

"Never seen anything like it before," she said.

I shook my head. "Me neither. And I've been around more than a handful of magic beasts."

As I was telling Clem my story about the hunt, there was pitter-patter of paws underneath my barstool. Angus, Clem's little dog, emerged from behind the counter. She was awfully fond of animals. The gentlemanly Boston terrier was her loyal companion and kept her company throughout the day's service. This little fella was the inspiration for the name of the Howling Beast Saloon, although I've never seen him howl, nor would I describe him as a beast. The old, snaggle-toothed pup had waddled out from his makeshift den and gave the scaly creature a good sniff.

"Angus, leave it," Clem snapped.

The little dog yelped and scurried back to safety as a gas bubble escaped from the beast's bloated gut. It had started to decompose a little, especially in a spot where a vulture had pecked off a few scales while I wasn't looking.

Angus's frightened retreat attracted the attention of a man eavesdropping from a dark corner a few seats away. I caught him glaring at me with wolfish eyes hiding behind a scrubby hairdo and sideburns that buried his ears. He stumbled out of his seat and wandered up close enough for me to smell the booze seeping through his yellowed teeth.

"Quite a prize there, ranger," he said with a thick Scottish accent. The neck of his bottle poked at me as he spoke. He slurred his words and had trouble focusing on my face. It took me a second to recognize him. His name was Colin, a werewolf and known troublemaker. He was laying low in town, too.

"Why don't you sit down, partner, pretend you don't know me, and mind that beer of yours before you spill it," I said. I got a real low tolerance when it comes to dealing with fools, not to mention drunken ones.

"Colin, don't start nothing," Clem said.

"I wouldn't dream of starting nothing," the furry man said with a high-pitched tone of innocence. He threw his hands up, stumbling from the sudden movement. "Wouldn't be smart of me to go against one of Willoby's inquisitors, would it, Miss Clem?"

I dropped my head low and let out a deep sigh into my whiskey glass. Willoby was a slimy political appointee who rubbed shoulders with the rich and powerful. I wasn't expecting to hear his name around here. Some say he was the architect of the Mortal Preservation Act, a law fashioned after the Indian Removal Act, an equally cruel piece of legislation that gave the government the right to commit genocide and forcefully relocate its 'undesirables' to remote locations, like Hexed Springs. Hanging outlaws and the extramundane had become his favorite hobby, one that earned him a great number of kickbacks. It was a well-known secret that he was itching for No Man's Land to earn statehood, so he could clean house and become the savior of the West with his hired gang of inquisitors, former rangers, and ruthless men who uprooted and displaced extramundane beings. He didn't believe in quarter or clemency and reveled in the power granted to him.

"Let's make a couple things clear," Clem said. "First, no one in this town can call me Clem. It's either Miss Clementine or ma'am. Second, Cal ain't an inquisitor and I'm not going to let you accuse him of being a government man."

"That ain't what I heard," Colin said, scratching at his porkchop sideburns. "Cal Cooper, wanted outlaw? I heard he cut a deal for his life with the cavalry before making his way out here."

I set my glass down hard, sending a shiver through the bartop. "Listen, partner. I've had a rough couple of days. I'm somewhat worn out, if you can't tell. Fact of the matter is, I'm just here to wet my whistle before I go along my merry way—"

"Cal," Clem interjected.

"—but if you continue to irritate me," I said, clenching my fists until my knuckles popped, "well, I might just have to add a mangy dog to my growing taxidermy collection."

The hairs on Colin's jaw bristled as his cheeks flushed red. He spilled out of his seat in a huff and charged at me, rearing back a hairy fist. Before he could throw a single punch, Clem whisked around the bar and caught him by the suspenders, yanking him so hard I thought she was going to snap his neck. To my amazement, she dragged a man twice her size from his stool and tossed him out on the street, all while giving him hell for trying to fight inside her saloon.

Colin dusted himself off and shouted back through the saloon doors.

"This whole town's gonna come gunning for you, boyo. Just you wait and see. I cannae wait until they discover who you really are," he yelled before stomping out of sight.

The atmosphere in the bar turned sour again. But since they'd already been told once to mind their own business, the patrons concealed any overt reaction to the scene. After all, you didn't want to find out what being scolded a second time was like. Even Cornelius barely missed a beat in the tune this time.

Clem stopped by the monster on her way back inside and peeled open one of its eyelids. Its eyeball rolled down and settled at the bottom of its socket, causing her to gag.

"So, what, are you some kind of monster hunter now?" she asked.

"Something like that. Hexed Springs doesn't have a ranger, so I reckoned I'd fill the role myself."

Clem cackled then stopped. "Wait, you're serious?"

"Sure, I am. You told me to find honest work, and this here is honest work."

"Misery me, Cal, 'honest work' means being a ranch hand, store clerk, something simple that lets you maintain a low profile."

"Well, I tried all that and didn't like it," I said, throwing my hands in the air. "You know I'm not one to work indoors. It's too boring. And you couldn't pay me enough to scoop horse shit for a living."

"So you decided to be a gun for hire hunting supernatural critters in a town known to be home to extramundane beings? No wonder Colin thinks you're trouble."

"I'm nothing at all like those bastards in the cavalry," I snapped.

Clem raised her eyebrows at my unusually sharp tone.

I softened up a bit and asked for her forgiveness with a small nod. "These new inquisitors and rangers from the old days aren't anything alike. Besides, all I'm good at is gunslinging and acting tough. You know that. I gotta make money somehow, especially on account of you blowing my half of the loot on this place."

"I told you, Cal," Clem said, thrusting her hands on her hips, "I've got to pay this loan off. When I do, I'll get you your money."

"That'll be the day, won't it?"

Clem smiled and leaned in closer. "You know, I could always count up the days you slept here, the meals you ate, the time spent with my girls. Toss your bar tab on top of that and we may just come out even."

"Fine, fine, you've made your point," I said, shaking my empty glass.

"I don't think I have," she said, topping it off with water. "You talk about money a lot, but I think you're looking for something else. I think you're trying to find your pride or some purpose in your little life since you can't afford to stir trouble no more."

"Be easier if you'd release me from my promise to go straight and just let me be me," I sighed.

Clem shook her head. "Cal, I—"

"Look, I don't want to talk about it." I kept my gaze down. "I don't know what I'm feeling, and I don't feel like having my head examined today." I paused, suddenly heavy with self-pity.

Clem wandered off to say something to one of her girls. When she came back, she leaned on her cash register and sighed. We'd spun this circle before. "I admit, your grotesque abomination is rather interesting, but I'd rather you not be bringing your work round here anymore. You're going to scare off my clientele."

"Cut me some slack, Clem. After the past few days I've had, I'm lucky to have staggered in here at all. I dragged this overgrown toad for miles in the summer heat, just so I could present it to Bill for proof and payment. No way am I letting it out of my sight."

"All right, but why bring it here? Why not take it to Bill's ranch directly?"

"Turns out I was closer to your saloon than I was to Bill's homestead," I said. "If I had to haul this thing in with my own two hands, I was going to at least save myself some effort."

"With your own two—?" Clem looked out the window at the hitching post outside. "Hold on, where's your horse?"

I pointed to the belly of the monster.

She groaned and palmed her face. "Good god, Cal. You've gone and got your horse killed?"

"I didn't *get* it killed. Not on purpose, at least." My protest came straight from my guilty heart. "This thing was faster than I expected, and that tongue whipped out at the speed of a bullet. It even had me inside its belly before I killed it."

"Lord above, you dummy. Don't you know? Monsters out here ain't like they are way out West. They're much stronger and stranger than anything else beyond the Black Mesa. Maybe you should have taken that into consideration before choosing your new career."

She used air quotes with the word 'career.'

I crossed my arms and huffed. "Yeah, well, thanks for the heads up."

"If you'd have read the newspaper," Clem

said, tapping a newspaper someone had left on the bar, "where normal folks like to post help-wanted ads, you'd have seen here that Ross Strickland's looking to hire men like yourself for a security detail. Maybe he'd find some value in your shooting skills."

I wrinkled my nose. "That city-slicker? He's in Hexed Springs? No way. I'll never work for somebody like him. I may have been dishonest once upon a time, but I was never as rotten as one of those big-wig financiers."

"You're telling me you'd turn down an honest paycheck in favor of endangering yourself by hunting puffed-up, wild critters?"

"Absolutely," I snarled. I was agitated by her willingness to trap me in a life indentured to some awful miser. "Trust me, my business is about to pick up. I have a gut feeling I'm about to rake in the dough with my revolver here pretty soon."

"You having one of your visions again?" Clem asked with a giggle.

"For the record, I am. Call me a fool or a superstitious man, but I think they're premonitions."

"Or delusions of grandeur," Clem muttered. "For your impoverished sake, I hope your little fairy tale comes true. If being the town ranger is your true calling, maybe you can better prepare yourself, lest you end up the one digesting inside the gut of some ungodly creature."

"You know, maybe I'd do better with a partner. What about Anne Red, the legendary sharpshooter? Could I peel her away from life as an innkeeper?" I said with a wink.

Clem wasn't amused. She rode under the pseudonym of Anne Red in our outlaw days, which was her middle name plus her most distinguishing feature, that thick red hair with a streak of silver that flowed out from underneath her riding hat. When she wasn't masking her appearance beneath a bandit's bandana, you could see faint freckles scattered across her sharp nose, accentuated by emerald-green eyes. Despite her prickly personality, Clem was a looker, a real Venus de Milo.

Nowadays, her hair was a little less fiery, more of a deep auburn, but the rest of her stunning features remained. Clem had traded in her chaps for an apron after nearly taking a bullet to the head, once upon a time. It had clipped the brim of her hat and sent it flying. I had watched as the sudden realization spread across her face. Outlaw life simply wasn't worth it anymore. She'd been talking of retiring, and that brush with death made the decision for her.

It wasn't hard for her to give it up and try something new. She was a versatile gal. The same couldn't be said about me, though. I was stubborn, grouchy, and had been happily set in my roguish ways.

Her hat, beautifully decorated with a bullet hole and an emu feather stuck in the band, hung behind the bar along with her bronze-scoped, custom Winchester repeating rifle. Together they were like a gunslinger's coat of arms. She told me it was a warning to those looking to cause trouble in her bar, but I imagined it was a trinket to help her remember the adventures she'd had as one of the Wild West's fiercest women.

She hushed me with a stern look, then took up a dishrag and started aggressively cleaning a spot on the bar. She'd use a little extra elbow grease in whatever she was doing while I was around. Must have been a coping mechanism for how often I got on her nerves.

"I've put those days behind me, Cal. Maybe you haven't figured it out, but the age of the gunslinger has come to pass and the smarter of us traded our weapons for simple, honest living. I run a saloon with Angus now, and I have no intention of taking up arms with you against man nor beast," she said.

"Come on, I wasn't that bad of a partner, was I? And gunslingers do too have a place in this world. I mean, Bill Conway must have heard about my legendary skill with a six-shooter and put me to work."

"Bill Conway hired you because I caught wind of his failing ranch sob story and wrote to him, asking him to throw you a bone. Didn't realize it was going to lead to this," Clem said, gesturing at the monster. She paused and took a deep breath. After a moment, she placed her hand on top of mine. "Cal, you've lost a horse, you're broke, and you were nearly killed. Being a lone monster hunter ain't practical and it sure ain't cheap, not to mention deadly."

"You think the paranormals in town really want to take their vengeance out on me?"

She gestured toward the door and exhaled sharply. "If what Colin says is true. Maybe this monster wasn't an intelligent being like we are, but it's supernatural like them, you know. Please, Cal. Won't you make something of yourself some other way?"

I sighed and shook my head. "Clem, I can't change. I am who I am. You know that."

"Well, then, you're gonna have to watch as the rest of the world leaves you behind. Either you move on or become a relic of the old days," she said with a stern shrug.

I hung my head and didn't say anything for a little while. Losing my horse really did eat me up inside, not to mention that I was out of my league in this business. Clem wanted the best for me, sure, but she's a practical person. My decisions had never made much sense to her. Where my mind gets made up in the moment, Clem needs a methodical plan to lay out her options.

My stomach churned at the thought that I'd been mistaken for one of those hired government killers, an inquisitor. My father had told me stories about my grandfather, who'd supposedly been a ranger. He rode across the plains, mingling with both mortals and immortals, using his wits and his revolver like one of those heroes who saves the day and rides off into the sunset, the kind you read about in pulp novels. The man stood for a code of honor, loyalty, and justice, righting social wrongs and the like. It used to inspire me. Nowadays, the feds had corrupted rangers into something horrible and vicious, changing their name to 'inquisitors,' so they'd evoke terror.

I decided to change the subject before I got too deep into my regrets. Clem wasn't pulling punches today, and I was already burdened with enough disappointment and frustration as it was. She cared for me, I knew that, but sometimes her honesty hit below the belt. A weight grew in my chest as I admitted to myself that I wasn't as successful in my post-marauder ventures as Clem had been with hers.

"Now that we've thoroughly dragged my confidence through the mud, let's talk about you, Clem. How's business been?" I asked.

"Folks in Hexed Springs are mighty thirsty lately. I swear, they'll even drink the dregs from the bottom of the barrel," Clem said as she rang up a customer. The whole time we'd been talking, she'd been working. "I get a few roosters in here now and then, taking to fighting and cursing, but they scare straight once I get after them.

As for the rooms, they're still full up, what with the workers, settlers, and extramundane coming in." Clem flipped over a bottle of gin and topped off three glasses without spilling a drop. Didn't even need to take her eyes off me while she was talking.

But when she slid the drinks down the bar, one of them skipped on the wood and sent the other glasses crashing to the floor. Clem wrapped her fingers around the back of her neck and blew out a breath to whip back a few strands of silver hair that had fallen out of place.

"To tell you the truth, I'm stretched thin, Cal," she said. Some of the weariness hiding behind those green eyes was beginning to show.

"Business is that good, huh? Most proprietors would call being too busy a good thing."

Clem stuffed shards of glass into her apron. I knelt down and gave her a hand.

"I'm just short-handed with the never-ending stream of new customers. One of my best girls ran off without telling me. She was good at keeping the customers drinking. Even took over the barback for me sometimes," she said.

"Did she run off or did you scare her away with that temper of yours?"

"Oh, please. I save all my outbursts for you, dummy," she said with a wink. "I know it's not uncommon for working girls to come and go, but not for mine. I make sure they're safe and paid well. They tend to be loyal and stick around."

"Well, who was it that ran off?" I asked.

"The one I least expected to. Rose disappeared a few days ago, about the time you'd left for your hunt. Last time I saw her, she was talking with that Montague fella. The one you met your first night in town. I reckon if she's in his favor, she doesn't need to work ever again. Man pays well and has a soft spot for human girls."

Rose took off with a vampire? That was disappointing. And disconcerting.

The Montagues were one of those socialite families that secretly ran the town, what with their riches and influence. Probably didn't hurt being immortals, capable of devouring humans, but most folks regarded them with an uneasy respect, given their proclivity to philanthropic endeavors around town.

Rose was a nice gal, so full of life, one of the few people besides Clem willing to give me the time of day. I liked the way she tied up her hair and enjoyed how her perfume lingered in the air. Her dark lipstick and olive skin could give any man butterflies in his stomach. She was fond of horses, too, and she liked Buck a lot. We got along grand.

We'd once gone out for a late evening stroll, just before she started a shift at Clem's, and we talked about our messy lives. We were both orphans, both had lived on the other side of the law. She talked about her dreams of running away and finding herself a proper adventure, somewhere far away from here. And I discovered a certain comfort in being around her. It felt like there were other people in the world like me after all, that I wasn't alone in this place.

I'd hoped we were friends enough that I could at least get a goodbye.

"She was probably just kind to me because she's paid to be nice to men," I said.

Clem huffed, a look of hurt and pity in her eyes. "You know that ain't true."

I feigned indifference. "Doesn't seem safe to run off with a vampire. You want me to track her down for you?"

Clem picked up on my disappointment and squeezed my arm. "I don't want you getting mixed up in vampire business, Mr. Ranger. Underneath all their fancy parties and fundraisers lies something sinister, believe you me. It's far too dangerous, even for a monster hunter like yourself. Besides, we both know you couldn't track an elephant in the snow."

I scoffed. "That's pretty funny, Clem. I've always thought you should tell jokes, as clever as you are. Maybe set that dog of yours on your lap and make it talk like a ventriloquist dummy."

"I didn't think you understood jokes, seeing how you've got nothing under that hat but hair."

I rolled my eyes and set down my glass. "All right, you win. Top me off one last time and I'll head out. I need to wire Bill for my money and let him worry about what to do with this damn thing. Unless you prefer I leave it here, that is. You could cook up a mess of frog's legs for Angus."

The little dog didn't react and stared at me with wandering, buggy eyes.

"Angus says leave the jokes to us. Now, I love you, Cal, but get the hell out and take that thing with you," she said, extending an open palm toward me.

Guess the whiskey wasn't free.

I patted my pockets and frowned. I honestly didn't have anything but the cost of the telegram to Bill.

Clem sighed again. She was good at it, seeing as she had to do it so much around me. "You know, for someone so concerned with money, it's odd that you sure don't mind depriving me of mine."

"Sorry, Clem," I said as I grabbed the monster by the tail. "I'll just have to owe you one."

"You already owe me more than one, Cal Cooper," she said. "And don't go poking around trouble. A mortal man's got no business with those vampires. Leave well enough alone. I'm serious."

I tipped my hat to her and scowled my way back through the crowd. The bar patrons watched me go with eyes as wide as saucers. I was too lost in my own thoughts to care, though. I came to Clem's looking for consolation, reassurance, anything to help me make sense of the past seven months and give me direction in this strange, new world. Sadly, I didn't find any comfort in the whiskey. Or in a conversation with my old friend.

I squeezed the fat lizard through the saloon doors once more, reminiscing about how the feel of well-earned cash used to ease my conscience. It was time to go collect my happiness from the rancher who owed me money.

CHAPTER THREE

I entered the August heat once more, bound for the telegraph office and the adjacent stagecoach freight yard. It would make a good hiding place for the dead monster until Bill could come look it over. The man had supposedly lived in No Man's Land his entire life, but dragons weren't common to North America, at least not anymore. Would he even believe me if I told him what I'd killed over a telegram?

I trod down the dusty avenue, barely rejuvenated by Clem's refreshments. My hands ached and my grip on the rope was weakening. The rope had started to fray in a few spots that bore the brunt of the beast's weight.

It didn't take long for a heavy sweat to build up on my brow as I crossed into the newer part of town. On days like this, if you didn't need to be outside, you weren't. If you were wealthy enough, you'd drop some cash and get yourself an ice box. Otherwise, you just suffered in sweaty silence. Me? I knew the best thing to do was settle down and do what the vaqueros do: take a siesta. I had hoped to arrive under the cover of night to avoid rubberneckers, not to mention more sunburns, but like the other parts of this particular job, it didn't work out exactly as planned.

Despite the sweltering temperature, there were plenty of people outdoors. Folks here were adept at coping with the sun's intense rays. It's just a part of life in No Man's Land. Working men rolled up their cotton shirtsleeves and dabbed their foreheads with handkerchiefs while complaining about the weather. Fancy ladies whipped hand fans back and forth as their gal pals tidied up their wilting hairdos. The farm girls wore loose dresses that flowed in the wind, and they covered their heads with pretty bonnets to keep cool. Then there was Amos, the local beggar who seemed to be missing a few screws. He dunked his head in a dirty horse trough and let the water trickle from his soaked cap down his scraggly beard.

And like the folks inside the saloon, every one of them was now staring directly at me. This part of town, full of city folks, probably have never seen a monster before. The homes and shops practically still smelled of fresh lumber they were so new.

One fella took his eyes off the road long enough to drive his spooked cattle into a cart of vegetables. The cart's owner was too dumbstruck himself to even notice the heads of cabbage rolling off into the dirt. A little boy ran up to poke my monster with a stick, but his mother swooped in and pulled him away. A young lady shrieked, her basket of dry goods spilling its contents on the wooden walkway, and she fainted into the arms of the man next to her. He'd been loudly explaining to the fella next to him that he'd seen me and the dragon in a carnival up in Dodge City last year.

Yep, so much for a quiet entrance. At least, I'd earned plenty of free advertising for my business as a ranger, right? Silver linings and all that, I told myself.

The young man running the telegraph office that afternoon also fell into a stupor as I approached his outpost. I slapped a coin on the counter, which snapped him out of it. I smirked at his ill-fitting, baby blue outfit. It made him look like a French soldier got his laundry mixed up with that of a train conductor.

"H-H-How can I help you?" the boy said, tucking the coins away. He kept stealing glances at the monster.

"I need to send a message to the outpost down by Conway Ranch. The recipient is expecting it. Just write: 'Back in HS.' Stop. 'Killed your creature.' Stop. 'Bring payment plus extra for incidentals. Cal.' Stop. You get all that?"

The boy nodded, never taking his eyes off the dragon. He couldn't have been more than fourteen, judging by his quivering voice and the hairs on his upper lip.

"Come on, son, I'm in a hurry," I said.

The boy stammered my message back to me and I told him to send it. Then he fumbled around in a drawer and pulled out a book with Morse Code translations, apologizing for not having them memorized already.

"You new at this or something?" I asked.

The boy looked at me with defeated eyes. As he lowered his head, I noticed scars on the tops of his ears. I winced. I was familiar with people who had scars like that.

"You're an elf, huh?" I asked gently. "Hold on, do I know you?"

The boy's eyes grew wide as he tensed up. "No, sir, I'm not. And I don't believe so."

"It's all right, son. I'm a friend to your people. I remember you from the wagon train to Hexed Springs," I said. I didn't tell him exactly how I remembered. It would have sparked some unpleasant memories for him.

Truth was, I had camped out on the convoy's flank near where the elves had settled for the night. A few of the elders sat around a fire playing a drowsy, forlorn tune on their stringed instruments. Their songs drowned out the screams of elven children whose ear tips were being cropped off. Passing for human wasn't a choice anymore for some extramundane—their survival depended on it. For elves it meant disfiguration.

Even though No Man's Land was the legally designated home for both American Indians and the extramundane, mortal human white folks weren't too fond of them. People do two things when they encounter something different: they get mad or get scared. Usually both. And now that there were far more humans than extramundane, they had to hide or conform in order to avoid becoming targets of prejudiced humans. The extramundane were running out of places to live, even before the government's edict forbidding them from inhabiting the states and outlawing their magic altogether.

I showed the boy my empty right hand, palm out and fingers stretched to the sun. It wasn't only a disarming gesture. It was a greeting. The open hand was a sign of the sunrise, a sacred time honored by the desert elves. "I used to be called Calam'avalar," I said.

"Avalar, a guardian who is human. Your name is Calam?" he asked, relaxing a bit.

"Close enough. I go by Cal."

The boy nodded. He didn't give me his name. Withholding your name might be suspicious to mortal folk, but it wasn't uncommon to the extramundane. Sharing your full, true name with someone meant having a special bond with them, one that could be called upon with magic, for good or for evil. Sharing my Elvish name was, at least, a show of good faith.

"So, you're working at the telegram office?"

I asked.

The boy nodded again, still noticeably tense. "It's my third week. My elleth is sick and my eldar only gets paid once per month. He works in the mines. I'm trying to help out by making money."

His father worked underground, a place more friendly to dwarves than elves.

"I'm sorry to hear that. I remember your elleth. She's a nice gal. Tailored me an enchanted duster that fits real nice. Looks sharp, too," I said with a hint of sympathy. "How's your eldar? He heal up all right?"

He nodded. "The doctor you traveled with helped. He still bears the battle scar."

"Scary stuff, those orcs. The Comanche made them even deadlier warriors by teaching them how to ride and fight from horseback. Or wolfback, I should say. I'm glad to hear your pa's doing all right. Never seen someone turn their flesh into bark like a suit of armor before. Beats taking an ax to the bare chest, I suppose."

A few moments of silence passed, each one weighing down the conversation.

"You go to school around here?" I asked, trying to lighten the mood.

"No, I don't go to human school." He sighed. "I can't go back because I cast a spell on someone."

"Whoa, what kind of spell?"

"A hex. I took someone's voice away for

calling me names."

I chuckled and knocked a fist on the counter. "That sounds like a good prank. I knew a desert elf kid once who—"

The boy's eyes flashed. "The desert elves aren't my friends. They don't like my people. I don't care what they do."

The boy's outburst made me take a step back. There were many different Elvish kindreds, but I didn't know there were hostilities between them. Shouldn't be a surprise, though, having people adapted to woodland life confined to an arid region and squashed up against land-hungry mortals.

"I didn't know that. I'm sorry," I said, searching for another subject. "So, your eldar works in the mines?"

The boy slowly hammered away at the telegraph machine. "Yes. He doesn't understand why so many humans are interested in the mines, though. Maybe it's gold."

"Lord, I hope not," I said. "Can't imagine what a gold rush would do to this place. Town's got enough people flocking to it without the allure of finding El Dorado beneath all this red clay. I don't know what makes this place so damn popular, tell you the truth."

The elven boy finished tapping out my message and handed me a receipt for my payment. He nodded toward the monster again. "The creature. Did it deserve to die?"

I looked back and sighed. "It was wiping out a rancher's herd, so I was hired to hunt it. I guess it's no crime to fulfill your role in the food chain."

The boy snapped his sullen eyes to meet mine, suddenly more confident. "I thought you said your name was guardian, Calam. You hunt supernatural creatures for money? If you were offered payment, would you hunt a supernatural person? Someone like me?" He kept my gaze.

I didn't know what to say. I pushed myself off the counter back to my full height. Yeah, I'd been offered money for hunting supernatural beings before. Not just monsters, but extramundane people, too. Killed a few dangerous ones that threatened my life while I was training under Marney. There was a difference between what the boy was suggesting and what I believed I represented as a ranger. But the line separating the two was growing thinner these days.

Poor kid. Oughta be out playing with others his age, not worrying about the problems of the world. I got a soft spot for sick mothers and god knows I owe plenty of good deeds to atone for my sins.

"Here," I said, tossing him my last coin. "For your elleth. In exchange, do me a favor and take this carcass around to the freight storage, will ya? Hide it good. Let's keep this secret between us and Bill Conway when he comes to retrieve it."

He thanked me as he stepped out of the mailroom, like a hotel bellhop coming for a guest's oversized luggage. I handed him the rope end.

"I'm Aldon," he finally said. "Aldon'asreal."

Aldon Leaf-Crown. A name reserved for elven nobility. His father must be a highborn wood elf.

Oh, how the mighty have fallen. Working in the mines would be torture for an elf. I pitied the boy and his kin. To be stolen from your homeland, your culture erased, and then forced to exist in conditions against your will was unimaginable to me. I felt a certain shame for wallowing in my self-pity earlier.

I shook the boy's hand. "Pleased to meet you, Aldon. You take care of your elleth. If you ever need anything, come find me."

The boy nodded. "Don't tell anyone what I am. Please."

"I'd never think of it," I said, squeezing his shoulder gently. "And may I be cursed with the permanent loss of my voice should I ever do it."

Aldon half-smiled and pulled the monster's corpse toward a good hiding spot. And when he thought I wasn't looking, he cast a spell to make the task easier.

I grinned and turned for home, ready to put the past few days far behind me. I longed for shade, a smoke, a glass of sweet tea, and a nice, long nap in a rocking chair.

CHAPTER FOUR

I lived in a shack at what used to be the edge of town, at least before it was swallowed up by new, trendy neighborhoods. My ramshackle wooden structure was an eyesore compared to the two-level, manicured homes that flanked it on either side, each one whitewashed with painted trim and little picket fences. My humble abode had no fancy exterior accoutrements, just raw wood arranged in the shape of a house that I'd built with my own two hands with materials I bought dirt-cheap.

Construction companies got smart during the rise and fall of boomtowns. Instead of setting a foundation and building a brand-new structure in every little town that popped up overnight, they designed little houses that could easily be built and stripped apart if the town dried up and relocated somewhere else. They came with blueprints and simple instructions, which was lucky for me, because I wasn't handy with tools at all. I got the build mostly right, except for a few odd angles in the kitchen and bedroom. The materials holding together my house weren't in the best of shape, which lowered its cost down to my price range. Despite its crude nature, my shack could withstand the strongest winds when they came sweeping down the plain, which was all I needed. Maybe it was a cart-before-the-horse situation, but I got a little ahead of myself and had painted 'Ranger' on the front window.

I turned the knob on my front door, but it wouldn't budge. Jammed again. One of these days, I'd be out of this dump. Maybe with Bill's payment I could afford to fix it up at least. I'd been stuck here since I moved out of Clem's saloon. Or kicked out, depending on who you ask.

I collapsed into the rocking chair I kept on the front porch and uncorked a canteen. I squeezed out the last few gulps of water. Triple-digit heat today, felt like. Summers were so hot you could crack an egg on a cast-iron skillet and cook it directly in the sun, no flame needed.

I picked up my corn-cob pipe and tapped out the old bits of burnt tobacco left in it. My tobacco pouch was empty, on account of me being broke. I sighed and stared up at the awning. My supply of vices had completely run dry. No money to gamble, no tobacco to smoke, no coffee to drink. And technically, the whiskey I drank belonged to Clem. I set my pipe aside and picked up a Jules Verne novel I'd left on the ground. It was somewhat relevant to my life, seeing as there were monsters in it. I considered it research.

At least I could afford to have an imagination.

A couple pages in, my exhaustion took over. I closed my eyes, pulled down my hat, and let the sounds of the town lull me to sleep. Wind chimes rustling in the distance. Wagon wheels creaking across the dirt road. Squirrels chattering among the leaves. Tension left my aching muscles and the beginnings of dreams started playing in my mind. My body had been through the wringer these past few days, a lot more than it was used to. I allowed myself to relax and prepared for a well-earned snooze.

Finally. Siesta time.

At least, it was, until some foul loudmouth interrupted it. Whooping and hollering replaced the soothing chorus of a lazy summer evening, and the thundering of hooves grew closer and louder. Then came the pops of gunfire.

All this was part of a classic outlaw routine. Ride into town with violent fanfare to pacify any weak-willed do-gooders. In other parts of the West, this might lure out any law enforcement stationed within town limits, which a few ruffians would then keep distracted while their posse pulled a job, like sticking up the local bank or something.

Not only did No Man's Land have no formal law enforcement, it didn't have any real government beyond the loose set of rules spelled out in a town charter. Most folks relied on each other's 'upstanding' ethics and morals to keep things straight, but the tragedy of the commons always ends in somebody else's personal gain. When someone felt cheated around here, they had to take the law into their own hands, which resulted in both justice and injustice alike in the form of duels, murders, or hangings by a mob of angry citizens. Or they could just hire someone like me to dispense their judgments. Rarely did anyone get it right, though. Justice being blind and all that.

A greasy young man on a horse came to a halt in front of my home. He wore a black shirt, half-unbuttoned, and a derby hat of the same color. He hopped off his saddle and hooked his thumbs inside white suspenders that hoisted up his britches, a pair of faded blue denim pants with mismatched patches over the knees. His face was mostly covered with a bright red bandana, and there was raw and puffy skin where the letter 'M' had been freshly branded into his slightly exposed chest. He leaned an elbow on his horse and tipped his nose up to me. "Ranger Cooper, I demand an audience with you."

I sighed and pushed my hat the rest of the way up to its proper resting place, giving up on my siesta. Rising out of the chair took a little effort, but I made it to my feet. "Boy, you better have a damn good reason for interrupting my nap with all that noise. You realize we find it illegal to fire weapons within town limits?"

A black stream of tobacco chaw streamed from the young punk's lips as he spit toward my feet. "As an outlaw wanted in six counties, I don't intend to obey your rules, nor do I recognize your authority to uphold them."

"Six counties, huh? Try five states. If you're such an awful big shot, what's your name?"

"I am Arnold Pollard, senior associate with the fearsome Matthews Gang," he said, puffing out his chest like a bullfrog.

I brought a hand to my mouth to stifle a yawn. "I've never heard of you, Bernard Palmer."

"It's Arnold Pollard, you imbecile, or don't you hear so good?" he snapped back.

"Buddy, I don't rightly care what your name is, so just get to the part where you tell me why the hell you're bothering me."

"I'm surprised you don't know. Figured word would have made its way out this far by now." He rocked back and forth on his boot heels.

"Probably got lost in all the other gossip we got floating around here. What do you know that I don't? Spit it out."

"Fact is, I'm here on behalf of a generous benefactor. There's a prize for folks who find and kill themselves a government man. I stumbled upon a few buffalo soldiers living out on the range. Roughed 'em up enough and they told me they'd heard about you, the man with 'Ranger' painted on his window. You wasn't that hard to find. Anyhow, I've come to this fair town to shoot you dead, right here"—he pointed at my front porch—"and collect my handsome reward."

I looked the young gunslinger up and down, sizing him up. "Marney send you?"

"I'm afraid that remains a mystery. In my business, an arranger organizes the reward on behalf of the anonymous donor," he said, sending another jet of spit into the ground.

"Oh, I'm familiar with your business," I said with a stone-cold face. "Not that long ago, I was in your boots. I threw in with gangs in the pursuit of freedom, fame, and, most of all, fortune, just like you do. It was grand, living like that. But the truth is, men don't live long in that life. They're too busy burning the candle on both ends to realize just how near the specter of Death stalks them. That is, unless they're too quick and dangerous to be caught. The fact that I'm still alive oughta concern you."

"I ain't seen any specters, nor do I intend to die anytime soon," he said, lazily stretching his arms wide. Awfully confident of him to leave himself open to a quick draw like that. "But I must disagree. We're not at all alike, you and me. I ain't a quitter like you. It ain't like you're one of the fastest guns in the West either."

As a matter of fact, I was. I was slightly offended that the punk didn't recognize me from my bounty posters.

By now, a few folks had overheard us and came to watch the show. Ladies peeked from behind window shutters, while the men acted brave and watched out in the open, but near the corner of a building for a quick escape. Maybe Clem had the right idea. I should start charging admission to the circus that was my life.

Arnold took notice and decided to strut about and peacock for the audience.

"People of Hexed Springs" he shouted, "I, Arnold Pollard, will now duel your ranger. Bear witness as I outdraw this man and gun him down where he stands. Should any of you come to his defense or take his place as an enforcer of the law, know that the Matthews Gang will deliver swift retribution." He bowed, as if he expected applause, then settled his hawkish gaze back on me. "Any last words, partner?"

I snickered and shrugged. "If you're dead set on a showdown, I guess I won't disappoint you. But before we draw, can you spell out your last name for me, Harold? I want to make sure the undertaker gets it right on your headstone."

His eyes seethed with fury, and I guessed that behind his bandana he was grinding his teeth. He scowled and placed his hand over his gun holster. His fingers wriggled, occasionally licking the butt of his pistol. I wanted to laugh at his theatrics, but I'd reached the end of my patience and wanted to end the little punk, so I could get to sleep again.

We squared up in a shooting stance. It was time to draw.

Bits of dust drifted by in the hot summer breeze. I forced my eyes open and tolerated the sting of sand pellets. I squinted to keep a clear view of Arnold's stance and tried to imagine the bullet's vector when he fired. I calmed myself with a deep breath, when a sudden chill shot up my spine. I winced and squeezed my eyes shut. When I opened them again, I was standing next to myself, watching the gunfight play out in a vision.

Arnold draws and fires. He's slower than me. Not as accurate. I move to my right. His bullet drifts wide and strikes the doorframe. The second one veers left and the third above my head. I shift and duck under the last bullet. After his second shot, I fire my gun. All it takes is one bullet. It strikes clean into his chest. His knees buckle and he collapses at the feet of his horse. It bolts away.

I exhaled. Moments later, Arnold made the move for his gun.

He drew and fired. He was slower than me. My hands and feet moved along the path foretold in my vision, like they were reciting the steps to a ballroom dance. I knew just when and where to be as the shots sailed by, missing me completely. After his second shot, I found my opening and fired. The bullet struck his chest, exiting through his back in an eruption of blood and bone. Fear and regret haunted his eyes in his last moments as his knees buckled. He sank to the ground near his horse. The mare panicked at the sight of its dead rider and kicked up dirt as it bolted for the horizon.

The dust settled over Arnold's body as I twirled my revolver with a quick flick of the wrist, slipping it effortlessly into its holster. Spectators emerged from their hiding spots and couldn't help but rubberneck at the dead outlaw. A man clapped for me, like it was some kind of street performance.

I gazed at my hands and tried to process whatever sensation had just overtaken me. Was this an extension of those visions I'd been having? The surge of energy running up my body, I'd never felt anything like it. Mundane mortals couldn't do what I'd just done.

Did I just cast a spell?

I buried my feelings as I returned to the world around me. I knelt down next to Arnold's lifeless body and rolled him over for closer inspection. The left lapel of his shirt flapped open in the breeze, revealing where my bullet had pierced his heart just beneath the bottom point of the 'M' on his chest.

"Boy's been branded like a cow," I muttered to myself.

"What do you think it means?" asked a stranger with a twangy Southern accent.

I jerked back to find Amos's dripping wet beard over me. Amos was a nice fellow, a bit touched, but mostly harmless in his curiosity. He once told me he was a mountaineer, then another time he was a famous playwright, and, finally, a Civil War vet. Still wore the cap from his Confederate uniform on top of his balding head, too. His gray beard was ragged and his face hadn't been washed in who knows how long, but people didn't mind him because he wasn't hurting anybody. He'd sometimes beg down by Clem's, and she'd give him leftovers and a warm beer because she has a good heart.

Everywhere Amos went, he was accompanied by a strong smell of hay and manure, probably from the barnyards he bedded down in. Surprised I hadn't smelled him coming.

"Christ, Amos, don't sneak up on people like that," I said.

"My apologies, Cal. On behalf of the community, I just wanted to compliment you on your quick shooting." He clenched one eye shut, made a gun shape with his hands, and started shooting imaginary villains.

"Amos! Amos, look here." I snapped my fingers a few times to bring him back to reality. "What do you reckon this mark is?" I pointed at the puffy scar.

"I don't rightly know. The boy said he was associated with the Matthews Gang. Could be the branding is some kind of gang initiation," he said. The curiosity in his eyes was replaced by a terrible revelation. "Or, you know what? I betcha somebody's using people like they *was* cattle. Branding them, harvesting them. Who knows what else."

How many marbles did Amos even have left, or had he lost them all already? We'd need to add 'budding conspiracy theorist' to the list.

"I'm gonna stick with the initiation ritual idea," I said.

I pulled Arnold's handgun out of the dust and looked it over. It was a newer firearm, recently cleaned and oiled, and assembled by a skilled manufacturer. I showed it to Amos. "You said you served in the Civil War, didn't you?"

He saluted the air. "I'm wearing a uniform, ain't I?"

"Well, it's good you ain't a sore loser," I joked. "What do you make of this gun?"

Amos twisted his face in a scowl as he silently mouthed his retort. He took the gun and turned it over a few times, spat on it, and rubbed it with his sleeve. He nodded and hummed like he knew exactly what he was looking at, then handed it back to me.

"Nope. Ain't a weapon I've ever seen on a battlefield."

I nodded and took the revolver back into my hands. "Just as I thought."

"Well, what'd you ask me for then?"

I stood up straight and tilted my hat back, trying to think. "The Matthews Gang is a bunch of small-timers that got run outta Waco a few years back for upending one too many stagecoaches. Reason I asked is because those gangs buy up military surplus, mostly Confederate issue, stuff you've probably fired before. They can't afford to outfit themselves with guns as nice as this one."

Amos shrugged. "Could be that his rich benefactor gave it to him?"

His bovine conspiracy, that didn't make sense at all, but Amos had a point.

"He did say outlaws were being paid to get rid of rangers in the region," I said. "Knock off enough of them and you could afford yourself something decent like this. Amos, you're not half bad as a detective."

"And you're not half bad as a gunslinger, Cal. They could write stories about us," he said with arched eyebrows.

"Wouldn't be a bad way to be remembered. I don't know, though. Seems like the only place you find legends anymore is in graveyards."

Amos frowned. He straightened up and squeezed some water from his beard. "Say, want me to go fetch the undertaker for you?"

I dabbed the sweat from my forehead with my sleeve. "Sure, that would be—" Without warning, a sharp pain swelled inside my head, just behind my left eye socket. I swayed, unable to keep my balance.

"Cal? Cal, you don't look so good," Amos said as he stepped up to brace me.

The sun flared ten times brighter and Amos multiplied in my blurry vision. I gritted my teeth and rubbed my temples, but the pain wouldn't subside, and soon nausea settled in. My ears began ringing loud enough that I couldn't hear myself calling for help.

Something was wrong. The sharp pain, emanating from the same part of my head where my 'vision' had channeled through, stopped me cold. All the bones in my skull felt as hot as a fire poker. I panicked and stumbled just as everything went dark around me.

NIGHTMARES I

"State your name," the lieutenant said.

"Wait, you don't recognize me?" I intended on acting as difficult as I could during this enlistment sham.

The tent door flapped in the wind as the beginnings of a snowstorm kicked up behind me. The canvas walls barely kept out the chill, which made for a rather uncomfortable workplace for the officer-turned-bureaucrat sitting in front of me. The lieutenant was hunkered down behind his desk, trying to stay warm. He tugged his coat up to his chin and dragged his fingers from his thinning hairline down through his thick mutton chops while emanating a phlegmy growl. He pulled a handkerchief from a drawer and blew his nose in it.

"I know damn well who you are," he barked. "Just state your name for the record."

My hands were bound behind my back. The skin around my wrists chafed from where the iron manacles dug into them.

"Folks call me Cal Cooper," I said, stringing out my words slowly.

"Mr. Cooper, do you now, or have you ever, associated with members of the extramundane, be they spirits, monsters, humanoids, or otherwise?"

I chuckled. "I kissed an elven girl once. That count as associating?"

The private who had escorted me from the brig jabbed me in the back. "Answer the question, scum."

"Come to think of it, I guess you could say I associate with them regularly. I have a friendly poker night with a halfling and his dwarven friends about once a month."

The lieutenant ignored my impudence. "Mr. Cooper, are you a strictly mortal or do you exhibit supernatural traits, abilities, and or the capacity to wield magic?"

"I'm all mortal. Plain as a bowl of vanilla ice cream," I said.

The lieutenant ticked checkboxes on a sheet of paper inside a green folder marked 'mortal offenders.' A bounty poster featuring my grizzled face was tacked to the corner of it.

"You sure about that?" the soldier behind me said.

"Look, I know my gunslinging borders on the supernatural, but I promise it's all me. Nothing magical about it."

"He's telling the truth," a harsh voice said

from behind the lieutenant. A gruff man sat in the darkest corner of the tent behind a table where little tin soldiers fought over imaginary positions on a map. For a moment, all I could see was his silhouette gently illuminated by a cigarette, until he put out his smoke and stepped out of the shadows. He straightened the black leather collar of his overcoat and placed his wide-brimmed hat on his head. There were all kinds of powder bags, vials, and pouches adhered to his utilitarian ranger's uniform. He had the appearance of a battle mage of some kind.

A fierce silver-toothed grin surrounded by salt-and-pepper stubble emerged from underneath his cowl. "Calamity Cooper here is a simple mortal. I detect no magic upon him," he said with the subtle charm of a Louisiana accent that had been dragged over gravel.

The lieutenant nodded at the man in black's assessment of me and scribbled down more words. "Mr. Cooper, do you know why you're here today?" He looked up at me for the first time during this little interrogation.

I chuffed. "I came to you looking for a deal. I heard you were handing out pardons in exchange for armed service. My intentions were pure, and yet I find myself in chains, stripped of my possessions, and held against my will."

The lieutenant let loose a laugh, which soon turned into a series of whooping coughs. His nose was bright red, chapped from the frigid wind that crept into the field tent.

"You reckless fool, did you think this was your chance at redemption? After everything you've done?" He shook his head with vigor. "Of course, we were going to apprehend you. Pardons are only issued to petty criminals. The United States doesn't negotiate with lifelong outlaws." He placed his ink pen inside the folder and snapped it shut. "Mortal or not, I'm afraid your long list of crimes outweighs Uncle Sam's generosity. I've scheduled you to be hanged in the fort's courtyard at dawn. Good day."

"Now hold on," I yelled.

My heart started to pound, panic and anger surging through me. I spit curses through my clenched jaw and lunged forward, but the private behind me wrapped his arms around my neck in a choke hold. The man in black stepped forward, gesturing his hand toward me. A wave of energy washed over me and my urge to fight melted away.

"I think you're being too hasty, lieutenant," the man said. His black iron gloves tipped with iron claws gently curled across the man's shoulder. "Calamity Cooper would make a fine addition to the Ranger Corps, don't you think? He has all the necessary qualifications, not to mention a wealth of experience on the frontier. Let's not waste his valuable skills with the noose."

The lieutenant let out a sigh, the kind from

a man who's been forced to cave to his superior's pressure far too often. In a way, his hands were just as bound as mine.

"Ranger Marney, if I release this man into your custody and he causes trouble, I don't want it to come back to bite me in my ass," he said sharply.

"Or perhaps I don't cooperate!" I interjected.

Marney and I stood nose to nose. He looked at me, revealing his stone-gray eyes. "Don't worry, Mr. Cooper won't be a problem at all. If he is, well ..." He plucked a dagger from a sheath on his chest and picked at the silver tooth. "I'll personally dispose of him."

I glared at the man, taking note of the various armaments decorating his outfit like war medals. *We'll see about that*, I thought.

"Well, then," the lieutenant said, standing from his seat. He ran his fingers through the remaining strands of hair covering his scalp. "By the power vested in me by Judge Roy Willoby, the legally appointed, federal judicial representative as mandated by the American Mortal Preservation Act, I hereby offer temporary clemency for all crimes and disturbances in exchange for your service in this United States military. Should you fail to meet the requirements of your duties, all pardons will be rendered null and void. Do you, Cal Cooper, agree to faithfully execute this agreement, so help you God?"

"I guess I don't have a choice, do I?" I hissed.

"Serve under me or hang. Simple as that," Marney said.

I took a deep breath and looked into Marney's eyes. Something about him didn't feel right. The man's swagger and focus were that of an apex predator, a panther lurking in tall grass. His threat to dispose of me wasn't an idle one, so any attempt at escape would need to be well conceived.

"Fine. I'll do it. Just give me back my stuff."

The lieutenant's sideburns bristled as he attempted a grin. "Very good then. You'll be stationed here under Ranger Marney's supervision. He will be your commanding officer and issue your orders from here on out." He opened a trunk at the back of the tent next to some filing cabinets and pulled out an oversized Colt Navy revolver.

My Cloudsplitter.

The weapon was more of a hand cannon than a pistol, as well as a family heirloom and my prized possession. Its handle was hewn from a ruby-red ponderosa pine, with gold filigree winding up the lock and stock like ivy. The mythological thunderbird graced its underside, carved into the charcoal-gray gunmetal. When it's fired, it sounds like Zeus himself unleashing a clap of thunder upon the earth. Many men have tried to win it from me, either by poker bet or theft. None of them have succeeded, and most aren't breathing anymore.

I let out a sigh of relief as the manacles were loosened from my wrists. I laced my gun belt around my waist and placed my revolver inside its holster with care, but this feeling of freedom didn't last long. Even though my hands were no longer bound, this government servitude was like a ball and chain.

Marney left the tent and motioned for me to follow. Flanked by two more soldiers, I begrudgingly trailed the man's imposing shadow outside, where a rolling plume of snow loomed large on the horizon. A bad omen for sure.

"Don't fuss, Cal. We'll begin your formal training in magical defense and tracking soon. You might be a plain mortal, but I can show you plenty of practical methods for dealing with the dangerous magics," he yelled over the driving wind.

"Just because you've rescued me from the gallows, don't think that I'll turn friendly and cooperate with you," I said.

Marney smiled that slick grin again and began walking. "Oh, come now. You'll make a fine apprentice, I just know it. You may even come to like me."

The private forced me down a path toward the barracks, a series of ratty tents that probably left recruits dead from frostbite. Marney tipped his hat and headed toward the much nicer and warmer-looking officer's quarters.

"Oh, and Cal?" he said, twirling back to face me. "Welcome to the cavalry."

CHAPTER FIVE

I sucked in a sharp breath and an unfamiliar world reappeared around me. A persistent pain pulsed down my back, which must have grown sore from lying awkwardly on a sofa. I rubbed my forehead and looked out a porthole window set inside the doorframe in front of me. The last few gleams of sunlight slipped away as dark purple tones painted over the soft orange sky. The rectangular room was lit by a lone oil lantern that cast a warm glow across a collection of knickknacks hanging above my head. My hat and gun belt hung on a nearby chair with my boots tucked neatly underneath the seat, and a full glass of water rested on a lace doily atop a polished oak side table. This room was far fancier than anything I was used to.

The air smelled of a woodsy perfume, masking an underlying whiff of mothballs and formaldehyde. I downed the water in one gulp and prepared to stand up, bracing myself in case I collapsed again. My feet, however, stayed firm beneath me, and I stretched my arms wide. My dizziness was gone, too.

Shadows danced across the room, drawing my eyes to some of the more interesting novelties within. The room was so littered with oddities that you could barely make out the pattern of the wallpaper. Jars of uniform size and shape lined shelves along one wall, each holding preserved fetal specimens of various life forms. Opposite those were large sheets of parchment, detailing the anatomical makeup of several vertebrates and invertebrates, which hung above a cataloging bureau. I peered inside one of the drawers. It was full of stuffed creatures, both natural and supernatural, each one labeled and classified. There were tribal masks, taxidermized predators, and unfamiliar mechanical gadgets, all on display inside this miniature museum.

I carefully placed the stuffed varmints back in their places—organized by genus and species, mind you—and examined the corner of the room. There was an eight-foot apelike skeleton beside a bookcase overflowing with encyclopedias, its back hunched over to accommodate the low ceiling. I tapped its ribs with a knuckle and discovered it wasn't made of bone. More like stone, maybe petrified wood.

"Welcome to my cabinet of curiosities. I see you're admiring my sasquatch skeleton," a dulcet voice said as the door behind me creaked open. It belonged to a Haitian fella I met on the trail while journeying to No Man's Land.

"Toussaint DuBois?" I asked.

Ever the gentleman, Toussaint bowed low and swept an arm across his chest. "Cooper Davenport," he said. "It's been some time, mon amie. Seven months by my count."

Toussaint was a confident and learned man. A polyglot capable of speaking several languages beyond his native Haitian Creole, he once told me, "Yon sèl lang se janm ase"—one language is never enough. He spoke English with confidence, and whenever he exclaimed or cursed, he preferred to do so in French. Even though he was brilliant and multilingual, he never used his smarts against me.

But as smart as the professor was, the man was even more handsome. His clean-shaven face sported a haircut cropped tight on the sides, with thick dreadlocks stacked on top. His smile made ladies swoon, and his good looks were complemented by tailored outfits comfortably wrapped around his caramel skin. Tonight, he wore a navy-blue, short-fronted riding jacket, its ebony buttons glinting in the lamplight. Frills spilled from the collar of his linen undershirt, which I believe is called a jabot, although I've never seen one, only read about them in fancy magazines. He had tan pantaloons tucked into knee-high black Hessian boots with black tassels hanging from the tops. Quite an ensemble for summer evening wear.

"Been a while, indeed," I said. I rubbed the back of my head sheepishly. "Look, I've got to come clean with you, partner. I'm afraid I gave you a false name last we met. The real name's Cal Cooper."

Toussaint let out a cannon blast of a laugh. "You would not be the first outlaw to use a pseudonym with me. May I ask, why the deception?"

"Too many folks on the trail with us. Any one of them could have snitched to that inquisitor escorting those wood elves. Luckily, I haven't seen a law man or any of Marney's brutes since then, so I've dropped the act."

"I see," he said, smiling and nodding. "I take it you have had no contact with Marney since?"

"None. Figure the magic behind the tracking spell must have worn off."

"A reasonable hypothesis," he said.

Toussaint was a true academic. And like an academic, he spoke in terminology more suited for a meeting between intellectuals, rather than sharing stew around a campfire with a layman. I knew about the supernatural, sure, but I couldn't make head nor tail of what he'd explained to me about extramundane biology when we had first met on the trail to No Man's Land.

Our trip here had been an eventful one. Buck and I happened to fall in with the same wagon train he did when we departed from the last train station in New Mexico, west of the Black Mesa. I shied away from the folks traveling with us, as I was a wanted man and all, not to mention hiding from the inquisitor escorting extramundane prisoners. Toussaint spotted me and reckoned I was a fellow outcast, so he struck up a conversation with me one night over a can of peaches. Turned out we shared the same opinions toward the government's treatment of the extramundane. The American Mortal Preservation Act was a brutal example of history repeating itself, since the federal government had already dabbled in mandatory relocations and genocide of Native peoples only a few decades back.

Neither of us were friendly toward the government man leading the elves in chains, so when we were set upon by a band of raiding orcs, Toussaint and I freed the elven kindred and escaped to safety. Can't say I shed a tear when an orc cleaved the inquisitor in twain with his great ax. I hadn't seen the professor again until tonight.

"I reckon I ought to thank you for saving me," I said.

Toussaint waved off the suggestion. "You merely needed a place to rest away from the sun. A man wearing a Confederate uniform dragged you here, saying you'd fainted after a gunfight. I was afraid you were shot and he'd confused me for a medical doctor."

I chuckled. "That's Amos for you. If I didn't know you were a naturalist, I might confuse you for a human doctor, too."

"My father wanted me to be a doctor, and I did train in medical school for a time, but once I found supernatural biology, I never turned back," he said.

I gathered my things and slipped my feet back in my boots, noticing the curated displays around the room. "So that's Sasquatch, huh?" I pointed at the gargantuan skeleton.

"*A* sasquatch," the professor corrected. "There are many. This one I excavated in a swamp in Louisiana. One of my first archaeological finds after leaving Haiti."

"Well, it's certainly a conversation piece. You've got a nice place here. Come to think of it, I've only ever seen it from the outside." I swirled a finger in the air toward all the interesting doodads.

"Thank you, Cal Cooper. I'm very fond of my collection. Many years of research and cataloging species from around the world." Toussaint smiled and waved at me to follow him outdoors, where he'd assembled a small campsite on the outskirts of Hexed Springs. We sat in chairs positioned near a cooking fire. "May I offer you a drink?"

I nodded. "I'd prefer whiskey, but something tells me I should have water instead."

"A wise decision," he said with a laugh.

Toussaint went inside his vardo, a special purple and gold wagon he called home. He'd customized it over the years, he told me, adding a system of gears and exhaust pipes and mechanical bits to create the first all-terrain locomotive. It's true, I'd witnessed the wagon drive itself, no horses needed. Just a crank of a handle here, a pull of a lever there, and off it went. It was a one-of-a-kind marvel engineered exclusively by Mr. DuBois himself. And he was certainly proud of it.

Toussaint returned shortly with a set of fine decorative glasses, two spheres of ice, and a matching water pitcher. He also brought back a hunk of bread and offered it to me. "A remedy for your liquid lunch," he said.

I plunged right into the bread. "Much appreciated," I said with a full mouth.

Toussaint's campsite was just as interesting as the inside of his wagon. A microscope and other scientific equipment sat neatly organized on top of a small table near a lean-to shelter, which was walled in by a colorful rug laid over a low-hanging tree branch. It flapped gently in the summer breeze. Liquid inside a glass sphere boiled underneath a small flame, hissing steam from the loose seal at its neck. Loose sheets of paper sprawled across the rest of the workstation and a pencil, chewed and worn down to a nub, rested precariously near the table's edge.

"Tell me, Cal, how has life treated you since we last met?" he said, pouring himself a glass of red wine.

"I've been better, Monsieur DuBois," I said between chomps. "My exile here hasn't been very prosperous. Figured there'd be more work for a man like me out here. I promised my friend, Clem, I'd give up my outlaw ways and live as an honest man, but I'm afraid I don't know how to do that."

"You feel as though you've lost your way?"

I nodded. "That's a good way to put it. I was a hired gun who'd spent his life living on the range, tangled up on the wrong side of the law. I look back and realize how many stupid decisions I made back then. Some of them I regret, some I don't. But this sort of sedentary life doesn't suit me. Doubt I'm going to find any kind of salvation out here."

"Mon Dieu, don't cast such a pall over yourself, Cal. You are not in need of redemption. For starters, I can tell you have a good soul."

"Oh, and how's that?"

"I saw pity in your eyes when you looked upon those elves. I've seen the kindness you give to your horse. You can tell much about a man by how he treats his animal and the less fortunate."

I sighed and stared into my glass. I wondered if he'd have the same opinion of me if I admitted that my hubris killed Buck, or that I've always called my horses by the same name so I wouldn't get too attached to them. Which, by the way, never worked.

It was nice to hear a compliment for once, though. And maybe Toussaint was right. Maybe I was being too hard on myself. Maybe, despite my flaws, I was a decent person with some value in this changing world. Sure, I'd committed my fair share of sins and then some. On paper, I read like a bad guy, but I've always lived by a code. One my pa instilled in me. *A man has to do what he thinks is right, but if he violates the tenets of chivalry, honor, and loyalty, then whatever he's doing is wrong.* I'd never intentionally murdered anyone in cold blood, stolen a man's lover away, or betrayed a friend. It's also my prerogative to stand up for the meek and innocent. I'm simply honor bound to do so. Even if, and when, it runs me afoul of the law.

"I appreciate you saying that, I really do, but I just can't seem to shake the feeling I'm too young to be obsolete, but too old to change," I said, watching the final sliver of the sun disappear from the horizon.

"I understand the feeling," Toussaint said. "Cal, have you heard of Darwin's finches?"

"Can't say that I have. Afraid I didn't get much science in school. Or schooling, in general."

"Among his many scientific endeavors, Charles Darwin once studied eighteen different species of finch. He found that, while they all came from a common ancestor, each bird evolved a unique style of beak specifically made to crack open the seeds available to them."

I scratched my chin and bobbed my head. "Afraid I don't follow, professor."

"Think of it like this: Every species must adapt to its environment if it's willing to survive. The extramundane here have done so. They've found a way to prosper, given the circumstances. Perhaps this land will change you for the better, too. If you let it."

"I hope you're right," I said with a sigh. "Not to nitpick, but what do you mean 'found a way to prosper'? The only extramundane I know of live in the rough and have a hard time making ends meet."

Toussaint poured himself another glass of wine and swirled it as the rising campfire smoke twisted in the wind. "You know, I don't believe I ever told you why I came to America, specifically No Man's Land."

"No, you didn't. We got split up before you could finish your story."

He began pacing around the campsite, one hand supporting his goblet, the other balled up and tucked into the small of his back. "For more than a decade, I've journeyed around the globe seeking to understand the diverse biology of our planet on each of the seven continents. As a result of my research, I have either studied or personally cataloged nearly every known species. It's a bold claim, yes, but it's true. There is little of the natural world that I do not already know.

"Mon Dieu, it was so distressing to me, to have reached the end of my knowledge with no path forward. That is, until one day I came upon an academic paper published by a man who claimed he had unraveled the secrets of vampirism, including treating patients afflicted with the disease before their transformation became complete. I was so desperate to make new discoveries again that I abandoned my medical studies and indulged my curiosity into the paranormal."

"Sounds like you took a pretty big leap. What happened then?" I asked.

"After writing my colleague, I traveled to Transylvania the following spring to find he had vanished without a trace. The only clues to his whereabouts resided in his field notes, which hinted at a hidden land in America that obscured the extramundane dwelling there from our reality."

"And so you journeyed across the pond and hit the trail toward No Man's Land?"

"After a time, yes. I first wished to study your country's legends and occult mysteries. That is how I stumbled upon something fascinating. Do you know what a ley line is?"

"Sure, I do. It's a vein of supernatural energy that amplifies magic around it."

"Precisely, but I discovered there is more to it than that," Toussaint said. He grinned and waved a finger in the air, drawing on an imaginary map. "Stonehenge, the Temple of Zeus, the

Pyramids at Giza, Machu Picchu, the Grand Canyon—these and many more of the world's most incredible wonders all have something in common: their relative positioning on the planet. Ley lines contain channels of raw mana, that is to say, the physical source of energy that fuels spells and the souls of supernatural creatures, and it just so happens that all of the world's wonders align in a very specific way. Humankind found inspiration in the mana streams underneath our feet and unwittingly created marvelous structures to celebrate them. Grandmother Earth herself created such natural wonders, too, but, unlike the mundanes, I suspect she knew what she was doing."

I scratched my head while digesting the concepts Toussaint was throwing at me. "I'm familiar with ley line energy, but I didn't know there was a physical component to it. Just sorta figured the energy floated out of the ground. What kind of mana did you say?"

Toussaint's eyes grew wide with excitement. I had the feeling he didn't have many people to talk with about his research, and the fact that I was able to somewhat follow along was a rare treat to him.

"Raw mana," he reiterated. "It's the viscous form of the primal energy that we thought only radiated from places of power. It was left behind by ancient deities many, many eons ago, before early human civilization. Or so it is said. In my own studies, I have witnessed creatures evolve rapidly or mutate into horrible versions of their prehistoric selves when exposed to it. Sometimes humans can be affected, too, though it usually enhances their latent or existing abilities."

That last sentence struck me. I waved my hands and interrupted his train of thought. "So you're saying a mundane human could, what, develop magical talent and become a wizard?"

Toussaint shrugged. "I suppose it is a possibility, yes. I hypothesize that long-term exposure may affect all manner of creatures, not just homo sapiens."

"A couple days ago, I was attacked by a monster that I've never heard of before." I described the fire-breathing lizard and how it nearly ate me whole. "Have you ever seen one of those before?"

Toussaint rubbed his chin and gazed up at the sky. "I am not familiar with that beast, no. I would be most interested in dissecting it. If it is a new species, we must give it a scientific name, no?"

A surprised smile spread across my face. I'd never discovered or had anything named after me before. "What do you have in mind?"

"*Anuragyga Cooper*"—he pronounced it ah-new-rah-gy-gah— "in Latin, it roughly translates to 'gigantic amphibious beast.'"

I chuckled, then let out a long sigh as the campfire crackled. "You're a rare bird, Toussaint, you know that? Mundanes nowadays are more likely to gather their torches and pitchforks than tolerate anything supernatural. Here you are venerating them in Latin."

Toussaint sighed and kicked a pebble into the fire pit. "The people here see me as a fish out of water. What is a fancy peacock of a Frenchman doing in the West? they wonder. I've been designated an outcast for both my elaborate sense of fashion and my study of the extramundane."

I watched the familiar expressions of a man contemplating loneliness even while enjoying the company of an acquaintance. I've become accustomed to it lately, to tell you the truth.

"To outcasts," I said, raising my glass of water.

Toussaint wagged a finger at me. "In France, it is bad luck to toast without a proper drink. May I interest you in a red wine? It is a fine vintage."

"Sure, I'll take a sip of your fancy firewater," I chuckled.

"That's the spirit," he said, offering me the bottle. Some kind of Italian was inscribed on the side of it. I tossed out my water and filled up the glass. The wine was smooth and rich, not like the smoky and sharp whiskey I was accustomed to.

"So tell me more about this raw mana," I said, smacking my lips from the dry liquor. "Is it something mundanes can get hold of? Could explain the influx of humans lately."

"It is theoretically possible, yes. It would be like drilling for oil, if one had the proper equipment," he said, swirling his glass. "You may find it hard to believe, as Hexed Springs appears to be nothing more than a common settlement on the open prairie, but it is actually one of the most magical places in the world."

"You're kidding?"

"Not at all. Let me demonstrate," he said, rising from his seat.

The professor hopped back inside the vardo and returned with a large globe and a plush, red pincushion. He gave it a spin before poking little red pins into each location that was home to a world wonder, natural or human made. With a thread of white yarn, he began stringing them together.

"As I said, all of the world's wonders correspond with a ley line. Old magic is actually quite detailed in ancient history, if you know which tomes to read," he said slowly, focusing his attention on his handiwork. "With our knowledge of the known world, and with the help of modern-day mathematics, we can calculate exactly where all the lines converge."

He tied a ribbon in the thread and presented his work to me. Every length of yarn tied to every little pin all culminated smack-dab in the center of No Man's Land.

Precisely where Hexed Springs was located.

"Voilà, I present to you the meeting point of all mana that courses through the veins of the earth. I calculated the exact position of this Nexus, but, curiously, it was not there. This led me to a grand discovery. Do you want to know what it is?" he asked, barely containing his excitement.

"The place you mentioned? The one obscured from reality?" I asked. I admit, the professor's excitement was infectious.

"Yes," he squealed. "The mana converges there, marked by a monument inside a veiled city that is hidden in the middle of Hexed Springs. And I. Have. Found it," he said, tapping his finger on the globe repeatedly for emphasis. He passed it over so I could study the crisscrossing lines for myself.

"You're saying there's a portal to another realm here? Right under our noses?" I asked.

"I know it sounds far-fetched, but it is true. Have you wondered why there seems to be fewer extramundane living in Hexed Springs than the number who have been forced here?"

"Actually, yes. You're saying they're hiding somewhere?"

"Many of them, yes. There is an elaborate spell that compresses reality, creating a sort of port city between our realms." Toussaint held his hands out wide and brought them together, like he was squeezing an accordion. "It also envelopes their city in an impenetrable veil, making it appear as if it doesn't exist at all. The city is centuries old. The original inhabitants wished to use it as an escape from the humans that battled them for supremacy in Old Europe. It was meant to shelter only the most wealthy and powerful extramundane, but in light of the extreme influx of supernatural refugees, the city has opened its borders. Many of the extramundane can now come and go freely, if they wish. Even some mundanes have been allowed passage, including moi."

"How in the world could anyone pull that kind of magic off?" I asked.

"That was my initial question. It would require many powerful practitioners performing the same ritual, true, but it would be possible, especially given the proximity to the literal fuel of all magic beneath their feet," he explained.

"They're in hiding," I said to myself, rubbing my stubbled chin. "If I were a government man, I'd say relocating the extramundane near the source of all magic was actually a bad idea."

Toussaint nodded. "It would seem so, but it could also be part of their plan. Perhaps they hope the mass exodus will destabilize the veiled city and reveal a new source of energy to exploit. It could be their ignorance is a boon for the extramundane; however, it is no consolation prize for being forcibly removed from your home."

I nodded. "Well, congratulations on your

discovery. What will you do with it?"

"It would be unethical of me to present my findings, given the current climate. My next steps will require some outside assistance. I had hoped that help could come from you. I can pay, of course."

I leaned forward and peered into the flames, curious about what kind of research the professor would possibly need my help with. I sat up tall, proud my skills were back in demand. "Much obliged. What did you have in mind?"

"Unfortunately, my studies are attracting attention and, with that, possible danger. My colleague, Dr. Van Helsing, the one whose work brought me here? He was murdered by vampires not far from here. I do not wish to meet the same fate, and as I cannot conjure magic myself, I require the services of a wizard," he said, gesturing toward me.

Well, that wasn't what I'd expected to hear. I furrowed my brow and paused to think about what Toussaint had said about mundanes manifesting magical abilities after prolonged exposure to raw mana. Which, I suppose, would technically mean they'd become extramundanes. Was that what was happening to me?

I looked back to Toussaint. He'd clasped his hands awaiting my answer.

"I'm afraid you're mistaken. I'm just a simple gunslinger. A talented one, sure, but I've got no magic in me. Besides, the price on my head is high enough without adding 'unlicensed wizard' to my crimes."

Toussaint didn't get the message and gave me an exaggerated wink. "Do not worry, your secret is safe with me. I reasoned that you wished to hide your name as well as your magic."

"I really don't know what you're talking about, partner."

"If you'll indulge me a moment," he said, holding up a finger. He rushed back inside and returned with a brass gadget that resembled a metronome combined with a dowsing rod.

"I hope you do not mind, but I took the liberty of running a few tests on you while you were incapacitated," he said apologetically.

"You what? What do you mean tests?" I growled.

"Please, please, allow me to demonstrate," he said. He flipped a switch on the gizmo and traced the air around me.

Nothing.

"Sometimes, the machines, they do not cooperate," he said. He chuckled nervously as he waved the invention around, but it still didn't do anything. He hammered at it with his fist while cursing in French. After the third whack, a warbling series of chirps bleeped from within the machine and the rods waved back and forth.

"Aha, it works. This device detects the presence of magic. People, objects, beasts, I can determine if they can wield the magic stirring within them. And look," he said, turning the machine toward me.

Each time the Y-shaped rods passed in my direction, the metronome ticked rapidly, and an eerie, high-pitched note wobbled in the air.

"I must confess, I spoke to the Confederate man. He told me many things, including how you won the gunfight. He said it was like you could see the bullets coming. It was not right of me to examine you without consent, I apologize. But, please, I cannot contain my curiosity. What magical abilities have you manifested?" he asked.

I suddenly felt exposed and vulnerable. I wasn't normally a person who shared much of anything with anyone, and now there was a machine giving away my secrets. *Imagine that in the hands of the government,* I thought. *The perfect device for America's second witch hunt.*

Maybe it was the wine talking, but I felt an urge to unpack my worries and tell the truth, all of it, and not hold anything back from my friend. He'd always given me the impression of being honest and trustworthy. Maybe he could use his superior intellect to shed some light on my situation.

Shadows danced around the campfire as I worked up the courage to share my secrets. "You said Amos told you I can see bullets coming? Well, it wasn't exactly like that," I said. "Right before we drew our guns, a cold shock ran up my spine and I received a vision. The fight played out in my mind's eye. When he was going to draw, where his bullets were going to hit, where I needed to dodge to keep from eating lead, it was all there. Like a warning bell went off in my head and told me just what to do in order to stay alive."

"Amazing," Toussaint said with a gleam in his eyes. He took out a field journal from his pocket and began jotting down notes. "You're a prognostic?"

I shook my head and shrugged. "I don't even know what that means."

"It means you're clairvoyant. You have knowledge of events before they take place."

"I suppose so. I've never really thought about it. I've chalked it up to déjà vu, but it's happened a couple of times since I moved here."

"Very interesting. And have you ever experienced a blackout after using your clairvoyance?"

"No, that's never happened to me before. This was the first time," I said.

Toussaint didn't respond. He sat silently, still rocking his head back and forth while writing on his pad of paper. After a moment, the silence became awkward.

"So, are you writing a book about me there or ...?"

Toussaint closed his notebook and slipped it back into his coat pocket. "A good scientist always records his data. I'll have to study your situation further. With your permission, of course."

"Sure, if you say so," I said. By now, the summer crescent moon was high in the sky, and the embers from the campfire tried their damnedest to reach it. The last of the red wine puddled at the bottom of my glass. Not a bad alternative to whiskey, but it wouldn't become my first choice of drink on the range.

For the first time in months, the feeling of stagnation that accompanied my new life drifted away, replaced by the familiar freedom of a starlit evening in the wilderness. I settled into my chair. It was nice to feel like the old me again. All that was missing was a good campfire story.

"Well, partner, wizard or not, I'd like to take you up on your job offer," I said.

CHAPTER SIX

The cool evening breeze walked me home after Toussaint and I parted ways. We had traded a handful of stories and let the logs burn down to ash before calling it a night. My head was swimming from all the wine in my belly and was ready to hit the hay.

I came to a fork in the road and considered heading for Clem's saloon, but after a day like this, I yearned to be home alone more than anything else. The walk wasn't too much farther, just enough to clear my head and think a bit.

Shops were closed for the night and most folks had finished their supper, but the night crowd was just emerging from the shadows. For me, evenings consisted of dining alone and scheming about making it big, without dragging my past back into my life. I used to go to Clem's for a drink, but that stopped being fun once all we did was argue over money.

My mind circled back to the events of this extraordinary day and the new acquaintances

I'd made. I thought about Colin, the werewolf, and Aldon'asreal, how both of them saw me as a threat to their existence. Humankind was destructive, no doubt about it, but I didn't like the thought of being feared by association. I could see why they found me frightening. A mundane gunslinger with a criminal history, trained in defense against the supernatural arts? Wouldn't inspire friendliness in me either, if the boot were on the other foot.

Then there was Toussaint DuBois. A fascinating fellow with a head full of crazy ideas. The man could live anywhere in the world but had come to the middle of nowhere to study the supernatural. Apparently, that middle of nowhere was also the concentration of all mana. I could still hear his weird invention trilling in my mind. Perhaps it really did work and sensed magic in me.

A couple folks turned their heads as I walked by chuckling to myself. They must have thought I'd gone batty, but I got a real kick imagining myself as some kind of wizard.

My mind painted a vivid scene. Mundane and extramundane folks strolling up and down the streets of this dusty old city. Me dressed in a tough-looking ensemble, as stylish as Toussaint's. And there, in a crowd of magical misfits, I spotted my bounty. I flicked a cigarette out of my mouth and marched into the middle of the street. My target, a wanted undead vaquero, spun around to face me in a high-noon duel.

Just like something out of a story book.

Even in my imagination, I was still a gunslinger. I could almost hear Clem scolding me. She wanted me to settle down so badly. But who was I without my revolver? I was no good with farm animals, that much was clear from my luck with horses, and I was a terrible farmer. Shopkeeping was too dull, and everything else in between too boring. That just left riding, shooting, and looting. Apart from those three things, I'd been a failure at everything else I'd ever done. Never happy with the life I was given. Gambling my fate. Wasting my life away wishing I'd wake up a Wild West legend.

No more than fifteen minutes after leaving Toussaint's, I arrived back at my little home. Arnold's body was gone and any record of our duel in the dust had been replaced by footprints, hooves, and the wagon-wheel treads that frequented these streets. The bullet holes were still there, though, lodged in the wooden frame that propped up my rickety house. I pushed my finger into one of the holes and felt the slug stuck inside it.

I rubbed the iron horseshoe on my front door, something I got to discourage evil spirits from entering my home, and took one final glance at the town. It looked a little bit bigger each day. There were some days when wagon trains rolled in, one after the other, all carrying beams of wood. A house, a store, or a workshop would pop up almost overnight. All they needed was a plot of land and some gravel to act as a foundation atop the red clay soil.

Nightlife in the old part of town was vibrant, and I could often hear the murmur of chattering drunks and the sounds of a band entertaining crowded bars. If you listened close enough, you could hear varmints rustling through the brush and the occasional yips of coyotes. Tonight, though, it was quiet, except for the faint sounds of the night drifting through the air.

I shouldered the door open and tossed my things on the dining room table. The bare wood floors creaked as I made my way to the large desk in the corner. A draft eked its way through the walls, chilling the place year-round. Facing my desk was a pair of rickety sky-blue chairs I'd bought from an estate sale, so clients would have a comfortable place to sit, but one of them's missing a chunk of cushion where a mutt took a bite out of it. Never had cause to use them yet, though. I flipped through the journal I kept locked in the top drawer, full of names and contract details, including who owes me money. Unfortunately, as of right now, it contained only one name, Bill Conway, and the agreed-upon total of thirty dollars. Bill got himself quite a steal, considering the creature I bagged for him. Not to mention what it cost me.

My place wasn't nearly as fancy as Toussaint's vardo, but it did have a few special trinkets from my life and travels. I'd built a rickety bookcase out of scrap wood and filled it with my favorite novels, like *Don Quixote*, *The Odyssey*, and *Moby Dick*. Next to the bookcase was a cabinet full of junk, but sitting on top were a series of sepia photographs. I blew dust off the photos, admiring the one of our family farm in the ruby-red hills of North Dakota. My twin sister and I were maybe nine years old, and still looked damn near the same. We were happy as clams when it was taken. A few years later, my whole family contracted cholera and died, and I was miraculously spared.

A Catholic boarding school took me in to shape me into a man of the cloth. I didn't care for their rules, so I ran away at fourteen years old and fell into a crowd of ill repute. In truth, though, that motley crew was full of the finest people I knew, who just so happened to be society's rejects.

Of course, I had a picture of those so-called deviants, too, of my time in the Beasley Gang. There was George and Henry, two Texas freedmen who had killed their master after he refused to recognize the abolition of slavery. They told me to submit to no master and always make my own luck. Millie was kneeled down in the front of the picture. She taught me to spin my pistols and do rope tricks. Then there was Harold, the camp cook, who told a lot of good campfire stories and even taught me a few simple recipes to survive on the trail. Next to him was our matron, Miss Hattie, who made me wash my face and scrub behind my ears every day. Standing behind her with his arm slung over my shoulder was Jeremiah Beasley, the leader of the titular Beasley Gang. I think I must have got my delusions of grandeur from him. He was always scheming and dreaming.

There were other men and women in the photo whose faces and names had slowly faded from my memory. That was the nature of living in a gang. People rode in and rode out. Or they were taken away, oftentimes at the end of a noose.

Everyone in this picture was dead now, save for me. I'll always remember them as my first family after my biological one was taken from me.

Clem never was a part of the Beasleys. She was somebody I met later in life, after I'd attempted to ride solo. We traveled around the country playing Robin Hood for a while, earning a good amount of notoriety.

Speaking of Clementine, I did have this one painting hanging in my parlor that she'd given me as a housewarming gift. It once belonged to a railroad tycoon, that is, until Clem swiped it during a raid on the wagon train transporting his valuables. The oil painting featured a dainty, red-headed Irish lass dressed in a pristine white gown standing in a field of shamrocks, a stormy sky behind her. She held out a severed head and had an ax slung over her shoulder. The head belonged to a grizzly-looking man whose corpse was lying prone underneath her feet. I've been told it's quite a conversation piece.

Some folks who get to know me are surprised that I'm not just a dumb outlaw. I also admire the arts and humanities. Hard to enjoy them too much without money. Not a lot of paintings out on the trail either. The only real times I've been able to enjoy art were during bank robberies. The nice ones had sculptures or fine paintings in their lobby, which I could admire while sticking up the teller and waiting for them to fill my bag with cash.

I placed my hat on a hook I'd crudely nailed to the wall and picked up an oil lamp. I struck a match and held it inside until soft, yellow light replaced the silver moonlight illuminating the room. I carried it to my bedroom, undressed, and flopped down on my bed. It wasn't a nice bed, like the ones at Clem's. The only support my back got was from a few ropes tied between the frame. One of these days, I could afford some wood slats. Otherwise, it was back to scavenging odd cuts of lumber in the carpenter's trash. My mind still buzzed with everything that had happened to me the past few days, making it hard to fall asleep.

Which was a good thing, I suppose, because no more than a half hour later, someone pounded on my front door. I groaned and forced myself to my feet after the third round of knocks. Lord help me, I'd spent the past seven months without so much as a mouse for a house guest. Now, all of a sudden, I've got unannounced visitors demanding my time. What is it with strangers thinking they can come calling whenever they please?

I threw on enough clothes to be considered decent and peered out my bedroom door toward the front window. Parked outside were four hulking Clydesdale horses pulling a fancy stagecoach. Its rich, dark wood was decorated with golden flourishes that gleamed in the moonlight. The coachman sitting on top wore a proper driver's uniform, and the lanterns flanking him were fashioned out of the same gold as the carriage's trim. As I leaned out a little farther, I could make out the words painted above the door. *Strickland Savings & Loan.*

"Ranger, I require an audience with you," a cold, assertive voice called out.

What the hell was a bank representative doing paying me a visit in the middle of the night?

Probably here to coerce me into selling my plot of land, so they could demolish my house and build something a little more revenue-generating. That sounded like something a slimy financier and developer like Strickland would do.

"It's awful late for a meeting," I hollered through the door. "Come back after sunrise tomorrow. Or, preferably, don't come back at all."

There was another knock, but this time, whoever had done the knocking nearly drove their fist through the door. Whoever had just caused my door to bow was strong. Like oxen strong.

"I apologize for my man's impatience, Ranger Cooper, but this is an urgent matter. There's no time to lose."

I growled and cracked open the door a hair. On the other side stood not a lowly bank employee, but Ross P. Strickland himself. The man had his chin in the air, as if he was accustomed to looking down upon underlings. Gray bags drooped under his cold, blue eyes. His skin was pale, probably because he spent most of his time inside a bank vault.

Even in the late evening, he was dressed like a titan of industry, sporting a black three-piece suit with white pinstripes and loafers that shone like mirrors. He was a regular J.P. Morgan and Andrew Carnegie rolled into one, except he made house calls apparently.

"I'm not interested," I said with a sleepy groan.

"I assure you, you will be. I know the hour is late, but I have an emergency," he said, tucking a monocle into a pocket of his vest. "As the town's ranger, you're the closest thing we have to a lawman in No Man's Land, and the only person I can trust with this case. I am in need of someone with your certain skill set."

"Oh, and why would that be?"

Strickland's face got paler as he glowered at me. "Because my daughter's been kidnapped by vampires."

CHAPTER SEVEN

It took me a second to fully process what I'd just heard. Strickland was right; I was interested, mostly out of morbid curiosity. For a moment, I forgot I was talking to the very type of man I despised most in the world. But his money spent like everyone else's, not to mention he had plenty of it. Enough to make me consider playing the role of ranger one more time.

Based on my experience with vampires, I ranked them as the most dangerous extramundane beings you could encounter. They were sly and cunning monsters, controlling folks from the shadows. When push came to shove, they were unrivaled in feats of speed and strength. Their skills represented a deadly combination that should be regarded with the same caution as a lit stick of dynamite glued to your hand.

The only peaceful encounter I've ever had with a vampire happened at Clem's on my first night in town. Clem described him as a popular philanthropist who represented all the old money and influence in Hexed Springs. His family was richer than anyone could fathom. Rumor had it they stashed heaping mounds of cash deep underground in vaults carved by humans brainwashed into do their bidding. Some of the currencies belonged to civilizations that didn't exist any longer. Even though they were extramundanes, they weren't afraid of hobnobbing in public.

Everyone in the saloon that night treated him kindly, perhaps out of both fear and respect. The beautiful woman hanging on his arm was drunk on his charm, not from liquor. He was of a light complexion, almost pale as the elves, and had a long, handsome face. His black hair cascaded down his shoulders, which the saloon gals couldn't help but twirl a finger through. He was dressed in accordance with his station, wearing a tailored suit accented with a pocket square the same color as his blood-red silk undershirt.

A tinge of fear wormed in my gut when we accidentally met eyes. His eyebrows shot up in surprise, like my presence there was serendipitous. Clem shot me a look of caution and slipped away to help another customer as he wandered over next to me. His arm slid around my shoulders and he extended a bejeweled hand. "Cal Cooper, I presume? Welcome to Hexed Springs."

I hesitated before taking his hand. It was ice cold. "How the hell do you know who I am?"

An exaggerated, apologetic look crossed

his face. "Forgive me, sir. That was too direct, especially in a land where most men prefer to remain anonymous. Do not worry, though, your identity is safe with me. Consider me a friend."

"Does my new friend have a name?" I asked.

"Lucius Montague. I'm quite pleased to make your acquaintance," he said, dipping his head low.

"You going to tell me how you know me?"

Lucius looked at the man seated next to me and smiled. The man promptly offered up his seat and the vampire gingerly slid onto the open stool and smoothed his untucked shirt.

"Please, Mr. Cooper, it's nothing overly devious, I assure you. I'm simply a well-informed man. I understand you're on the run from the army," he said.

I didn't say anything.

"Word of your deeds has reached all the way out here," he continued. "Some folks aren't sure if they can trust you. A man trained to be an inquisitor is a threat to the extramundane here."

"If you're so well-informed, you'll know I'm not like them. I've never hurt anybody who didn't already have it coming."

"Of course, of course. The Inquisition is extreme at times, yes, but as a higher being of the extramundane world, I understand the need to cull lesser magical beings, particularly wild beasts. I do not hold your experience against you."

I furrowed my brow and pulled away. "I appreciate your leniency."

"I believe you're a man with good judgment, which is why I've come to speak with you. Should the need ever arise, I trust you'll be considerate of my family in any future work you may undertake. I do so hate to see mundanes become mixed up with those around here who don't know their place."

I enjoyed the last drop of whiskey in my glass and calmly set it aside. "Is that some kind of warning?"

"Just some friendly advice. Hexed Springs isn't like other towns. Mundanes have conquered most of this country, but No Man's Land should always be a realm of cooperation between our peoples. It's no secret my family has much influence in the region, and personally, I'd much prefer to have a man of your talents working for me rather than against me."

I squared my shoulders to the vamp, staring straight into his dark eyes. "Frankly, Lucius, I don't care too much for veiled threats. Next time, save your breath and make me an offer. I go where the money leads me. You should already know that."

Lucius returned my stare with a face of stone, his brow revealing only the slightest crease of discontent with my direct approach. After a moment, he lightened up, clapping me on the shoulder. "I will remember, sir, and I do so appreciate your time." He knocked his obsidian ring on the bartop. "Pardon me, but I must return to my … date."

Lucius gestured to a woman sitting in a booth in a secluded, darkened corner of the saloon. She hadn't moved an inch since he'd approached me. I noticed she had a birthmark, a small splotch of brown that crawled up the side of her neck. She tried to hide a pair of fang marks in the middle of it, covering herself with a lace collar that wrapped around her like a Victorian princess. Hard to forget their extravagance, let alone the lady's elegant beauty.

"Lovely gal," I said.

"Yes, she certainly is. She's captivated with me. And I with her. We share an uncommon bond, you might say," he said, his gaze brimming with lust. After a moment, he cleared his throat and nodded back to me. "I'll let you return to your conversation with Miss Clementine. I do hope you'll consider working alongside us someday. No offense, but mundanes have such a way of mucking things up. Man's greed corrupts like no other."

I reckoned I should have felt honored. My first full day in the territory and a prominent paranormal was already lining up for my services. Seven months later, the most powerful of the mortal folks around here would be standing on my front porch doing the same.

I reluctantly lit the lamp and pulled open the door, inviting Strickland inside. He was tailed by an associate, a man unlike any other I'd seen. Nearly as wide as he was tall, he had to stoop to get inside my doorway.

His knuckles bulged in his metallic gloves, at least as thick as two of mine. He wore a sickly green cloak over a bronze suit of armor and carried a long, blunted executioner's sword. His helmet was reminiscent of a Bronze Age warrior and peeked out from underneath a pointed hood. I could only see black where his eyes should have been. Without a doubt, he was the one trying to break down my door.

"Why don't you have a seat, Ross?" I said, playing host and gesturing to my half-eaten chair. Strickland sneered. The man had probably never sat on anything so poor. I imagine he preferred the comfort of a goose-down cushion or, hell, maybe even a gold throne. I'm sure he found my home to be downright offensive.

"I'll stand. And, please, I insist that you address me as Mr. Strickland."

I chuffed at that. I reckoned Strickland was a pompous ass based on the rumors I'd heard about him. Anyone demanding to be called 'mister' only wanted their ass kissed, or was so high and mighty they thought they'd naturally inherited the right to command others. Strickland was probably both.

I played along, intoxicated with the

thought of how much money I could squeeze out of him. "Forgive me, *Mr.* Strickland. Can I offer you something to drink? You and your eager associate—"

"Never mind him," Strickland interrupted. "I'm ready to get down to business. I do not wish to linger here and attract unwanted attention." He wandered through my parlor and scanned my meager belongings, settling at my bookshelf, and swiped a gloved finger across the top. He sneered at the thick layer of dust that came off.

"Like I said, my only child has been kidnapped by a vampiric abomination, and I shouldn't have to tell you how dire that sort of situation is," he said. He wiped the dust on my one nice chair. "I'm prepared to negotiate a handsome contract for you, including a down payment for your services, if you agree to find my daughter and eradicate whatever infestation of these vile creatures exists in the area immediately."

Got down to business. Prepared to negotiate. All this man knows is how to talk money.

"Hold on," I said, brushing off the chair. "Just how sure are you that it was, in fact, a vampire that took your little girl? Pretty brazen of a being known to work from the shadows to abduct someone of such a high profile."

"Indeed, it is, but I'm sure of it. I have four eyewitnesses who can corroborate a description of the creature. The men who patrol my estate's grounds at night, as well as my daughter's nanny, each encountered the vampire."

"All right, then, tell me what they told you."

Strickland stopped pacing and continued. "In the early hours of the morning, approximately twenty hours ago, my men noticed a disturbance in the hedge maze outside my mansion. They reported witnessing the topiary rattling as if something was muddling through it. One man assumed it was a raccoon and went to scare it off. When he held up his lantern to investigate, something charged at him. He believes the flame in his lamp frightened it and caused it to leap over his head onto the eastern side of the property. If you had ever seen my mansion grounds, you would know that distance is quite impossible for a human to manage in one jump. In the moments it took for my security team to run from the hedge maze to the main house, the creature had broken into my daughter's second-floor window, plundered her room, and stolen her from her bed. My servants caught a glimpse of the horrible thing just before it departed with her."

"And? What did the creature look like?" I asked.

"It had a contorted face and large fangs, and it measured about the same size as the average person. My servants could not tell if it was male or female, but it was not at all human. The creature reeked of blood and left a trail of soot on my Persian rugs, presumably tracking it in from its filthy lair. It struggled to fly away but managed to do so with the assistance of a thin membrane attached to its wrist and connecting near its waist, similar to the wing of a bat."

I knew just what Strickland had seen. He was describing a feral vampire. Truly the most dangerous kind. Feral vamps are unpredictable, caught in a state between an addled human and a bloodthirsty demon. They have all the powers of a vampire with none of the mental faculties.

I was going to charge a big fee for this sort of a job.

"That's a vampire all right, but why would it want to attack your daughter? I mean, it could have assaulted anyone else in the house," I said.

Strickland stood over my chair and gripped the back of it with his gloved hands. "I believe it is personal, ranger. Ever since I established myself in No Man's Land, my extramundane counterparts here seem to be collaborating in their efforts to diminish me. This is why I must also ask for your discretion in handling this matter."

"I don't understand. Why the secrecy?"

"I have a substantial vested interest in the success of Hexed Springs. I don't expect a man like yourself to understand, but I'd prefer my prestigious reputation remain untarnished and not become associated with rumors concerning the paranormal. My business partners, let alone the regional markets, would not react well to this series of events. I will not let anyone jeopardize my plans for this territory, nor will I allow anyone to interfere with what is mine. Certainly not those filthy abominations." The lone oil lantern cast an ominous shadow across the spidery, purple veins in his cheeks.

I waited a moment for his anger to simmer before jabbing back at him for the personal insult he'd conveniently buried in his diatribe. "You're right, I guess I don't understand. I'm just a simple man who can't comprehend the complicated subject of social stratification among the elite. Why did you come to this part of the world if you didn't want to be near the extramundane?"

He snorted and turned his nose up before walking away from me, his hands clasped behind his back. "You don't get to be a man of my status by being meek and simple. Seize what you can before someone else does or risk becoming a footnote in their biography."

Strickland paused near the window and peered out over the town. The superiority drained from his voice, replaced with ambition and hope.

"I've been having dreams of a new and improved Hexed Springs, ranger. My vision for the town will affect every man and woman here, including the extramundane. Soon, mechanical marvels will revolutionize the way we live. The men of industry in my network tell me they are on the cusp of great transformation. Imagine, if you will, a cable car running through our town square alongside wagons that need no horse to pull them. Lanterns that burn without flame but are a hundred times brighter. Automatons that obey their master's commands. A utopia, right here in the Wild West, within our grasp," he said with a growing fervor.

Like a locomotive releasing its steam, he exhaled and turned from the window. He inspected his associate, who hadn't moved since he'd walked in, his silent gaze focused straight ahead on nothing in particular. The blunted end of his sword pointed toward the floor and his weight rested on its hilt.

"I am neither an optimistic nor a pessimistic man, ranger," he continued. "I am simply determined. I can make life better here. For everyone. I know I may come across as a raging bull sometimes, but I assure you, I have the best intentions for every soul in this future American state. As such, I cannot be too protective of my generous investments."

I'm sure everyone sounds like the good guy in their own version of history. Ross P. Strickland was actually a hard-ass whose other 'dreams' for humanity included cheap labor wages, extended sentences in debtor's prisons, and exempting the excessively wealthy from taxation—all things that made him richer and fatter than anybody else. As I looked at him from across the room, I could picture his face on a poster announcing his candidacy for governor.

One thing was missing from the long-winded job offer: the details on his daughter. Curious how he'd expounded more on his vision than his own flesh and blood who'd been stolen during the night.

"Whatever you say, Mr. Strickland. But I need to consider a few more details before I take on your contract. Do you have any idea where this thing took your daughter?"

Strickland begrudgingly shifted his priorities back from his dreams to reality. "My men followed it southwest as far as they could, but it was too difficult to track in the night with its speed."

"Predators usually don't tend to carry their prey over long distances. Can't imagine your daughter would be far away from your grounds. What's her name? What does she look like?"

Strickland grunted and dug through his coat pockets. "Her name is Abigail," he said, holding up a photograph. "She's aged since this was taken."

I scanned the photo and frowned. Something was off. Abigail's eyes telegraphed a sense of fear, and her smile was clearly forced. She was a dainty thing with a sweet face, chunky cheeks, and a bow in her hair, bobbed off just above her shoulders. Her hair appeared to be nearly white in the sepia image. She was surrounded by stuffed horses and wore a pretty dress with a floral pattern that complemented the canvas backdrop behind her. Her lace collar had no ruffles in it, and she sat straight and tall, like she would be punished for taking a bad photograph. On the back, it read *Abigail Ames Strickland, age 8* handwritten in a lady's cursive.

"And how old is she now?" I asked.

"She's nine, maybe even as old as eleven, I forget," Strickland said, shrugging his shoulders.

I arched an eyebrow. "You're not sure how old your only daughter is?"

"Why should I be?" he said with a nonchalant laugh. "Youth is such an insignificant stage of life. A male minor cannot own land, cannot vote, and his earning potential is pitiful. For a girl, all these things are nonexistent. I would have preferred a son, as any father would. Girls her age despise their fathers. Although I seem to have very little in common with her, she is my blood and only heir, so I am willing to do whatever it takes to retrieve her."

I shook my head in disbelief. The joy of rearing children was wasted on such an awful man. He didn't deserve to be a father. I'm sure he sensed my seething disapproval.

"I heard you put an ad in the paper looking for security guards. Why not send one of them? Why not send this guy right here?" I asked, pointing to the quiet man near the door.

"Unfortunately, that is out of the question. I cannot divert their attention from protecting my assets. That is why I'm seeking outside help. And, as I mentioned earlier, this must be discreet, which is why I didn't just advertise it in the newspaper as well."

He couldn't even spare a single man to save his only little girl? Strickland chimed in before I could fully express my judgment. "I hope you're not insinuating that I'm a bad father. I can assure you the accusation would be false. Despite her being born the wrong sex, I provide Abigail with food, shelter, and all the toys she could ever want. Besides, I'm not paying you to judge me," he said.

The anger continued to boil inside me. *Just keep your trap shut and think of the payday,* I thought. That's the sort of attitude that would make Clem proud.

"Mr. Strickland, you've mistaken me for a man with empathy. I don't care what kind of father you are, and, as of this moment, you're not paying me at all. I haven't agreed to go searching for your—"

Strickland's hand shot up. "Two hundred dollars will be paid to you upon my daughter's return alive. Twenty dollars will be offered as a down payment. I will also include an additional fifty dollars for proof of every vampire you exterminate."

I had a great poker face, but even I

couldn't conceal my shock at that potential payday. Strickland saw the greed in my eyes. "I take it you'll agree to these terms," he said.

Two hundred dollars, plus at least an additional fifty dollars, was nothing to sneeze at. As of right now, my total earnings was zero—a big, fat goose egg. I'd earned bigger payouts pulling heists just as risky as what I assumed this vampire hunt would be, but, as they say, beggars can't be choosers. I was simply trying to eat and live, all while improving my station, just like everybody else. Takes a lot of money to do that, and I had a long list of basic necessities I lacked, starting with coffee grounds and a better mattress.

Seconds ticked by as I thought over the offer, and I could feel Strickland's patience wane. "I asked you a question," he said.

"Hang on, I've still got questions of my own. What happens if I can't return her alive? You can't possibly expect me to guarantee her condition, especially not after she's spent a day or two with a vampire."

Strickland's frustrated stare began to bore a hole in my head. I wasn't going to take the chance of being conned out of payment due to an overlooked detail hidden in the language of a contract. I expected that from men like him.

"My terms assume you'll spare no effort in slaying every single one of the creatures while rescuing her, even if that means putting yourself in the way of great harm. You may return her in any condition, as long as she is breathing," he said.

Strickland's terms felt designed to cheat me out of my pay. There were too many subjective variables up for interpretation.

"I'm going to need more money. Call it hazard pay, if it makes you feel better, but no way am I risking my skin hunting vampiric beasts for a measly two hundred dollars, while I know you're good for more. Make it five hundred. And I'll take half of it right now," I demanded.

Strickland threw his arms up. "Despicable. Bargaining with an anxious father whose only precious child has just been stolen away! By unholy monsters, no less. I'll give you two hundred and nothing more. I'm not willing to entertain any other amount."

"Then I'm not willing to entertain your contract." I stood up and motioned toward the door. "Now, I believe it's well past all of our bedtimes. If that's all, gentlemen?"

Strickland turned and nodded to the armored man guarding my door. He gripped the doorknob as if to open for his boss, but instead he wrenched my door off its hinges, wood and metal creaking under his strength, and chucked it straight at me. I ducked and scrambled for my gun, barely missing being struck by the door. Before I could take two steps, the cloaked enforcer snatched me up by my throat and hoisted me up to his height. I kicked him in the chest as I swung back and forth in his grip, sinking my heel into his brass chest plate. He jolted me, which knocked loose the latch and caused it to swing open from beneath his robes.

He wasn't a man at all.

A series of gears, tubes, and wires connected to a glowing pink crystal were hidden beneath his armor where one would expect a heart and lungs. I looked up into the automaton's eyes. In lieu of pupils, a pair of glowing, violet orbs flickered deep inside the metal helmet.

I couldn't shake the feeling that pieces of the metal man looked awfully familiar.

Without much effort, the automaton turned me out to face Strickland, who was grinning from ear to ear as I swayed back and forth, choking for air.

"Do you like him? He was constructed recently. I obtained his blueprints as collateral in a deal with a rather resourceful individual. My man has a convincing way of doing business, wouldn't you agree?" Strickland suppressed a maniacal laugh. "Oh, ranger. You just had to go and force my hand, didn't you? This is your fault, you know. You should have been thankful for the opportunity to work for Mr. Ross P. Strickland. Any offer I put on the table, you should have gobbled up like a starved rat in a larder. I suppose we'll just have to try something else then."

He reached into his coat pocket and pulled out a yellowed roll of parchment. He unfurled it and pushed it up to my face. "Read it," he commanded.

In big bold letters, accompanied by a crude sketch of my handsome mug, the paper read:

WANTED: 'DEADEYE' CAL COOPER
Reward for the capture of one Cal Cooper, $20,000, paid upon delivery of his DEATH.
Age: 32. Height: 6 feet, 2 inches. Weight: 220 lb. Light complexion, dark hair, dark eyes, solid build. Wanted for felony MURDER of HUMAN SOLDIERS; DESERTION and TREACHERY; ROBBERY of $5,000 in GOLD BARS from a train near Albuquerque, NM; SILVER THEFT of $2,500 from a Federal depository in Silver City, NV; HORSE THEFT in Waco, TX; and numerous BANK and HIGHWAY ROBBERIES across the Southwest. Known associate and accomplice to violent acts committed by an Extramundane.
He is believed to be ARMED and VERY DANGEROUS. Do NOT approach alone.

Strickland came so close I could feel his spit and smell the garlic on his breath. "I know who you really are, Cal Cooper. You're a wanted man who thinks he can cower in my town. But everything that happens in Hexed Springs does so with my permission," Strickland whispered sharply into my ear. He rolled up the paper and slipped it back into his coat pocket.

I tried to croak out a response, but nothing

came out. Strickland smiled as he took pleasure in watching the air trapped in my lungs go sour.

"I hear you're a friend to Toussaint DuBois now. You could learn a lot from a man like him. Smart. Obedient. I'm financing his studies, you know. He gladly welcomed the opportunity to work for me. People who are loyal to me tend to do well in society. But men like you, you're nothing but wastrel scum, always and forever. Only I can save you from your fate. And those who are disloyal to me?"

Strickland drew a line across his throat with his thumb and squelched.

He continued to savor my struggle for air before speaking again. "Let me make myself clear, ranger. Either you cooperate with me or I will have you eliminated in the most painful way. You see, I'm very good friends with Roy Willoby. My friends in Washington welcomed my suggestion to appoint him as a federal judge. If you do not obey me and quietly return with my daughter within twenty-four hours, I will see that you are charged with her murder and then happily collect the bounty on your mutilated corpse." He patted my cheeks and smirked in his crooked triumph. "Do we have an arrangement?"

I almost preferred death to submitting to him. Almost. I nodded as best as I could and squeaked out a 'yes.'

"Good boy," he said.

Stars popped in my vision and my face was

hot and flushed. Before I could pass out, Strickland gestured for his lackey to drop me. With an obedient hum, the automaton tossed me across the room like a ragdoll.

"Thank you for your cooperation, ranger," Strickland said as I rolled on the floor in pain. "It's a shame it had to resort to this, though. You could have just done business like an honest man. Instead, you reverted to your criminal ways and tried to extort payment from me. I'll still offer you a down payment for your services, since I am the better man, but your actions will not go unpunished." Strickland withdrew a large wad of two-dollar bills from his pocket and tossed five of them at me. "Remember, ranger: Twenty-four hours. And tell no one of what you're doing. Good night."

The automaton picked up his sword and escorted his boss through what used to be my front door, then climbed aboard the rear of the stagecoach, nearly buckling its rear axle. The driver slapped the reins against the horses and the stagecoach disappeared into the night.

I rubbed my crushed windpipe and stood up after the blood returned to my extremities. The rumors were true—Strickland was no different from a gang boss who turned to blackmail and violence if money didn't buy him his way. If he and I swapped places, and I were to blackmail him? You can imagine the swift response from the authorities. The rich were privileged that way, and laws are interpreted differently for those with enough money and influence. That little fact actually inspired most of me and Clem's heists.

I'd been an idiot for inviting them inside. Not like I had a choice, though. Strickland would have let his mechanical pet bust in even if I'd declined to see them. No matter the outcome, that bastard came to me tonight knowing, one way or another, he was going to have his cake and eat it, too.

My mind was racing to catch up. The cold, metallic skin concealing cogs and pistons. The burning purple eyes. I suddenly recognized where I'd seen the metal man's gadgetry before. Strickland said he got the schematics to build the automaton from a business deal, a deal that must have involved Toussaint for something that complex. And Toussaint had knowledge of the paranormal, including an extensive academic knowledge of vampirism. He also had access to the veiled city of the extramundane. Surely there must be a lead in there somewhere. What's more, he trusted me, even though my faith in him had just been shaken for working with a man like Strickland, a category I now reluctantly belonged to. A parade of thoughts marched around my head. I could barely keep track of them all, and the ones I could led me down a rabbit hole of dead-ended questions. I paced around the room and scratched at my stubble. My first concern was with Strickland. Obviously, I was going to have to play his game or else my jig was up. He'd leak my identity to the territory, then sic his guards, bounty hunters, and the inquisitors on me until I was captured and hanged or brought in dead on arrival. Even if I did bring his daughter back, what if he forced me to do even more of his dirty work? I'd have to cross that bridge when the time came.

Running away from him wasn't much of an option either. I had nowhere safe to go and now my attempt to lay low in No Man's Land was in jeopardy. Even if I did tuck my tail and run, I wasn't going to get very far, very fast without a horse. Plus, who knew where Marney was lurking. I couldn't assume he'd forgotten me, even after all this time.

Now that I thought of it, being horseless was also going to complicate finding his daughter, too. I could steal one, I reckoned. After all, it was a crime already printed on my bounty poster. Damn that little voice in my conscience. It was telling me I couldn't break my promise to Clem that I'd be good.

Plus, this job could be my chance to prove to people like Aldon and Colin that I was a peacekeeper eliminating a threat, and not another exterminator. Who's ever heard of a good vampire? But I couldn't let Lucius find out about this. I doubted the feral vamp would be related to the Montagues, and usually vampires take care of their own. I crossed my fingers and hoped there wouldn't be any repercussions from all this.

Strickland's deadline didn't leave me much time. At first light, in less than five hours, I'd go see Toussaint and get what I could from him. Then I'd procure a horse and make my way to Strickland's manor to begin my search.

CHAPTER EIGHT

There's nothing like a life-threatening deadline to get you going in the morning. One of nature's alarm clocks wandered in through my missing front door, crowing and cawing at the sun streaming through my windows. I hollered at the wayward rooster to shut up before I realized he was actually doing me a favor. I'd dozed off while waiting for the early dawn and slept in too late.

I flew out of the chair and lit a fire in the stove to heat up some breakfast. I groaned while rubbing the sleep out of my eyes. Still no grounds, still no coffee. A damn shame.

I rinsed my face off in the water barrel behind the house while breakfast heated up. I took a long look at my reflection in the shaving mirror and rubbed a hand over the stubble growing long on my face. It was well past a five o'clock shadow but wasn't quite at the scruffy stage yet. I could put off shaving for another few days. Besides, depending on the eye of the beholder, I was either gritty or handsome. Two things I didn't mind being.

I pushed a comb through my black hair, even though it was just going to end up smothered underneath a hat. The smell of buttery biscuits wafted into my bedroom as I dashed back inside to pick through my wardrobe. I threw on a cream-colored, button-down shirt and tied on a black neckerchief—for filtering out trail dust, not robbing folks—and pulled tan pants over my dark leather boots. Next, I slipped a hawk-skull amulet around my neck. It was enchanted to protect me against hexes, something I'd picked up from a sorcerer during my travels. Three feathers were tied to the leather cord, each one capable of absorbing a damaging spell thrown my way, but each time it burns away a feather. I was already down two feathers and didn't have any more to replace them.

Last, but not least, I slipped on a golden locket that belonged to my twin sister. It was my lucky charm. Nothing fancy or magical about it, just pretty and sentimental. I tucked it safely into my shirt, alongside the neckerchief, then threw on the elven duster and hat Aldon's elleth had tailored for me, on account of me saving her husband from an orc. Magic-imbued threads lined the inside of the moss-green leather jacket, offering me extra protection against blunt forces via a bark-skin enchantment.

Back in the kitchen, I ripped off a fistful of biscuit and sandwiched a helping of fried egg.

Performing a delicate balancing act, so as not to spill my only meal, I rummaged through the cabinets for my trail rations—a couple strips of pemmican and some hardtack. I learned how to make it from my father, whose full-blood Cheyenne grandmother had taught him to make it. These pieces came straight from a family recipe, real fatty and tender, and I could still taste the blueberries mashed in.

I sat at the table, plugging bullets into my bandolier in between bites of bread. I wasn't good at keeping my larder stocked, but a good gunslinger always keeps plenty of ammunition around. Perhaps I was a little paranoid, but I never knew if or when I'd need to shoot my way out of a situation.

Cloudsplitter, my revolver, was a dependable piece of machinery and probably my most prized possession, one that I took care to clean and oil regularly. The Colt Navy revolver once belonged to my father. It was a family heirloom, and Pa had intended to give it to me when I became a man. Since he died before my teenage years, he never got the chance. Before the church took me in, I stowed it away and kept it hidden, never telling anyone about it. I took it with me everywhere I went after being orphaned. Since I don't have any heirs to pass it on to, I'm afraid it's more than likely going to die alongside me. Maybe they'll bury me with it, who knows.

I rubbed my palm across the ornamental

flourishes and floral patterns of my belt buckle to give it a polish, then slung my stocked bandolier across my shoulder. I downed the last of my breakfast, then wrapped a few pieces of pemmican in parchment paper and stashed it in my pocket. Given my late start, I was making good time.

Dammit, the door! I might not have the most valuable possessions in town, but they're mine and I'd be awful pissed if they were stolen because I'd left the door wide open, or, in this case, completely ripped from its hinges. I grabbed a few nails and a ball peen hammer from the junk drawer and hastily nailed a chunk of wood from the ruined door across the gap to deter anyone from messing with my belongings while I was gone.

"That'll do, Cal," I muttered to the half-assed attempt before me. I blindly tossed the hammer inside and didn't look back when I heard something crash to the ground.

I made it to Toussaint's camp in half the time it took to walk home last night, despite the growing number of people, horses, and wagons bustling through the crowded morning streets.

As I wandered up to the vardo, I practiced confronting the professor on his business with Strickland. The worn leather in my gloves squeaked as I nervously rubbed my hands together. Normally, coming on strong and slinging accusations was my kind of talking, but given that I'd come to know the man, badgering him from the get-go felt wrong. It would be a good way to alienate the only person who'd given me the time of day lately, not to mention offered me a job investigating the occult.

Maybe I could give him the benefit of the doubt and assume foreign academic types aren't well acquainted with the who's-who of rotten Americans to avoid. Sometimes it's hard to see a snake before it bites you.

To my luck, Toussaint was already awake and seated near the lean-to with a newspaper pinched in one hand and the smallest coffee cup I'd ever seen in the other. He was dressed in a white, long-sleeved shirt and gray pants with the same black boots he wore last night. His shirt was cut in a deep V-shape with an interesting design on its front lining the row of vertical buttons. There were extra bits of cloth shaped like feathers that crisscrossed over his chest all the way up to his neck.

"Professor, I need to have a word," I said as I sauntered up, interrupting his morning routine. "About Ross Strickland."

"My goodness. Bonjour, Cal Cooper. I did not expect to see you again so soon." He folded up his newspaper and tossed back the last drops in his cup. His curiosity and excitedness hadn't diminished at all from last night. "Yes, of course. Please sit."

I waved off his offer. "No time. I need to get to the bottom of something. Late last night, I got a visit from Ross Strickland. He offered me a job."

Toussaint rocked his head back and forth, taking in my words. "I suppose that is good, no? Strickland is a man of means who can pay well. I could postpone my research, if you wish to consider his offer."

"About that ..." I said, trying to look intimidating by hooking my thumbs into my gun belt. "Strickland isn't the kind of man who I'd choose to associate with. In fact, I think he's a real piece of shit. Only reason I'm taking on the work is because he's blackmailing me into it. He brought along an enforcer, an automaton who nearly choked the living daylights out of me." I walked over to the vardo and tapped my boot on the brass pipes snaking down its side. "The mechanical man looked an awful lot like some of your engineering."

The professor shrank back and held a hand to his chest. "The Sentinel?"

"If that's what you want to call it," I said. "You want to tell me what you're doing working like some kind of personal mechanic for Strickland? I know you're on his payroll."

Toussaint's eyes continued to grow wider by the second. "Are you suggesting I am involved with his blackmail scheme?"

A shadow cast by the brim of my hat crossed my face as I scowled. "I reckon you're the only person around who can engineer something like that. So, yeah, I am."

"I am offended, Cal Cooper. Have I given you the impression that I would condone such behavior?" He rose to face me, folding his arms across his chest. "If you must know, Strickland's investment firm awarded me my first research grant and funded my work investigating ley lines. It's how I was able to afford the journey to Hexed Springs in the first place."

"How could you take money from a man like him?" I snarled.

The professor threw up his hands. "How could I not? I may not be an American, but I know how things work here, mon amie. The rich and powerful dangle their resources in front of men like us. It is unjust, yes, but tell me, how else can I complete my research? How else can I pay to eat and travel and live?"

"You suck it up and do without. You dress like you're doing more than fine. I may live in squalor, but at least I have my honor."

Toussaint scoffed and turned away from me. "Forgive me for not living by your scoundrel's code, but I reside in the real world. If I must swallow my pride and work for a 'piece of shit,' as you say, so be it. Without this grant, I would be penniless, stuck in a country that finds both myself and my work untrustworthy. At least with his funding, I have been able to make some breakthroughs, some progress with my goals. It sounds to me like you've done nothing but wallow in self-pity."

I growled and kicked at a rock in my path. For a moment, I thought I was back at Clem's enduring another browbeating. Part of me didn't want to admit it, but they were both right. Perhaps I've been holding myself back in fear and remorse, stuck in the rut I'd made for myself. But I couldn't just abandon my principles and take work from people I fundamentally disagreed with. I'm no bootlicker.

Toussaint sighed and rubbed the back of his neck. "I'm sorry, Cal, that was too harsh. It's not my place to judge your principles. But I wish you wouldn't judge me for mine. I admit, I did build the automaton as a favor to Strickland. But, if it makes you feel better, I did not consider it would be used in such a fashion."

That did make me feel a little better. Deep down I knew the professor wasn't interested in engineering things to hurt people.

"What do you mean?" I asked as curiosity overtook my anger.

"To my knowledge, there is no way to power the machine. I assembled the Sentinel from ancient schematics, but had no knowledge of how to give it life. I assumed it was a suit of armor meant to serve as decor in his home," he said with a shrug.

"But what the hell is it, really?"

"The automaton was a guardian created

by the subterranean Talvir dwarves. They were powerful constructs immune to a number of spells, including a vampire's charm. The few known copies of the schematics that survived that ancient civilization are incomplete and do not detail how to power or program one."

"But somehow Strickland did and has it doing his dirty work."

"It appears so," Toussaint said, stroking his chin. "May I ask what you were blackmailed into doing?"

"Strickland ordered me to find and rescue his daughter from what sounds like a feral vampire within twenty-four hours. Otherwise, he'll give up my location to the cavalry, Marney's inquisitors, and anyone else looking to cash in on my bounty. If I don't get a move on, I'm worried the task might be impossible."

Toussaint swung his tiny mug around and sighed. "I am sorry this happened to you, Cal Cooper. I would not have constructed the automaton if I knew it would be used this way. Only bullies and cowards threaten violence to achieve their ends. Intimidating a man with death. It's reprehensible."

He was right. Death isn't pretty. Whether you're shot, hanged, or an old man dying in your bed, it's all ugly and frightening. Maybe somebody who's lived a long and purposeful life would feel differently, I don't know. But I'm not one of those people.

"Reckon you're right," I said. "Look, I'm sorry for hollering at you. Strickland's a bastard and I shouldn't have let him get me so riled up. I think we've both been taken advantage of."

"How do you mean?" he asked.

"Way I see it, Strickland knows just how to get what he wants. He exploited your situation and eagerness to learn about the supernatural. I was an easy target since I've got one too many skeletons in my closet."

"Perhaps you are correct," he said.

I extended a hand. "Mind if we put this one behind us?"

"I suppose we can." He shook my hand. "Now tell me: What are you going to do about this vampire hunt?"

"That's the other reason I'm here. I don't have many friends in the extramundane community here, not like I did outside the territory. I was hoping you may have a lead for me or know someone who might have the lowdown on what goes on around here."

Toussaint crossed his arms and paced around the camp. "As a matter of fact, I do know just the person. He's an extravagant man who sells exotic potions and poultices."

"Sounds like a snake oil salesman," I said.

The professor laughed. "He does come across as duplicitous, but I assure you, he is the one you seek. He's an alchemist who runs a trading outpost, selling mostly elixirs, chemical reagents, and occult artifacts, but he's also an information broker dealing in gossip and secrets."

"Great. Sounds like another untrustworthy person to fall in with. How do you know him?"

"It just so happens he provided me with the schematics for the Sentinel. And, yes, let's just say I would not want to be a fly trapped in his web. However, given the unique nature of your situation, I think it would be wise to pay him a visit. I'm confident he will have something to outfit you with for your encounter with a vampire, be it knowledge or potions."

I sighed and placed my hands on my hips. Something in my gut told me this was a bad idea, but it was the only lead I had. "You mind introducing me?"

"Not at all. I have business in Strayhaven this morning and was preparing to leave myself."

"Strayhaven?"

"The veiled city between our realms. That is its proper name."

"Interesting name. If you don't mind, can we leave now? I don't have much time to mess around," I said, hooking a thumb toward town.

Toussaint nodded and strapped on a shoulder holster holding two flintlock pistols, each with flared barrels and ebony grips. They were decorated with golden, floral patterns, and an odd assortment of gears, tubes, and casings coiled around the hammers.

"My own design," he said, holding one out for me to see. "The veve markings honor the loa of intellect, Damballa. The mechanisms here automatically reload ammunition into the barrel and cock the hammer. I cannot, how do you say, hit the broadside of a barn, but as a mundane with no magical ability, I welcome the extra protection."

Made sense to me. Even with my trusty revolver, I wished I was packing a little extra assurance against hostile paranormal forces, too. Like a lot of TNT.

Toussaint leapt up into the driver's seat of his vardo and patted the seat next to him. I climbed aboard as he pushed buttons and pulled levers, bringing the wagon engine roaring to life. He pulled gold-rimmed goggles down over his eyes and kicked the wagon into first gear.

"I'm curious," I asked as I clung to the seat. The trail into town was getting bumpy and I'd nearly tumbled out of my seat when we hit a rock. "How will we get me inside? I don't imagine a man whose past includes hunting the supernatural would be welcome in a city full of extramundane and their refugees."

Toussaint looked me up and down, then pressed my hat down tightly and pulled the duster's collar up to my ears. "Your garments appear vaguely elven, which will help you blend in. Don't worry, my contact has given me a unique item that will allow us to pass through the veil undetected."

"Just how does that work?"

Toussaint grinned and kicked the wagon into higher gear.

"You'll see."

CHAPTER NINE

Toussaint's motorized vardo careened around corners like a bat outta hell. I clutched my hat and hung on for dear life as folks shook their fists at us. Even a few hungover cowboys had to dive out of the way as we rounded the corner by Clem's saloon. Toussaint shouted his apologies, but I don't think anyone could hear him over the howling engines. I breathed a sigh of relief as we came to a halt. The engine sputtered as Toussaint twisted some knobs and disengaged the throttle.

He pulled the goggles over the brim of his hat, revealing a streak of dust that had formed around his eyes. "We are here," he said, wiping the dirt away.

We'd pulled up outside of two abandoned buildings located on the opposite side of town. I recognized the old S. J. Curtis five-and-dime store. On the leftmost side of the dilapidated building was an advertisement for absinthe, its paint peeled and weathered, featuring a lime-green fairy floating above a curly arrow that pointed down an alleyway. A little golden-haired sprite's wand rested upon the words 'Leave your reality behind.'

"A little on the nose, huh?" I asked.

"Not discreet at all," Toussaint joked. "This way."

I followed him down the darkened corridor between the two buildings, curving around corners left and right, like some kind of maze. There were far too many turns based on how the two buildings were situated. At the end of the trail sat some barrels; crates and chicken-wire cages lined up against a solid brick wall. It was a dead end full of trash.

I searched around for anything interesting. "This isn't what you wanted to show me, is it?"

"Not quite." He pried a loose top off one of the barrels and reached his arm all the way inside, pulling out a bottle of shiny, green liquid. "Normally, I wouldn't dare serve absinthe without first observing the traditional preparation ritual, but since you say time is short, this will have to suffice."

Toussaint took a light swig from the bottle. His lips puckered and he shivered as the drink hit his stomach. He vigorously cleared his throat, then offered the bottle to me.

"A little early, don't you think?" I asked.

Toussaint winked. "A little trick to getting inside. This is the item the eccentric alchemist gifted me. It's an enchanted liquor tinged with mana. The guardian wards woven into the veil will think we are a pair of extramundane beings and let us pass."

He hiccupped once, then gently swirled the contents of the bottle. I carefully accepted it and peered down the neck of the bottle. It was decorated with shooting stars that gave some texture to its green, transparent glass. Apart from being effervescent and pungent, the liquid seemed all right to me.

I've experienced my fair share of weird before, but I never pictured myself chugging a magic potion behind some abandoned buildings in the middle of town. I chuckled at what Clem would think of me if she saw me doing this. Now, Amos, he'd probably go right along with it.

I set aside my reservations and knocked back the bottle. As soon as the drink hit my tongue, my tastebuds lit on fire with a crackling and fizzing sensation followed by a sweet nectarlike taste—like a bolt of lightning dipped in honey.

I wheezed out a few coughs and stared at the bottle. "This stuff's stronger than a hillbilly's moonshine."

Toussaint nodded approvingly and snuck the bottle back into its hiding place.

"Allons-y, Cal Cooper," he said as he walked headfirst into the brick wall.

And then disappeared.

I blinked a few times, wondering if I was hallucinating. As a buzzing sensation coursed through my veins, I witnessed something strange happening to the wall. I crept up to it slowly, squinting to get a better look at the subtle transformation materializing right before my eyes. The bricks were becoming translucent, like a sheer gown flapping in the breeze. My hand brushed against the surface and slid right through the veil.

I steeled myself to step through the portal, knowing everything I'd ever perceived as true about this backwater town was about to change. "Al-on-zee, indeed," I said as I departed from the mortal plane I called home.

Pushing through the veil felt just as it looked, like walking through laundry on a clothesline. Toussaint beamed as I emerged, waiting for me with his hands on his hips. He clapped a hand on my back and spun me around to face the most extravagant view I'd ever seen.

"May I present Strayhaven, the city within a city, bridge between the mortal and immortal realms," he proudly exclaimed.

I could hardly believe my eyes. Strayhaven wasn't a dinky station the size of the back alley we'd just wandered through. It was a sprawling metropolis.

Toussaint wrapped his arm around my shoulder and carried me forward, leading me down the crowded streets as I stumbled along slack-jawed. We were packed in tight among a variety of extramundane species, walking in the opposite direction of foot traffic on the dusty side street, like salmon swimming upstream. I tried not to be rude and stare, but I couldn't help being a tourist in a magical land that, until now, had been hidden right under my nose.

The professor played tour guide, pointing out important locales. Funny enough, most of the area looked and felt familiar to me. It shared the same aesthetic as a Western town like Hexed Springs. Many of the buildings were either brick-and-mortar structures or wooden, one-level homes. Every now and then you'd see one featuring a hint of medieval-village flair, but the street mostly resembled the main drag in any Western town. Even some of the people here were dressed like cowpokes, if you counted the occasional tunic juxtaposed with a ten-gallon hat.

The first thing I noticed was the diverse population of mystical beings living in this district. Just about every kind of paranormal species were wandering the streets this morning. Elves, halflings, gnomes, dwarves, trolls, centaurs, kobolds, even the rare catlike Kanaanis. A hulking gray ogre with two heads sat against a tobacco shop. One of the heads was smoking from a pipe, while the other one was exhaling the puffs of smoke. I got a real kick out of that.

On down the road, we walked through a tunnel carved through a massive tree. It looked at least four times taller than any of the buildings surrounding it. At the base of the tree, highborn elves cozied up inside ivy-covered gazebos and babbling fountains, and walkways spiraled up to bungalows built along its enormous trunk, where elves mingled in its thick boughs. The tree's strong branches sprawled out in every direction, blanketing the block in shade with its canopy. I'd hate to be responsible for raking its human-sized leaves in autumn.

The plant growth around the great tree crept up the sides of nearby buildings, leaving no brick uncovered. Dryads, who looked like wooden ladies, danced among the flowers that bloomed on the vines as little pixies skipped along their petals. A young girl with short green hair and pointed ears was selling flower bouquets from underneath an awning made from twigs. One of the pixies floated over her shoulder, calling to the passersby to stop and look at their stock.

We came upon a grand archway leading down a side street, which was clearly some sort of red-light district. The skinny street dead-ended at a fancy house, painted deep red with black trim. It resembled a Victorian mansion with its delicate facets and lots of windows full of lush red curtains with golden tassels. Good for obscuring nosey folks from peeking inside.

Despite the early hour, a buxom gal stood on the corner, swishing her frilly dress back and forth. She winked at me while singing a beautiful melody, beckoning me to join her. I slipped free from Toussaint's grasp and politely removed my hat. Just before I could talk to her, I bumped into a tall green orc lugging around a bear trap on a chain. He looked like he outweighed me by fifty pounds of pure muscle, his spiked nose ring and cracked tusks more than intimidating. I excused myself and did an about face to avoid accidentally starting a fight.

Toussaint hadn't stopped talking or noticed that I'd stepped away. "Unbelievable, is it not?"

"You ain't kidding," I said, drinking in the surroundings. "So, this is all considered Strayhaven?"

"This quarter is called 'the Dust.' There are other quarters above the surface, too."

"Above the surface? You're saying there's more below us?"

He nodded. "There are three areas of note beneath our feet," he said, holding up three fingers, counting on each one as he talked. "The Catacombs are where the living dead congregate. Sentient ghouls, skeletons, zombies reside there. Then there is the Underkeep, a dungeon for the supernatural's most wanted. It is like a prison and asylum combined. And, finally, there is the Nexus, the hub of all mana on Earth."

Toussaint pulled me aside to an empty brick and pointed off into the distance. I stood on my toes to get a better look at the jet-black obelisk reaching up to the sky. It had a golden eye with a half-shut lid etched into its peak, sort of like an Egyptian hieroglyph.

"That monument marks the central point of the mana streams. An elaborate temple the shape of a pentagram rests at its base, but its doors have not opened in eons, nor has anyone ever traveled into the depths."

"What do you reckon it's protecting?" I asked.

"I can only guess it has something to do with the convergence of the ley lines." He sidled up close to me, lowering his voice to a whisper. "Just out of curiosity, have you any experience with breaking and entering into warded locations?"

"And here I thought you'd only hired me for my charming disposition and good looks."

Toussaint nudged me with an elbow. "It would be a shame if someone slipped past the barriers and cataloged the secrets of the temple, no?"

We shared a laugh, then turned down a cobblestone path leading to a bustling marketplace so full that folks stood shoulder to shoulder. Barking salesmen shoved their wares into my chest as I bumped my way through the crowd. Intoxicating spices tingled the inside of my nose, alongside the smell of greasy foods and grilled meats. As I was eyeing a tamale cart, pushed by a skeletal vaquero, a tall and gangly troll bounded toward me with speared hunks of meat, slow-roasted and dripping with fat. Ghoul haunches. While they looked delicious, they were actually poisonous to humans.

"No, thank you. I'm happy with being a vegetarian," Toussaint said to the troll. His face twisted up as we pressed on through the market. The troll didn't appreciate being told no but moved on to other potential customers.

The crowd came to a standstill as we reached the outer edge of the market. Shuffling along was the only way through. We were stuck behind a long line leading up to a popular food stall manned by an ogre selling huge wheels of cheese, salted meats, mead, mulled wine, and jars of honey. Those of us pushing through started cursing at the people standing in line, who were cursing at the guy holding us all up —a dwarf with a long braided red beard buying what looked like one of everything. I couldn't help but gawk at the ogre's wares while I waited. His garden vegetables were bigger than any I'd ever seen, and the links of sausage hanging from a hook behind him made me salivate. Together, they'd roast well over an open fire and make a fine meal.

I ignored the grumbling in my stomach as a path to the exit opened up in front of me.

"Toussaint? I found a way out," I called.

But there was no answer. The professor

was nowhere to be seen.

The street was clear, so I wandered ahead and called his name, figuring he hadn't gone too far without me. Not like he wasn't hard to find, after all. I hadn't been paying much attention or else I would have noticed everyone scrambling to make way for a chariot full of gray and green goblins. They blew past the crowd in a vehicle pulled by a squealing warthog the size of a wolfhound. I figured fire brigades here would be a little more ... magical. And less pig-powered.

Someone grabbed my shoulders and yanked me out of the path of the oncoming chariot. It careened around a corner and headed toward smoke rising in the distance. Tripping over my own feet, I spilled backward onto a wooden sidewalk, where people carelessly walked past me. I dusted myself off and turned to thank the kind stranger who'd saved me. To my unpleasant surprise, it was Colin the mangy werewolf.

"Fancy seeing you here, ranger. Almost didn't recognize you in this get-up. First time here?"

"That obvious?" I replied.

He leaned against a wall and lit a cigarette. He took a deep draw and blew it out, a little too close to my personal space. "Not many mortals find their way into Strayhaven. Some of them never find their way back out," he said with a sly grin.

I feigned a laugh and took a step closer to

him. "Look, Colin, that's a cute saying you've got there, but I ain't here to start trouble. Let's put what happened at Clem's behind us."

Colin was growing more agitated. In my experience, werewolves don't have much patience and hold grudges a little too well. "I don't care about what happened at the saloon. I care that you murder my people for money."

I leaned in and lowered my voice so no one else could hear. "You ever stop and wonder if some of them deserved it? Monsters killing animals, killing mundanes. What about you, huh? Ever lose control during a full moon and feast upon a few humans?"

Colin bared his teeth and laughed. "Trying to get a rise out of me, boyo? You might get away with causing a scene on your half of the realm, but here, you'd be dead meat."

"Your quarrel ain't with me, you half-wit mongrel. I don't pick sides between normal and paranormal. I dispense my own justice with equal opportunity."

"Like when you were a ranger? You know what 'rangers' like you are doing right now? Don't tell me you haven't read the papers. You and the rest of Willoby's inquisitors are wiping out my people so they can steal their land. And I, for one, won't stand for it," Colin said, hardening his gaze.

I wished he'd stop bringing up Willoby and his private army. He had no idea what he was talking about. I wasn't one of Willoby's men. It hadn't been like that at all.

"Goddammit, you fool. I ain't ..." I started to yell, then lowered my voice again. "I ain't a federal inquisitor."

Colin stepped back, his wolfish grin beaming. "Semantics, ranger. You know, I'm curious to find out what some of these folks would do if they knew that Cal Cooper was standing here in the flesh."

The werewolf eyed a trio of hobgoblins strutting through the crowd. Hobbies are notorious human haters and talented spell-slingers from birth. They can twist arcane energies into painful hexes and curses that can turn your stomach or even blind you, all so they can slip in and shank you with their poisoned blades. They don't fight fair and I'm sure they'd want to get a piece of me.

I heard Toussaint's voice yelling my name. He spun around and spotted me. The hobgoblins were only steps away.

My heart rate quickened. I needed an escape route, preferably one that would avoid stirring up trouble and prevent any unnecessary bloodshed. I don't know how well folks around here knew my face, but anyone with ears would have heard the rumors about me. Chances were somebody would recognize me if they put two and two together.

I made a break for my partner, running

against the flow of the crowd, but didn't get very far. A male faun shoved me back with his ram horns and flipped a finger at me. Colin cupped his hands to his mouth and took a deep breath in.

"Oi, hobbies. You look like a fine coupla mercs," he hollered. "I've got a fresh bounty right here for you: the infamous inquisitor, Cal Cooper."

The head hobgoblin eyed me as he shuffled closer, twirling a green dagger between his knuckles. The chainmail under his leather jerkin rustled against his gray skin. His pale blue eyes squared me up from head to toe while his two companions circled around me.

"What do you know? Furball's telling the truth. I'd recognize this face anywhere," he said through blackened, sharklike teeth. "How'd a mundane fella like you get past the veil?"

"I'm full of surprises for a mundane," I said. "For starters, I'm as resourceful as I am handy with a revolver." I peeked over the hobgoblin's shoulder and saw the professor approaching. He was tugging out his pistol when I stopped him with a shake of my head.

The hobbies laughed. "We love surprises. Suppose you'll come along quietly with us then? I hear vampires are looking for you."

"No, you're going to let me walk on by and attend to my business." I pulled up my back duster to reveal Cloudsplitter.

"Now that's not going to work either," the

lead hobgoblin said. He jerked his head toward the female hobgoblin behind him. "Blind him."

She muttered something and flung a hand at my face, projecting a black, oozy, tarlike liquid toward my eyes. The sludge dissipated as it struck an invisible magic barrier surrounding me, and one of the feathers on my pendant burned away as it absorbed the spell. I shoved the lead hobgoblin down just as his partner lunged at me with a blade. It nicked my duster, missing any flesh. I answered back with a hard right hook strong enough to crunch cartilage. He was already off balance with the swipe, so my punch landed clean and spun him to the ground.

The crowd circled around us now, creating an impromptu boxing ring. Toussaint emerged on the opposite side of me and pulled out his flintlock. "Now?" he asked.

"No, not here," I yelled as I jumped back from the female hobgoblin's blade.

The lead hobgoblin came to his feet and charged Toussaint. He muttered a few words of the ancient language while drawing shapes with his hands. He was going to hex the professor.

I grabbed the hobbie slashing at me and threw her into the barrel Colin was using as a viewing platform. The werewolf fell from his perch and landed on top of my attacker, giving me a chance to help Toussaint. He'd buried his face in his arms and twisted his body to the side, but the hobgoblin stopped suddenly. He held a hand to his mouth. He looked like he was speaking, but nothing came out, and the hex he was conjuring failed.

"Run," I yelled to Toussaint, but he was already on the move.

We pushed through the onlookers and searched for an exit. Just before I made it out into the open plaza ahead, a familiar face came into view.

I grabbed Toussaint by the collar and steered him toward Aldon, who was waving us down an alley. We followed him down a short path that ended at an old, boarded-up shop. Aldon tugged open a shuttered window and motioned us inside. We dove through it just as our enemies came around the corner. Aldon poked a finger out from between the slats of wood and whispered something in Silvis, the elves' native language. Seconds later, the crackling and popping sounds of fireworks ricocheted down the alley away from us, drawing the hobgoblin's attention away.

"Well, I'll be damned," I said once the commotion outside died away. I gave the kid a friendly punch on the shoulder. "Reckon you saved our skins back there, buddy. Aldon, this is Toussaint DuBois."

The elf boy nodded and created a ball of light in his hand. Toussaint was in awe of his magic. "What are you two doing in the Dust?" Aldon asked.

"Just a little business. What about you? What are you doing here?"

He ducked underneath a beam of wood hanging between a felled wall. "I snuck in. My eldar says my kindred aren't welcome here, but I like it. I want to make friends with the other elves. I don't like people in Hexed Springs."

"Humans are often unkind," Toussaint said.

Aldon rubbed the tips of his cropped ears. "My boss calls elves 'knife ears.' He speaks ill of me and doesn't even know I'm elven."

"I'm sorry, kid. You point him out to me next time you're working the telegraph and I'll give him a talking to," I said, holding up a fist.

Aldon rubbed his hands together in embarrassment. "I may have been fired from the telegraph office. I lost my temper and started a fight with some Pony Express riders." He pulled up his sleeve and showed me a purple bruise on his arm.

"I'd scold you, son, but I'm not one to speak. I've been in scuffles like that before."

Aldon smiled and stepped through an empty doorframe. On the other side was a child's room, empty and barren except for a collection of elven clothes, toys, and games stuffed in a corner of an impromptu hideout.

"My eldar doesn't know I was fired or expelled from school. This is where I hide during the day or when I want to be alone," Aldon said.

He tossed the ball of light in the air, where it hung like a chandelier, revealing dozens of paintings tacked to the walls.

"Young elf, these are stunning," Toussaint said, admiring a particular piece depicting an elven goddess holding the moon. "Did you paint these?"

Aldon nodded. "The storyteller told me legends about my ancestors. I like to paint the stories to remember them. My eldar says our people have forsaken us and won't let elleth teach me."

Toussaint was absorbed with the boy's work and poured over them with intense focus. "It is good that you stay connected with your heritage. Learning about my Creole ancestors, their revolution, and my namesake, Toussaint Louverture, filled me with pride and inspires me to this day."

"You're both lucky. I didn't have anything but memorabilia to remember my folks," I said.

"You do not know your heritage? Nothing at all?" Toussaint asked.

"Never had anybody to teach me."

Aldon tilted his head. "No one from your kindred?"

"Humans don't really have a kindred, kid. Not like the elves, at least. My parents died when I was little, so I never got to learn about my ancestors. I was sent to an orphanage, and they only wanted to teach me about being Catholic. They sure weren't going to teach me my Cheyenne roots."

"Genealogy is a fascinating study. I'm sorry you were denied the knowledge, Cal Cooper," Toussaint said.

"Yeah, well, I reckon I turned out okay without it. It wasn't easy growing up not knowing who I was or where I belonged. I never really felt like I nailed down an identity, just floated between personalities based on who I was with at the time. You get pretty jaded as a kid, being forced to learn to be something you don't want to be. But I made my own way. Right or wrong, I did it according to my own rules."

I stood back and took in the boy's work. He had some talent, all right. Seeing his assortment of memorabilia reminded me of my room at the orphanage. I'd latched onto odds and ends that reminded me of my family and my childhood. Instead of facing my emotions, I'd bottle them up and assign them to a trinket that I kept with me wherever I went. Aldon was doing something similar with his elven toys and paintings, but instead of burying his feelings, he was experiencing them, even going so far as to contribute to his culture.

I nudged Toussaint who was admiring a whittled figurine. "Your hideout's pretty spectacular, partner, but we've got a deadline to keep. I'm afraid we've got to be going."

Aldon hung his head and shied away from us. "It's okay. I think it's safe now anyway." He pulled back a blanket hiding a latched door. "My eldar accepted the coin you gave me and bought medicine for my elleth. She's better today. I didn't tell him it came from you, though," Aldon said as we walked outside.

"Fair enough. And don't worry, I understand. All that matters is she's feeling better," I said.

Aldon stared at his foot as he twisted it in the dirt. "When you said you were doing 'business,' did you mean hunting someone?"

I sighed and leaned against the wall next to the door. "Something like that. It's sort of complicated, but I've got a good reason to do it. A human hired me to find his daughter. She's been taken by something very bad and her life is in danger."

"That doesn't sound complicated. Are you going to kill it?"

"Probably so, partner."

Aldon stuck his hands in his pockets and looked up at me. "I guess I understand. You're doing it because you're a guardian."

No, I'm doing it to save my own skin from a greedy, double-crossing bastard.

"If you say so," I said.

We exchanged our final farewells, and Aldon pulled the door shut after us. It didn't feel right lying to the kid. I don't know if I was inspired by the small kinship I felt with the boy or just eager to change my reputation from killer to guardian, but the little white lie weighed on me more than I expected it to. I don't think I could ever tell the boy about my days with the cavalry.

As for Abigail, of course I had sympathy for the little girl. I'm no sociopath. Even if she was the daughter of a megalomaniacal asshole, I'd make a real effort to bring her back alive, though having the richest and most powerful man in the region threatening to unleash the equivalent of hellhounds on my trail motivated me more than anything, and I wasn't ready to face whatever waited for me beyond the boundary of No Man's Land.

Like Aldon, perhaps all I needed was a blank canvas, one unmarred by my past regrets.

CHAPTER TEN

Toussaint and I hiked up a bridge that connected to a wide plaza walled in by shops built of white stone and terracotta tiles. Buildings in Strayhaven were older and towered over the courtyard below. Glass orbs hovered above braided-iron street lamps that bordered the square. Folks walked like they had someplace to be, their fine garments swaying in their wake. A tower jutted up out of the center of the square and displayed the location of planets, the phase of the moon, the position of the sun and the current time, all in a series of concentric rings. I wasn't sure if it was decorative or served some higher purpose.

A few elven children sat in a circle underneath the clock tower with a faun and a kid with elk antlers, one of them bobbing behind the others, patting heads and counting. Then came a *thwump* followed by a puff of smoke. One of the kids had been transformed into a goose and was chasing down the others, who were running away and screaming in delight.

West of the clock tower was an underpass that cast a deep, black shadow as far down the path as I could see. Past the outer walls of the town square, I could make out Gothic stone towers with castle parapets poking out of them. Creatures with glowing eyes and people covered in thick dark robes mulled about in the twilight section.

"What's back there?" I asked.

"That darkened path leads to the oldest part of Strayhaven where vampires and other creatures of the night live. The Montagues' main manor resides there, but they have separate minor estates back in Hexed Springs, too. To get to the more decadent parts, you'll have to cross through slums as well as hideouts known for harboring illegal goods for blood mages and dark sorcerers. Dubious transactions happen there," Toussaint said with a hint of caution.

"Don't tell me that's where your contact is …"

Toussaint laughed. "Although my contact prefers to do business in the shadows, he is far too eccentric to live there. We can brave that district another day. For now, we are here."

We stopped in front of a curious building at the back of the plaza. All kinds of paranormals were shuffling in and out. Swinging on hinges above an arched entrance was a wooden sign that read 'The Elixirium.' The shop itself was a mismatched feat of architecture composed of several fairytale cottages smashed together. The roof was made up of numerous rounded towers covered with blue tiles shaped like wizards' hats. The shop was several stories high, each with its own balcony, giant window, or smoking chimney. A sparkly, pink puff of smoke trailed from one of the portside windows. The center of the store was topped with a geodesic dome; a greenhouse full of tropical birds and blooms sunned underneath the glass.

Toussaint went in first and greeted the blue-haired fairy girl working the cash register. She was surrounded by displays of flower petals, gnarled roots, and empty vials with cork stoppers. All of it was for sale.

An interesting mix of smells floated up from bubbling potion cauldrons that were at least half as tall as me. The air deeper in the store was mostly stale and musty, like moldy soil, but wasn't terribly off-putting. I thumbed through some of the merchandise resting on a pedestal. Potted plants sat at the top of the display, enjoying a wash of sunlight from a large, eye-shaped window in the back of the store. Each plant was accompanied by a card listing its name and alchemical properties, along with recipes for budding potion-makers to try at home. Sumac, milkweed, yucca, wheat grass, persimmons were but a few of the plants on display.

Stewing potions wasn't my thing. I was downright awful at brewing anything other than a cup of coffee. I preferred to buy my potions from Indian shamans. They were the premiere alchemists of the West, in my semi-professional opinion.

The back of the store was organized like a library; shelves full of jars and tubes were topped off with every color of liquid you can imagine. Dried garlic and chili peppers hung from a rack above various bulk goods in barrels, just like your average general store. I observed a stout dwarven gal filling her basket with crystals and gemstones, before my line of sight was interrupted by an ogre carrying in freight boxes labeled 'fragile.'

Toussaint jumped aside before the ogre absentmindedly walked through him. "Is Oliver in this morning?" he asked.

The blue-haired fairy girl nodded. "He is, but he's about to perform."

"Perform?" I asked.

Toussaint leaned over and whispered, "A theatrical sales exhibition in the plaza. I said he was eccentric, no?" He turned back to the fairy, who was all smiles, and said, "Thank you, Cass."

"Actually, it's me. Sandra," she politely corrected.

"Forgive me, I should have recognized you from your cheery disposition," Toussaint said.

He leaned over to whisper again. "Cass and Sandra are one fairy girl split into two beings after a horrible accident with an echo spell and a polymorph potion. Don't ask unless you wish to spend the rest of the afternoon listening to the argument of who was at fault."

"Noted. I'll avoid the topic," I said.

Another fairy girl, identical in appearance, tramped around the corner holding a box under her arm. "Your specimen arrived yesterday, Mr. DuBois. Take it before it tries to kill one of Mr. Van Pelt's crows again," Cass said. She huffed and thrust the box at the professor.

Toussaint beamed, too excited to notice her discontent. "I hope it was not too much trouble to obtain."

Cass and Sandra answered at the same time.

"Not at all. Our pleasure," Sandra said.

"Pain in the ass," Cass said.

Sweet Sandra and Crass Cass. That's how I was going to remember how to tell them apart. They were exact copies, like identical twins, each with matching blue hair, hooped ear piercings, and tattoos of the moon phases on their forearms. They even wore the same laced-up, forest green vest and flowing goldenrod skirt.

Toussaint turned to me and showed me the box, which thumped and wriggled in his hands. "For my research. I've been dissecting rare magical abominations recently. I believe it will give me insight into your condition, mon amie."

I smiled half-heartedly. "What all do you sell here?" I asked the girls.

"All manner of potions, elixirs, and even spell scrolls," Sandra said. "If you're looking for something specific, we can usually track it down for you."

"Buyer beware in the experimental elixir section, though. Half of the potions have weird side effects or don't really work," Cass said.

Before I could find out more about the side effects, carnival music interrupted my thought. The customers in the shop perked up, leaving behind their baskets full of items, and hurried toward the exit.

Cass smiled brightly and tucked her fists under her chin. Sandra rolled her eyes. "He's back," they said simultaneously.

Toussaint and I fell in line for the exit and made our way through the crowd forming in the plaza. A large wagon bigger than a prairie schooner rolled up on oversized wheels. It really did look like it belonged in a traveling carnival. An organ grinder built into the rear of the vehicle piped out a playful tune and blew colorful bubbles for kids to chase after. The wagon, painted ruby-red with golden flourishes on its trim, was reminiscent of something straight out of Vaudeville. It read "Dr. Van Pelt's Traveling Apothecary: Potions, Elixirs, and Patented Medicines" in swirling golden letters.

The wagon came to a stop in the center of the plaza with a level of fanfare befitting the arrival of a foreign dignitary. A stream of confetti erupted as a trio of horns embedded in the organ announced Oliver's arrival, and a stage unfolded from the walls of the wagon. Posters depicting bottles and jars unfurled from the bottom of the platform, calling buyers to action with slogans like "Don't miss your chance" or "Limited time only." By the looks of his production, I reckoned the man must have a silver tongue that could sell ice to a polar bear.

The crowd fell quiet with anticipation. I looked over at Toussaint who had a gleam in his eyes waiting for the performance to start. After a moment, a drumroll purred from the wagon, punctuated by a cymbal crash as the red velvet curtains opened wide and Oliver emerged, arms raised in triumph as the crowd applauded.

The man looked like a circus ringmaster who had the color drained from his apparel. He sported a black- and gray-striped tailcoat with a bolo tie shaped like a skull. A thin mustache stopped short of the corners of his mouth, and his facial features were accentuated by a subtle amount of stage makeup. I had expected to see a cheap copy of P.T. Barnum, but so far, Oliver was just as captivating.

"Ladies and gentlemen, boys and girls, it is I, Dr. Van Pelt, here to ignite your imaginations with my wondrous, stupendous, and absolutely marvelous selection of curios," he said, gesticulating wildly across the stage. "I've returned from a long journey across the mundane realms, mingling with magicians, pondering with physicians, and surmising with shamans to curate a fine selection of distillations. Find a cure for all ailments, maladies, illnesses, and more, here at my traveling apothecary or just down the street at my Elixirium."

"What'd I say? A snake oil salesman," I whispered to Toussaint.

"Trust me, Cal Cooper. He is, as you say, 'bona fide.'"

I rolled my eyes and turned my attention to the crowd. One by one, Oliver called them up on stage to demonstrate some new whatchamajig. The sales pitches on stage bordered on outright lunacy. Oliver rubbed purple goop on a dwarf's hairless chin and told him to wait three nights for thick chin whiskers to appear. Then he claimed to cure some man of his back pains with electric shocks. Finally, he fed powdered bull horn to an orcish brute and cracked a crude joke about preparing himself for a rowdy night in the bedroom.

After he'd exhausted his bundle of wares, Oliver bowed low and bid farewell to his customers then disappeared back inside his wagon. Toussaint wandered up to the stage and examined some bits and baubles. I looped my arm around him and dragged him away before he could get too distracted.

"Let's get what we need from this fella and get out of here," I said.

Oliver had his back to us when we approached the rear of the wagon. He was having a lively discussion with the shop ogre from earlier, who was holding a large, wooden crate.

"No, no, can't you see? The big red arrow on the box should point this way, not that way. Oh, and look, this one is leaking," he said.

The big gray and single-headed ogre inspected the boxes carefully, then shrugged and dropped the crate with a thud. Oliver shooed it away and cursed.

"Mr. Van Pelt," Toussaint called out.

Oliver spun around and clasped his hands together, swapping out his anger for the same vigor and showmanship he used on stage. A delightful little smile drew across his face, and he removed his top hat and bowed.

"Oh, my! Toussaint DuBois, as I live and breathe," he said, reaching out his hand to exchange handshakes with us both. "And Cal Cooper, the lone ranger of Hexed Springs. I've been dying to meet a fellow mundane as captivating as you. The name's Oliver Van Pelt, purveyor of the occult and alchemist extraordinaire. I'm sorry for causing a scene there, but in the case of ogres, two heads are absolutely better than one. Twice the brain power."

He chuckled and socked me in the arm. His speech pattern was a performance in itself. Certain syllables were cut short while others played out to maximize their dramatic effect. I must say, it was catchy and effective. The man exuded charisma.

"Hold on, partner. How do you know me?" I asked.

"I wouldn't be a good salesman if I didn't know my customers, both normal and paranormal, now would I? Don't tell anyone, but I only do market research on the most fascinating individuals," he said, giving me a reassuring wink.

The showman held up a finger and pranced up the ramp and returned with a small container filled with a variety of his products.

"I have a special elixir for you gentlemen to try today. Perhaps not you, Mr. DuBois, your voice is already like that of an angel, but maybe I can interest you, Mr. Cooper, in this incredible singing tonic I invented. Two squirts down the throat, like this," he said as he mimicked the action of squeezing the spray bottle's bulb, "and your voice will transform from your brusque tone into something more melodic and pleasing."

"You saying you don't like the way I sound?"

"Oh, no, it's not that. I love a man with a commanding voice. Gruff and intimidating," he said as he bobbed his eyebrows.

"No, thank you. Look, I'm here for—"

"One moment, I have another new product I want to show you." He dug through the crate and pulled out a vial of golden liquid.

"Mr. DuBois, how about I toss in a bottle of this lusty perfume with your purchase today? One drop of this intoxicating aroma conjures an olfactory echo mimicking the great redwood cedars of California and the cinnamon trees of Saigon. Strong enough to make any gal spin on her heels and fall into an unbreakable trance of love."

Oliver uncapped the tube and offered it to Toussaint, who swirled the vial and let its contents waft into the air. Toussaint jerked away from the bottle and rubbed his nose. "That is certainly a unique aroma."

I pinched my nose and waved the smell away. "Lord almighty, what is that stuff? I can smell it over here. Reeks of dog piss and fir nettles."

"I may use some unusual and exotic ingredients, but I suppose this fragrance isn't for everyone. However, I can attest to its potency to win over a lover," Oliver said, clearly unimpressed with my olfactory palette.

I checked the clock tower behind us as Toussaint continued to politely decline the man's offer to fix him up with a nice gal. I cleared my throat and shot an impatient glare at my friend and the wannabe matchmaker.

"Pardonnez-nous, but I'm afraid we don't have the luxury of time today. Cal Cooper here has a *special* request for you," Toussaint said.

"I'm thrilled to be of service, Mr. Cooper. Why don't we step inside my office at the Elixirium? I prefer to handle 'special requests' there," Oliver said, gesturing toward the building. He turned back to his ogre assistant. "Felix, pack up the wagon and unload our goods in the storage room. And be sure to read the directions on the crates this time, please."

Oliver whisked us inside and led us to a hidden room at the back of the store. "Cassandra, sorry, Cass and Sandra, will you hold any visitors for me? I'll be in my office with two of my favorite clients."

We settled into plush chairs in the cozy, private office. The room was lined with bookshelves full of ledgers. An assortment of alchemy equipment was displayed on the hearth above the empty fireplace behind his desk.

"Fewer wandering ears in here, if you know what I mean," Oliver said, lighting a long, thin cigarette. "Please tell me exactly how I can be of service."

I spread my arms across the chairback. "Let's start with you telling me how you really know me."

"Very well." He clasped his hands together and sat forward in attention. "I'm not just a traveling alchemist, Mr. Cooper. I deal in a great number of things, including managing an incredibly complex trade operation between the mundane and extramundane realms, both in and out of the port of Strayhaven. In my journeys, I come across gossip, rumors, facts, and fictions. That is to say, information of all sorts, which I broker between parties that interest me. You, sir, belong to one of those parties."

"I'm flattered, pal. I haven't been outside No Man's Land in months. What are they saying?" I asked.

"Well, the newspapers have ceased running your mugshot. The cavalry, however, is still in a tizzy over the incident at Rusted Butte. The inquisitors have another priority at the moment, but you're still a persona non grata."

"What do they say about Rusted Butte?"

Oliver leaned forward. "That you betrayed our kind. Massacred your platoon to save a few elves."

I glowered, unsurprised at the allegations.

"Was it truly murder, Cal Cooper?" Toussaint asked.

"No. I was acting in self-defense," I said, sharply. "What did you mean by 'our kind'? I didn't reckon mortals got around the immortal plane that often."

"Not many do. However, mundanes who prove themselves useful to the people here are granted passage. I proudly hail from Maine but have resided here for quite some time."

"Granted by who?" I asked.

"My, my. You do have many questions," Oliver said. He removed his top hat and placed it upon a faceless wooden bust. "As fate would have it, I met a vampire on a trade excursion in the mundane realm, one belonging to the Nightingale brood of Old Europe. They value trade and saw me as a valuable partner in creating commerce here."

"I'm only familiar with the Montague brood," I said.

"They reside at the top of the food chain around these parts. There is also the Tiberius, the Nightingales, and a few minor houses not worth naming. Many of the elder vampires who reside in Strayhaven were here when it was founded. They've accrued substantial wealth and a large sphere of influence, each vying for power and status."

"You have any kinship with the vamps?"

"In my line of business, my boy, one must stay neutral in political affairs. I claim no allegiance to any party here and simply desire the best deals for my clients." He tapped the ash off his cigarette and looked into my eyes. "Why are you so curious about these vampires?"

I shifted in my seat and blew out a breath. "Long story short, I've got less than twenty-four hours to find a missing little girl, and I have to believe you can tell me how to find her."

Oliver folded his hands and shook his head. "Now, now, Mr. Cooper. Elixirs aren't the only items I sell. I've given you a decent amount of information for free. If I gave away all my services, I'd be a poor businessman in more ways than one."

Finally, here were the terms and conditions part of the sales pitch. Just after I get suckered in, I get hit with the price tag. I was afraid this one would cause me to have some sticker shock.

"Name your price," I said with a growl.

Oliver hummed to himself for a moment. "One favor. At my discretion and at the time of my choosing."

"Depends on the favor. You gonna have me breaking the law?"

"Would that be a problem?"

I took a deep breath and thought it over. "In a previous life, no. But I've promised someone very close to me that I wouldn't do that anymore."

"All due respect, sir, this is the real world we're dealing in. One that just so happens to be on the cusp of a very pivotal moment. I'm afraid your presence here in No Man's Land has accelerated a series of events already in motion."

"Why me?" I asked.

"You're a wild card. A last-minute entry into the horse race. You're a thumb on the scale that can tip the balance of power and upset the status quo of our linked worlds," he said, exhaling a puff of smoke that smelled of cloves.

"You're talking about the bad blood brewing between the mundane and extramundane?"

Oliver blew out another long breath and stroked his mustache. "It would be more accurately described as a powder keg. Certain members of humankind have been vying to unseat the reign of vampires. Making good progress at it, too, if you ask me. The elven kindreds could make a case for power, if they were willing to wage war on the Families. The orc clans are far too shattered, but someone is uniting their warbands and enlisting wayward Comanche boys to learn their battle tactics. As for the rest? They simply don't have the means to be considered a threat."

"Does Lucius Montague wear the crown in No Man's Land?" Toussaint asked.

"He's the eldest son of the family's Patriarch, so yes. Strange man for a vampire. Has a fondness for human women, especially ones that aren't available, if you catch my drift. He's rather diplomatic when it comes to working with humans, something that his brood father isn't happy about. Some say Lucius is willing to sacrifice a part of the family's dominance to accommodate a more peaceful future between the realms. However, the other families smell blood in the water."

Maybe I should go into politics with as much as I was learning about the social hierarchies of No Man's Land.

"Here's why I'm asking," I said, showing him the photograph of Abigail. "Abigail Strickland. Daughter of Ross Strickland. She's the missing little girl."

"And Strickland hired you to find her," Oliver said, gazing at the photo.

"More like forced me to," I said. "He says she was abducted by a feral vampire. I need to know where she may be and if I'm about to incur the wrath of one of the Families."

Oliver's bright green eyes grew wide. "Well, that is certainly quite the job. The wealthy financier who thinks he can invest his way to the top is turning to assassination. How interesting." He chewed his lip. "Feral, you say? If that's true, it couldn't be a member of the Families. The heirs take care of their own kind and would never let one spoil and atrophy like that. Sounds like your quarry is some poor soul that contracted vampirism after being fed upon and discarded."

I breathed a sigh of relief knowing I wouldn't be picking any more fights with the rich and powerful.

"I'm curious, aren't vamps immortal? Why the need for heirs?" I asked.

Toussaint chimed in with his expert knowledge of supernatural biology. "Vampire minds are highly intelligent, and their bodies are stronger and faster than any human, but they can be destroyed. Given their superior physiology, vampires deteriorate rapidly without proper sustenance. Animal blood is an insufficient nutrient source that can cause serious health repercussions for them."

Oliver nodded. "Mr. DuBois is correct. Plus,

immortal life can be so droll. Assassinating each other is the only thing that brings them any joy after hundreds or even thousands of years of life." He set the cigarette down in an ashtray and reached inside his desk. "Let us think where your feral vampire may be."

Oliver pushed aside some papers and spread a thin, yellowed parchment across the desk. It was a map, but one enchanted to update itself with information in real time. It was covered in markings denoting who owned which land tracts, where Oliver sourced his alchemical supplies, safe routes free of bandits, and other symbols I didn't understand.

"Show me the location of all vampire-related sightings within the past six months," he said. The map redrew itself to portray the town of Hexed Springs. Hundreds of dots appeared in red ink across Hexed Springs. "Nothing unusual there. Let's try a twenty-mile radius around Hexed Springs."

The map zoomed out to show more of the surrounding area. More red marks cropped up, but they were scattered and didn't hint at any kind of pattern.

"Try west of the Strickland estate," I said.

Oliver repeated my request to the living document. Its black ink shifted and focused upon a radius around Strickland's land. Within seconds, a dozen markings revealed themselves across the fields southwest of the estate, concentrated at one spot.

"A coal mine," Oliver said, pointing to a symbol shaped like a cave. It was located at the edge of Bill Conway's land. "It was abandoned recently when miners began disappearing inside. If I were you, I wouldn't march in there ill-equipped."

I got up and walked over to the window, anxious to get going. "I reckon you're about to sell me something. Let me hear what you've got for vampire removal."

Oliver laughed. "Holy water is the obvious choice. A wooden stake is also a sure-fire bet, but this is a potion shop, not a hardware store. I could brew a potent poison to inject into your bloodstream, should the vampire overwhelm you. It would prevent you from transforming and maybe take it down with you."

"Yeah, no thanks on that last one. You've really got nothing else that can help me?"

"Is the knowledge I've imparted upon you not sufficient?" Oliver asked with wounded pride.

"I've never heard of anyone teaching a vampire to death, so no." I couldn't contain my impatience.

Oliver arched an eyebrow and unlocked a chest in the corner of the room. He placed a clear liquid vial in the shape of a crucifix on the table. "My last vial of holy water."

"And how much will this run me?" I asked.

"Whatever the cost, Mr. Van Pelt, please put it on my tab," Toussaint said.

Oliver waved a hand. "It's on the house, gentlemen. But be careful with that now. That stuff's rare these days. I'm under contract with the Montagues not to sell any of it to anyone else but them. Seems they're worried about a growing mundane population armed with the stuff. But only a fool brings a knife to a gunfight. I can't help it if I keep a stock of my own. Shame if a vial goes missing from time to time."

"Can't we just have one of the ordained around here bless some regular water?" I asked.

Oliver chuckled. "Water is scarce in Hexed Springs, Mr. Cooper. Folks prefer to drink it."

I stuffed the vial in my satchel and thanked him. "So why is it that you've decided to help me? How can I trust you not to flip on me as fast as you've flipped on the vamps?"

Oliver smiled. "I am on your side, Mr. Cooper. I'm a fellow mortal looking to keep the peace between our two worlds." He rolled up the enchanted map and locked it back in his desk. "The normal and paranormal have always struggled to coexist. Humans have always sought to dominate nature. Even though they possess immortality and exist on various planes outside the human realm, the extramundane want largely the same." After a short pause Oliver continued. "There are more mortals than paranormals nowadays. We simply outnumber them. The new guard wants the old guard to fade away with the past."

"And what do you want?"

Oliver shrugged and leaned back in his chair, letting the silence hang. "Selfishly, I'd say it's what's best for trade, but it's more than that. I want what's best for everyone, be they human or monster. Even when that breaches contracts or violates the law. Mr. Cooper, we all must choose sides sometimes. As someone who has a solid foot in both worlds, like it or not, you may find yourself the peacekeeper."

I chuckled. "I appreciate that, but don't hold your breath. You won't catch me dispensing law and order. Besides, it feels wrong supporting the new guard, as you called it. Especially when it's represented by men like Ross Strickland."

"Strickland is a son of bitch," Oliver said. "He may have money, but he's a poor man. I can guarantee you, whatever consequences he has in mind for you are much less devastating than what the vampires can do. As awful as it may seem, it might be best for us mortals to stick together right now."

"That's just great. Sounds like I'll be caught in the middle of this struggle."

"Don't worry so much, Mr. Cooper," Oliver said, rising from his seat and motioning toward the door. "I'll be here to navigate the ever-changing political landscape with you. Although I sincerely doubt it will be an issue; if the need should arise, I will convince Lucius that you were doing the family a favor by knocking off a feral vampire attracting unwanted mortal attention. Finish this job and you'll have both Strickland and the Montagues satisfied for the time being. Just remember that favor you owe me."

"I'll agree to those terms," I said, shaking his hand. Oliver's eyes flashed and he cracked his biggest smile yet. Thankfully, he wasn't an extra-mundane sorcerer, otherwise I'd just indentured myself with a powerful magical IOU.

"Wonderful. I truly believe you have a big role to play here, Mr. Cooper. Come see me after you save that girl and I'll help keep that eight-hundred-pound-gorilla Strickland off your back."

I tipped my hat to him and thanked him again for the advice and the holy water. I stopped just shy of opening the door when I remembered I had one more question.

"Got any advice for destroying a Sentinel? Strickland powered the one Toussaint built with your schematics. He's using it for muscle. Damn near killed me, too," I said, rubbing the spot on my neck where the metal hands had crunched my windpipe.

Oliver froze for a moment and stuttered. "I'm sorry. What did you say? Mr. DuBois, is this true?"

Toussaint nodded, eyes down. "Strickland says he was gifted the energy source by someone powerful."

A drop of sweat broke out on Oliver's forehead, smearing the powder on his face. Underneath the tan layer of makeup, his skin had turned ghostly white. "Well, that's a horse of a different color. The translucers haven't been able to enchant the old crystalline technology. This is happening ahead of schedule."

I raised my eyebrows. "You got something you want to tell us?"

Oliver paced the room, his chin on his fist. He clicked his teeth together a few times before focusing his gaze back on me. "No offense, Mr. Cooper, but this information is far too valuable for anything you've got to trade. But rest assured, I will inform you when I know more."

I cocked my head to the side and laughed. I hadn't come to Hexed Springs to become a puppet in the schemes of the rich and powerful, but here I was, having my strings pulled by two prominent and ambitious men. Three, if you counted Oliver. Dancing to someone else's tunes wasn't my idea of freedom. Way things are going right now, though, Oliver was right. I needed to pick a side—right or wrong, mortal or immortal, legal or illegal. Not really an easy choice, to tell the truth. Seeing how I may have some magical ability of my own, I wasn't so sure which side I belonged to anymore. Which me would I betray? The mortal one who gave his word to be an honest man, trying to lay low? Or the potential wizard gunslinger itching to return to a more thrilling life?

Either way, I had to deal with Strickland and Montague. Strickland represented new money and mortals getting rich off exploiting land and people. The Montagues represented old power, immortals so ingrained in extramundane society that simply mentioning their name elevated your own status. Pick the wrong side and it's goodbye Calamity.

As I grabbed the doorknob to make my exit, the door flew open, nearly catching me in the face. One of the fairy girls stood in the doorway. She was shivering in fright.

"I'm sorry, Mr. Van Pelt, but I tried to tell them you were with guests and weren't to be disturbed. He insisted I let him through."

A pale hand emerged from the shadow behind her, pinching the tip of the fairy girl's translucent wing. She yelped in pain as a man with skin the color of ash forced her out of the way.

"Lord Montague is waiting for you, ranger. Follow us, please."

CHAPTER ELEVEN

Three vampires escorted me across town to the slums, where various ghouls and goblins stalked the shadows. The quarter was unusually dim, as if the sun couldn't quite penetrate the air around it. A product of magic, no doubt. Any remaining light was filtered out through grimy canvas sheets the size of sailcloths, like a jungle canopy, each cloth tacked to the corners of the rundown buildings huddled together here. Vandals etched vulgar symbols into crumbling walls and broken gargoyles decorated the arches overhead. The loud bickering of aggressive creatures trickled through the alleyways, their grunts and howls trailing behind as I was led through the cobblestone streets.

Toussaint said this area was known for its 'dubious' nature, which didn't bother me much, seeing as I'd mingled in similar places in the mortal world. The only difference between here and out there was the addition of bloodthirsty, deranged monsters who prey upon the weak.

Actually, it didn't sound that much different when you really thought about it.

It hadn't taken much for the vampires to separate me from my mortal allies back at the Elixirium. Oliver had tried to smooth things over with the vamps, while Toussaint tended to Sandra, and I lost my temper and tried to sock the one who'd hurt the girl in the mouth. That ended the peace talks real quick. In a flash, the ashen vampire had my arm twisted behind my back and his two compatriots had drawn their fangs and knives. They surrounded me and pushed me out into the morning sunlight, careful to draw up the hoods of their black cloaks, filtering out the sunlight. Despite how easily they had subdued me, none of them were dressed for a proper fight; they looked like they shopped at the same tailor as Toussaint.

My escorts stopped shy of a heavy oak door, like something you'd expect on a medieval castle. They knocked out a rhythm with the door knocker, which was shaped like a clawed fist. The door creaked open and the stench of ammonia wafted into my face. The lead vampire gave me a hard nudge forward.

The room inside was cavernous, lit by crude torches and supported by tall stone pillars about every ten feet. Lush, red tapestries draped down the pillars and all kinds of pillows, lounges, beds, and rugs were scattered all over. A haze filled the room, while creatures of the night perched lazily on the furniture provided.

It was an opium den.

Two of the vampires peeled off and joined a group of similarly dressed men and women, all with sleek facial features and black or silver hair. Their voices were low, but I could tell they were saying something smug and haughty, just by the way they smiled, fangs out and eyes sharp. Hobgoblin guards, posted at the four corners of the room, kept a watchful eye on their clientele. I wondered if they were the same ones from that scuffle this morning.

The lead vampire brought me up to a door, a smaller version of the entrance, and held up a finger before disappearing inside. I took a good look around while I waited. None of the creatures noticed me or even cared to look away from the long pipes stuck in their hands and mouths. I heard a muffled cough coming from underneath a pile of pillows and blankets. I crept toward the noise, taking care not to provoke the guards, and tugged at the frilly tassel on the corner of one of the cushions. As I pulled, another cough erupted and a man—a human man—fell at my feet.

"The hell?" I muttered.

I spun around and looked over the place with fresh eyes, ones now accustomed to the dim torchlight. The people strewn across the place weren't just extramundane—several of them were mortals.

The fella moaned and giggled as he

sprawled out before me. A thin streak of orange light crept across his thigh, which led my eyes to a door that was slightly ajar. I carefully stepped over the man and hugged the wall, still evading the guards' sight, until I sidled up close enough to peek inside the room.

There was a man inside, another human man, one who I'd met before. Wilbur Cromley, the Hexed Springs' undertaker. You could never confuse Cromley with the wrong person. The man had porkchop sideburns, shaggy as a dog's, but was bald as a cue ball on top. He wore little round glasses made of brass wire, which constantly slipped down his nose.

Cromley strolled toward a wooden slab with a bundle of medical instruments, humming a little tune. Something, or rather someone, was lying on the table covered in a sheet. All I could see were their bare feet, which lay motionless, toes pointed straight up at the stone ceiling. Cromley bent down and pulled up a long tube, like something you'd see in a surgeon's bag, and jabbed a needle into one end and placed the opposite end into a bucket.

"Don't worry, you won't feel a thing," he sang as he pulled back the sheet and pressed the needle into the person's thigh. Blood flowed through the tube and clanged into the tin bucket. Cromley put his hands on his hips and smiled, following the length of the tube with his gaze. He muttered something and turned to the corner of the room where a fire was blazing. Resting in the flames were three iron rods, which he grabbed and rotated in the fire.

A hand grabbed me by the shoulder and yanked me away.

"Oi, get away from there," said the vampire who had led me here.

"What's he doing in there?" I asked, pulling away from his grip.

"Nothing that concerns you, filth. If you weren't a guest of milord, I'd claw out those curious peepers and eat them like grapes," he said, pinching his thumb and forefinger together.

"Bartholomew, that will be enough. Ranger Cooper, come in, please," a man said. He knocked an obsidian skull ring on the doorframe. Lucius Montague.

I reluctantly entered the room without the henchman's help. It was cozier than an office, but not personal enough to be someone's quarters. A beeswax candle burned in the corner, blanketing the room in a fine perfume, snuffing out the smell of the den on the other side of the door.

"Forgive him, he's one of my sister's men. I don't care for the help she hires, but I have little choice in allies these days," he said. He gestured toward two chairs, both upholstered in black, with gold-leafed and polished oak lining the arms and legs. "Please, have a seat. Would you like a cup of tea?"

I waved him off. "I'd rather get right down

to business. I've got places I need to be, Lucius. Or should I call you 'my lord'?"

"Let's forgo the titles and speak to each other as equals." He poured steaming brown liquid into a fine teacup and topped it off with a little cream. "I won't waste your time, Cal. It's come to my attention that you've taken employment with Ross Strickland and his associates."

I crossed my arms and huffed. "And just who told you that?"

"Word gets around quicker here than one expects. But, please, don't play coy. You've been tailed ever since you arrived in Hexed Springs."

"Whoever you hired to spy on me must be feeding you lies, Lucius. My life has been as uneventful as can be, until just a few days ago. You're wasting your money."

"Oh, money is of no concern to me. I'm blessed with both immortality and the lack of a need for a budget." He stopped to sip his tea, then cleared his throat. "No, the decision to observe you came from my father, the Patriarch. He views you and the ghosts of your past as existential threats to our family, as well as the realm of Strayhaven. I must say, after hearing you'd allied with Strickland, then to be discovered conversing with that trickster Van Pelt, I admit I now share his concern."

I didn't like where this was going. "If I'm such a threat, why didn't you kill me that first night at Clem's? Why not take me out now, on your home turf?"

Lucius pointed at my revolver. "Same reason I didn't have you disarmed when you were brought in. I believe in diplomacy with mortals. Both of our kinds may see the other as inherently evil, but I choose not to believe that. My philanthropic endeavors into mundane livelihoods should speak for themselves."

"That's *awfully* considerate of you," I said, rolling my eyes. "Speaking of Clem's, someone reported you'd taken off with one of her saloon girls a couple days ago. That true?"

The vampire furrowed his brow. "I don't know what you're talking about. My courtships are no one's business. But if you must know, my heart belongs to another human woman, so I'm afraid that person would be mistaken."

"And I take it that's one of the reasons why you're at odds with your own family?"

The air seemed to get heavier. Lucius's tone snapped into focused attention. "I suppose it was Van Pelt who told you that? A friendly word of advice: Beware of how much trust you put in that man." Lucius let out a barely perceptible sigh. "Yes, it's no secret that my fondness for mortals has put me in a delicate position among my siblings, who are, frankly, a group of overly ambitious brats. I've learned recently that it's bought me no favors among the humans either, particularly Ross Strickland. What business do you have with that man?"

"No offense, Lucius, but my business with Strickland is just that—my business," I said, shifting in my seat but forcing myself to keep his gaze.

Lucius set his teacup in its saucer and gently placed it on the onyx table between us. He stood up, folded his hands behind his back, and began pacing around the room.

"I wish you would enjoy a cup of that tea. It's a marvelous blend of flavors—a burst of sweet from the fruits and berries, then a finish of clove and cinnamon. I drink it habitually." He nodded toward a painting hanging on the back wall—a vast blooming orchard against the backdrop of blue sky and white-capped mountains. "Everything in the tea is grown in my father's gardens in Szentabraham, a quaint stretch of land in Transylvania. Lovely place. Most visitors are surprised at how lush it is. Speaking of my father, did you know he is a direct descendant of Nosferatu? He's a member of the first brood of the first vampires, created in the initial corruption after the Eternals fled."

"Is that supposed to impress me? Is Dracula your favorite uncle or something?"

Lucius wasn't amused. "No, I'm telling you this so you'll appreciate the weight the Montague name carries. Vampires have played a pivotal role in extramundane history, all the way back to the dawn of the common era. We've greatly impacted your mortal world, too. I'll spare you the history lesson, but my father's father had a role in creating Strayhaven."

"And you're worried some mere mortal, like myself, is going to cause this good thing you've got going to come crashing down? I'm flattered you think so highly of me."

Lucius spun around, clapping his hands together in frustration. I jumped back into my seat.

"Enough," he yelled, hard enough a fleck of spit flew from his mouth. "Test my patience no longer. Either you're playing stupid or you really are a fool mortal caught up in something he doesn't understand. I ask again, what are you doing for Ross Strickland? And what is your association with the engineer that rebuilt the Sentinel?"

My heart thumped hard in my chest. I still might have had my gun, but it wouldn't help me in a close-quarters fight with an elder vampire. I had to calm Lucius down, while convincing him to buy some half-truths. I had a feeling telling him everything I knew would probably get me killed.

"Take it easy there, your highness," I said softly. "Listen, I'll help you and you help me. What do you say?"

Lucius closed his eyes and took a deep breath. "How very human of you. Make your offer." He settled back into his chair, reining in his powerful energy a little.

"To also spare you a history lesson, I'm not on friendly terms with most people in the United States. A lot of them would like to capture me and sell me to Uncle Sam. Others would prefer to shoot me dead. Strickland knows this and aimed to take advantage of the fact by using the Sentinel to coerce me into taking a job. As for the engineer? He's just a bookworm with a sense for high fashion, nothing more. Y'all can take him out of your crosshairs."

"You cannot expect me to believe a man who builds a weapon does not understand its true function while he builds it."

"I'm telling the truth. Cross my heart, hope to die. He thought Strickland hired him to build a suit of armor for his drawing room, or whatever the hell rooms you rich folks have to display old shit," I said, hoping the beads of sweat on my brow would stay in place.

Lucius's lip curled up in a sneer. "It's so like you mundanes to meddle in things you don't understand. Sentinels are not merely 'old shit,' but powerful weapons capable of easily neutralizing vampires. The existence of one is an imminent threat, even more so in the hands of my mortal nemesis."

"You're telling me. The metal man nearly killed me. Strickland's no friend to me, let me make that clear."

"Noted," Lucius said. His voice was calm again. Menacingly calm. "I ask again, for the third time: What did Strickland hire you to do?"

Here it was: The biggest lie I'd need to make. Two players are left, a big pot of chips is up for grabs, and I'm holding jack squat. Time to put on my best poker face and stick the bluff.

I leaned forward and looked him in the eyes. "Light security detail. You may have read the advertisement in the newspaper."

Lucius held my gaze for several seconds without speaking. "You know, they say you can tell a human is lying by observing the change in their pupil size as they tell the lie."

My heart skipped a beat. Without thinking, I glanced at the door, then at my revolver, then back to Lucius. A bead of sweat fell from my brow.

The tension in the air shattered as he looked me over, then chuckled. "Cal, you look like you've just seen a ghost. I'm sorry, I didn't mean to insinuate that *you* were lying to me just now. Sometimes I can't help but recall interesting tidbits about humans when I talk with them."

I faked a laugh. "Sounds like someone else I know."

"In light of our shared contempt for Strickland, I believe I can help you be rid of him," Lucius said, reaching to pour a fresh cup of tea. "But I have one favor to ask in return."

"And what's that?"

"It goes without saying that if Ross Strickland asks you to do something against the family, you'll decline, but if he should ever assign you to any … subterranean adventures, you'll let me know in advance."

Subterranean adventures as in the coal mine? A little uncanny for both Oliver and Lucius to suggest the same place, if you ask me. This was starting to feel like a setup.

"You mean like delving for monsters in mines?" I asked.

"Precisely. Decades ago, men like Strickland came to the South to drill and mine the earth. Some of them wiped out their fortunes in search of products like oil, gold, or diamonds. To be frank, I don't understand your kind's fascination with crude. In No Man's Land, they came up empty-handed. I've heard rumors that Strickland has developed an interest in mining, which means he's found something. I'd like to personally be the first to know his intentions."

"Whatever you say," I said. I sat back in my chair, disguising my nervousness as comfort. "I'm a man who enjoys wide-open skies, anyhow. I promise you, I won't be delving into any mines, and I'll give you a holler if he does."

Even though I'd dodged a bullet, I was still recovering from that close shave. I didn't want to press deeper into the issue of the coal mine. All I wanted was to get a move on and stop wasting the little time I had left to find Abigail.

"Are you sure you don't want some tea?" Lucius asked again.

"No, thank you. I need to be going, if you don't mind."

He took a deep sip before continuing. "If you've told me everything you know about Strickland, then, no, I don't mind at all. But, Cal, I'm afraid I must end our friendly conversation and speak to you now as Lord Lucius Montague, first son of the Patriarch Alexandru Montague, Keeper of Strayhaven, and brood descendant of the Unholy Nosferatu." He shrugged and tried to make light of the comment while maintaining his authority. "You know how it is. I must appear to administer my father's wishes from time to time."

I gritted my teeth. "I'm listening."

Lucius laid a heavy hand on the table. The light within the room evaporated and a chill pricked my skin. The vampire's black pupils grew until they filled his eyes.

"Humankind's greed is driving us all toward the precipice of an endless abyss, and the Montague family will no longer tolerate beings who threaten extramundane existence. Your ignorance does not excuse you from your role in these matters. You broke our laws by penetrating the veil into Strayhaven, and you're lucky I'm letting you leave here alive, given your association with known mortal threats. If you so much as cross the veil again, you will be apprehended and given a swift death. At your earliest convenience, you will flee No Man's Land."

Light and warmth quickly returned to the room after Lucius finished his speech. So did my impatience for being told what to do. My temper flared and I lost control of my tongue ... again.

"Now let me speak to you as Cal Cooper, gunslinger and ignorant mortal. I don't give a goddamn who your brood daddy is. I've gunned down two dozen men from here to the Rio Grande and twice as many monsters. That includes laying slick-talking vampires like you in the dirt, who never again rose to see the moonlight. I'd love to leave this godforsaken land, but seeing as I may be exiled here for the foreseeable future, you're either going to have to kill me or tolerate me for a little longer."

Lucius didn't react. He simply shrugged. "Very well. I suppose we'll see what fate holds for you."

I stood up and squared up with Lucius. We were the same height but I had more mass. "Lucky for me, I'm a gambling man and fate is my currency."

Lucius waved a hand and called out for Bartholomew, who was standing on the other side of the door.

"Yes, milord?"

"Bartholomew, Mr. Cooper is taking his leave. I don't know how he stumbled into Strayhaven, but make sure he doesn't find another entrance, understood?"

The sickly, ashen vamp nodded. "What

about his friends at the Elixirium?"

"Pay them no mind. Your attention is needed elsewhere."

I sauntered over between Lucius and Bartholomew, thumbs hooked in my gun belt. "I appreciate the hospitality, Lucius. Maybe not as much as those guys out there getting higher than kites. But there's one last thing I need to know before I go see a man about a horse. What's the deal with the town undertaker collecting blood down the hall?"

"You'll have to ask my sister, Lilith, should you ever meet her. All of this—the opium, the addicts, this awful place—it's all part of her disgusting pet project," Lucius said with a curled lip. "Farewell, Mr. Cooper."

And with that, he nodded to Bartholomew. Before I could turn around, my head was shoved in a sack and my hands were bound with rope.

CHAPTER TWELVE

Little flecks of light poked through the burlap covering my face. Not enough to see clearly, but I could tell I was in Hexed Springs again. The bright sunshine and fresh air were a dead giveaway we'd traveled across the veil. I'd worked up a sweat, which was soaking into the bag still stuffed over my head.

My hands were still tied, too, which made it impossible to scratch the itch on my arm left behind where the vamp had sunk his claws into my flesh to force my obedience.

I wasn't the most agreeable passenger along the journey. I'd kicked and cursed all the way here, wherever here was. Both mine and Bartholomew's patience for each other had run out long ago, so he reckoned it was best for us to part ways and tossed me out of the moving stagecoach.

I hit the ground hard. "Damn it, you bloodsucking son of a bitch!"

"Jeez, mister. No need for naughty words,"

a small voice said.

I jerked away from the bright sunlight as someone pulled the bag off and untied my hands. It was some rosy-cheeked kid sucking on a lollipop.

"Thanks, kid. I owe you," I said, dusting myself off. The stagecoach was gone from sight, and I didn't have anything to gain by wasting time bickering with vampires. I adjusted my hat to block the noon sun. "Hey, can you point me toward the livery?"

The boy pointed east and sucked the spit off his lollipop with a big slurp. "What are you doing tied up, mister?"

"Don't worry about it, kid," I said, heading off in the direction he gave me.

The little fella trotted after me. I turned a corner and dodged through workers unloading lumber from a buggy, but the kid kept pace with me stride for stride.

"Who were those men in the fancy wagon? They looked funny. What kind of gun is that? Can I hold it?" He reached for my holster.

I growled and walked faster. "No, you'll shoot your eye out. Now, go bother somebody else."

The kid wasn't deterred and skipped around to my other side. "Are you an outlaw? Pa says there are a lot of outlaws living here. Ma says the army oughta come clean this place up so kids like me can play outside and not get kidnapped.

She said, 'stay away from those grubby knife ears or they'll turn you into a tree.' I know an elf kid, he's weird and—"

"Chrissakes, kid, I said to git!"

I threw my arm out wide, pointing off into the distance. My skin prickled and a pressure built inside my eardrums until they popped. Just then, that same pressure blew off my glove and channeled electricity through my finger, which sent a bolt zipping down an alley and right toward a stack of barrels. The lightning bolt screeched as it flew, exploding the barrels upon impact.

The kid froze. The lollipop slipped from his hand and landed sticky-side down in the dust. I stood there equally dumbfounded and slack-jawed.

"Wizard!" he screamed.

"Kid, wait," I hollered. The little boy didn't listen. He took off running for his life as a few folks started searching in my direction. I slipped my glove back on and made a quick escape before anybody could interrogate me.

To my surprise, I didn't feel any sickness after casting the spell. All the pressure, stress, and anger from my ordeal had come to a head and burst out of me. Whatever was happening to me, I needed to get it under control.

But first, I needed to find a horse.

I followed my nose all the way to the livery, its unmistakable smell of hay and manure serving as my guide. Old Mr. Eriksen ran the stables like a zoo, collecting all kinds of farm animals. In addition to a few horses, he's got a trio of pigs, some billy goats, a dozen chickens, and a mule named Herbert that he lets the little kids ride around on.

With so many ranches fighting land barons and going belly up, a lot of critters get overlooked and forgotten. If one of these crooked people offered you money for your acreage and you didn't take it, they'd find ways to devalue your claim and cripple your livelihood, until you caved or you died. Rather than let the animals suffer, Mr. Eriksen takes them in and loves them as his own. He used to care for Buck, too. He really liked that horse.

I pulled off my hat, ran my fingers back through my hair, and rubbed out a few creases in my undershirt. Maybe the old livery man would cut me a deal. Not that he owed me any favors, but the old man was kind like that. Give-you-the-shirt-off-his-back sort of kind.

The barn door stood open, so I walked on through, hat in hand. A few stalls down from the entrance I got an unexpected view of a person's denim-covered backside as they leaned over the top bar of the stable gate.

I cleared my throat. "Excuse me, sir, I'm looking to rent a horse."

To my surprise, the owner of the backside wasn't a man, but rather a tall and muscular woman. She wore a gingham shirt underneath overalls, which were stained with telltale signs of someone who works with barnyard animals. She had a very light complexion, complemented by two blond braids tucked beneath a blue bandana tied around her head like a bonnet. She looked just like the fabled Valkyries.

She hopped down from the gate and wiped her hands with a rag from her back pocket. "I'm no 'sir,' but I'd be happy to help you today."

I bowed and placed my hat over my heart. "I was expecting to find the old fella who runs these stables. I apologize, Miss—"

"Astrid is my name. I work the forge out back. Anders is my father. He's who you want to talk to," she said as she hoisted a saddle in the air with one arm and gently placed it atop the gate of another stable.

I blinked in amazement before offering her my hand. "Cal Cooper. Pardon me, but did I understand you correctly? You're a blacksmith?"

Astrid returned my handshake with a grip as tight as a vice. "I am. I learned the trade from my pappa and took over for him when his bones started to ache. I make all of our horseshoes."

"Amazing. You learn that from him, too?"

"I did," she said with a smile. "Our family boasts a proud tradition of smiths dating back to the era of Vikings."

I thought about how the Sentinel had ripped my front door off. "You wouldn't happen to make some door hinges, do you?"

"Cal, I can forge swords and helmets and anything else you can imagine. I can certainly forge door hinges," she said.

The rear door of the stables swung open and a hefty old man hobbled through. Anders waddled side to side more than forward when he walked. His eyesight wasn't so good and his hands were turning knobby, but his lengthy beard hadn't lost any of its vigor. I reckon it could rival a dwarf in a beard-growing contest.

"Astrid, my dear," Anders said. "I can't find Herbert's sugar cubes and he's not very cooperative today. Can you find them for me?"

Astrid sighed. "Pappa, you give that mule so many sweets and his teeth are already falling out of his skull."

"He's old, dearheart. Just like your pappa. Don't deny an old creature his only pleasures."

"Yes, pappa. I'll find them," she said, effortlessly throwing two bags of feed atop her shoulders. "I'll leave you to it, Cal. Come see me in a few days for those door hinges."

"Cal? Cal's here?" Anders asked.

"Right here, Mr. Eriksen."

The old man shuffled toward me and reached out his wrinkled hands. "Good to see you, Cal. Where's Buck? I haven't seen him in a few days?" he asked, squinting to see my face.

A pang of sadness washed over me. I felt like I was about to tell a kid I'd had to put down his dog.

I hung my head and let out a heavy sigh. "Buck suffered a mortal wound out on the range a few days ago, Mr. Eriksen. I'm sorry to say he didn't make it."

Anders groaned and slowly shook his head. "Oh, no. That's awful to hear. I was so happy to stable that beautiful animal. Such a shame. I'm sorry for your loss."

"Our loss. I know you loved him, too," I said, balling a fist up inside my hat. "I'm afraid that's why I'm here, Mr. Eriksen. I was hoping you could lend me a horse."

Astrid overheard and peeked out from inside the pigsty.

"Pappa, remember what we talked about," she said. Her voice was firm.

Anders sighed. "But this is Cal, he's the town ranger. Stopped that hooligan from shooting up town, remember?"

"Pappa."

"What's wrong, Mr. Eriksen?" I asked.

He rubbed his hands together. "I'm sorry, Cal. But I can't rent horses anymore. I've lost three in the last month from people never returning them. Astrid says I am too trusting."

"Until we have a lawman who can track down horse thieves, pappa, we can't afford to lose another one," she said firmly. "I apologize, Cal, but, no, pappa cannot rent horses."

"She's right. I have to make money to keep

my little petting zoo open," he said, admiring a red hen who was scratching around our boots. "I can't let these animals starve because of silly land wars between greedy humans."

I rubbed my knuckles inside my hat, not ready to give up yet. "I'm sorry about the thefts, Miss Astrid, but I swear I'm an honest man. Mr. Eriksen, I'd have your horse back by morning."

Anders looked at his daughter with puppy-dog eyes. She responded by placing her hands on her hips and raising an unyielding eyebrow.

"Miss Astrid, I'm not supposed to go into specifics, but there's a little girl missing and her father is worried sick about her. I've been hired to find her before something bad happens to her. Your pappa loves you. Can you imagine what it would do to him if that little girl were you?"

My mouth felt dirty as soon as the words left my lips. I didn't mind twisting the truth, but I hated lying to manipulate good folks.

"That's awful. What's the world coming to?" Anders said. "If you were captured, I'd go to the ends of the earth to retrieve you. Let Cal have a horse."

Imagine if Ross Strickland talked about his little girl like Anders had. Strickland probably never gave Abigail the time of day, let alone pass down the family trade. Guilt dug itself deeper and deeper into my conscience, but this was my only legal option for obtaining a horse.

"Please, Miss Astrid. I'll give you ten dollars for good measure," I said. I turned over the money that Strickland had thrown at me like a begging dog. Astrid palmed it and chewed her lip. Butterflies in my stomach multiplied every second that ticked by. A few moments later, she smiled.

"Pappa," she said. "What about the palomino?"

His eyes darted over to a stable in the far corner. "Yes. Yes, I believe that's a fine horse for Mr. Cooper."

The old man waddled toward the far stable, whistling a trill series of notes and clicking his tongue. Hidden among a lump of hay was a palomino appaloosa with a chestnut brown coat and a snow-white rear with brown speckles. Her mane was a light blond, about the same color as Astrid's hair. It was a little on the chunky side, likely accustomed to the comfort of its messy pen.

The horse lifted her head and stared at me like I'd disturbed her beauty sleep.

"She came from one of those failing ranches we talked about. Instead of renting," Astrid said, nodding to her father, "we will sell her to you for ten dollars. Won't we, pappa?"

Anders squinted his blue eyes and nodded slowly.

"I'm not one to look a gift horse in the mouth, but is there something I should know about a ten-dollar animal?"

Astrid winced and put her hands together in a steeple. "There's nothing wrong with her, per se, she's just a little grumpy sometimes."

"That's no problem. I've had horses like that before. They've all got their own personalities. Just gotta know how to deal with them," I said with a shrug.

"And she doesn't like to listen," Anders said.

"That's okay. Horses take a while to bond with a new rider."

"And she's stubborn. And won't do anything unless motivated by food," Astrid said.

"It won't ride, it won't listen. So what does this horse have going for it?"

Astrid's brow furrowed and she exhaled sharply, throwing her hands out to her side. "She's beautiful. Look at how pretty she is."

She was awfully pretty, but it's personality, not beauty, that most riders are looking for. I needed an animal that had a strong will and quick feet, something that wasn't afraid of a little gun smoke and could outrun anything. I didn't have much room to argue, given that I was asking for a horse with only ten dollars to my name, but I couldn't help but feel like I was the one getting the rotten end of this deal.

"So you're telling me she's gone barn sour," I said.

Astrid nodded hesitantly. "She might not like to go anywhere or do anything, but she's only ten dollars. I'll even throw in a saddle. Deal?"

Astrid held out a hand and waited for me to shake it. No matter how bad the horse was, I only needed it for one job. One job and then I could find myself something better, with more time on my side. I shook her hand and thanked her.

"Wonderful. Pappa, let's get her ready to go," she said, bubbling with newfound enthusiasm. The old man lured the horse with an apple and Astrid slapped a saddle on her before she could finish the treat.

"You know, she didn't come with a name when she arrived from her old home. Why don't you give her one?" he said.

"I've got a certain naming convention when it comes to my horses. I've named them all the same name, so I can never forget it," I said.

"How strange, yet fun. What do you name them?" Astrid asked.

I took the reins from her hands. "Buck."

She winced. "Buck is a boy horse's name. Why don't you call her something like Penelope? Or maybe Sandy because of her color?"

"Nope. Gonna call her Buck."

I tugged on the reins of my new horse and tried to walk her out of the livery, but she wouldn't budge.

"Maybe she hates her name," Astrid suggested.

"No, I think she's just spoiled and lazy," I

said.

"She likes sugar cubes."

Buck's ears perked right up and she trotted after the old man, nearly dragging me behind her. I clawed my way onto the saddle as she beelined for the door, mesmerized by the bag of sweets Anders was holding out.

"Come on, dearheart. A little farther," he said with a gentle exuberance. It was working.

Astrid waited at the exit as the horse came through. "I'll shut the barn door behind you while she's distracted."

Mr. Eriksen stroked the horse's shoulder and looked up at me, wagging a knobby finger. "Cal, remember, barn sours are only difficult because they've lost their herd. They're lonely."

I tipped my hat. "I know that feeling, Mr. Eriksen. Miss Astrid. Thank you for your help and your kindness."

Astrid raised a hand to her forehead to block out the sun. "I hope you find that little girl, Cal."

"I'll do my best, ma'am. And I'll come back for that door hinge."

Astrid and her father stepped inside the livery. She waved a silent farewell to Buck and me, then slid the barn door shut once her father made it inside. The heavy door scraped along its irons until it latched with a loud *clank*. Buck was so lost in eating her sweets she didn't realize she'd been tricked into going outside. She stopped chomping on the cubes and gave a pitiful whinny.

"C'mon, now. It's not gonna be so bad riding with me," I said, followed by a very reassuring, "I hope."

I clicked my teeth and steered her toward the coal mine at the edge of the Conway land, but Buck wanted to go the opposite way.

"Wrong way, horse." I bobbed up and down. Nothing I did seemed to matter, Buck was going to go where she pleased. Which, at the moment, was toward that little boy sitting on a fencepost eating another lollipop.

"Oh, no. Not him. Leave him be," I begged. I pulled out one of the sugar cubes and stuffed it inside her gums. Sure enough, the big, dumb horse started trotting in the right direction.

"I'm glad we could come to an agreement," I said.

* * *

Buck slowed as we approached the edge of town and the long, empty road west. Open ground stretched before us, reaching from one end of the earth to the other. Tall grasses swayed in the wind and summer wildflowers bloomed damn near everywhere. I don't care where you are in the world, there's nowhere else you'll see anything that compares to the prairie. Endless wilds and sapphire skies.

But just as there's beauty in the skies, there's also terror. What may seem like a benign cloud puff in a gentle wind can build into a tower of Grandmother Nature's own fury; colossal thunderstorms that announce themselves with drumming explosions and purple streaks of forked lightning; storms that hurl down hailstones as big as your palm and unleash torrents that flood the land, followed by a particularly strong maelstrom that'll carve away swaths of earth with tornadoes. The Wild West has a bit of everything.

I took a deep breath. Despite the calming summer wilds, anxiety welled up in my chest. I was finally off to retrieve Strickland's daughter, but I had no idea what condition she would be in when I arrived. Would I be too late?

Armed with a vial of holy water and my trusty revolver, I was out to save my skin and make my own fate.

CHAPTER THIRTEEN

Riding in the doldrums across the wastes can be a bore. Most cowboys sing along the trail to help pass the time, but I prefer to whistle. Although I know my fair share of tunes, even my repertoire isn't deep enough to fill the stretch of a long ride. Three hours went by without much fanfare. I spied a buzzard sitting on top of a buffalo skull and a few tumbleweeds crossed my path. Nothing special.

But something caught my eye as I crested a short hill. Up ahead was an upturned wagon. Behind it was another horse, stamping its hooves and eyeing us with fear. A streak of red ran down its hind leg. It was injured, but not critically; at least it wasn't showing signs of limping or pain. Just fear.

"Whoa, now," I called to Buck. She slowed to a halt and I climbed off, keeping her reins in my hand. I didn't trust her enough not to wander away and leave me stranded. She was wary of the wreckage. The other horse had tried to bolt, but its reins were tied to something.

I held up my hands and shushed the horse, which seemed to calm it some. The wagon rocked each time it tugged at its tether. I reached for my knife to cut the creature loose when a black heron swooped in out of nowhere, scaring us both; it perched on top of the wagon and cawed. I swear it was the same one I saw the other day. It looked me straight in the eye, just like before. Like it was attempting to search my soul.

I crept closer to the cart, careful not to make any sudden movements. Quick as a flash, someone spun out from behind the wreck, a rifle pointed right at my head.

"You man or monster?"

I jumped back, my hands held high. My heart beat in my ears. "Hold up, what?"

The lady cocked the rifle. "I said, are you man or monster?"

The black heron spread its wings and flew off.

"Man! Man. Name's Cal Cooper and I am not a monster," I said, watching the bird escape from view.

The lady kept her aim trained on me as she approached. A wide-brimmed sun hat rested precariously on her head, pinned to the curly silver hair underneath. "Ranger? Ranger Cal Cooper? If you are who you say you are, tell me what you know about Bill Conway."

I scrunched up my face and stammered. "What the hell is this? And who are you, lady?"

She tilted her rifle skyward and fired a round. "Next one goes in your skull, sonny. Answer me."

"Chrissakes, what kind of a stick-up is this?" I hollered. "Bill Conway is a rancher who hired me to kill a monster eating his herd. That's the long and short of it. You happy?"

She kept her rifle steady, eyes hard.

If I was quick enough, I could draw my revolver and shoot the rifle out of her hands before she got me. I wasn't going to shoot an old lady, but I didn't want to be shot by one either.

Then, the old gal lowered her aim. "Yep, suits me just fine. Apologize for the aggressive greeting, Cal, but something came after me and Big Gus here. You know as well as anyone, you can't be too careful outside of Hexed Springs. Monsters lurk out here. Some of them impersonating people. You never know."

I breathed a sigh of relief and lowered my hands. "Something came after you? Hang on, do I know you?"

"See here?" she said, nodding toward the wreckage. "Wild ghoul, I reckon. Didn't get a good look at it, but I've seen 'em out here before, preying upon lonely travelers. I'm Rita Conway, by the way. Bill's sister. I was on my way into Hexed Springs after receiving your message before I got walloped."

Now that I wasn't staring down the barrel of a gun, I could catch a glimpse at the silver-haired gal. She wasn't as old as I thought, maybe in her mid-fifties. A wide-brimmed sun hat rested precariously on her head, pinned to the curly gray hair underneath. She sported a navy-blue split skirt. Not the kind of formal gal who rode side-saddle apparently.

"You hurt?" I asked, pointing to the purple bruise on her wrist. Her white blouse, the kind with tight sleeves and puffy shoulders, was covered in orange dust, no doubt from where she'd been thrown from the cart.

Rita sighed and pushed her rifle in the dirt like a walking stick. "Only my pride. Thought I was a decent shot, but I couldn't hit whatever got me. Can't tell if it's gone or tracking me either."

The tension between us dissipated and the horses were less jumpy. Buck came along with me and stood near Big Gus as I inspected the wreckage. Rita's cart had only toppled on its side. Lucky for her it hadn't completely rolled over. Down the side of the cart was a long trail of claw marks and peels of wood curling backward from the gashes. The back wheel was bent in on its axle.

No way this cart was going to travel anymore without repair.

"You think ghouls did this?" I asked, handling the bent metal inner ring of the wheel.

"Yessir, I do. Seen more and more of them

recently. Something's got monsters out here stirred up."

I nodded, turning back to Rita and her horse. "You said you were going into town to see me, huh? Bill too busy to go?"

She shook her head and looked down at her feet. "I trust you to keep this to yourself, but Bill's been dead since last year. Fool got hisself so drunk he went to cussing a rich fella's name, then wandered into the cold looking to find him and kill him. Instead, it was he who found his death. Frostbite."

I slapped my hand on the wooden cart. "Bill's dead? Then who have I been communicating with? Better yet, who's gonna pay me?"

"That would be me. And also me, but I ain't paying you for a job unfinished," she said.

"What do you mean?" I damn sure had finished that job. I thought of poor Buck.

Rita picked up the rifle and cradled it in her arms. "I mean, to the first point, I'm the one who hired you. Secondly, I'm still losing cattle, so whatever you killed wasn't the right monster. I followed a fresh trail of blood this morning, right to the entrance of the old coal mine near the corner of our land. I was coming to town to get you and take you there."

That damn fire lizard. If I'd tracked the right monster, I wouldn't have lost my best horse and ended up with the laziest one in town.

A knot twisted up inside my gut as I

thought this all through. Lotta trouble seems to be connected with this coal mine. What if the cattle were being eaten because one little girl hadn't satisfied a vampire's hunger? I didn't know who I could trust about what awaited me down in that mine, but I got the feeling I was walking into something much more deadly than I'd ever faced before.

"Well, lucky you, then. I was just heading to the mine right now. Seems you're not the only one having trouble out there," I said.

Rita looked down the long stretch of road. "This trail will take you pretty close to the mine. It'll take you two hours by horse if you stick to it. Tell you what, I'll take you down a shortcut, but only if you take care of my job first."

A trio of birds soared overhead. My eyes tracked them as they flew in the direction I needed to go. "As enticing as that sounds, my other job is very time sensitive. Once I finish it, I'll attend to your matter properly, I promise."

"What could be so time sensitive that you can't help little ol' me? You told me in our initial correspondence that I was your very first client. Surely that gets me some special treatment?" She was nearly pouting.

"I honor loyalty above all, Miss Rita, but this job is a matter of life and death."

Big Gus flinched when she tossed up her hands. "You think mine isn't? I got cattle dying left and right, and if I continue to lose them, I will lose my ranch."

"A human life. A little girl's, to be exact."

Rita stiffened. "That's a little different, I suppose. I'll show you the shortcut, but on one condition."

I sighed. "And what's that?"

"I'm coming with you."

I pinched the bridge of my nose and huffed. "You were just attacked and your horse is hurt. Maybe you should go home."

I prefer to work alone, even when the odds are against me. I believed Rita when she said she could fend for herself, but having her along felt like a liability. The shortcut would save some time, though.

She patted the black horse. "Big Gus has a little scratch, that's all. He'll be fine."

"You said it yourself, it's dangerous out here. Just point me in the direction of the short-cut and I'll find it myself."

Rita slung her rifle over her shoulder, then looped a foot in the stirrup. She tapped her boots onto her overgrown horse's thighs and trotted into the brush without me.

"If you want that shortcut, you'd better hurry along. Giddyup, Gus," she called out.

Buck tugged at her reins.

"All right, girl. Let's go," I said, scrambling into the saddle.

Buck pulled up alongside her equine counterpart, minding the stray rocks and brush, and matched pace. A few hills, if you could call them that, provided some texture to the landscape as we galloped through the pristine sea of grass that would take us to the coal mine.

"So, who's got you monster-hunting out at the coal mine on my land?" Rita asked, shouting into the wind.

"Can't say. Rules of the contract, I'm afraid."

Rita groaned. "I already gave you an important bit of information about my situation. Not fair to hold out on me, ranger."

"What's so important about you telling me Bill was dead?"

"Pretty damning, to tell you the truth. Don't you know nothing? An unmarried woman can't own land. If anyone found out Bill had gone off and died, it would make it easier for that son of a bitch Strickland to squeeze me out of what I've got left." She tightened her grip on the reins. "He's been interested in what's underneath my soil."

My blood boiled hearing that. Leave it to men to think up some cockamamie rule about women not being able to hold onto their family's land. Rules like that were what urged me to rebel—to lash out against it all. Rules were nothing more than injustice disguised as law.

"Did he make you an offer for your land?" I said.

Rita laughed. "That cheap bastard made

Bill an offer that was way under value. We weren't about to give up the family farm, so we declined. Politely, of course. Ever since then, he's been sending men to strong-arm us."

I shook my head. "Sounds about right. What's he done?"

"Bill caught some of his men plowing salt in our fields once. Another time we both saw them moving our fence posts inward. My brother claimed to have witnessed them poisoning cattle, too."

I expected to hear something dastardly, but that was conniving and vile. Evil, even. "Good lord, Rita. What did Bill do about that?"

"Started carrying this rifle around with him everywhere he went. He caught Strickland's men in the act once and shot at 'em. Only wounded one of the bastards, but Strickland sent an angry letter to the house threatening retribution." She paused, a frown replacing her smirk. "That was actually the reason Bill died. He read that letter and stewed over it for days. Got piss drunk one night and decided he was going to put an end to the fight. I found him frozen to death the next morning."

I could find no redeemable qualities for the man who was turning out to be a plague upon the living in this part of the world. Strickland held power over me, knowing my history and being connected to powerful folks who could do me in. But I couldn't let him get away with terrorizing these good people. "Between you and me, Rita, I'd like to finish what Bill started. I want to take Strickland out."

"You and me both, Cal, but I just don't have it in me. I don't have anyone else, you know. I never married. Neither did Bill. Life passed us by while we tended a farm that needed constant supervision. If I'm honest, I'm barely surviving on my own without him." Her voice lowered. "I could never handle fighting a war against the man who wants everything."

"Who will take over for you when you're gone?"

Rita shrugged. "I imagine Strickland will. I've got no heirs or extended family, so when I'm gone, I reckon that's it."

Seemed like I wasn't the only one Strickland held power over.

"I know you don't want to, but ..." I needed to word this just so. "You could use the money to travel and enjoy yourself somewhere more exotic than No Man's Land."

"I hear ya, Cal," she said with a chuckle. "But I've got plenty of years left and I'm not selling to that devil. It's the principle of it. If he's gonna force me out, I'm gonna make him work for it."

I laughed. "I appreciate your stubborn nature. It's inspiring."

She smiled and said nothing more. I couldn't tell if she was just focusing on the path ahead or thinking back on her life, and the monsters, literal and figurative, that haunted her past.

I needed to find my way out of Strickland's clutches. Out of the man's plot for dominance disguised as utopia. His business empire with its army of guards would be tough to take down, though. I'd have to be smart and hit him where it hurts. Perhaps there were others who'd join me.

I chuckled quietly to myself as we rode. I was starting to think like an outlaw again.

And it felt pretty good.

CHAPTER FOURTEEN

"Here we are, Cal. Welcome to my little homestead," Rita said.

Miles of barbed wire tied to wooden posts parted at the entrance of Conway Ranch, an archway decorated with interlocking 'C' and 'R' on top. Rita's home sat atop a low rolling hill guarding a dense thicket of trees and brush behind it. It was an idyllic country home, with room to house a whole family and a few ranch hands. We crossed through a small herd of cattle on the way toward a red barn; its doors swung open for animals to come and go from the heat. A couple of pigs sniffed around the water well at the base of the windmill, its tin blades creaking along as it spun in the wind.

"These critters are about all I've got left," she said. "That's why it's so important that we get the right monster, and quick, before it wipes out the rest of 'em."

"Where's this shortcut you're telling me about?" I asked.

"Back through this mess of trees. About a quarter mile south of here runs a creek. Pretty good size one, too. If you follow it around a few bends, you'll come to a clearing and the entrance to the coal mine."

I sat up tall on my horse and scanned the thicket. "Looks pretty crowded back there. Is it safe to bring the horses through?"

Rita dismounted Big Gus. "Afraid not, ranger. Too many stray branches and gopher holes. They're likely to break an ankle in that mess."

I followed her into the barn, where both our horses were more than pleased to be. I pulled the vial of holy water from my saddle bag and placed it in my shirt pocket while Rita rewarded the horses with a carrot each.

"Y'all be good now. Me and Cal will be back before you know it," Rita said to the animals. I followed her through the rear door of the barn and back into the wilderness behind her house, stepping lightly over downed branches, thorny bushes, and a mess of dead, crunchy leaves.

Rita stopped shy of a slope where a fallen tree trunk acted as a ramp down into the creek bed. The ground in front of our feet sloped downward sharply, until it leveled off near the water's edge. On the opposite was a ten-foot-tall sheer ridge of red clay and exposed stone with the occasional tree root poking through the earthen barrier. The only way forward was to follow the long and bendy banks of the creek.

The water wasn't moving very fast and it didn't look that deep, but it was too much for a person to cross easily. I guessed it to be about twenty or so feet wide, probably no more than waist deep at its deepest point. It was hard to tell because the water was stained red from all the silt it carried.

I took Rita's hand and helped her climb down the tree trunk. She held her rifle in her other hand for balance as she took slow and careful steps down to the ground below.

"My pa took Bill and I fishing for crawdads here when we were little. Be careful, now. The ground can get soft in places and the mud'll pull the boots right off your feet. There's also copperheads hiding along the banks," she said.

We walked along the bank, dodging sloppy patches of mud and anything that resembled a hidey hole for snakes. When I wasn't being a gentleman and helping Rita get across the softer surfaces, I was swatting at the mosquitoes and gnats buzzing around the banks. Bugs are a fan of stagnant water. It makes a good place to lay their eggs. Any catfish that call these shallow waters home burrow deep in the mud and snack on the swarms of bugs until they become the size of dogs.

This would be a great place to bring Clem and Toussaint noodling, if I could convince them to get muddy and wet.

"So where do we exit this creek? Are we

looking for a certain geographic landmark or something?" I asked.

Rita was walking in front now, stepping gingerly through a sand bar. "If I told you, you wouldn't need me, would you?"

"Yeah, about that, ma'am. What I'm hunting is pretty dangerous, and I don't think it's safe for you to tag along once we get there," I said, trying to sound forceful.

"You don't think I can handle my own out here?"

"I don't doubt that, but you didn't hire me for my good looks."

"Ain't that the truth," she said with snort. "I hired you because I was too busy to go hunting monsters. They don't threaten me. I could wrestle a two-thousand-pound bull to the ground, if I wanted."

I chuckled. "If you say so, ma'am."

"If there's a will, there's a way, Cal. And I've got lots of will." We squeezed through a choke point in the trail where the land hugged an ankle-deep inlet. As we rounded the corner of the bank, we found a thick tree trunk that had fallen and lodged itself in the ground.

"Well, that's new," she said. "No way around it. Help me climb over."

I clamored up the log with ease and bounced on top of it. It was good and steady, its roots still gripping the soil on the ledge. Rita steadied herself against the clay wall and offered me her hands. I hoisted her up next to me and prepared to ease her down the other side. Just before she hit the ground, I yanked her back up.

"Copperhead. Right there," I said, pointing to a coil of brown scales camouflaged in a patch of grass below.

Rita gasped. "Sharp eyes, Cal. We either get a running jump or wade out into the water a little bit. Should we shoot it?"

"No, best leave it alone. We're trespassing on its home. Here," I said, picking up a fist-sized stone. "I'll get it to move."

The rock bounced against the cliff nearest the snake. The noise startled and it slithered away into the water. Another one followed behind it.

"Two copperheads. That second one might have got us," Rita said.

I sighed in relief and helped her back over to the other side. A few steps later, the clay barrier receded, opening up a wider swath of ground and plenty of space to walk.

"Here we are," Rita said in a sing-song voice.

Across the bank was a large boulder that, at some point in geological time, had slid down the red wall, creating a ramp out of the creek. A long stretch of rope ran across the water, tied to two stakes on either bank. The rope ran through a pulley connected to a hand ferry, maybe big enough to fit four people.

"The water's deeper here. Runs quick enough to pull you along, too. We get across and head up the hill and we'll be at our destination," she said, boarding the raft. "Come on. Put those big muscles to use and hoist us across."

The gears and handrails were rusty with age, but still functioned perfectly.

"All set?" I asked.

Rita nodded. The raft lurched forward as I dislodged it from the muddy bank. The corroded joints screeched as I tugged at the rope hard, enough to get us into motion. The ferry jerked against the current, but soon we were halfway across and the ride smoothed out. Luckily, I didn't get my fingers caught in the pulley.

Rita chuckled as we made our way across. "Poor Bill. He was always a hothead, you know? I remember once when we were kids, he wanted to pull the raft across the water, but he wasn't big enough and—"

She screamed and fell off the raft. I nearly lost my footing but whirled around to see a ghostly white arm gripped around Rita's body, pulling her under the water.

"Hold on!" I hollered.

Rita fought to the surface and gasped for air in between cries for help. I leaned out and tried to grab her hand, but she was too far away. Her hat was floating down the river in the opposite direction, and her rifle was lodged in the mud out of reach. She thrashed herself free from the pale arm when the man it belonged to surfaced.

It was the bandit I'd shot and killed in the duel.

I recognized Arnold Pollard from the bullet hole just beneath the letter branded into his chest. His eyes were engorged, swollen to excess from being soaked in the water, and his jaw was slack. He let out a terrible moan while he grasped for Rita, who was swimming back to the ferry.

I drew my pistol and aimed, but the rushing water sloshed the ferry around too much for a clean shot. Rita bobbed up and down, violently splashing water and stirring up the silt in the creek. Arnold grabbed her head and pulled her back down.

He was trying to drown her. And he was beginning to win.

I needed to do something, and fast. I pulled my silver knife from its sheath and dropped my revolver and bandolier on the ferry. The warm water splashed as I leapt in feet first, the knife gripped between my teeth. My feet met the bottom of the creek and I hustled to reach Rita, but the creek bed was soft and pulled at my boots as they pressed deep into the muck. I stretched out my arm and felt her leg. I grabbed Rita's ankle and tried to pry her away from Arnold, but the drowned man had her in a headlock. With a hard yank, I pulled the two toward me, close enough to plunge my knife into Arnold's forearm. I twisted it hard, severing the tendons below the elbow. Arnold roared and his grip loosened while Rita surfaced behind me.

"What the hell is that thing?" she sputtered between coughing up water and choking for air.

"Get to the ferry," I yelled.

Even with only one arm to swim, Arnold was still quite capable of moving through the water. He closed the distance between us and dove for me, grabbing my head and dunking me underwater. I gulped a mouthful of water on the way down. My lungs spasmed and the air forced its way out. I shoved hard to push Arnold away and surfaced, hacking and rubbing the silty water from my eyes. Arnold floated backward, giving me just enough time and distance to get my feet set under me.

Arnold screamed and lunged for me. I was ready this time and drove the knife right into his skull, through his bloated eyeball. He went limp and foam gurgled out his mouth. The fluid from his punctured eyeball slid out like egg whites and ran down to the hilt of my knife. I yanked it out and made sure, for the second time, that he was really dead.

Rita was sprawled on the opposite bank when I hauled Arnold onto the shore. She scrambled as far away from the soggy corpse as she could until her back met the edge of the slope out of the creek bed.

"You're all right now, Miss Rita. Take a second to catch your breath," I said.

I knelt down beside the twice-dead man. He looked just as he did when I shot him: cocky, but afraid, the bright red bandana still tied around his neck. I grabbed him by the hair and rolled his head around in the mud, inspecting what was left of his face. His skin was waterlogged and squishy. On the left side of his neck were a pair of puncture wounds. Two perfect holes, side by side. All the blood had been drained from him, leaving a porcelain white corpse.

"What the hell was that thing?" Rita asked in between breaths.

I sat down next to Rita. "This 'thing' was a member of the Matthews Gang yesterday. That is, until I shot and killed him."

She brushed her wet hair from her face as the pace of her breathing returned to normal. "So what's it doing floating down my creek?"

"Beats me. Last I knew, he was spending the night at the undertaker's. But look here," I said, pointing out the bite wounds. "My best guess is that Arnold is a vampire's thrall."

Rita gasped. "Lord above, you're saying a person can be killed and still wander around like that?"

"Seems that way. I guess the curse doesn't end with the servant's death. Alive or dead, or in Arnold's case *undead*, thralls are mindless husks that obey their master's bidding."

"Do you think some vampire bid him to

kill us?"

I shook my head. "No, I think he was a sentry keeping watch over the area."

"So how do we know he isn't going to get up and try to kill us again?"

I pried apart the shattered bone of Arnold's skull with my knife. "Judging by this pink mush that used to be his brain, I think he's really done for this time."

The fluids inside the skull made a slurping noise as I slid the blade out of the curdled goo. I wiped it off and slid it back into its sheath. "Rest here for a moment. I'm going to go retrieve your things from the creek."

I didn't find Rita's hat, but I was able to get her rifle unstuck from the mud. The barrel was poking out of the water like a reed.

"I think this belongs to you," I said, wiping the mud from the butt. She took it and thanked me before laying it down next to her. I cinched up my own gun belt and bandoliers again and sat down on a stone shaped like a stool.

"So you said you shot this boy? Is that your bullet hole there?" she asked, pointing to Arnold's chest.

"Yes, ma'am, it is. He rode into Hexed Springs and told me he was going to shoot me because I was once a ranger and collect a bounty on my head," I answered.

Rita looked surprised. "A bounty? Because you're a ranger?"

I winced. I had proudly advertised myself as a ranger to Rita, but the title was quickly losing its charm. "Not sure if that's how I want to be known anymore."

"But you're the town's monster hunter, aren't you? You can ride and shoot and know plenty about the extramundane. I think that's plenty enough to make you a ranger."

"If you say so." I shrugged as I wiped away the mud caked on my boots. "I'll have to get some answers from the undertaker when I get back to town. Seems he's working for a vampire."

Rita shook her head for a long time, then let out of a heavy sigh. She rubbed her bruised wrist. After a few moments, she held out her hand for me and nodded toward the slope out of the creek valley. "Ready if you are."

* * *

By now, the shortcut was no longer useful but we pressed on nonetheless. Bright light streamed through some of the boughs of the forest canopy, enough for me to guess it was late afternoon. We walked up the natural elevation created by the rock outcropping and followed the creek.

I decided I liked Rita. She was a tough old gal living under a false identity in order to protect her secrets. Reminded me of some of the outlaws I had rode with, except Rita wasn't hiding something immoral. She was an honest woman lying in order to hold on to everything she and her family had worked for. That didn't sound unethical to me.

I have a lot of respect for women, especially those with both tenacity and grace. And Rita reminded me of Clem. They were both willing to do what was necessary to live life on their terms, and didn't bellyache and quit when things got tough. Clem puts up with me, and Rita put up with her brother, both of them having to tolerate the social expectations placed on them. But neither of them really gives a shit about those standards. They do as they please. Good for them.

The ground beneath us leveled out as we exited the creek and came upon a series of low rolling hills, bare, bumpy mounds, save for a few stones jutting out from under the soil. We were back to the mostly barren plains that dominated the prairie. A wall of exposed limestone came into view as we crested one of the hills. The opening to a natural cave sat smack in the middle of it.

"Ah, hell," Rita cursed.

She trotted up toward the mouth of the cave and shooed away a pack of vultures. The birds were hollowing out the corpse of a cow steeped in a puddle of its own blood. The kill was recent.

"One of yours?" I asked.

Rita pointed to its hindquarters. "That's the brand I use on all the cattle. Proves they're mine if someone rustles them and tries to sell them."

I followed the trail of blood leading toward the mouth of the mine. "And this wasn't here earlier?"

"Not when I came out this morning," she said.

The blood crossed over a rough spot in the grass, which was worn by the wagon wheels that had come and gone when the mine was still in operation. Minecart tracks ran parallel to those, leading around the mine's entrance to an empty wooden shed, where the lode could be dumped into the bed of the wagons. I approached the mouth of the cave. A sign was nailed to a post announcing the recent sale of the mine to the Allen Mining Company, financed by the one and only Ross P. Strickland of Strickland Savings & Loan. The mining operations were supposed to resume two months ago.

I scoffed. Saving Strickland's daughter and protecting his latest investment? The way I see it, I oughta earn double for this job.

Darkness overtook the sunbeams before they reached inside the cave. I'd have a hard time getting around without light to guide me. Luckily, there was an oil lamp on a drafting table at the entrance, along with pickaxes and helmets, presumably left over from the last shift before the operation shut down.

"Blood trail continues into the mine. Looks like whatever got that cow dragged some of it down there," I said, peering into the darkness.

"You reckon we can lure it out?"

"That's not a bad idea. Why don't you get behind that dead tree over there and get ready to shoot," I said, pointing in the distance. A thick tree, covered in claw marks, stood not fifty feet from us. It had a clear view of the mine.

Rita positioned herself behind the trunk and peeked out of the corner with her rifle trained on the cave.

"I'm ready," she called.

I nodded and raised a hand to give her a signal. The mine was still and silent. The only noise came from the vultures angrily squawking at us. Three were perched in the nearby tree line, waiting for us to leave so they could resume their feast.

I let out a whoop that echoed down the cave, then scrambled back to a safe spot. I held my breath and listened. Even the vultures got quiet for a moment.

Nothing.

I kicked at the dirt while scratching my chin. "Keep your eyes on that entrance while I try something else."

Rita nodded and propped herself up against the tree for balance.

I suddenly remembered that vampires

prefer human blood over animal blood, but other vampiric creatures don't care about the source. They all react to the scent of human blood like a shark reacts to chum in water.

I approached the cave mouth once more.

"Careful, Cal," Rita said.

I pressed the blade of my knife into the meat of my palm and wiped the trickle of blood along the entrance of the cave. The breeze was light, but strong enough to carry a scent, hopefully down deep enough to attract my prey.

I crouched in my hiding spot and waited for a solid minute.

"My shoulder's getting tired and I can't hold this position much longer, Cal. Maybe you should go up and holler again?"

"Give it a minute longer," I said.

"Want me to go holler?"

I turned toward Rita and put a finger to my lips. A faint growl was coming from somewhere nearby.

"Cal, look out!"

Before I could look up, something pounced on me, sending me tumbling end over end. My revolver slipped out of my hands as I rolled. I sprang to my feet and spun around: a sickly, yellow creature about five feet tall was circling me. Its face looked like a cross between a short-nosed bat and a dog, but it had the scales and spines of a lizard.

It was a chupacabra, a known killer of cattle.

"Get clear so I can shoot it," Rita yelled, chambering her first round.

The creature snapped its head to look at her. It took off, darting side to side, easily dodging her shots. The monster pinned her against the tree with its claws and Rita screamed. It bared its teeth and licked the soft flesh of her neck as she struggled in its grip. She punched and kicked at it, but it was no good. The chupacabra hoisted her even higher, its blood-red eyes flashing with fury as it prepared to tear out her abdomen.

I needed to take a shot. There wasn't any time to get into a better position. I had to make a quick decision.

My sixth sense. Maybe I could conjure up the same spell I'd used against Arnold in our duel. I didn't care if I risked hurting myself—it was the only way I could save Rita.

I took a breath and closed my eyes. The same chill shot up my spine and my head was abuzz with power. When I opened my eyes, time had slowed to a crawl. I could feel the direction of the breeze, hear where the vultures were perched, smell the blood on my hand. My senses were heightened to a level I'd never experienced before.

The chupacabra's jaws were slowly closing in on Rita. I had just enough time to take aim on the monster's exposed flank. As I pulled the trigger, a bright light flared in my vision, returning time to its normal speed. My bullet split the air, but sailed off its mark, hitting the tree trunk instead.

Pain flared inside my left eye, like it'd been impaled with a white-hot iron rod. I stumbled, clutching the left side of my face.

Sensing my weakened state, the chupacabra threw Rita to the ground and charged me. I was too woozy to fire my gun again, so I tossed it aside and reached for my knife. The monster roared, unleashing a sound like a dog's bark mixed with an alligator's growl, barreling toward me on all fours. I glanced back at Rita. She wasn't getting up. The chupacabra had thrown her down hard enough to make her bounce, and she was laying limp on the ground.

When the monster was just feet away from me, I lunged for its heart. It effortlessly dodged, swinging a huge claw at me. I countered by driving my knife into its shoulder. We collided hard, then stumbled apart. My blade was lodged in the creature's right clavicle. The chupacabra hissed, then turned back to me, its long, pointy tongue raking over its fangs.

My vision cleared and I eyed my revolver on the ground. I circled toward it, trying not to telegraph my next move, but the chupacabra was smart enough to figure out what I was going to do. Each time I took a step toward the gun, its spines bristled, and it would feign a swipe in my direction. Its right arm was useless, the knife had taken care of that, but it was still dangerous.

If I turned hard and dove fast enough, I could scoop up the revolver and squeeze off a shot before the creature piled on top of me. I chewed my lip for a moment. My stomach was queasy from the attempt at spellcasting, but adrenaline was kicking in, blocking out the pain and boosting my confidence.

I bolted for the gun, and the chupacabra followed. I stretched out my body as long as I could as I dove, but came up short. The chupacabra stopped short, turning on a dime, and pressed its back legs into the dirt, preparing to pounce. It would dig its fangs into my jugular any chance it got.

The creature leapt, one arm dangling limply at its side, its mouth agape. I braced myself for impact when I heard a crack. Rita had intercepted it, thrusting her rifle into its jaws. She held it like a baton, one hand on the barrel and one on the butt, and the creature bit down hard. She twisted the rifle sharply, and the creature's fangs scraped off the metal as it stumbled backward. Rita drew up her aim, point-blank right between the eyes, and pulled the trigger.

The creature sank to the ground, convulsing and hissing. Rita shot it again and again, until she had no more bullets left.

"Whoa, there," I said, after her fourth shot. "You got it, Miss Rita. It's dead."

She dropped her rifle, suddenly spent, and dry-heaved. The creature smelled like rot and death and looked about that ugly up close. She stared with empty eyes at the creature's yellow blood dripping down its snout, then shakily pointed at the dead chupacabra, still so stunned she could barely get the words out. "That ... that was the creature that attacked me on the trail."

It must have been tracking us ever since I found the overturned wagon. Chupacabras are clever. Probably thought following us to its lair would make for an easier hunt.

I sidled up next to her and fixed my eyes on the creature. "Rita, you saved my life."

"I don't see how you do it. Hunting monsters, that is," she said.

I laughed. "Apparently, I'm not that good at it. Without you, I'd be monster chow right now."

She didn't react. She stood still for a moment, then turned back toward the creek. "I want to go home now."

"Rita, I appreciate everything you've done, but I can't leave here yet. I don't know if you're safe wandering home alone. Or in the condition to, for that matter," I said.

She picked up her rifle and slung it over her shoulder. "I'm fine. I'm fine. I have some bullets left. I'll be all right."

I reached out to stop her. "Rita, I—"

"I'm fine!" she barked, swatting my hand

away. She hung her head and her whole body shook. "I'm sorry, Cal. It's just ... I thought we were going to be killed."

I patted her on the back. She wasn't feeble, but her tough outer shell had cracked. I'd felt this way before, too, when I first experienced mortal danger in a firefight. Once the adrenaline drains away, fear and regret settle in.

"It's okay to be frightened. It's natural. Hell, you nearly drowned and then this? I don't blame you," I said. The side of her body where she'd been thrust into the ground was one big bruise. I was amazed she was still standing.

"I always knew there were creatures beyond our imaginations. Unexplained mysteries out here are nothing new to me. But how am I supposed to defend myself against something as fast and strong and bloodthirsty as that? Creatures are tougher and smarter than they used to be."

I blew out a breath and squeezed her shoulder. "Not a fair fight, is it?"

Rita shook her head and limped toward the trail. "I can't make it down the creek again, so I'll take the long road home. I'll take care of the horses, too. Now, I insist you let me go and that you don't worry about me."

I sighed. "If you insist. If you don't mind, give Buck one of these, will you?"

I passed her the last sugar cube and she smiled.

"Come by the homestead when you're done and I'll have your payment ready. I think you've earned a little extra for taking out two monsters," she hollered from down the path.

"Thank you, but the original agreement is enough," I shouted back.

It didn't feel right to take double the payment. It felt wrong to take any payment at all, really. When she was gone from sight, I put my boot against the chupacabra and dislodged my blade from its shoulder. Viscous yellow and pink fluid poured out of the monster's exposed veins. I inspected the corpse while I wiped away the sludge from the knife. Just like every chupacabra I've heard about, this one had no membrane running from waist to wrist, just puss-colored scales with short gray hairs poking out of them. This wasn't the vampiric creature Strickland had described.

"You wouldn't happen to have seen a little girl around here, would ya?" I asked the dead monster. I dusted myself off and gathered my weapons. My head still hurt, but the pain had subsided enough to be tolerable.

I turned back to the vultures still waiting and watching for their chance to peck at the dead cow. I wondered if they'd eat dead chupacabra, too.

"All yours, fellas," I yelled.

I grabbed one of the lanterns sitting on the drafting table by the cave mouth. It was dusty and the handle had rusted over, but it still had oil in its reserve. Enough to last a few hours, at least. I struck one of the matches I carried in my pouch and lit the charred wick inside. The light battled for control of the darkness that tunneled down as far as I could see.

The wind whistled as it swept across the jagged and rocky maw of the mine. Somewhere down there was a little girl, scared and alone, waiting for her rescue.

CHAPTER FIFTEEN

The darkness in the mineshaft overwhelmed the light of my borrowed lantern. I should have been able to see my boots, but everything below my knees was pitch black. The cave was unnaturally dim, just like the shadows in Strayhaven. This amount of gloom could only be achieved with a spell.

Someone was trying to keep humans out.

The tunnel was small, barely wide enough for the minecarts that conveyed the nuggets of coal to squeeze through. I pictured the workers struggling to file in one after the other, entering and exiting the depths together to avoid clogging the production line.

Black soot lined the walls and hung in the air. The gritty residue of the deep earth clung to my throat with each breath. I carefully set down my lantern, keeping in mind that I was surrounded by flammable dust, and pulled the kerchief over my nose. Walking in the darkness wasn't easy, but walking in supernatural darkness with minecart tracks and the rocky terrain was downright frustrating. The unending silence didn't help and made it feel like the cave walls were pressing in on me. The wooden braces that lined the ceiling resembled the ribs of a beast, and I was being willingly devoured.

Not a single sliver of sunbeam could follow me after I passed the one-hundred-yard mark, not this far down. Even with the lantern, I could barely see my own hand in front of my face. The tunnel ahead was completely void of light, and a chill radiated from the stone walls, replacing the summer heat my skin was accustomed to. I skidded across loose chips of stone, which crunched and echoed down the corridor with each step. As I steadied myself against the wall with my free hand, the soot found a way inside my knife wound, sending a shooting pain through my palm. I yanked my hand away and hissed, my voice bouncing down the endless mine shaft.

The cavern opened up slightly as I entered a new chamber. This must have been an outpost of some kind. A drafting table, similar to the one outside, sat in the corner next to a cabinet with more mining tools and helmets, which hung like hats in a saloon. Stretched on top of the table was a large sheet of paper, its corners held down by pieces of coal acting as paperweights. I swiped off the layer of dust covering the parchment, revealing a map of the shafts. According to the map, the shaft descended fifty feet via a corkscrew turn, then opened up into another chamber. I couldn't tell what was beyond that. Someone had scratched out the next chamber and written the words *NO* and *GET OUT*. Underlined them, too.

How reassuring. At least I knew I was going the right way.

I pressed on. Just as the map said, the mineshaft shrank back to its petite width, and the corkscrew turn came next, gently curling down and to the right, deeper into the earth. My eyes shifted back and forth between the ground and what was in front of me. The terrain was getting bumpy again and one wrong step could mean a rolled ankle. Or worse. I don't know if the silence and tight quarters were getting to me, but a small, panicked voice started filling my head with scary thoughts. If there was something down here, did it have any idea I was stalking it? Maybe it was stalking me. Ever since I entered this place, I felt like I was being watched. Like something knew I was down here. And it was expecting me, leading me down, down into its lair.

My senses heightened as my heart pumped harder and quicker. The temperature in the cave took a nosedive and goosebumps spread down my forearms. The winding slope spiraled downward many feet before becoming a flat pathway again, still lined with the rickety wooden ceiling supports.

With the lantern held high, I entered the

last-known room on the map. I searched the room for its contents when something in the darkness moved. My heart skipped a beat as I whipped out my revolver and did a sharp double-take in the direction of the movement.

It was nothing. Just a shadow playing off an overturned minecart down the line. The cart was empty, save for a few chunks of coal and a mound of coal dust. My mind was playing tricks on me.

At the end of the chamber was a natural archway, one not carved by a miner's pickax. It opened onto a much larger cavern. The black soot lining the walls didn't contaminate this part of the cave.

A pleasant sound greeted me as I crossed the threshold of the natural doorway. At first, I confused it with rain, the slow and steady pattering of water droplets, as if a cloud had got trapped down here. I held the lantern out and saw that it was a wayward waterfall. The water flowed forth from a crack in the cavern wall and glowed a faint violet when it splashed on the limestone floor far below.

This section was the complete opposite of the mineshaft I had just left. It was spacious, big enough to fit the drinking parlor of Clem's saloon inside it, chandelier included. The air was clean and the stone floor was wet and slick, which made walking difficult. The rocky slope down to the cavern floor was round and smooth, like a stone snatched up from the bottom of a river.

Just as I started down the steps, a noise split the silence. A hollow clang rang out from the upended minecart behind me. I lost my footing on the slippery surface and stifled a yell before it could jump halfway out of my throat. I fell backward down the rocky path, losing my grip on the lantern in the process.

I landed on my ass, coasting through the cavern and down into another room, until I slammed into one of those spiky rocks made from eons of sediment dripping from the roof of a cave. My lantern chased after me, clanking end over end, and I caught it on the last bounce before it could tumble into the unreachable darkness below. Its glass bulb had shattered, but the flame was still burning strong. My hand quivered as I aimed my revolver into the abyss.

But, again, nothing came.

My heart was stuck in my throat. It took a second to return to its home. When I'd collected myself, I continued exploring the new cavern, keeping my gun drawn for good measure. I didn't intend to be ambushed again, not by a chupacabra or anything else that might be stalking me.

It was a good thing the stalagmite had stopped my fall. The sheer drop appeared deep enough to shatter bones. The faint rush of water bubbled up again from far below. A subterranean body of water, perhaps fed by Rita's creek.

The platform on which I stood was of natural origin, but a new set of stairs in front of me weren't. They looked hastily carved by an untrained hand. Each step was irregular in size and shape and led to a wrought-iron door wedged into a small mouth of stone.

Once I was sure I wasn't being followed, I descended the steps to the door. Its hinges were rusty and probably hadn't moved in ages. I gritted my teeth and prepared myself for the noise. With a shove of my shoulder, the door jolted ajar with a sharp squeak, then groaned as it swung all the way open.

If there was something down here, it would know I was here. Every muscle in my body tensed as I listened, separating the faint rushing water from the quiet stillness surrounding me. My eyes grew wide, trying to gather as much light as they could. I felt exposed. My heart pressed against my chest as it beat faster and faster, waiting for something to reach out from the dark and drag me into its jaws.

But none of that happened.

I crossed the threshold into the new cavern. The orange glow from my lantern was no longer the only light source here. Just around a bend, a flickering light beckoned me forward. I prayed that there was a little girl—and only a little girl—around that corner holding a candle.

I set my lantern down and removed the holy water from my pocket. I gripped it so tight I was afraid it would shatter in my palm. I crept along with my back to the wall, nearly gasping in shock when I peered around the corner.

Six people, four men and two women, were huddled together around a brazier in the middle of the room, each one bobbing up and down from their rapid and shallow breathing. Their eyes were closed and their mouths hung open as they huffed, emitting an eerie chorus of wheezing and panting. Every now and then, one of them would let out a throaty rasp and gulp down as much air as they could. It made my blood run cold.

I crept up to the man nearest to me and waved my hand in front of his eyelids. Neither the motion nor my presence stirred him, so I leaned in closer for a better look. He was approaching middle age, probably in his late forties, gray hair with some longer stubble on his face. His hands were black and his nails were bloodied and raw. He wore a worker's coveralls, probably a mining outfit, just as two of his compatriots beside him. Under his left ear were two puncture wounds surrounded by a pale purple bruise.

I searched the necks of the other men. Same puncture wounds. I checked on the two women. The fire in the brazier shone bright and helped me get a good look at their faces. One was particularly beautiful.

It was Rose, Clem's girl.

She was still pretty, despite her blue lips and pale skin. She wore a corset with a white shoulder-less blouse and a flowing maroon skirt, just as she did when working at the saloon. On her exposed flesh underneath the left collarbone was a branded 'M,' just like the one burned into Arnold.

Without thinking, I grabbed her by the waist and cupped the back of her head in my hands. She didn't react. Her eyes stayed shut and she continued her ragged breathing.

"Rose. Hey, can you hear me?" I whispered in her ear.

Still no response. As I pulled my lips away, I noticed she had the same puncture wounds on her neck. I let her go and backed away.

A helpless panic struck me, like watching someone choke and not knowing how to save them. She needed to see a doctor. Maybe Toussaint could treat her, since he knew about a treatment for vampire infection. Once I'd found Abigail, I was going to get them both out.

I examined the woman standing next to her. She wore a cowhide dress adorned with elaborate glass beads. The veins on her face, which flushed as she panted, contoured her sharp jawline and deep-set eyes. I slowly reached for the neck of her dress. As I peeled it back, there it was —another 'M.'

Obviously, none of these people were members of the Matthews Gang. The brand had to represent something else. That's when it hit me. The iron rods at the opium den, the ones in the room where Cromley was draining blood from a human. Could those have been brands heating up in the fire?

I stood dumbstruck for a moment. Rose and the others must have been enthralled, just like Arnold. But what were they doing stored away in a catatonic state in this cave? They'd each been bitten. Either they were infected and being transformed into vampires or they'd been issued a fate far worse—a living, breathing buffet line for the feral vampire who took Abigail. I prayed I wasn't going to find a little girl in near death up ahead.

I didn't want to leave these people like this. To have been robbed of their free will and their minds corrupted into worshipping a master? That was wrong and beyond judgment. Maybe I could still save Rose. I wasn't sure what to do with the others. I could pierce their hearts with my knife, one after the other, and lay them down quietly to avoid making noise. My reflection looked back at me in the mirrored blade. In between the streaks of fluid left behind from killing the chupacabra, I could see the fear and indecision in my own eyes.

I went up to the first miner and placed the point right between his ribs, where the heart was vulnerable. I steeled myself and counted to three. After a moment, lowered my knife. I couldn't do it. If I could save Rose, I owed it to these people to try and save them, too. Perhaps Toussaint would know what to do and could journey back down with me after I purged the mine of whatever evil lived inside.

Something up ahead let out a whooping cough just as I secured my knife. It was a harsh noise coming from what sounded like a small child. My heart leapt for the umpteenth time. *That has to be Abigail,* I thought. She didn't sound well at all. I could tell from the gurgle in the cough that there was phlegm in it. I left the resting thralls in their place and crept down the corridor toward the noise.

The trail ended in what would be best described as a lair. Sconces, driven into the cave wall, held burning torches. In the middle of the room, an open coffin leaned against the back of the rock wall, surrounded by wax candles that had nearly melted down to the stump. The coffin was made of a fine wood, rich and dark, and lined with red velvet cushions. Inside it lay a woman, or what appeared to be one, with her arms folded across her chest. She was nude, but her stomach and breasts were covered by a flap of skin that hung from her wrists and connected near her hips, just like a set of wings. Her hair was light brown and she had fair skin, almost as white as porcelain, that appeared radiant in the candle glow. Her nose sat twisted up like bat's snout on her face, and two exposed fangs rested on her lower lip, dangerously close to piercing it.

She also had a birthmark, a splotchy field

of brown resting on her neck. Not only was this the monster Strickland described, it was the woman I had seen with Lucius months ago at Clem's. She was resting peacefully, and if she didn't have the crude features of a vampire, I would have confused her for an angel.

Another muffled cough, this time from the corner of the room. A young girl was curled up in a fetal position. She let out a soft, yet pained, moan. I darted over to her and cradled her on my chest. Her head burned with a fever while the rest of her body was cold and clammy and covered in sweat.

Sad memories washed over me, as I flashed to my twin sister. The last time I saw her, she was laying on her bed, blue in the face after choking on her own vomit. I was the one who draped the sheet over her dead body, just as I'd done with my parents. Despite my hatred for the man, Strickland's request felt personal to me now, seeing this helpless little girl sprawled out on the cold stone floor, sick and in pain.

"Abigail?" I whispered. "Sweetheart, your daddy sent me and I'm going to take you home now."

Her eyes tried to focus as she made an effort to sit up, but she collapsed back into my arms. She was talking but didn't make any sense.

"I want to stay with mommy. Daddy, stop ..." she murmured.

"Sugar, I'm not your daddy, but I'm here to

rescue you. It's gonna be all right," I whispered, brushing the hair from her cheek.

The creature inside the coffin had to be dealt with first. If I were a betting man, and I am, I'd put my money on this thing being the master to those poor folks down the hall. I gripped the vial of holy water in a quivering hand, dread creeping up my arms.

Only one problem, though. The membrane of her wings covered her body, obscuring her chest. Holy water needs to melt into a vital organ to be lethal. It was too dangerous to take any chances. I needed to expose her heart.

I had one chance and I couldn't let my nerves get the best of me. Better to do one calm and confident movement to avoid waking her up.

I gathered my courage and gently peeled back the wing, exposing her chest. Her hand was cold and rough. Her ribs poked through her pallid skin like nails, and purple veins snaked down her entire body. I uncorked the vial with my teeth and lowered it over her heart.

Her nostrils flared and her eyelids fluttered. That's when I noticed a trickle of blood dripping from the knife wound in my palm. She must have smelled it.

The feral vampiress let out a piercing screech, one capable of shattering glass. A crack appeared in the vial and I felt the water trickle down my arm. We wrestled for control, but her demonic strength won out, bending my arm in the wrong direction and nearly breaking it. I hollered in pain and stumbled backward as the vial of holy water shattered on the cavern floor.

The vampiress lifted herself majestically from her resting place. We both shot a glance at Abigail. The little girl was still slumped on the floor and hadn't reacted to the scream. I thought about scooping her up and making a run for it, but Strickland mentioned that this thing was fast and agile. No way I could outrun it with a little girl in my arms.

And Rose. How was I going to save her, too?

The monster sprang from its coffin and landed between me and the little girl. It held its wings out wide and hissed.

"Mine," it said.

"Over my dead body," I snapped back.

The creature cackled like it enjoyed the thought of adding me to its collection of thralls. I reached for my revolver, but the blackened and bloodied hand of a miner clamped down on my shoulder like a vice. I twisted and felt the hand slide off, but others took its place. The thralls' scratched at my face and neck, their long fingernails narrowly missing my eyes, and then they seized my wrists. As they tried to drag me down to the ground and pin me, I pressed my feet into the earth and launched myself backward. We all spilled onto the ground like bowling pins.

I rolled behind the mass of writhing bodies

and fanned the hammer of my revolver, booming out five shots in rapid succession. The blasts were even more deafening than the vampire's piercing wail, but they got the job done. Each found its target and all but one of the thralls slumped to the floor. The barrel of my gun shook as I aimed at the last one.

"Rose, snap out of it," I pleaded.

It was no use. Rose stood up with disjointed and jerky movements. She gurgled and growled, lurching toward me. I looked into her eyes and couldn't recognize her anymore. The spirit and vibrance of my new friend was gone. All that was left was brainwashed bloodlust that would only be sated by killing me. She was too far gone.

Sadness washed over me. I could do nothing for her.

I lowered my gun and drove my blade into her heart as she crashed into me. Her body went limp in my arms as she slid down to my feet, lifeless and, hopefully, at peace.

As soon as the last thrall stopped convulsing, the vampiress left her defensive position over Abigail and rushed me. Even in undeath, she moved with speed and grace. I fired my last round, hitting her in the lower abdomen. The shot didn't faze her, barely causing her to waver. She hissed and sprinted toward me, fangs exposed.

We grappled and stumbled toward the

coffin in the middle of the room. Her clawed hands dug at my throat, knocking me off balance and sending us both to the ground. I pressed my hands into her face, trying to gouge her eyes with my thumbs, but all I managed to do was smear black coal dust across her face. She was too strong.

And that's when I had an idea.

I fumbled around for the candles. Hot, gummy wax stung my skin, but I finally managed to grab hold of one, cramming the burning wick right into her eye. The black coal dust sparked and flashed like a fuse, and fire engulfed her face. The vampiress shrieked, burying her burning face in her hands.

I lowered my shoulder and rammed her from behind, shoving her back into the coffin. I flung the lid closed and tugged hard at a corner, throwing all of my strength into the effort. The coffin creaked loose and fell in slow motion, like a tall tree falling in the woods. It crashed to the ground, trapping the monster and crushing the bones in her wings. A muffled wail wormed its way out from inside the coffin.

I sprinted for the exit. Without missing a step, I scooped up the sick little girl in my arms. She was still barely fazed by all the commotion. I said a final goodbye to Rose as I hustled out of the vampiress's chambers with Abigail clinging to my shoulder. The iron door screeched closed and I hastily wedged it shut again.

"Hold on tight, baby doll. I don't wanna tumble and lose you," I said.

With all the strength she could muster, she gripped my shirt, the color leaving her little fists. A piercing screech rushed up behind us, echoing up to the second miner's outpost. The vampiress was breaking free from the wooden trap.

"Mine!" she repeated over and over.

As I passed the overturned minecart, the metal door behind us groaned as it was nearly ripped off its hinges. I wasn't sure how much longer it was going to hold. If I could make it out of the cave first, the feral vamp might be crazy enough to follow me into the sunshine and roast to death. Maybe. There was no way I could outrun her if she broke through. I had to make my last stand right here.

I searched the waystation for anything useful. Hitting her with a pickax would do some damage, but probably wasn't the best idea. I didn't want to go toe-to-toe with the monster again. Firing in close quarters had already proved ineffective. And none of the wooden handles of the mining tools were sharp enough to pierce her heart.

"This is gonna have to work," I said. "Abigail, hang on."

I chucked the lantern at the overturned minecart just as the vamp glided into the chamber. The flames landed just shy of the cart, but had enough momentum to roll the lamp forward. The oil inside sprayed out as it tumbled, throwing flaming droplets at the minecart. The fire licked at the edge of the coal dust.

I squeezed the little girl to my chest and took off running. A second later, the coal dust exploded. We were thrown forward by the force of the blast. I tripped and fell, but managed to land on my back and not crush the poor girl. Without the lantern, everything was pitch black again.

Dust swirled around us, making it even more difficult to breathe. Other than the ringing in my ears, the mine was silent. But there was a new noise slowly rumbling out of the depths. Vibrations rippled through the tunnel and I could hear the faint cracking of stone.

The mine was caving in.

I set my hand on the mine wall and started running. We made the corkscrew turn and dashed past the first outpost, coal dust thick in the air. Before long, I could see a faint light cutting through the darkness. I sprinted for it as hard as I could, a plume of dust close on our heels.

I burst into the sunlight seconds before the plume could overtake us. I set Abigail down and collapsed near the dead chupacabra, huffing and puffing in between gritty coughs. The deep rumbles shook beneath me as the mine crumbled in on itself, soot floating into the air like smoke, flying right up into the purple and pinks of the sunset, where storm clouds were brewing.

The sunset? I'd been down there longer than I thought.

The ground around the mine went still again. The vampiress was dead, surely killed in the explosion or crushed by the collapsed stone. The mine was also ruined. The Allen Mining Company executives would be pissed. Strickland, too, I reckon.

Then I remembered that Rose was down there, too. Clem would appreciate the closure if I told her I'd found her, but maybe I could leave out the part about her being turned into a mindless victim of a vampire. Rose didn't deserve any of that. None of those folks down there did. All I could do was pretend that I did them a favor by releasing their bodies from that sick creature's servitude.

A rumble of thunder brought me back to the present. The black clouds that towered above us were tinted with a green hue, and an opaque sheet of rain fell in the distance. Locals say you can tell how strong a storm is by its glow. Green skies means something bad was coming your way. The air was thick and soupy, a recipe for hailstones and lightning, maybe even tornadoes. It was no more than an hour away.

Even if I rode hard for town, I wasn't going to make it before the storm hit. My best bet was to find Rita and hold out at her house. If I stayed there until the storm passed, I was going to miss

Strickland's deadline. Surely, he wouldn't mind since I'd lived up to my end of the bargain. But I wouldn't put it past him to dock my earnings. Especially, if I told him the mine he was investing in had collapsed.

I patted Abigail on the back, trying to rouse her from her feverish stupor.

"I don't know what that thing did to you down there, darlin,' but you're gonna be okay now. I've gotta get you somewhere safe and let the storm pass over before I get you home. Does that sound good? Abigail?"

The sick little girl didn't make a peep.

CHAPTER SIXTEEN

"Abigail?" I rocked the little girl gently in my arms.

Still nothing.

I panicked and placed my hand on her chest. A faint heartbeat fluttered beneath her shallow breaths. She was still alive, but unconscious. Any color left in her face was gone now. She was completely pale except for the soot stains that had accumulated in her sweat.

The storm clouds overshadowed the setting sun, which blanketed the creek bed in a gray wash. Raindrops scattered across the ground as I ran back through the creek, the little girl in my arms. I pulled us across the water on the hand ferry, nearly wearing a hole in my gloves. Thankfully, there weren't any copperheads waiting to surprise me in the weeds and grasses as I rushed by. The rain started to fall more steadily, bouncing off the water's surface and causing the creek to swell.

I burst through the thicket behind Conway

Ranch just as the last light left the sky. The rain was heavy now and pooled in low spots around the homestead. A lightning flash illuminated the brick chimney and covered back patio. There was a light on in one of the windows.

The weathervane on top of the barn twisted wildly and the windmill creaked as if it were about to spin loose in the gusting wind. I could hear Buck and Big Gus causing a fuss as we passed the red barn.

The lightning bolts carved into the ground and back up to the clouds more frequently now, lighting up the old oak tree in the front yard. It shielded us from the rain as it swayed in sync with winds rushing through it. A makeshift cross made with two sticks of wood tied together marked a burial plot at the base of the tree. I assumed it was for Bill.

I banged hard on the door.

"Rita, it's Cal. I need help," I yelled over the storm.

A few seconds later, a candlelight rushed toward us, moving from window to window until it reached the door. Rita appeared, wrapped in a night gown and holding a candlestick. She craned her neck to see what I was holding and gasped when she saw it was a little girl.

"She's sick, Rita. I don't know what to do," I said, presenting Abigail's limp body to her.

She opened the door, her eyes wide as saucers, and pulled us inside. "Go lay her down on the bed. I'll fetch a washcloth and see what I can do."

I entered the foyer, a dank and dusty room full of furniture covered in white sheets, like ghosts in an empty house. A family portrait, two kids and two parents, hung above an empty hearth tucked away in the back of the room. A grandfather clock, the only thing not covered in cloth, sat next to a staircase. It was primed and ready to chime out nine times.

Abigail coughed something fierce.

"Use that bedroom." Rita pointed to a doorway in the corner. "I'll be right back."

I barged inside and laid Abigail down on the bed. It was a small, undecorated room with a wood-framed bed, a feather mattress, and a potbellied stove that provided warmth in the winter. The bed was flanked by two windows with a clear view of the barn and the expanse of flat land the Conways owned. I pulled out a chair that was tucked into a secretary desk, where Rita wrote her letters, and placed it next to the bed.

Abigail's hand was cold and clammy inside mine. I brushed the hair out of her face, which was wet as a mop now. Her breathing became more of a wheeze, and she let out a few violent coughs as Rita came in with a glass bottle and a wet cloth.

"I found some camphor oil. That oughta help with the coughing," she said.

She blotted away the girl's sweat and shook

out a few drops of the oil onto her palms. She rubbed them together to warm the liquid, then massaged it just under Abigail's throat. She stopped under the neck of her shirt.

"What's this?" Rita said, feeling around.

She tugged back the shirt a little. Above Abigail's heart were two puncture wounds, swollen and purple.

I slammed my fists into my lap. "Son of a bitch!"

Rita shrank back, her face unchanged.

"Vampire bites, Rita. This is Ross Strickland's daughter. I found her in the bottom of the coal mine along with some half-bat, half-woman vampire. I think it was feeding on her."

Rita took a step backward, mouth open, shock filling her eyes. "What's going to happen to her?"

I shook my head. "I genuinely don't have a clue. I think I know someone who does, though, but they're in Hexed Springs and I can't get there because of the storm."

Rita looked out the window and jumped as a hailstone slapped the glass. Purple light flashed across her face and a loud rumble shook the house.

"Nobody could make it through this. You're going to need to stay here tonight, or at least until this storm passes," she said.

My boots hammered the floor as I paced around the room. "Remember the timely job I mentioned? I'm supposed to have her back in Strickland's custody by midnight. Alive, no less."

"Cal, there's nothing you can do right now. Surely, he'll understand that circumstances were out of your control and held you back."

"I doubt he'll sympathize, especially since he threatened to find me and have me hanged or —"

"Hush now. Let me serve you some supper. I have beans and ham stewing in a pot underneath a fire in the kitchen. Come, let me set you a place at the table," she said, patting me on the shoulder.

"Thank you, ma'am, but I don't want to leave her alone in this state."

Rita gingerly shuffled toward the door, her bruises peeking out of her sleeves, and stopped inside the doorway. "You're quite the guardian angel. You stay put and I'll bring you a bowl."

Abigail curled herself up in the blankets. Was she sick from the cold, damp cave or had the vampire infected her when it fed on her? If she could hold on a little longer, I could get her help.

Abigail's breathing was improving, at least it seemed like she was taking in deeper pulls of air. Poor thing was nestled under a mound of blankets and pillows. She wasn't so pale anymore, but the way she was laying there, I couldn't see anything else but a little girl laying in a casket.

Rita came back a few minutes later with a

bowl of stew and a wedge of cornbread. I nodded in thanks. It was the only real meal I'd had since breakfast.

"I salted a ham hock and let it soak with beans. The pork was grown and fed here on Conway land," she said with pride.

"It's awfully good," I replied between bites.

Rita swirled her beans with a spoon while I chowed down.

"What's her name?" she said, placing her bowl on the nearby nightstand.

"Abigail Ames Strickland. She's nine or ten. Her father wasn't sure," I replied.

Rita touched Abigail's arm. "So young and sweet. For the last year, I've been cursing her father's name. The man's been a plague upon us. Put a lot of folks out of business then stole their land out from under them. I've been praying that someday he gets a taste of his own medicine and loses everything he holds dear. Wasn't that terrible of me?"

I wiped my mouth on my forearm. "You're not the first person to wish ill upon that man. I doubt you'll be the last either. Vampires did this to Abigail. I don't think your wishes caused this to happen."

Rita sighed. "I'm gonna have to sell to Strickland. I tried to avoid it, but it's inevitable."

I stopped mid-chew and looked at her. She was so full of defeat. "I hate to hear that, Rita. I'm sorry."

"I am, too," she said. "I'm not sure if I'll do it this winter or next spring. I'm hoping he'll let me stay in the house my brother and father built. Let me work the land as a tenant farmer, at least until I pass on."

"No locals are willing to buy it?"

"Not anyone willing to fight against Strickland. He's just too rich and powerful. I've heard he intends to buy up all the land from here to the Black Mesa. Don't know what for, though, but there's not many folks left to stand in his way."

We sat silent for a minute as the rain beat down upon the roof and thunderbolts cracked the sky. I felt pity for Rita. The old gal was alone, poor and scared, her relatives dead and gone. It was hard to hold out against these land barons gobbling up the county. They couldn't wait until she died to seize her farm. They needed to bleed her dry, like they were on some sort of deadline.

"I know it's not the same situation, but I can't tell what I'm going to do with myself after this either. Strickland's jeopardized my future, too," I said.

"What do you mean?" Rita asked.

I stared at the raindrops streaking down the window. "Strickland blackmailed me into this job. Who's to say he won't do it again? I can't live underneath his thumb. Not when he's so close to Judge Willoby."

"What's the judge have to do with it? He's after paranormals, not humans."

"The man knows my face and my long history of breaking the law. I've sat in his courtroom before, back when I was a government ranger."

Rita put a hand to her mouth. "You were an inquisitor?"

"Sort of. I thought I was learning to be a true ranger, protecting mortal folks from monsters, like my ancestors did once upon a time. I refused to participate in the removals, so I went AWOL."

"How did you end up in his courtroom?"

"Testifying against an innocent man. I'd been called in to hunt a desert elf, one wanted for murder. I knew who he was. Didn't like the fella, so when they told me to track him down, I didn't ask any questions. The judge exaggerated the results of my investigation until the case against the elf was airtight. He was so slick, he had me having doubts about my own words."

"Oh, Cal, I'm sorry. You shouldn't be so hard on yourself, though. Those trials don't have juries. The elf would have been condemned even if you weren't there."

"The elf wasn't even allowed a lawyer. They shoved a gag in his mouth when he protested," I said. I tapped a fist on my knee. "I shouldn't even have agreed to track him down. They killed him that day. I felt so guilty for falling in line with their lies that I ran off for Rusted Butte."

"You don't have to tell me anymore," Rita

said. "I've heard the rest of the story."

Rita saw my empty bowl and offered to get me another serving. I didn't want to impose, though, and declined. She smiled and nodded.

"Rita, I don't want you to pay me. I want you to keep the money," I said.

I sensed relief in her soft eyes, but it was soon replaced by stubbornness—the kind a person gets when they're down and out, and a simple kindness or favor unintentionally adds to their sense of worthlessness.

"Nonsense, Cal. I hired you and you provided me a service. How much do I owe you? Tell me true now," she said as she pulled out a checkbook from the desk.

"Forget it, really."

"No, I insist." Her pen scratched out figures on the paper and she tore it from the binder. "Here. Take this. It's enough for both creatures you killed."

"I'm not taking your money, Miss Rita."

Rita shoved the paper into my chest. "Dammit, Cal. Give me the dignity of being able to pay a man for something I hired him to do."

I wanted to argue with her more, but the shouting stirred Abigail. She groaned and hacked up phlegm. The final cluster of coughs turned into a wail as she sunk her head into the blanket and sobbed. Rita and I looked at each other, then turned back to the crying little girl. She sat down at the foot of the bed next to Abigail.

"Honey, you're all right now," Rita said in a gentle, calming voice. It was very grandmotherly.

"My throat hurts. I don't feel good," the girl sobbed. She pulled the blankets down and I could see snot running down her nose. Rita reached to wipe it away on her nightgown sleeve, but Abigail recoiled from her touch.

"Who are you?" she said. She was shaking.

"My name is Rita and this here is Ranger Cal. He saved you and brought you here to get better before he takes you back to your daddy."

The little girl's eyes grew wide. "I don't want to go back to my daddy. Don't make me."

Rita and I exchanged another look, this time more of confusion than concern.

"Your daddy's looking for you, Abigail. He found me so I could get you out of that place and away from the creature that took you," I said.

"Daddy's not looking for me, he hates me."

"What do you mean, honey?" Rita maintained her calm and loving demeanor.

Abigail sniveled and wiped her eyes. "Mommy and daddy had a big fight about me. Daddy said he needed something from me, but my mommy was scared and she was going to run away and take me with her. Daddy started hitting her a lot. He said mommy spoiled me and she wouldn't be allowed to. I couldn't find mommy after that. Daddy locked me in my room and told his men to spank me if I came out."

Another coughing fit overtook her. Rita patted her back and shot me a grave look. "You can't take her back to that man."

I nodded in agreement and knelt down next to Abigail.

"Why would he do that, darlin'?" I asked.

"He was crazy!" she screamed as tears ran down her cheeks. "He kept telling me the secret was in my blood ..." Abigail stammered, the words lodged in her throat, then vomited on Rita and the bed. Rita took it in stride and shushed the little girl's sobbing.

"She's out again," I said.

Rita turned to me, trembling with anger. "That bastard has lost his mind. How could he ever hit a little girl like this? He abuses everything he's got while wanting even more."

I chewed over Abigail's story for a minute. "'The secret is in her blood?' What the hell does that mean?"

Rita shook her head. "I can't help you there, Cal. But, no matter what, you're not taking that girl back to Strickland."

"Agreed. Until I get to the bottom of what's going on, she'll have to stay here. I'll ride back to town when the storm passes and bring my friend Toussaint back with me. He's a doctor and will know what to do."

"Let me go instead, Cal. Strickland and his men will be looking for you, not me."

True, Strickland's men wouldn't be looking for her, but with this web getting more and more tangled, I'd rather handle things myself. And, truth be told, Rita needed a doctor just as bad as Abigail did.

"Good point, but I want you to stay here. I don't want you getting mixed up in this anymore than you already have. You stay here and rest those bruises."

Rita conceded with a solemn nod. "Well, we should all plan to get some sleep then. I expect it could storm all night. I'll freshen up Abigail's washcloth and change this blanket out. I'll get you situated after that."

"That'll be just fine, ma'am. Thank you."

I think Rita must have found some comfort in having purpose again, even if it was only for tonight. There were still good and honest people in the world, even if she seemed to be out of place in it. I looked at the check. She'd written it for three hundred dollars. Far too much.

I tore the check to shreds and settled down into the chair, watching Abigail breathe as the storm raged outside. The poor thing was tired from coughing so much and moaned in her sleep. Even in the dim light of the lantern, I could see she was older than Strickland had guessed. She wasn't quite a teenager, but she wasn't a child either. Her hair was platinum blond, almost white, and she had outgrown her chubby cheeks. Her arms and legs were long and lanky compared to her torso. She looked just like your average kid suffering from growth spurts.

I tugged off my glove and pulled her photo from my pocket. I held it up to the sleeping child. How could Strickland not know how old his daughter is? There was a rough texture on the photograph's corner. Flipping the photo over, I noticed a thin piece of adhesive tape placed delicately on its edge. I scratched at the tape with my fingernail, trying my best not to damage the image, until it came loose. The photograph had been folded and sealed shut for some reason. I collapsed into my chair in disbelief as I stared at the whole picture.

Abigail wasn't alone in the picture. Her mother stood by her side, hands folded over her stomach, her smile crippled by the same fear that lived in the little girl's eyes. Peeking out from underneath the woman's collar was a splotchy birthmark.

Guilt, anxiety, fear, pain. I couldn't pinpoint the emotion ripping out my heart, but it was one of them.

I'd killed Abigail's mother.

NIGHTMARES II

The peanut gallery shuffled out of the courtroom, pleased at the guilty verdict delivered in the murder case. Kael'un, the desert elf, glared at me as the bailiff led him away, muzzled and in chains.

"You're a hero today, Calam'avalar. You've sent an innocent man to die," he said.

I hung my head and thumped my fist on the witness stand. I didn't intend to condemn him with my testimony, but that damn judge had put words in my mouth. The irony of him using my Elvish nickname wounded me.

After the murmur of the crowd waned down to nothing, the judge called us into his chambers. I hid my shame in the far corner of the room, arms crossed and head down. Marney slid in next to me. I could feel the glee radiating off him when Willoby acknowledged him.

"Magnificent, Marney. We're one step closer to achieving our goals," he said, hanging his robes on a brass coat hook. He grunted as he settled into a large leather chair, lit up a cigar, and blew the smoke straight up into the air. His sharp facial features softened in his revelry.

"Couldn't have said it better myself, sir. One less killer roaming the West, destined for a jail cell," Marney said.

Willoby laughed. "No, not a jail cell. It's not practical locking up an immortal being. He'll be put to the firing line later this week." I glanced in shock at the judge, then back at Marney, who noticed.

"Is there a problem, ranger? You've been mighty quiet since you got off the witness stand," he said.

I opened my mouth, but nothing came out. I settled back into the shadows and plucked a book from the shelf, tracing a finger across one of the pages.

"Cooper's been around for executions before, hasn't he? He's been with the Ranger Corps for, what, two years now, Marney?" Willoby asked.

Marney turned to face me. "Just about. He's the finest ranger we've got, judge. Runs in his veins, apparently."

"That's fine, boy, very fine," Willoby said, sucking on the cigar. The smoke obscured the malice telegraphed in his cold, blue eyes. "We need men like Cooper for the next phase of the project. Have you filled him in yet?"

Marney tugged at his gloved hands and

cleared his throat. "Judge, on that subject, might I have a word? In private?"

Willoby nodded and jerked his head to the door. I snapped the book shut, put it back in its home, and shut the door behind me. My boots tapped out the fast tempo of my walk upon the marble floor of the courthouse. I wandered down a hallway where two marshals were talking about today's case. I tuned them out and opened my journal, flipping to a blank page. Words started appearing before my eyes.

I'd left an eavesdropper in the judge's chambers, a special rune symbol in one of his books, one Marney taught me in our ranger training but likely didn't expect to be used against him. Non-magical folks could cast it with the right ingredients and proper knowledge of the symbols. The reagents for the ritual are hard to come by, but I'd swiped a handful of an imbued powder seized from a band of sorcerers operating illegally in Arizona, which powered a lot of this kind of magic.

Their conversation was coming in fast.

"Just what the hell happened out there today, Marney? Cooper stuttering on the stand, nearly wiping out the evidence we'd planted? I don't care if he's your best man, his performance was unacceptable."

"I agree, your honor, which is why I haven't brought him into the inner circle. Not yet. Not without a proper display of loyalty,"

Marney said.

I had a bad feeling about whatever Marney had in mind. I was reluctant to serve under Marney, but he turned out to be an okay mentor. My gunslinging fit in well with his training, and when I told him I liked to read, he made his personal library available to me. He had a selection of old spellbooks, which weren't of use to me as a mundane, but interesting nonetheless. To tell you the truth, sometimes I'd forget that I had been unfairly conscripted and held against my will.

Within a year of my service, though, he was pushing for us to be the 'tip of the spear,' he called it, when it came to enforcing the Mortal Preservation Act. We started out capturing bounties, mortal and extramundane alike, but nowadays it seemed like we brought in more of them dead than alive. Now that Judge Willoby was involved, Marney had become more and more deranged, hiding out in his homemade alchemy laboratory reading god-knows-what ancient tome. He'd become obsessed with our mission, taking our orders to every extreme. I spied him slicing off the ears of a bounty one night for some sick experiment. I swear the man isn't who he says he is. I started to wonder if he was a blood mage, hiding in disguise, right under the government's nose.

"You know outlaws are only motivated by money. How else do you expect to gain loyalty from someone like him?" Willoby said.

"Simple, my good judge. Cooper responds well to acceptance and inclusion. He's prickly to begin with, but I've made serving as a ranger something that gives him purpose, value, and a home. As long as we offer him a level of significance, he'll fall in line," Marney said.

That stung. Was I so easy to read? To manipulate? Marney's mentorship and my commendations in the Ranger Corps were all an illusion. I clenched the book and seethed as the words scribbled themselves before my eyes.

"I don't care about that shit, Marney. We're representing the goddamn United States of America. Uncle Sam needs real men to rid the frontier of extramundane before they use up what's ours by God-given right. Or worse, weaponize it against us."

"Of course, sir, but might I recommend caution when announcing our inquisition. If we throw the frog in boiling water, it may jump out."

"Very well," Willoby said. "But I need a firm commitment from Cooper. We're going to do things my way. I want you to—"

Four fingers waved themselves in front of the book. "Howdy there, bookworm. You that ranger from the trial today?"

I growled and looked up. The two marshals stood on either side of me, one chewing on a toothpick, the other wiping up the brown spit dribbling down his chin after taking a bite of too much chewing tobacco.

"Yeah, that was me," I said, turning back to my book.

"Is it true what they say about rangers, Frank?" the toothpick one asked.

"I don't know. What do they say, Rodney?" the tobacco-chewer said.

"They're nothing but criminals and low-lifes. Law don't mind sending them to the front-lines to get hexed into toads."

"I reckon his family tree is a shrub."

Frank laughed and grabbed his partner's arm. "Probably couldn't hit the ground with his hat in three tries!"

They both doubled over laughing until Rodney shoved me. "I'm talking to you, you sum-bitch. You think being a ranger makes you too good to listen to me?"

"Piss off, if you know what's good for you," I said.

"Listen to this guy, Frank. He thinks he's tough. What'll you give us to leave you be?"

Between getting manipulated in the court-room and double-crossed by Marney, I didn't need this. I threw the book down, and in one fluid movement drew my revolver from its host-ler and smashed tobacco-dribbler across the nose, then grabbed toothpick's collar and pinned the barrel of my revolver to his Adam's apple.

"I'll give you nothing and let you keep your lives," I growled, cocking the hammer.

Toothpick's knees went limp and all the color left his face. His friend rolled on the floor, cupping his bleeding nose while he groaned.

"Take it easy, partner. We were just having a laugh."

"Tell better jokes next time then," I said. I shoved the man away and picked up my book, searching for where I'd been in the conversation. I ran my finger across the pages, murmuring the words as I went along until I found my place.

"... I want you to have Cooper execute the prisoner. Right now. Do it out back."

My blood ran cold. Adrenaline already coursing through my system.

"Sir, I don't think—"

"That's an order, Marney. You carry out my wishes or I'll find some other deviant to lead the removals. After this landmark case, we'll have public opinion on our side. I want to be ready for war within one week. It's time we take control of our destiny and eradicate these magical abominations."

"Yes, your honor. You can count on me. If that's all, I'll fetch Ranger Cooper."

I snapped the book closed as the sound of Marney's spurs jingled around the corner.

"Cooper, a word, please. Cooper?" he said.

I took off down the long hallway, leaping over the marshals writhing on the ground. Marney was slow to pursue, and appeared confused at the scene he'd stumbled upon, which gave me a head start.

I wasn't wasting any time. I knew what betrayal felt like and I wasn't going to tolerate it happening to me. Not again. To hell with the rangers, the cavalry, the pardon. No way was I going to fight in some war schemed up by a wannabe politician and a man hellbent on genocide. Cal Cooper is his own man.

I reached the holding cells underneath the courthouse and wedged a chair against the door. Kael'un was muttering a prayer to himself but jumped up when I broke into the room.

"Get back, we're leaving," I yelled.

A few of the other prisoners hopped out of their beds and pleaded for me to take them with me. I ignored their calls and stuck a small explosive to the cell lock.

"A silver dust grenade? You'll cut off my magic and blow me to pieces," he said, clamoring against the far cell wall.

"It'll only dull your magic for a while. Now get back or lose your eyebrows."

Marney yelled for me while ramming the jammed door. I crossed to the other side of the room and aimed my gun, and the other prisoners dove for the floor. Kael'un wrapped his arms around himself, huddled against the wall as close as he could.

The explosion sent a shockwave through the room, shaking dust and cobwebs from the rafters. Silver particles floated in the air as the smoke cleared, revealing a half-bent cell door and an elf scrambling over the top.

"You crazy bastard. The silver's in my eyes. I can't see," he said.

"This way," I yelled.

Marney burst through the door just as I'd helped Kael'un up through the cargo hatch on the other side of the holding area. He drew his guns and took cover behind a wooden beam.

"You've made a big mistake, partner. Wil-loby was about to promote you, too," he said.

"I know it's all been a lie, Marney. You want me to commit genocide for you and that sick bas-tard. I know how to eavesdrop from afar."

Marney cackled. "How clever. I suppose it's best not to drag on a bad relationship, Cooper. It's a shame, you had real potential. You were on the cusp of a real transformation."

"What do you mean?"

"Stay here with me and I'll tell you. You walk out that door and I'll report you as AWOL and get your pardon rescinded post-haste."

"Follow me and I'll kill you," I said, inching toward the exit.

Marney holstered his gun and walked out from behind his cover. "You're too good to kill in cold blood, Cal. You know it. I know it. Or per-haps I'm wrong. Shoot me, if you can muster the balls."

I drew the barrel of my revolver right over his heart and cocked the hammer. Sweat dripped down my forehead. *I should kill the bastard, end it right here.* My finger jiggled on the trigger.

"Just as I thought. Weakling," Marney said. He snapped his fingers and a blue flame engulfed his hand. With one quick motion, he launched a ball of fire at a prisoner in the next cell. Marney giggled and stared me down. "See? It's easy, Cooper. Do it. Do it!"

I felt sick to my stomach and stood there shaking as the drum of horse hooves thundered above me. It was Kael'un.

"Let's go, Cal," he hollered.

I scrambled up the stairs as Marney shot another blue fireball, which narrowly missed me as I escaped into the sunlight. I jumped on Buck's saddle and lit out for the horizon next to Kael'un and the horse he'd stolen. Gunfire echoed in the distance and bullets exploded in the dirt around us. Kael'un yelped. I looked over to see the elf clutching his chest, holding back a gush of blood. A bullet had cut clean through his back.

He looked at me and smiled. "Thanks for trying, Calam'avalar."

His eyes rolled back into his skull, and he slipped from his horse. There was nothing I could do but press on and ride as hard as I could.

Marney's voice echoed in my mind.

"I will hunt you down, Calamity. I will find you in your nightmares."

CHAPTER SEVENTEEN

A blast of thunder shook me from a nightmare. Bolts of lightning continued their assault on the plains into the night and the rain was still beating down hard. I'd seen hundreds of storms in my life, every one just as magnificent as the last. I rubbed the sleep from my eyes, trying to shake off the hangover of a bad dream.

Abigail was resting peacefully. Her breathing was stable again, but her coughs sounded awful, and she was likely infected with vampirism from the two bites. But worse than any of those things was how much she would suffer when she found out I'd inadvertently killed her mother.

"I'm not sure what I'm gonna do with you, but I won't leave your side, little gal. I promise," I said, stroking her hair.

The lightning flashed again and lit up the room. But something was different this time. Something was out of place. Out of the corner of my eye, I caught the outline of a shadow. A figure was standing right outside the window. I grabbed my revolver and peeled back the thin curtains. Another crash of lightning, but nothing was there. I waited, eyes trained on the dark, searching for any movement. I didn't enjoy feeling like prey.

There was a knock at the front door. I dropped the edge of the curtain and walked into the main room where Rita was standing with a clean blanket and wash bucket. We both eyed the door with caution.

"You expecting company?" I whispered.

Rita shook her head. I crept up beside her with my gun drawn. There was another knock. We nodded to each other, then she cracked the door open. The air smelled foul.

"Good evening, Miss Conway. I'm here on behalf of Lucius Montague. I'm looking for Ranger Cooper. I believe he is inside. May I come in?" It was the vampire lackey, Bartholomew.

Rita wedged her foot against the bottom of the door. She was struck for words and went white as the sheets covering her furniture.

"Well, Miss Conway? Do I have your permission to enter? Please, I seek both the ranger and shelter from this awful storm," the vampire said, laying the charm on thick.

Until they were invited inside, vampires were incapable of crossing a home's threshold. It was Grandmother Nature's way of giving us mundanes a chance against dangerous immortals. Ancient laws of magic, rooted in the creation of life, deemed original vampires unholy abominations unfit to walk the earth. It's why they're susceptible to nature. Fire and sunlight, holy water, hallowed grounds and such.

Rita glanced at me for an answer. I shook my head and mouthed the word 'no.'

"I'm afraid you're mistaken, young man. Ranger Cooper isn't here. Lit out on his horse just before the storm hit," Rita lied.

I eyed her to get a sense of what was going on outside the door. The vampire clicked his tongue.

"Please, Miss Conway, do not lie to me. There are two saddled horses inside your barn, one of which matches the description of the ranger's. I must insist that you invite me inside."

Rita was flustered, so I pulled the door open and stepped in front of her. Bartholomew's black riding cloak was drenched and dripped into a puddle at his feet. Fingernails as sharp as daggers hung from his fingertips and his eyes emitted a faint glow, like a predator on a hunt.

And I, his prey, was cornered.

"Here I am. And, no, you may not enter. Now, piss off, before I fill you with lead and send you back to Lucius with my regards." I cocked my revolver and the vampire giggled.

"That weapon is harmless to a vampire, mate. I'm not surprised you don't know that. You're just another common American dimwit."

He rolled his eyes.

"Harmless? It might not have the stopping power of, say, a stake through the heart, but stick around and find out just how deadly it can be. I've already killed one vampire today and I don't mind adding one more to my tally."

The vampire's red eyes flashed. "Lord Montague told you to lay off family business."

"Never was a very good listener. So, let me guess, Lucius send you to find me? Do his dirty work?"

"Surrender yourself to me now or I'll kill the old woman."

I laughed and spun my revolver lazily around a finger. "And just how are you going to do that from out there?"

A lightning bolt flashed, blinding me for a brief second, and the vampire was gone, vanished into thin air. I barred the door and turned to Rita, who was cowering behind me.

"Is there another way inside the house?"

"There's a back door in the kitchen."

Abigail was still feverish and in no condition to be moved. Bartholemew wouldn't give up this easy. I donned my gear and prepared to keep watch at the door.

"What are we gonna do, Cal?" Rita said, still carrying her rifle.

"Vampires can't enter a house unless they're invited inside. As long as we don't give them permission, they can't harm us here. I say we hold out until dawn. Our vampire will turn to ash if he's exposed to the sun for too long. Reckon they'll have to scatter before morning. As soon as the sun's out, I'll ride for town and you stay here with the girl, just like we planned."

"What if one of those thralls comes back? Can it force its way in?" she asked.

That was a good question. As far as I knew, thralls weren't bound by threshold magic, and they certainly didn't mind the daylight. Given her home only had two entry points, I had faith that Rita was a good enough shot to manage any thralls while I was gone. Besides, I didn't have much choice. Someone had to stay here with the girl.

"Whatever comes through these doors that isn't me, put it out of its misery," I said.

A cloud of dust lifted as I yanked the sheet off one of the chairs. I dragged it to face the front door and sat down, making myself comfortable for an extended sit.

"Don't think I'll get much sleep tonight, Rita. You should take a load off. Maybe get some shut eye if you can," I said.

"Hell if I'll find any rest tonight either." She moaned as she pulled up another chair.

"I'm sorry I dragged you into this further. I didn't know I was being tailed. I was too focused on the little girl and getting somewhere safe," I said.

Rita didn't respond. She held her up hand

to me, listening intently, and looked up.

I didn't see anything. "What is it?"

Rita raised a finger to her lips and then toward the ceiling. Every few seconds, a trail of dust would float down from the beams that supported this part of the house.

Bartholomew was up there. Step after step, we followed the falling dust with our eyes, through the living room and into the kitchen, where Rita's pot of stew sat inside the cooking hearth. Something clanked its way down the chimney and, before we could react, an oil lantern landed in the middle of the cooking fire and exploded. Flames splattered the sides of the kitchen table, igniting it in a flash. The fire roared and spilled onto the wooden floor, moving so fast we could barely react. The smoke, which should have gone up the chimney, billowed out right behind the flames.

I took Rita's arm and hauled her back into the foyer, curls of smoke already strangling us.

"He's stuffed the chimney shut."

She pointed toward where Abigail slept. "Get the girl!"

The glow of the fire turned the white sheets to orange as I dashed into the bedroom. Abigail was oblivious to the mayhem unfolding and slumped into my shoulder as I picked her up and ran. Rita had opened the front door, which gave us some breathable air and a view of the outside. Standing just beyond the threshold was

Bartholomew, smiling as if this was a big gotcha moment. His fangs and claws at the ready.

But he wasn't alone. My obstinate horse's head peeked out of the barn door. The vamp must have left it open when he went to check for me.

Immortal dimwit.

A beam supporting the roof cracked and crashed down, inches from our position, exposing the stormy sky above. The fire had now consumed the kitchen and was crawling up the walls and stairs behind us. It was too powerful to be extinguished by the rain now trickling in, and our window of escape was closing by the second. Poor Rita watched in horror as her family home succumbed to the blaze. The home she had grown up in. Where she had buried her brother.

I felt a sense of remorse as I shook her out of her trance. "Get ready to move. Follow me," I shouted. I whistled for Buck. To my surprise, she reared up and kicked the barn door the rest of the way open. The vampire dove aside as she and Big Gus galloped out of the barn.

That's when I made my move. With Abigail slung over my shoulder like a sack of potatoes, I fired lead and made a break for it. I shot Bartholomew in the shoulder, but he shrugged it off and lunged for me. Rita swung the butt of her rifle and plowed it right into his face. This gave me enough time to toss Abigail on Buck's back, but not enough to get her secured before Bartholomew leapt clean over my horse and sunk his claws into my skin.

We both fell to the ground and rolled until I was on top. I gripped his throat with my off-hand and ground his head into the mud. He hissed and writhed as he continued clawing at me, until one swipe connected with my jaw and I flew off him. I forgot just how strong vamps can be.

He was already rushing back toward Rita. She cried out as he cut a deep gash on her fore-arm. As they circled around each other, Rita with her gun ready, the vampire lazily licked her blood off his fingertips. The blazing fire cast an eerie red glow, and the house was now completely en-gulfed, sending plumes of smoke into the sky.

"Mount your horse, Rita. I've got you covered," I said, gun trained on Bartholomew.

Rita kept her eyes on him and shook her head. She wouldn't be moved. "You and the girl get out of here while I hold him off. Don't stop until you reach town. This bastard burned down my home and I aim to see him pay." She never took her eyes off the vamp.

"Don't be a fool. You can't kill that thing."

"I said get out of here, Cal. Now!" Rita fired her rifle in the air and slapped Big Gus on the rear, causing him to bolt.

Buck was startled, too, and started to pull forward, but I held her reins tight and reeled her in. She didn't like that and fought harder.

Rita had had enough. She aimed at the vamp and fired, only to hear the click of an empty chamber. Bartholomew doubled over laughing, which really pissed her off. This was all a game to him. She dropped the gun and launched herself at the vampire head on, gripping him with the full strength of a tough, old rancher, and drove him inside the burning house.

"Burn, you son of a bitch!" The roar of the inferno engulfed them both and a few seconds later the roof caved in. All I could hear were Rita's defiant screams as a burst of flames erupted from its center.

I wiped the rain from my face and sighed. That stubborn old woman. Why did she have to go pull a stunt like that and die for nothing? I couldn't understand the attachment to a homestead or a plot of land. But then again, I'd never had a place like that to call home. As I watched the fire burn, I vowed to never let Lucius or Strickland interfere with the lives of good folks out here again. No mortal or immortal was going to use these people like pawns, human capital to risk and sacrifice on a whim for their own gain. Not if I could help it.

I reluctantly let the reins go slack and Buck flew at full speed toward the road.

The storm was still rowdy, and riding in it was dangerous, but I didn't have any choice. Who knew if Bartholemew was the only vampire tracking me? I was in no state to encounter any more foot soldiers, no matter who they belonged to. Neither was the girl. She was hot as a stovetop and had lost the color in her cheeks again. I wasn't sure how long the poor child was going to hold out. I'd heard that the infection doesn't always turn the victim into a vampire—sometimes it kills them outright as their body rejects the transformation.

Anger welled inside my chest as I thought about what Abigail said. I would see to it that Strickland never touched her again. My best bet now was to ride to town and seek Toussaint's help, while laying low to avoid Strickland and his mechanical man.

My little barn-sour mare puffed and snorted as she bravely plowed through the darkness, while I kept an eye over my shoulder for trouble. I knew Buck could sense my desperation. I think she also understood Abigail's condition and felt compassion for the sick child.

Horses are smart like that.

CHAPTER EIGHTEEN

Hexed Springs was dark and quiet when we arrived. The storm settled and a steady rain had replaced the violent torrent from a few hours ago. The aftermath remained, though. The street was a muddy slop and a number of streetlamps were extinguished or toppled over completely. Lucky for me, no one was outside and I rode in silently under the cover of night.

"We're going to make it, sugar. I promise you, I'll get you to safety. Just hang on."

Abigail's condition had worsened during the long ride. She looked so delicate in my arms. I couldn't have her die on me. I was responsible for her safety, and I wasn't going to bury another sick little girl.

"Professor! Professor, I need help," I hollered, pulling on Buck's reins as we approached Toussaint's vardo. She huffed and puffed, foam flinging from her mouth as I brought her to a halt. I ran my fingers through her mane and thanked her with a sugar cube.

All was quiet and the windows were dark. The lean-to was gone and the campfire had been rained out. Looked like no one was home. I hopped down from my horse and pounded a heavy fist on the door.

No response.

Buck neighed and champed at her bit. She was afraid and sending me a warning. A warning that we weren't alone. Horses may be finicky creatures, but when they tell you they're scared, you better listen.

Something didn't feel right as we'd entered town. It was too empty and too quiet. Sure, people usually stay inside during a storm; they light lanterns, they watch the rain from a covered porch, they stir and mingle inside their homes. Right now, there wasn't any of that. Only eerie tranquility—and darkness. In my time as an outlaw, I'd both been ambushed and done my share of ambushing. Right now, I felt like I'd walked into a trap.

Although the streets were empty, Buck was still on edge. I decided to search higher, following across the rooftops. Perched on top of a butcher shop was a silhouetted figure, its red eyes blazing in the dark. It was leaner and more pale than Bartholomew, and its sleeves and pant legs were torn open to accommodate its beastly transformation. It was following me.

I pulled out my gun, hoping to get a jump on it, but the vampire was too quick. It sailed through the air and down onto the muddy street, landing cleanly on its feet. In a heartbeat, it burst forward toward us.

Buck turned and bolted, which gave me enough room to get a clear shot. My revolver thundered and a bullet hit the vampire just above its left ear. A chunk of its skull exploded in a slurry of tissue and blood. It was a blow that nothing natural could survive—but somehow the vamp stumbled for a moment, and didn't lose much ground in its chase. The vampire swiped for Buck's tail, but came up empty-handed, hissing and cursing in some kind of ancient tongue.

I didn't know where to run. My house was most likely being watched, either by Strickland or vampires, and Toussaint had either met trouble himself or wasn't home. I hoped it was the latter. The only other place in town where I was welcome was Clem's saloon. It was also probably the safest, given my old partner's skill as a sharpshooter.

Buck tore through the mud as we veered to our new destination. We rounded the corner, and I could see a faint yellow light spilling out over the double doors.

The Howling Beast Saloon & Inn was the only place open for business on the street.

I hopped off my horse and tucked Abigail under my arm. I rested my forehead against Buck's. "I take back all the means things I said about you. You're all right, girl. Now go find Mr.

Eriksen. Giddyup!"

Buck took off toward the livery. She'd get herself home safely. Barn sours are like homing pigeons; they always know their way back home.

With Abigail in my arms, I shouldered through the doors and found myself in an empty saloon. Clem was standing at the bar back, rifle in hand. Concern spread across her face the instant I came in. "Cal, what's going on? Who's this?"

"Abigail Strickland. No time to explain. She's deathly ill and needs a bed to rest in," I said, out of breath.

"This isn't the infirmary. Take her to a doctor," Clem said, picking up her skirt as she jogged around the bar.

"I tried. He didn't answer. What's going on? Where is everyone?"

Clem scooped up Abigail from my arms. "Something's going on. A gunfight broke out in the town square between a gang of vampires and a bunch of Strickland's men. Folks are sheltering in place, I reckon. And now, here you are, holding that man's daughter?"

"Long story. I'll tell you later. For now, I need you to watch her."

"Where do you think you're going?"

Footsteps plodded along the wooden walkway bordering the saloon. The footfall didn't follow the typical rhythm of walking, more of an awkward, club-footed shuffle.

It was the vampire I shot. It tailed us here.

The vamp stopped in front of the entrance, unable to cross the threshold. I spun my revolver out of its holster and quickly fired a double bulls-eye, two shots right in between its eyes. Seems a wooden stake through the heart isn't the only way to kill a vampire. Three bullets to the head and the vampire's eyes finally rolled back in their sockets as it fell, stiff as a board.

"I've got to find answers. We were ambushed by vampires twice now. Both dead," I said as I plucked out a few bullets from my bandolier and reloaded. "I saved this little girl from a feral vampire living in a coal mine and now the Montagues are after me in revenge. I don't know what the hell Strickland and his men are doing, but they want a piece of me, too." We were all caught in the crossfire of an attempted coup for control of No Man's Land.

Clem rolled her eyes and groaned. "You just had to pick a fight with the most powerful men in town, didn't you?"

The gunshots had stirred the girls who worked in Clem's saloon. Three gals dressed in their night clothes, with their hair let down, leaned on the banister of the staircase that led to the upstairs brothel. Clem turned to them and handed out orders.

"You two. Seeing that we have no customers whatsoever tonight, I want you to take this girl and set her up in one of the rooms. Get her under some covers and place a wet cloth on her head. Check my washroom for medicine bottles and figure out something to give her. And you, take care of my sweet Angus. Cal, you and me need to talk."

The women took Abigail and Clem's little dog upstairs. Abigail was in good hands.

I told Clem the long and the short of it. How I'd been blackmailed by Strickland, confronted by vampires, rescued Abigail from the mine, all of it. I half expected her to slap me, hopefully knocking some sense into me in the process, but instead she looked at me square in the eyes and nodded.

"You did the right thing, Cal," she said.

I was taken aback. "So, you're really not mad at me?"

"I ain't mad. Concerned, but not mad," she said. "I've known you for a decade, Calamity Cooper, and even though I give you a hard time, you always seem to do the right thing in the end. Besides, if causing trouble is what you do best, then who am I to judge?" She laughed, then hooked a thumb at the entrance. "Plus, I think you've finally started listening to me. I'm thankful you didn't kill that monster in here and leave me a mess to clean up on my nice floor, like you did last time you were here."

"Lucky for us, vampires can't cross thresholds unless they're invited in. Didn't think the laws of magic would protect a sleazy joint like this, though," I said with a wink.

She shook a fist at me, playfully. "You better pray the laws of magic keep me from busting you upside the head for that remark. Don't worry, I'll make sure the girls know not to invite anyone inside tonight."

"Good," I said. I prepared to deliver the bad news. "Listen, there's one other thing. Down in the mine? Before I rescued the little girl? I found Rose."

Clem placed her hands on her hips and looked down, chewing on her lip. "I take it she didn't fare so well?"

"She was already gone. Her personality had been wiped away. Her smile, her laugh, her spirit, all of it stolen. All that was left of her was a mindless husk."

Clem shook her head and stared off into the distance. She sighed and pushed back a straggle of hairs that had slipped out of her bun, then wrapped her arms around my neck in a soft hug.

"Thank you, Cal. I'm sorry you had to see her like that. She was a great gal."

I didn't say anything back. Just returned the hug and patted her back a couple times.

Clem let go and looked up toward the hallway to the rooms. One of the girls was hustling back and forth, bringing items to care for Abigail and make her more comfortable.

Clem collected her rifle and put on a serious face. "What do we do now?"

"I need to figure out what's going on between the Montagues and Strickland before I have to deal with one or the other. I also discovered our resident undertaker works for the vamps. I'll see if he knows something I don't."

"What if the undertaker isn't willing to rat out his employer? Lucius might seem like a pleasant socialite, but I reckon he's got an iron grip on his operation."

I held up my fist and winked at her. "I can be persuasive."

"So I'm supposed to just stay here and watch over the girl? That's all?" she asked. Clem always was thorough on the details when it came to planning.

"That's all," I said. "Worst case scenario, we wait until the sun comes up and the vampires retreat. But I'd like to get the girl some professional care right now. I hope to catch my friend, Toussaint, while I'm out. He might have some kind of treatment."

Clem nodded and made her way back behind the bar, standing watch over the saloon, while I straightened my hat and smoothed out the front of my duster. Once more into the pouring rain and imminent danger.

"Hurry back," she called after me as I walked through the doors.

I carefully scanned the rooftops and along the streets for good measure. All was clear. I planted a boot on the dead vampire's cheek and rolled his head to the side to make sure he was really dead. As far as I could tell, he wasn't breathing, wasn't blinking, and was missing half his skull. I think that qualified as dead, all right.

* * *

I ran headlong into the wind toward the undertaker's office, eyes and ears alert. Clem was right, I could hear the occasional pops of gunfire in between rumbles of distant thunder. Perhaps one side would eliminate the other and save me the trouble of fighting a war on two fronts.

When I reached the undertaker's office I found the door locked and windows darkened. Outside the door, a gas lantern flickered wildly from a hook and a swinging wooden sign read 'Wilbur Cromley, Mortician.' I peered inside the window. Light flickered from underneath a doorway inside the parlor at the back of the foyer. I pounded on the glass. A pair of shadows crossed over the light inside the room, two legs casting black streaks from behind the door.

I hammered again. This time, there were no shadows.

"All right, if you insist," I muttered to no one. I pulled out Cloudsplitter and smashed the glass in the door with its pine handle. As I let myself in, the door to the back room flew open. It was Cromley.

He whimpered as I marched in with my

gun drawn. His thick sideburns quivered as he rubbed the blood on his hands onto his white apron.

"What is the meaning of this? I have nothing for you to rob. The dead do not arrive in my care with any possessions," he said, his voice shaking.

"I'm not here to rob you or the dearly departed, but unless you want to join your customers in a coffin, you better come clean, Cromley," I said.

"Clean? Whatever do you mean?" he squeaked, trying to hide his face in the shadows.

I stepped into the lamp light and took a better look. "Is that blood on your mouth?"

Cromley quickly wiped his lips on his sleeve.

"I can explain, ranger. It's not what you think. Look, I'll show you," he said, beckoning me to follow him into the other room.

I waved the gun toward the door. "I can't imagine any explanation of blood on a mortician's lips being a good one."

Cromley nodded and shuffled backward. The overpowering stench of formaldehyde tainted the air of the back room, mingling with the pine tar on the coffins to create a horrible amalgamation of smells. The room was lit by a series of lanterns arranged to provide adequate illumination for a man who worked primarily at night.

Cromley was a feeble man, but all men can be dangerous, no matter their size. I kept my gun trained on him in case he tried something funny while I looked around his laboratory. Four pinewood coffins rested in a row, the same style as the feral vamp's, and two of them were occupied. A young woman in the first, her eyes closed and hands folded over her chest. She was dressed plainly and had a bonnet wrapped around her head. The other coffin held a young man in a blue cotton shirt and britches patched at the knees. His arms rested on his chest, fingers grazing the edge of a familiar bright red bandana tied around his neck.

In between was a metal tray displaying several medical instruments, including a scalpel with wet blood on its blade. I leaned in to inspect the two corpses and noticed something interesting.

Neither of them were actually corpses.

The woman's chest rose and fell softly with each long breath. She was in a deep trance-like sleep. The man, however, breathed normally, like he was merely snoozing. I pulled his hands off his chest, revealing a blood stain on his unbuttoned shirt. I pulled back the flap of cloth where a letter 'M' had been burned in.

I tugged back the young woman's shirt, too, and found a bloodied bite mark. Not puncture wounds like a vampire bite, but the impression left from human teeth.

Cromley let out an audible gulp and backed into a corner of the room.

"Shut your whining and tell me just what's going on here," I said, raising my revolver.

"Please, if I tell you, will you let me live?" He cowered against the wall.

I tilted my head and grinned. "Depends on what you tell me. Start with why a mortician has two *living* people on slabs."

Cromley wiped at the blood on his lips again and sputtered, barely squeaking out his words. "I'm only doing as I'm told, I swear. As he commands."

"Who commands?" I asked.

"The Patriarch. I provide his family with blood from the embalming process, and he pays me in return." He would say no more.

I laughed, incredulous that such a twisted setup had gone undisturbed for so long. Cromley tasked with taking the blood of the dead to feed the undead. Nobody complains and nobody gets hurt. Seems innocent enough, in its own sick way.

"Why do I get the feeling that's not all that goes on here?"

"Please, I don't know."

"Sure, you do. I had a little meeting with Lucius in Strayhaven at the opium den. Managed to catch a peek at your handiwork."

Cromley fidgeted with his glasses. "Despite its salacious nature, the opium den is a perfectly legitimate business."

"Is it, now? Getting folks high and draining their blood is legitimate over there?"

Cromley stuttered as his gaze shifted to his victims. "If—if you must know, the opium den is where men and women willingly surrender themselves in service to the Families. The drug allows their minds to be opened."

"Fancy way of saying they surrender their free will to a vampire. And the letter burned into their chests?"

"The Patriarch instructed me to mark the family's thralls. It's how he keeps track of them so no other vampire family can interfere with them."

"Just like branding cattle to deter rustlers," I said, shaking my head.

Goddamn, Amos was right after all.

"Yes, I suppose you could say that. He allows some of them to return to their consciousness and only calls upon them when he needs them."

"How thoughtful of him," I said. "And her?" I gestured at the little lady in the coffin. "There's teeth marks on her. You got an explanation for that, too?"

Cromley flushed. "I—I just wanted a taste for myself. To feel the hot blood wash across my tongue."

"You sick bastard, is she some kind of gift to you?"

"Oh, no. She's not for me. She will serve one of the master's children. I believe she'll make a wonderful hand maiden. Or perhaps one of the young lords can use her for ..." Cromley paused to dab sweat from his upper lip "... for pleasure."

My stomach tightened into a ball. The other Montagues had no respect for humankind, enslaving us for their sick pleasure. How many people in Hexed Springs were walking around with letters scarred into their skin?

In the distance, several vampires screeched in pain, shattering the temporary calm outside. The rain had subsided, but the fighting raged on.

"Have the Montagues started a turf war with humans?" I asked.

Cromley waved his hands. "No, no, nothing like that. Lucius would never. He believes the fight would be too lopsided and vowed never to use force against humans."

I chuckled and nodded toward the darkened window. "Sounds to me like he might want to rethink that strategy."

A cuckoo clock chimed eleven, which startled Cromley. He rubbed his hands together and peeked around me toward the foyer. Almost like he had someplace to be.

"Have I answered all your questions?" he asked.

"Not quite," I said. "Tell me why six people with the same brand as this fella were living in a coal mine and protecting a vampire who kidnapped a little girl."

Cromley's face drooped. "I can't tell you about that."

"Can't or won't?"

"Lord Lucius wouldn't approve. It's not my place to tell my lord's secrets," he said.

I slapped Cromley with the back of my hand, sending him reeling through the doorway and backward into the darkness of the front room.

I followed him, keeping intimidatingly close. "You're a fool, talking like you're a member of their family. You're human, dammit. Tell me right now why Lucius's woman was feral down in the coal mine," I growled.

Cromley was frozen in place trying to conjure up a suitable lie. He gazed over my shoulder and an excited grin skittered across his slap-happy face. He scurried to his feet, nearly tripping over his apron, giggling with glee. A shadow darkened the door behind me, and I spun around to see a hulking abomination, a mass of flesh and bone crudely stitched together, in some places, bursting at the seams.

"Ranger, meet my gift to the Patriarch," Cromley said with a newfound pomposity. "A scientific marvel, a thrall composed of pieces from the most-talented outlaws in the region. Introduce yourself, my good man."

The abomination groaned and swung its

fist. Its arms were as thick as tree trunks. I dodged backward, barely avoiding the punch, but tripped on a loose floorboard and fell on my back.

And that's when things got worse.

There were two vampires outside the front door, one male and one female. Both wore the same black get-up as the one I blew away outside of Clem's, like it was some kind of vampire assassin uniform. They looked down their noses at me and smirked.

"Good evening, Mr. Cromley," the vampiress purred. Her red eyes sparkled. She licked a fang and came closer to the door. "May we come in?"

"Be my guest," Cromley answered.

CHAPTER NINETEEN

The two vampires took turns stepping across the threshold.

The vampiress strode in first and wrung the water from her hair. Her counterpart entered behind her and smoothed out his shirt, then rolled his sleeves up to his elbows. Neither seemed in a hurry to kill me.

"Take another step closer and I'll shoot him," I said, coming back to my feet. The abomination's breath was hot on my neck.

The vampiress smiled as her eyes slid mischievously over to the undertaker, who didn't seem to mind the sight of my barrel trained on him with his associates present.

"You wouldn't dare," Cromley said.

"And cut off their supply of blood? Why not?" I barked back.

The female vamp feigned a gasp and slinked over to Cromley. She slid her hands up his arms and rested them on his shoulders. "Have you been giving away family secrets?"

Cromley fiddled with his hands. "Well, no. I mean, yes, but it was an accident. It doesn't matter, though, the ranger's not going to live long enough to tell."

"Perhaps," she said in a soft, teasing croon, then turned her sultry gaze to me.

"Speaking of secrets," Cromley said, jumping between us, "the ranger here confided to me that he has killed Lord Lucius's bride."

I did a doubletake. "His bride? What the hell?"

Cromley turned innocently toward the vampires. "I thought he already knew that. Forgive me. Please don't tell your master."

"Who cares about that human harlot. Filthy half-blood. Most of us wanted her gone anyway, including the Patriarch," she said. Cromley was taken aback and clutched at imaginary pearls. The vampiress rolled her eyes and turned to her partner. "I believe we're obligated to inform Lord Lucius of the death of his pet. Go and tell him. I'll handle the ranger."

The vampire snarled with disappointment, then turned to leave, but the vampiress snatched his arm and pulled him back.

"Wait," she said with a menacing smile. "Tell his sister first. She'll be very interested in this development."

Her partner darted off into the night, leaving me with one traitor, one vamp, and one freak of nature. I'd been outnumbered worse before, but with a vampire involved, I didn't like my odds of getting out of this alive. I counted the exits, including the ones I remembered behind the mass of flesh blocking the back room.

"Sounds like I did you a favor, getting rid of a feral vamp no one liked," I said as I sized up the vampiress.

She stalked over to a clock on the wall and ran a finger down its polished brass face. She didn't have a reflection in its mirrored surface.

"You did, and we would be so forever grateful, if we hadn't sworn fealty to Lucius. Alas, I'm afraid I'm going to have to capture you."

"That's a shame. I was just getting to know your family. Made plans to kill a few of them, too," I said.

She laughed, adjusting her derby hat, then reached behind her back and produced a long, slightly curved blade the length of her leg. The abomination was standing by, waiting for instruction. I was caught in the middle of a standoff. My hand hovered over my revolver.

I gritted my teeth and drew my gun as the abomination shoved me forward. My head snapped back as I crashed into the vampiress, and we both sailed out the front door, where I fell flat on my back in the mud, while she, with her catlike reflexes, landed coolly on her feet. The abomination plodded into the street after us, bursting through the door, leaving it much wider. I dragged my hands through the mud, searching for my revolver, but came up empty-handed. The thrall seized me by the arm, pulling me onto my feet. The vampiress leaned on her sword and watched.

"After you," she said.

The abomination was taller and thicker than me, and certainly out of my weight class. It groaned and slugged a putrid fist into my stomach. Adrenaline surged through my veins as the 'fight' part of 'fight or flight' kicked in. My quick punches hit its ribs with a nauseating crunch, the last uppercut connecting with its jaw.

The thrall jolted backward, absorbing most of the impact of my attack with ease, and kicked me in the chest, sending me back down into the mud. It dug a knee into my chest and pinned my shoulder to the ground. Cromley was cheering from the sidelines. I looked up at the thrall's mismatched eyes. It was missing teeth and its neck muscles were coming unstitched. The last thing I saw before raindrops blurred my vision were two meaty fists hoisted high in the air, ready to drive me into the ground like a hammer hitting a nail.

I clenched my teeth and prepared for pain. Suddenly, the seams holding together the top half of the thrall ripped open, severed by some kind of blade. I pushed myself free, and finally found my revolver, as the mangled corpse landed with a *thunk*. The vampiress shrieked and leapt over me, attacking whatever it was that had just saved my life.

I rubbed the water from my eyes. Metal sliced through the air, followed by a metallic clank and a hollow thud. I turned to find the limp body of the sword-wielding vampiress flying through the air like a doll. She crashed through the glass window and landed in a heap on top of Cromley. In the distance, halfway cloaked in darkness, with its executioner's sword gripped in its bronzed hand, stood the Sentinel.

The vampiress tried to push herself up but sagged to the floor in a pool of her black blood. Cromley wriggled and squawked for help from underneath her. The Sentinel squared its shoulders to me and pointed its sword at my chest. With not enough room to run, I tossed up my hands and walked backward into the funeral parlor.

I stepped over the two vamps sprawled in the doorway, avoiding the one coughing up blood. The robed automaton stomped in after me and surveyed the room. Gears clanked and whirred as its arm revealed a compartment tucked inside its forearm. Three short lengths of metal clicked into formation and a wooden stake slid into place.

It was assembling a crossbow.

The Sentinel aimed at the vampiress's back and finished her off with a stake through the heart. With all the supernatural threats neutralized, the automaton stepped away from the doorframe, revealing none other than Ross P. Strickland.

Strickland was staring at a pocket watch and humming a little tune as he entered. He didn't quite look like himself. His skin was sallow and pitted, and he had dark circles under his eyes. When his eyes met mine, he threw his arms out wide, like an exuberant child reunited with its plaything, and a sardonic laugh escaped his thin, gray lips.

"What a coincidence, Mr. Cooper. Here I am, out tying up loose ends when I should run into you. Speaking of loose ends, pardon me for a moment." He pointed at the undertaker. Cromley's eyes shifted back and forth in confusion as the automaton raised its sword. And brought it smoothly down. Cromley's head rolled off into the shadows, his expression frozen in a permanent panic and disbelief.

"Where were we?" Strickland asked, pinning his arms behind his back again, as if this were the conclusion of a standard business deal. His monocle rose as the rounds of his fat cheeks propped up a smile. "I believe you have something for me? Or, should I say, someone?"

I kept my eyes focused on the crossbow. "I won't tell you where she is, you sick bastard."

"Tsk, tsk, ranger. I didn't think following instructions would be so hard." He took one lazy step toward me. "Tell me, if she isn't with you, where can I go to collect her?" Running just beneath his once stoic reserve was a crazed look.

I took a step back, angling myself toward the back room, one eye on the Sentinel. "I don't reckon I'll be sharing that information with you, just like how you didn't tell me I'd be killing her mother."

Strickland clapped his hands together. "Ah, so you really did rescue her. For a moment there, I thought you were lying to save your skin. Did Abigail say anything about me?"

"She told me you beat your wife and sent her away, then sent her to the mine. That's some complicated kind of punishment."

"Her account of the events are mostly true —from a child's point of view," Strickland said, holding up fingers to count as he recalled memories. "Yes, I beat her mother. Yes, I sent her away. Yes, I left her in a cave. And?"

"I'm afraid I seem to be missing what parts are false."

Strickland chuckled and wiped a smudge from his monocle so hard it cracked. He replaced it, seemingly unaware of what he'd just done. "I'm happy to explain. Abigail's mother was a gentle woman who pampered her with my riches, too much for my liking. She complained that I was a bad father. In exchange for my wife's habitual insolence, I showed her the back of my hand, as every man has the right to do." He grinned.

"Surprised you didn't hire someone to

carry out your spousal abuse," I said.

"In matters of the house, if you want something done right, you'll do it yourself."

I sneered at his blasé attitude. "So what's with this guy, if you're so keen on doing things yourself?"

Strickland tapped the hollow chest of his metal enforcer. "One of my better acquisitions, I must say. Although I am capable of a great many things, I often find myself in need of muscle, so to speak. Having an unquestioning and nigh-unstoppable servant do my bidding has tipped the scales in my favor, wouldn't you say? Or perhaps we should stroll down the avenue and count the dead vampires."

I didn't need convincing. The memory of cold metal denying me air was still fresh in my mind.

"So how does all this relate to Abigail?" I asked.

"As I was saying, my young and impertinent wife grew accustomed to mouthing off, instead of appreciating the lavish lifestyle I bestowed upon her. Soon, she took to disappearing altogether. I paid an employee of mine to follow her and record her whereabouts."

"I know where this is going," I said with a sly grin. "She got herself a man on the side. Someone who loved her like you couldn't."

Strickland wasn't offended, or at least he didn't show it. "A common storyline, no doubt, among lowlifes like yourself. I dug further into her escapades and discovered something very interesting—a plot to destroy my wealth and seize my every possession."

"Not your precious money. Anything but that," I said, mockingly.

"You sound like my wife," Strickland said between roaring laughs. Just as quickly, he got quiet and continued. "She was, in fact, seeing one of the Montague vampires, whom I believe you're familiar with, so I called in a favor and had her sent to an asylum back east. To my surprise, however, her transport never arrived."

Even though I'd been stalling for time, waiting for the right moment to act, something in Strickland's story struck me as odd. I might not be the sharpest, but the methods of Strickland's madness were beginning to reveal themselves.

"I wasn't the first person you'd sent to find her, was I?"

"Very astute of you, Cooper," Strickland said. "I needed to find a gunslinger who could handle himself in a battle with vampires, should the need arise. Lucius Montague, as duplicitous and treacherous as he is, has a brilliant network of spies and can be tough to outmaneuver. To avoid arousing suspicion, I hired petty thieves to test the abilities of gunslingers in the region, filtering out weaker candidates. I must say, though, you have performed well beyond my expectations, Cooper." He replaced the cracked monocle as it slipped down his cheek.

"That boy from the Matthews Gang. But he was a thrall for the Montague family," I said.

Strickland was again impressed with my discovery. "Ironically, the young men I hired were the very same individuals Cromley here had marked as the Montague's chattel. But, as I learned in a research journal published by Mr. DuBois' mentor, thralls retain a sense of free will when not actively performing their duties for their master. Perhaps next time, vampires will think twice before leaving their assets vulnerable to interference."

Strickland's plan was convoluted, but clever. I hated that he had dragged me into all this mess. Used. Again. I'll make sure there won't be a next time.

"What are you going to do with me?"

Strickland glanced at his pocket watch again and adjusted his broken monocle. The man looked like he was starting to crack. "As I said, I'm tying up loose ends, before time runs out. Now, let me ask you, ranger. Have you ever played chess?"

"I don't see how that has anything to do with this."

"Of course, you wouldn't," he said. "That's why it was so easy to manipulate you."

I felt the urge to draw my gun and start blasting but somehow restrained my itchy trigger finger. "Get to the damn point already."

"The game of chess has millions upon millions of positions, but the best players make creative use of the pawns. You must never leave a pawn totally exposed; you add layer upon layer of protection from other pieces. Abigail, too, is a pawn, but she is vital to the endgame. If I play her piece all the way to the end of the board, she can become something much more valuable." His eyes were vacant as he spoke.

"I truly didn't anticipate losing Abigail the night before I realized my vision for Hexed Springs, but my other pieces prevented an untimely checkmate. You, Cal Cooper, may seem to be a knight, but you, too, are one of my pawns. A sacrificial one, I'm afraid."

"You think you can kill me and achieve utopia? You're a crackpot," I growled, my fingers creeping toward my holster. They had a life of their own, and I didn't know how much longer I could hold off. The Sentinel detected the movement and blared a tone from its core.

"Hands back where I can see them, ranger!" Strickland warned. "I admit, I haven't quite felt like myself for the past few weeks. I hear voices when I sleep. But all that will end soon, once I've kept my end of the bargain. I'll be a proud father as my child helps me transform humankind and enter a new age." He let out a smug laugh and the boastful pride returned to his face, flushing his sickly skin. "To a simpleton, it all seems convoluted, having twisted my enemies and obstacles in such an intricate fashion, but in reality, I had every avenue covered."

There was a slight breeze at the back of my neck, and the earthy smell of rain flowed into the room. Strickland, so transfixed by his grand vision, was oblivious. It must be the window in Cromley's lab, and it could be my ticket out of here. No way was I going to become the next loose end tied up forever.

"You're no genius," I stalled. "You're sick. You're hearing voices because you've gone insane with greed and jealousy." I inched back toward my escape. "This isn't just about revenge against your wife, is it?"

Strickland laughed as he shot another impatient glance at his watch. "I cannot be late to this meeting, but I do so love to gloat when a plan comes together so flawlessly. Are you even aware of the endless streams of mana coursing beneath our feet?" He couldn't help it. He stamped his feet like a child. "After tonight, I will seize control of it all. While the most powerful supernatural family is distracted by my forces and searching for the local ranger who killed their leader's lover, I will seize control of it and secure humankind's destiny."

Strickland was asking for full-blown war with the extramundane. They would never let some mortal hijack their sacred life force. Only a delusional, greedy bastard like him could believe it.

"Thousands of humans will die because of you," I said.

"They are merely collateral."

He turned sharply toward the door, everything on schedule, as the clattering of hooves trotted toward us. His gold-plated carriage had arrived, pulled by the same massive Clydesdales. "Apologies, Mr. Cooper, but I'm afraid I have an appointment with my associates in Strayhaven that I can delay no further. Thank you for spending the last few moments of your life with me. You were useful."

He waved a mocking farewell, his double chin flexing underneath his grin. He signaled to the Sentinel and ordered my execution. I'd stared down the barrel of a gun in tighter squeezes. This one just happened to involve an overpowered automaton with a deadly medieval weapon built inside it.

Time slowed down, and a familiar chill shot up my spine. I steadied my breath as the scene unfolded before me. I saw myself drawing and firing my revolver, the tinman launching a bolt from its arm-mounted crossbow, Strickland reeling back as my bullet pierces his shoulder, the bolt grazing my left cheek.

I exhaled as time caught up. Everything had played out as in my vision, and my cheek burned from my fresh wound. I winced and dashed through the open window in the back room in a dead sprint, toward the only safe place I could think of—Clementine's.

As I rounded the corner of the undertaker's office, the wooden exterior splintered and cracked in twain as the automaton burst through, flinging beams clear across the street. Hot on my heels, the Sentinel was gaining ground so quickly I could hear its internal gears whirring and its metal joints creaking with each step. A shiver shot down my spine, a warning from my still semi-functional sixth sense, telling me to make a hard left. As I did, I felt a whoosh of air brush my shoulder as a crossbow bolt pierced the ground right where I'd been running.

My premonitions lead me down an alleyway, zigzagging from left to right as I avoided the hail of bow fire. After the third or fourth turn, I came upon a familiar intersection. The saloon was right up ahead.

Golden lantern light washed over me as I rushed through the back door. I hollered for Clem. Someone else was shouting her name, too.

It was Toussaint.

The booming of flintlock pistols and shattering glass echoed from the main saloon parlor ahead. I stumbled through the dimly lit larder, dodging obstacles along the way. I banged my head on a cast-iron skillet hanging from the rafters and almost plunged headfirst into an empty beer barrel. I cursed, rubbing my forehead where the metal had met my thick skull.

"Toussaint?" I hollered back.

"Cal? In here." His voice told me something was very wrong.

I emerged from the storeroom to find my friends in the middle of a brand-new heap of trouble. Clem and Toussaint were pinned behind the bar by a squad of armed men. Some of them were providing cover fire while others were turning tail.

Seconds later, the Sentinel burst through the back door.

Danger on all sides.

Talk about a rock and a hard place, huh?

CHAPTER TWENTY

Imagine the look on my face as I crashed into the saloon, nearly falling into the arms of four armed men holding down the saloon door. I locked eyes with a fella, who was just as surprised to see me as I was at seeing him shooting up Clem's saloon. I dove behind cover, pulled out my gun, and prepared to add my fire to the gunfight.

There wasn't any time to make a plan. The automaton was charging up behind me, and my friends were pinned against the back wall by a barrage of gunfire.

"Sentinel behind me," I yelled toward the bar. Or what remained of it.

"The hell's a Sentinel?" Clem hollered back.

The golden gleam of the Sentinel's armor burst through the stockroom door, buckling the wooden supports that held up the second floor.

This guy must really hate doors.

I opened fire at the automaton and showered it with however many bullets remained in my six-shooter. Two shots pierced its metal frame, joining the flecks of pellets scattered across its torso as Toussaint blasted it with buckshot. The click of an empty weapon was all that came out on my third pull of the trigger.

None of our shots did anything more than surface damage to the metal man. The Sentinel ignored Clem's and Toussaint's gunfire, refocusing its eyes on me. It stomped its tree-trunk legs through tables and chairs like they were forest brush. I scrambled to my feet as it swung a thick arm at me, sliding just underneath its fist as I dove for new cover.

"Backup's here, boys," said one of the armed men. "Rendezvous back with the boss and let the metal man handle them."

Out of the corner of my eye, I saw Clem pop up from behind the bar and wing one of the men as they retreated. Veins bulged from her neck and her hair wisped wildly in every direction. I thought she was going to crack her teeth, she had them clenched so tight.

"Damn you, all of you. Get out of my saloon!" She slid a long, sharp bullet into her rifle's chamber.

I wanted to chase after the men, but the Sentinel was closing in on me, its gears clanking and whirring as it raised its sword high. I wasn't quite ready to depart from my head just yet. Trying to draw the automaton outside, I made a run for the front double doors and away from my friends. I burst through the saloon doors and rounded the corner, looking over my shoulder to see if it was following me, ready to fire at any stragglers from the retreating squad.

There was no one in sight. And the Sentinel hadn't crashed through the doors behind me, like I thought it would. I chewed on my lip and wondered if I should risk going back in. I kept my eyes trained on the entrance, waiting for it to emerge.

Seconds ticked by. Then, gunfire erupted from inside.

"Come on, dammit. Come get me," I mumbled to myself.

I peeked inside the saloon window just as it shattered, sending shards of glass flying toward my face. A cold metal hand grabbed my shirt and yanked me through the busted window. The Sentinel buzzed and growled as it slammed me to the ground, pinning me to the floorboards with its pneumatic strength. As I lay in wait for the automaton's blade to drop, a pulse of energy coursed through my body and pricked up the hairs on my neck. The sensation felt familiar, like the few times I'd tried calling up my magic. But this time it wasn't me drawing up mana.

"I said, 'Get. Out. Of. My. Saloon.'" Clem's voice boomed across the room.

The bang of Clem's rifle thundered, the force of it shattering the liquor bottles on the shelf behind her. The reverberation rattled through my chest and I recoiled, in both shock and fear. Dust floated down from the rafters. The sniper's round had pierced the Sentinel's armor underneath its mechanical armpit and exploded through the other side. Its golden armor was split open, spewing out springs, gears, and shattered crystal shards like a gush of blood and guts, and it fell forward onto me. Its fiery eyes faded to black, and its joints creaked as they locked in place, creating a cage around me.

I crawled out from beneath the tinman's bulk and glanced over at my former partner in crime. Toussaint and I both stood dumbfounded, our mouths agape.

Looked like I wasn't the only new wizard gunslinger in town.

The barrel of Clem's weapon sizzled and popped as white smoke drifted from the orange-hot barrel. A blast of heat swirled around the saloon. Her eyes were full of emerald fury and her hair blazed like wildfire. She had channeled her wrath into a single devastating round.

Finally, she relaxed her grip on the gun, unclenched her jaw, and lowered the rifle. Her eyes cooled to their normal state as the frenzy seemed to drain from her body. "Y'all better close your mouths or else you're going to catch flies," she chided, her voice raspy from so much hollering.

"How did you just do that?" I asked, stepping lightly toward her. I pointed at her hair.

Clem looked at her reflection in the last remaining piece of mirrored glass in the bar back. She tugged down a strand of red hair, still the bright orange of hot iron. Her eyes grew wide at the sight of it.

It took a moment for her words to flow. "I don't know how to explain it, but—"

"You're a witch?" Toussaint asked.

"No, I ain't a witch," Clem snapped. She examined her rifle and rubbed her forehead. "It's like my eyes suddenly became a rifle's scope. I could see through that thing, and I knew exactly where to put my bullet. It didn't feel like I was the one pulling the trigger, though. I lost control of my thoughts and surrendered to someone else. Someone angry, some sort of loose cannon alter ego."

"Conjuring up Anne Red? Sounds like something a witch can do," I joked.

Clem's eyes flashed with fury again and she threw me a not so friendly punch. It hurt.

"Hold on, I was only kidding. What's wrong with being a witch anyhow?"

"I don't know. Nothing, I guess," she said. She threw up her hands in dismay as she surveyed the remains of her saloon. "I'm just freaked out right now, okay? You show up with some near-death child before running off, the doc here appears and offers to treat her, another one of those vampires stops by to inspect the corpse of the one you left behind, and then some of Strickland's men ambush it and lay siege to my business. Oh, and then you come crashing through the back door with some metal monstrosity."

"Thanks for taking it out for me. Solved one of my future problems," I said.

"And yet again, Cal Cooper owes me one," she said, rolling her eyes.

I shrugged. "Look, Strickland ordered that thing to take me out while I was fighting another sort of monstrosity at the undertaker's. What's your story, professor? I came by your place looking for you."

Toussaint adjusted his tailored outfit and tucked his flintlocks back onto his chest holster. "I was actually looking for you, mon amie. Based on what you have said, I think we are all in grave danger."

Clem held up a finger, trying to take her usual charge of the conversation, but she stumbled and caught herself on a nearby barstool. She grimaced in pain.

"Is this your first time using magic?" Toussaint said as he felt her forehead.

Clem inhaled sharply. "If that's what you call what I did, then yes."

Clem let out another sigh, and her little dog Angus emerged unscathed from a pile of rubble, as if this were just a regular evening at the bar. He trotted over and curled up in her lap. She stroked his head and closed her eyes, taking slow and controlled breaths.

A wave of queasiness had washed over me, too, but it didn't hit me as hard this time.

Toussaint looked at me and frowned. He produced a research notebook from his pocket and began jotting down some notes. "I think you two have confirmed one of my theories. I came to Hexed Springs to study the supernatural, remember? What I did not tell you, Cal, was that I was here to study you as well."

"Me? Why me?"

Toussaint looked up from his notetaking. "Forgive me, not 'you' exactly, but 'you' as in the people of Hexed Springs. It was a lead I came across while following Dr. Van Helsing's work. Exposure to raw mana can cause unstable effects in people not born with innate supernatural abilities. To those born with the abilities, it can amplify them greatly."

"So, which are we: born or mutated? I've ridden with Clem for years and never saw her do that before," I said.

He shook his head. "I'm afraid the answers elude me. This will require further study."

"It'll have to wait," I said. "Before we do anything, I want to check on Abigail."

Toussaint and Clem exchanged glances.

"She's gone, Cal. Those men came and took her," Clem said, stone cold in her expression.

I clenched my hands into fists and cursed. "How the hell did they manage to do that? You too busy worrying about defending your lousy firewater to protect her?" The words seemed to fly from my mouth before I could stop them.

Clem shot up to her feet, pushing through the pain, and poked a finger right in my face. "Before you go and shoot your mouth off saying something you'll regret, let me tell you something. That girl was not my responsibility. I feel pity in my heart for a suffering child, just like anyone else, but I've got my own girls to worry about." She surveyed the devastation—tables broken in half, chairs splintered into kindling, bullet holes scattered like pockmarks on the walls. It was going to take a lot of time and money to fix the joint up. At least the chandelier seemed all right.

"And as of right now, I don't know whether they're alive or dead. Half the town might be slaughtered for all I know. So before you go projecting your guilt onto me, look around and see just what I've lost getting dragged into your affairs."

We had all been reluctantly dragged into the middle of a cold war between normals and paranormals, new wealth and old power, greed and jealousy. All of which had just exploded into a full-on assault.

"Fine," I snapped. "Just tell me what happened."

Toussaint spoke up first. "I came looking for you, hoping you'd returned from your hunt.

Miss Clementine told me everything. I tried to treat the girl, but there wasn't enough time to complete her treatment."

My heart sank as I assumed the worst. "What do you mean?"

"He means we ran out of time before those men arrived. They were only after the lone vampire but opened fire once they discovered we had possession of their boss's kid," Clem said.

"I was, however, able to diagnose the girl. I'm afraid she has an advanced case of pneumonia." Toussaint pulled off his top hat and sheepishly clenched its brim. "And I was able to confirm from her blood that she is infected with vampirism."

My heart sank. "How the hell do we fix her? You've studied vampires, professor. Said yourself your predecessor was close to a cure. Can we treat her before it's, you know, too late?"

Toussaint opened a satchel on his hip and unrolled a leather sleeve of vials and tubes filled with chemicals. "I am not sure. See this vial? The concentration of the vampiric essence in her blood was only half of what I typically find in the blood of full-fledged vampires."

"So, the only way to find out is to get her back?" I asked.

"We don't have any clue where they took her, Cal," Clem said.

I chewed my lip and thought things through. "I know where they're going. I heard a man say they were going to rendezvous with Strickland, and Strickland told me he had an appointment with someone in Strayhaven."

Toussaint inhaled sharply. "If this is true, we should go there now. After our appointment with Mr. Van Pelt, I made a visit to a man who calls himself the Archivist. He's a hobbyist historian with detailed records of the happenings within Hexed Springs."

"Van Pelt, the snake oil salesman?" Clem asked.

"Long story. I'll tell you later," I said. "Go on, professor."

"Among his collection, I found records of Strickland's recent business acquisitions. All of them are strategic sources of the earth's natural resources, particularly one very valuable reservoir."

Strickland had financed and drew up contracts across No Man's Land. I remembered the sign in front of the mine.

"He must have found a way to tap into the ley line energies," I said.

"The Nexus may be vulnerable amidst all the fighting," Toussaint added.

"Get the girl, save Strayhaven. Two birds, one stone."

Clem looked around the room and laughed. "We and what army? There's only three of us. Four, if you count Angus, but, trust me, he ain't any help. No offense, professor, you're not a great shot either."

I turned to Clem, squeezed her shoulder, and looked right into her eyes. "Clem, I'm sorry about your saloon and I'm sorry about earlier. Really, I am. I didn't mean to get you caught up in this. But I'm going after Strickland and I'm finding that little girl and getting her the help she needs. Whatever is happening tonight, we have to put a stop to it. You told me coming to Hexed Springs would change things for me, but truth is, trouble still follows me all the same. And just like every other time, I sure could use your help."

Clem sighed. "Save the sad puppy-dog eyes routine. You know I'll always ride with you, you idiot. Besides, I've got a mind to punish some vamps for Rose and everyone else they've enslaved. But that's after we stop whatever that rich bastard is planning on doing."

I smiled at Clem and turned to Toussaint. He nodded in agreement.

Clem reached up and plucked her hat, still somehow hanging from a hook above the bar. The long feather bounced as it came to rest on her head.

"Well, what are you standing around for, gentlemen? Let's go millionaire hunting and save a little girl."

CHAPTER TWENTY-ONE

The three of us snuck down the alley toward the secret entrance into the Strayhaven. The storm had let up not long after we left the saloon, but suspense still hung heavy in the air, clouding our faces with unease.

On our way through the mazelike alleys, I filled them in with what had happened with Cromley and Strickland along the way. Unsurprisingly, Clem had a number of questions, especially about the shambling horror of mismatched body parts that nearly wrestled me to death; it grossed her out. Toussaint was more curious than concerned about the abomination, but by the time I got through the whole story, the professor was most alarmed about the potential coup fomenting within the extramundane community.

"Strickland said he has help from the inside? What paranormal would help a mortal upset the balance between worlds?" Toussaint asked as we approached the secret entrance.

"I was hoping you would know. That, and how Strickland got control of the Sentinel. You're the one that's handy with machines, after all," I said.

"Perhaps both of those questions have the same answer," Clem added.

Clem and I didn't slow down as we crossed the veil into Strayhaven. Even though she'd been debriefed on what to expect, she still spun around, slack-jawed at her new surroundings. Things were different than earlier, though. The bellies of the dark clouds were lit by the orange hue of fire, casting more gloom over everything.

Toussaint appeared moments later and did a double-take toward the veil. "You both just walked through the brick wall without drinking the potion?"

"What brick wall?" Clem asked.

It suddenly hit me. Magic wielders can cross the veil freely without the help of Toussaint's concoction. "Guess you and me really are magical folks now, Clem," I said. "Look at this." I reached past Toussaint and touched a strip of the translucent veil. It disintegrated into a fine powder in my hands. "Looks like the veil won't be a problem for anybody before much longer."

"I don't know anything about what y'all are talking about, but I imagine that ain't a good thing," Clem said.

Toussaint reached up and touched a strand. "Merde. I don't like the looks of this."

We didn't have much time before Strickland pulled off his big plan, but I had no clue where to begin. "Should we split up?" Toussaint asked as Clem took in the back alleys of Strayhaven. "Cover more ground?"

"No, we need to stick together. Strength of the pack."

Clem guffawed. "You don't hear that coming from ole 'Deadeye' Cooper too often."

I gave her a look, then turned back to Toussaint. "Would Strickland head straight for the Nexus? Or is there another way inside?"

"I don't believe so. Unless Strickland has found an alternate entrance," he said. He paused and rubbed his chin. "If only there was a trail we could follow."

"Hey, boys," Clem shouted. "Why don't we just follow the trail of destruction?"

Toussaint and I both raised our eyebrows, until we saw where Clem was pointing. I was surprised we hadn't seen it earlier. Bodies of men, vampires, and innocent bystanders riddled the road leading toward the black obelisk in the distance, which peeked over the rooftops. Among them were the four men who'd attacked the saloon and taken Abigail.

"The girl's not here," Clem said.

I nodded. "Means she's still out there."

I started down the trail of destruction.

CHAPTER TWENTY-TWO

I used to get nervous before I pulled off a job. Even though I'd run through the plans in my head at least a hundred times, I'd still get butterflies right before I robbed a bank, stuck up a train, or engaged in whatever banditry I'd been involved with. Gunfights were the most nerve-racking. It's natural to panic a little each time a bullet whizzes by or chips away at the cover you're ducked under. After a few years of breaking the law, I settled down and found myself one with the chaos, completely at peace with the havoc and madness around me.

But all those years of being an outlaw weren't helping me at all right now. My nerves were frayed and my thoughts rattled in my head like dice. I'd failed my promise to keep Abigail safe. And not only that, now the lives of hundreds, maybe thousands, of innocents hung in the balance.

The chaos caused by Strickland's ambush was recorded in the dusty avenue—a trail of dead that led toward the Nexus. Some of Strayhaven's denizens were armed and guarded their shops and homes, paying the three of us no mind as we made our way through the aftermath. Glass from broken windows littered the street and the intermittent shouts of battle echoed down side alleys. Every few minutes, a violet light surged from underneath the obelisk, and waves of energy pulsed through the air, making my stomach churn and head buzz. Clem was looking a little green around the gills, too.

That buzz of power was growing inside me again, and it was intoxicating. I wanted to reach out and grab hold of it, like seizing the reins of a bucking bronco.

The sky was still cloudy, but I hadn't felt a single raindrop for a little while. The only booms came from a nearby alley, around the corner from the massive elven tree, whose vines were overtaking the plant shop. A familiar face caught my eye as we walked past.

It was Aldon.

The elven boy's back was pressed against the alley wall. A vampire was hunched over him, twisted and ugly from its transformation into a demonic predator. Before I could shout his name, Aldon thrust his hands into the earth. Leaves from the giant tree shook loose, and one of its gnarled roots erupted from the ground, coiling around the vampire like a boa constrictor, cracking the vamp's bones within its wooden grip. The monster screeched until the snakelike root crushed its lungs and yanked it down into the earth. Aldon waved his hands over the ground, burying the vampire and the root.

Seeing that the danger had cleared, no thanks to me, I strolled up to him. "Come on, kid, I owed you a rescue. You should have let me make us even."

Aldon didn't have time to joke around. His eyes flashed.

"I knew humans couldn't be trusted. You're here to invade our home, too, aren't you?" he growled through gritted teeth. There was a real frustration and sadness in the boy's voice.

"Aldon, take it easy," I said, grabbing his balled fists. "I'm here to put a stop to all this. Have you seen a stagecoach come by here? Gold trim, pulled by big horses?"

Aldon nodded and searched around, unsure of the direction.

"Come on, Cal, we don't have much time," Clem said. "Leave the boy be and we'll find him ourselves."

I waved Clem off and drew up close to the young wood elf. "It's going to be all right. Go home to your family, your eldar and elleth, and let me take care of this. Trust me to be your guardian."

Aldon mulled it over and found his voice

again. He pointed toward the center of town.

"That way. I saw a large wagon going that way," he said.

"Good lad," I said, patting him on the shoulder. "Now get yourself home safely."

Aldon grabbed my arm as I turned to leave. "I'm coming with you."

"Kid, I know you can handle yourself in a fight, but I can't risk it. Bullets can be as deadly as a spell. If you won't go home, then at least help out the folks around here. Deal?"

The elven boy looked down at his feet. "Fine," he muttered. He pushed past me and jogged down the way toward cries for help.

"Good luck, kid," Clem called after him.

* * *

Aldon's direction led us right up to Strickland's gaudy stagecoach, which was parked outside the obelisk. The adjoining temple marked the entrance down to the Nexus.

"Look." Toussaint stopped and pointed ahead. "Someone has disabled the magical barriers. The Nexus is vulnerable."

"Be ready for anything," I said, gripping my revolver's handle tight.

We approached the stagecoach and looked around. The driver was still there, presumably waiting for his boss and tending to those big

Clydesdales. He didn't hear Clem sneak up on him.

"Don't move, don't holler, don't do nothing," she snarled, resting her gun barrel on the back of the driver's skull.

"Yes, don't do nothing. Where is your boss? Tell us before I dislodge the brain inside your cranium," Toussaint said, waving around one of his pistols. It was more comical than frightening, unfortunately.

The man held his hands up and froze, probably his first stick-up. He didn't say a word. "Well, the man asked you a question," Clem said, pressing the barrel down harder.

"Please, please, I'm just the driver. I just go where I'm told, I swear," he pleaded.

"Strickland down there?" I asked. The man nodded nervously. "How many others are with him?"

He stammered and shook in his boots. "Wh-what?"

"Men. Armed guards. Humans," I yelled.

"One. One human. There are others, but—but I don't know what they are," he said.

"Sentinels? Metal men?"

He shook his head. "I've never seen anything like them before. Hooded figures with tentacled faces. I swear that's all I know."

Clem looked at me and I jerked my head to the side. "Let him go."

She pulled back her rifle and unhitched the

big horses. "You better get gone and don't look back, you hear?"

The man took the hint and awkwardly clambered aboard one of the tall horses. I gave Toussaint the pleasure of slapping the Clydesdale's hind flank. He giggled as the driver and the horses scattered.

He was grinning. "I can see why you two like the outlaw life. That was invigorating."

First-timers usually get a little slaphappy from an armed ambush.

"Keep that ego in check there, Freud. We ain't done yet," Clem said.

We circled up to make our plan of attack. Charging in blindly would be risky, but it was our only option.

"Abigail's down there with her father and some squid-like, hooded figures? Pardon the pun, but something smells fishy. Toussaint, you have any idea what else awaits us past this gate?" I asked.

"This is a sacred place for some, strictly forbidden to mortals. I'm afraid I do not know."

"What do we need a plan for? This is a classic run-and-gun, smash-and-grab," Clem said.

"Like robbing a bank, huh?" I asked.

Clem winked and smiled. Anne Red was back. "Follow us, professor, and do what we do."

We left the stagecoach and crept up to the temple, eyes peeled for any trouble. The stones were slick to the touch from the earlier rainfall, but showed evidence of erosion from what must have been eons of exposure to the harsh plains winds. The obsidian monolith stretched straight up to the sky, supported by granite stones stacked about eight feet high. I peeked inside the entrance: a stone archway revealed a set of stairs that spiraled around the black obelisk and extended far below the earth.

Clem looked over the temple grounds. "Doesn't much fit in with the look of the rest of town, does it?"

"According to my studies, the monument is very, very old. I believe it was constructed first, before anything or anyone else was here. A monument to an ancient time," Toussaint said.

The powerful energy, which was both making me sick and hungry for power, was at its strongest here. Whatever awaited us down there was both repelling my presence and begging me to continue onward.

"We'll study it later. Let's get down there," I said.

Even if there wasn't a little girl needing to be rescued, I would have pushed past my body's warning signs and indulged my temptation for its offering.

We descended a narrow staircase into the depths of the temple, one behind the other. The walls surrounding us were carved from layers of red rocks, their striations ranging in depth from a few feet thick to no more than a few inches.

I shivered as the hollowed-out tunnel got colder the deeper we went. Lighting the way were glowing orbs, wedged inside the stones above each step. They flickered to life as we crossed. Eventually, the layers of rock became dull, gray stone embellished with symbols and characters. The ancient words scrawled on the walls made it hard for Toussaint to focus on the path ahead.

"Are these hieroglyphs of some kind? Runes maybe?" I asked him.

"I've never seen anything like this before. It's not Egyptian or Mesopotamian," he said, rubbing a hand across the carvings as we passed. "It appears to chronicle some kind of history. The symbols vaguely resemble those of ancient times, particularly the Age of the Eternals."

Faint chanting echoed from the depths, and we followed it until we came to the bottom of the stairs. I held a finger up to my lips and waved Clem and Toussaint forward. We pushed inside a chamber and surveyed the octagonal expanse. Clustered all around us were pink crystals jutting sharply out of the cavernous stone room, like the inside of a geode. They varied in size, but the smallest crystal was still bigger than me. Above us, thin, ethereal lines of violet energy fluttered and curled lazily through the air, emanating from the eight corners of the room. The energy wasn't quite liquid or gas, but something in between. The streams culminated in the center of the room where an enormous, perfectly spherical black orb hovered silently, absorbing each wave of energy that poured over its surface. When one of the streams would wander off course and cross into another strand, a violent crackling would erupt and unleash a shockwave of energy. Those were the pulses we'd felt outside.

"The ley lines ..." Toussaint whispered. He pointed to the strands of energy. "That's raw mana."

As we stepped forward, an observation platform came into view underneath the black orb. My attention quickly shifted to the four robed figures chanting around a stone tablet in the center of the platform. They were performing some kind of strange ritual. Strickland was there, his injured arm wrapped in a makeshift sling; he was gripping Abigail's limp arm. She looked like a rag doll being dragged by a gorilla.

"Toussaint, you handle the robed people. I'll take care of Strickland, and Clem, you grab the girl. On my mark," I whispered. They nodded.

The creeps continued their chant in an ancient and vile tongue. Their words wormed into my ears and left a slimy, disgusting feeling inside me. We waited, hidden in shadows, as they repeated the ancient song. Toussaint translated the song and whispered it back to us.

According to the professor, the leader chanted, "Break the chains that bind our power. Smash the seal that oppresses our destiny. Release the masters so they may grant us this day our share of mana."

"Can I shoot them now?" Clem whispered.

I waved her off. As much as I wanted to charge down there and save Abigail, I felt compelled to watch the ritual unfold. Toussaint's eyes darted around the room, taking it all in.

"This ritual cannot be for summoning anything good," he said.

The leader and his three shrouded companions held their cupped hands out toward the orb. "We choose this day to free all creatures of Earth"—they spoke the common tongue now —"We choose this day to empower all mortal and immortal flesh in service to the ancients. So it was prophesied, so shall it be done." They lowered their hands and stepped up to the stone tablet on the pedestal. It had two cupped wells and several intersecting lines that met at a drain in the center. "I hereby offer the blood of the ancients to the sacred seal," he said, producing a vial from his sleeve. His robes fluttered, but I couldn't make out his face. He emptied the contents of the vial into one of the wells and watched it swirl through the maze of carved channels and down the drain.

"Do you, mortal, willingly offer the blood of the pure?" the leader said to Strickland.

"I do," he said, adjusting his sling so he could better hold onto Abigail. "I offer you my daughter's blood. Take what you need."

The leader produced a small knife and poked Abigail's forearm, allowing a pool of blood to flow onto the blade. She didn't react to the cut.

"Now?" Clem hissed, poking me with the butt of her rifle.

I held a finger to my lips as the robed man smeared the blood on the other side of the tablet.

But nothing happened. The hooded figures all stared at Strickland.

"This blood is not pure," the leader said.

"What do you mean?" Strickland said, inspecting the tablet for himself. He slammed a fist on it when he realized he couldn't understand the markings.

"This blood is tainted."

Strickland gritted his teeth. "How dare you? She has the blood of my ancestors coursing through her veins. I am a pure-blooded American, I can assure you." He wasn't used to not getting his way.

One of the other robed figures stepped forward, took the knife, and tasted the tip of the blade. "It is not from a pure heart," it mewed.

Strickland stomped his foot like a child ready to erupt into a tantrum. "Surely you are not suggesting my bloodline is impure. I get the feeling you four are attempting to alter our agreement and cheat me of my destiny. Need I remind your master that I control the Sentinel?"

The robed figure wiped the blood from the dagger and ignored Strickland's antics. "The machines do not serve you, nor will they ever. Its servitude was a temporary boon to achieve our ends, nothing more."

Strickland was dumbfounded, unable to comprehend not having the upper hand in every deal. He tucked Abigail underneath his arm like she was a sack of flour. "Then what are you trying to say about my daughter?" he demanded.

"That she isn't your daughter," I said, emerging from the shadows, my gun drawn.

Strickland jumped at the sound of my voice. He spun around and clenched his jaw, his eyelid twitching. "Cooper? How ...? Explain yourself."

I smirked and twirled the revolver around my finger to goad him. "It's not hard, if you think about it. You don't seem like someone that dense. Come on, make a guess."

Strickland's nostrils flared and I could hear his shallow breaths over the clashes of violet energy behind him.

"Allow me to elucidate, partner. You were too busy being a megalomaniac that your estranged wife found herself somebody else. You thought she ran off to your extramundane rival to hurt you, but they must have honestly loved each other."

The robed figures murmured amongst themselves in a huddle, then one said, "The interloper speaks the truth."

"This must not be discovered," said another.

The leader peered over his shoulder at me and sneered, exposing rotten teeth and pallid tentacles hidden beneath his hood. "Do not worry, there will be blood spilled tonight. Our vengeance is still at hand."

And with that, they all bowed their heads. Their leader waved his hand in front of the group and a portal of swirling black and green fire appeared. Strickland dropped Abigail and chased after them as they floated through, one by one, and disappeared. The portal vanished with a pop, leaving the five of us alone in the chamber.

Strickland dug his nails into the sides of his head and stared me down with bulging bloodshot eyes. "Why aren't you dead, ranger?" He was seething.

"You ever hear the legend of John Henry? Used two sledgehammers, one in each hand, to beat a steam machine in a race to drive the most rail stakes. Man triumphs over machine, Ross. Or, in this case, a red-headed barkeep triumphed over one." Abigail, still in a heap on the floor, coughed. "I suggest you move away from the girl. Clem, grab her," I said.

Clem stepped forward, but Strickland tugged the girl up by the shirt collar and pulled a small pistol from his waist belt. From a distance, it couldn't kill a quail, but up close, it was still very lethal, especially to someone so frail.

"Another step and I'll kill her. If she isn't

mine, why should I care?"

Strickland grunted and searched for somewhere to run, but the only way out was behind us. A leap over the edge of the platform meant certain death, either by the fall or the jagged crystals below. Strickland's confident swagger melted away, exposing a desperate old fool who'd risked it all, and lost. He cocked the hammer of his gun. "Do you three realize what you've just done? They were going to give me the power of the gods in exchange for her blood. I could have used it to guide mundanes to a never-ending golden age," he yelled.

"Best laid plans of mice and men often go awry," I said. "Shame we didn't have the same vision for humanity."

"No. Please," Strickland begged. His image of dominance was cracking the more he realized he was just a cornered rat. Desperate. "Help me disengage the seal behind me and I'll show you how truly benevolent I can become."

I looked at him with disdain. "I prefer to live life on my own terms, not ones set up in an eternally-binding contract, thank you very much."

"The ritual. We could still complete it somehow," Strickland said, his desperation painted on his face. It was pitiful, really. "Yes. The voices are asking you to offer the pedestal your blood, Cal. They want you to break the seal that dampens this fountain of unlimited power. The ancients can empower us, empower humanity. I'll give you, all of you, permanent roles in the future. With our new powers, we'll bring the world medicine, energy, endless sustenance. Every person, a purpose. No hunger, no pain. We'll be seen as gods. New gods!"

Strickland arched his back in pain and grimaced, never losing his grip on the girl. "Can't you hear them? They're screaming your name, Cooper. Their power is here, locked behind a silly, ancient ritual and our blood—pure mortal blood—is the key. Please, ranger," he begged. His eyes were wild and gleaming as he all but groveled at my feet.

"No chance. You've sent men and machines to kill me, blackmailed me into killing your vampiric ex, and now you expect me to help you achieve omnipotence? Forget it. Nobody's blood is completing this ritual, not today. Now, for the last time, let go of the girl and put your hands up."

Strickland started to sweat.

Toussaint tried to calm the situation with the soft, smooth voice you'd use to soothe an infant. "Trust me, you do not want to strike bargains with any ancient gods. It is over, Strickland. Let her go and Cal will let you live."

Before Strickland could think it over, I cocked the hammer on my revolver and aimed at his ribcage farthest from Abigail. It would have been a tough shot for anyone.

Other than me, that is.

"The hell I will," I said, then fired.

Toussaint and Clem both jumped as Cloudsplitter boomed. Strickland's shoulder erupted into meat and blood, and he stumbled backward, still clutching the girl as blood welled up under his shirt.

Clem rushed up and whisked Abigail from him. She brushed the hair out of her face and hummed a sweet song as she took her over to the professor. I strolled up to Strickland, spurs jingling one after the other, my gun still trained on him. He scrambled away from me with all his fleeting might, until his back reached the pillar holding the stone tablet.

"You know, Ross, this is all your fault," I said with a smile. "You could have done business like a decent human being. Instead, you'll die within arm's reach of your twisted little delusion of grandeur. I'd ask you what you were doing down here, but I don't really care. I'm just happy to see you squirm."

Rage fluttered between the panic in his eyes as I twisted his own words back at him. Flecks of blood sprayed from his mouth as he choked out his retort. "No green shall grow upon your grave either, Calamity. You're someone else's pawn now. You'll always be."

I pressed my boot heel to his bullet wound to shut him up. Strickland squealed in pain and blood puddled his chest where my boot was planted. He tried to spout out words, but his mouth was filling rapidly with blood. He slumped down, his breaths beginning to grow fewer and farther between, his eyes fixed upon the coursing mana.

I cursed and strode back to my companions who were stationed by the doorway. Clem had Abigail clenched tightly to her chest. I patted the girl's head. "He's bleeding out. Let's leave him here to rot and get her some help."

"Think the fighting's cleared out above ground?" Clem asked.

"No idea. Maybe Aldon's cleared an escape route for us. That kid can sling magic, all right."

"Cal?" Toussaint said, his eyes fixed on something behind me.

I turned to see a crack forming in the black orb. My bullet must have exited Strickland and struck it. The lines of mana licked over the surface, groping for the fracture. Each time the energies converged, they pulsed, and the crack widened. Soon, larger chunks began to chip away, exposing the hollow innards of the sphere, along with the bottom tip of the obelisk, shaped just as the tip pointing to the sky.

Strickland, in his dying breath, spit out a mouthful of blood and forced his arm upward. His hand landed on the stone tablet and he smeared some of his blood across its surface. His liquid viscera swirled through the maze of grooves and washed down into the gaping hole in the middle. The ley lines perked up, their parabolic wave patterns whipping around the chamber, the crystals humming and glowing brighter and louder into a chaotic frenzy. The orb began to crumble into massive shards that crashed into the abyss below. The entire chamber shuddered.

"The voices, they're singing. Singing my name," Strickland muttered. "I told them I was pure-blooded. The power of the gods ..." Strickland slipped into an intense coughing fit. Then, his eyes glazed over and he stopped moving.

Pale green lines drew across the cracked orb as Strickland's blood mixed inside the tablet. They etched strange runes across its surface, the same ones marking the descent down the stairwell. Every line converged at the center, carving what looked to be an eye with a keyhole as its pupil. The colors faded and the parts of the orb that hadn't chipped away separated into rows, each spinning in alternating directions. The ley lines ignited the metal and dissolved it into violet dust.

As the last hunk of the seal burned away, a fury of light and sound filled the cavern. We all stood there transfixed as the ley lines converged on the obelisk, and the strength of the vibrations coursing through the crystals intensified. The whole place shook as pink lightning coursed up the obelisk's shaft, and the air was filled with the cacophony of brass horns and banshee screams.

"Run, everyone, now," I finally was able to

yell, pulling my companions in front of me.

We bolted for the steps just as the crystals lining the cavern ceiling began caving in. Pulses of energy and the echoes of shattered crystal lashed at our heels as we raced up the stairs, the converging ley lines flooding the space with invisible quantities of mana.

All my hairs stood on end. Was this the power Strickland had mentioned? A voice in my subconscious was telling me to let go and find out. The invitation was frightening and invigorating all at the same time. Something inside me wanted to harness it, to go back into the chamber and accept omnipotence. But the image of Strickland's dead body, laying at the base of the fractured obelisk, was enough to shake off the temptation.

We clambered up the stairwell as the tunnel shook around us; tiny chips of rock peppered our heads as we reached the upper tunnel. The orbs of light on the steps dimmed and flared in time with the pulsing shockwaves.

We emerged above ground into a new level of pandemonium. The dying storm had regained its strength and lightning energized the clouds. Rumbles of thunder shook the air and the ground quaked. In the distance, we could see folks of Strayhaven pouring into the streets, fleeing homes shook loose from their foundations, and we could hear the terrified screams coming from the central elven tree. A great roar burst from the temple behind us, more notes from the ghastly subterranean orchestra.

We ran from the temple, just as a force of pressure nearly sucked us back in. The temple was imploding, shattering the towering obelisk and compressing its lower stone base into the earth. It sent a violet shockwave into the sky, revealing an opaque dome that encompassed Strayhaven, like it was nothing more than a colorful swirl inside a marble. We looked back at the hellscape—the smoldering rubble and carnage. A bolt of pink lightning flashed from the remains of the obelisk, as if cleaving the sky, tearing the opaque dome above the town to shreds.

"Mon Dieu," said Toussaint, looking up in awe. "The veil between worlds."

There, sinking down through the clouds, was the city of Hexed Springs.

CHAPTER TWENTY-THREE

It was impossible to tell where the shouts and screams were coming from. Human men and women pointed to their sky, which was our ground, and we pointed right back at them as Hexed Springs grew closer. Some folks fell to their knees and covered their heads to protect themselves from being crushed. Others cried silently as hell broke loose from the sky above.

Clem, Toussaint, and I huddled around Abigail and I thought my goodbyes. Clem squeezed my shoulder and Toussaint looked resigned, not sure what to say or do in his final moments.

Just before we all became sandwiched between the earth, the two terrestrial planes stopped and stood still for a moment, perfectly parallel to each other.

A gust of wind blew past us, ruffling my duster and whipping Clem's hair about. We all held our breath. During the moment of peace, I scanned the horizon and noticed that the temple behind us had crumbled into a pit of boulders, with raw mana seeping through the cracks. The obsidian obelisk had fallen into the earth, except for its upper half, which floated ominously above the ruins, surrounded by electrified splinters. Strickland's stagecoach was dinged up, and one wheel was elevated off the uneven ground, but it was still in one piece.

Even though my heart hadn't slowed down, I let go of my companions and looked back toward the town for a way out. People were still panicked but had slowed down during the relative calm, uncertain limbo. That's when I spied a familiar face in the crowd—the unlikeliest hero, one I'd never bet on seeing in a moment like this.

It was my horse.

"Clem, I'm gonna need a mess of sugar cubes when this is all done," I said. I whistled to Buck and waved my hands real big. Her ears pricked up and she spotted us immediately through the chaos of the crowd. Clem looked surprised. Confused, and somewhat dazed, but mostly pleasantly surprised.

Clem squinted to get a better look at the brave barn sour while Toussaint pulled down the brass goggles from the brim of his hat. One of the lenses extended like a spyglass. "I see a clear path toward the alleyway into Hexed Springs," he said. "I don't know what will happen if we cross back into our realm, but I am curious to find out."

"It doesn't surprise me that you'd be thinking of research at a time like this," I said as Buck nuzzled her nose in my palm. "Listen, you and Clem get the girl and pile into the stagecoach. I'll hook Buck up to the front and drive. She's no Clydesdale, but I think she'll be able to get us out of here."

Clem and Toussaint got everything ready while I affixed Buck to pull us home. I climbed into the driver's seat and slapped the roof. "Y'all ready?"

Clem popped her head out of the passenger window. "Hit it, Cal. Let's go."

The ground began to twist and shake again, more violently than before. The sky, or rather the ground, slowly lifted away again, this time inclined at an angle, until it appeared as a wall perpendicular to us, like opening the pages of a book. Fissures snaked through the ground across both realms, creating small pieces of land that began to shuffle around like dominoes.

Buck didn't wait for me to slap the reins. She took off, whether it was safe or not. Crowds of extramundane species made way as we careened toward our way back into Hexed Springs.

"The hidden city is not so hidden anymore," Toussaint yelled from the passenger window as we passed through the alleyway. "We are witnessing the land returning to its original tectonic layout."

I didn't have time to appreciate the geological marvel playing out before my eyes. Swaths of land churned and entire buildings were rearranging, combining into a totally new city. The stagecoach's wheels groaned as Buck made sharp, erratic turns, avoiding the whirlpools of mud and dirt and falling debris. We twisted and turned, down street after street, completely lost, until I finally spotted the Howling Beast Saloon & Inn, dead ahead, standing firm as a lighthouse in a raging sea.

"Angus, baby, I'm coming," Clem hollered.

If there was any sort of incline left between the two planes, I couldn't tell. They were just one piece of land now. Buck seemed to recognize the landmark, and her turbulent course-correcting settled down as we drew near.

The swinging doors were within reach when all the quaking and twisting suddenly stopped. Everyone, including Buck, lurched forward from the sudden lack of momentum as the tracts of land settled into their new homes. I fell off the stagecoach and landed on my back, which, although painful, at least afforded me a good view of where we'd come from. The sky was the sky again and not a terrifying view of the rooftops of Hexed Springs.

The storm clouds had gathered again, picking up strength as the pink bolts of lightning sporadically erupted from the obelisk. The gentle violet light returned, its glow painting the underbelly of the violent skies and the flat prairie.

The buzz of mana still flooded the air. It hadn't dissipated and in fact felt stronger now. My skin tightened into gooseflesh as a static charge ran up my arms. My head swam like I'd drunk one too many whiskeys.

Buck trotted over to me as I got to my feet. "All right, girl, it's over now. No need to panic." But Buck wouldn't calm down. Her ears were focused forward and her eyes dialed in on something behind me. She champed at her bridle as the gentle rain fell on us like a fine mist. She whinnied and twitched as more lightning lit up the sky.

"Wizard," a voice hissed.

Confused, I peeked over Buck's shoulders and saw a whole gang of vampires, half of them fully transformed into demonic beasts, converging on the stagecoach.

When it rains, it pours, don't it?

CHAPTER TWENTY-FOUR

Toussaint was halfway out of the stagecoach when he saw the pack of vamps surrounding us. He quickly shut and locked the passenger door, and peeked out the window, waiting. We were outnumbered four to one by monsters capable of incredible feats of speed and strength. Cunning and vile creatures capable of killing me and raising my corpse in eternal servitude. It was going to take a miracle for us to get out of this one alive.

But I had other plans, none of which included dying at the hands of vampires.

Toussaint and I locked eyes. I nodded to him and he nodded to me—the universal signal for 'watch what I do.'

"Who you calling a wizard, vamp?" I asked, strutting into the muddy street.

A lone vampire stepped forward from the crowd of about a dozen. Compared to the other vampires I've met, he was dressed for work, not for socializing. His white cotton shirt, half-unbuttoned and drenched with rainwater, outlined his lean muscular frame. He tugged off a black cloak and let it fall into the mud. When he looked back at me, his eyes were blackened pools of malice.

"You have tried to steal the power of the ancients. Underneath your human aura, I can sense their presence. That power does not belong to you," he said.

"I'm not the mortal to blame for all that. Just an innocent bystander. Y'all work for Lucius?"

The vampire slinked closer to me, fangs exposed and claws at the ready. He stepped lightly and slowly at an almost hypnotizing pace. "You, ranger, are not so innocent. The Patriarch demands your presence. You will follow us and bring the child," he said.

I took a step backward toward Buck. "Oh, I'm afraid the girl's too ill to be traveling right now. How about I deliver her another time?"

The vampire flexed his hands and frustration flashed in his eyes. Behind his pack of companions, a portal ripped open and six more vampires stepped out. I gripped my gun belt to keep my hands from quivering. I didn't want the vampire to see my fear, although I suppose he had already sensed it, along with my spell-slinging abilities.

"You will come now, willingly or dead."

"I claim his blood," a vampiress shouted from within the crowd. A few snickers bubbled up, and the vampire talking to me grinned.

My attempt to play it cool had failed. My eyes shifted quickly between vampires, as if I was going to think up the right combination of bullets to plug into each one. My fingers twitched over my revolver. My breathing shook with every exhale. The fact was, there were too many of them, and they were too strong, capable of handling more bullet wounds than humans could.

Unless I could harness my sixth sense, see what was going to happen before it happened. Maybe I could let go of myself, reach out and seize the very power Strickland had described. After all, I could still feel it buzzing underneath my skin and in my soul.

All I could think about at this moment were my friends. Abigail, too, even though we hadn't formally made introductions. I couldn't help but think of how everyone I knew, friends and enemies alike, had somehow contributed to my role in this pivotal moment. And, for better or worse, I was going to finally seize my destiny, even if it meant falling to a pack of bloodthirsty monsters.

My mother told me she had a vision before I was born. She said she'd seen me grow, from a baby to a man, in her dreams and that I was always up to no good. I couldn't keep myself out of trouble, couldn't stay away from mischief, and reveled in the chaos that inevitably followed. And that's how she picked my name.

Even now, in the face of death, I wasn't about to let her down.

I ran my hand across Buck's flank. "Thanks for coming to get us back there," I whispered. "Run for the hills and don't stop until you get to safety. And be good, ya hear?"

Clem and Toussaint were halfway out the window when I slapped Buck on her rear. She plowed forward with all her might, preparing to crash right through the line of vampires. The stagecoach wheels spun for a moment before finding their grip in the mud and jerking forward, sending Clem and Toussaint back into their seats. I could hear Clem call me something endearingly rude as she sailed by. I tuned it out, took a deep breath, and focused my thoughts and my will on the energy around me: the mana permeating the earth, the sky, and every living being around me.

The lead vampire cursed and yelled for his companions to follow after them. I'm not sure what I said that made them stop dead in their tracks. But whatever it was, it was as loud as thunder and drove fear right through their blackened hearts.

When I opened my eyes again, I had changed. The raw power flowed freely through my veins, and I knew I could manipulate it. It was mine. I was its master. The emotions inside my head cried out all at once, drunk with the power I'd seized. One voice sifted through the rest and told me to be afraid. Afraid of the responsibility for the magnitude of a weapon I now possessed. I drowned it out and let my other emotions go along with it. All of them, except my desperation.

More portals split open, and vampires and their thralls spilled out into the street, swooping up along the rooftops. The lead vampire leapt for me, and his companions followed suit.

That's when my desperation turned to rage. I channeled that feeling into a spell that somehow felt as natural as shooting a bullseye, even though I'd never intentionally slung a spell before. I could see the mana now, flowing freely through the air. It surged forth from the earth like a river bursting through the dam, the Nexus having collapsed. I steeled my nerves and exerted my control, channeling the energy of the storm strengthening around me.

And I became chaos—or should I say calamity—unbridled.

Droplets of rain ceased to fall. My enemies froze in place, their bodies suspended in midair, stalled in time, which I now controlled. Everything around me was motionless, but I could still move, albeit at a fraction of my natural speed. My thoughts were unhindered. I reached up to touch a raindrop and pushed it aside, forever changing its terminal vector.

Now my rage turned to greed. The power continued to well up inside me, channeling itself in a way I didn't know how to manage, but still I wanted more. I wanted to wield more than I needed, begged for it, enough to finally obliterate my enemies.

Electricity pricked my skin and coursed through me as I drew my revolver. I aimed at the vampires and sensed their panic, their thoughts manifesting inside my own head. I heard them beg for their lives. I heard them pray to the unholy masters they served.

It mattered little to me.

Physical tension gripped the world around me. Nature pleaded and recoiled in a newfound fear. Like a stuck gear, I felt the earth resist my hold, crying out, beseeching me to free it from my grasp.

And I said no.

My revolver thundered out its rounds, not bullets but bolts of lightning this time. In that moment, I finally understood why my hand cannon had been called Cloudsplitter. The thralls went down first, each shot rupturing their chests, littering their ribcages. The vampires fell next. Their skulls split in two as I speared them with lightning.

Now my greed turned to lust. I continued to feed upon power until it was something I could no longer control. The eyes of the heavenly entities turned their gaze upon me. I had become a conduit for a power forbidden to humankind, one reserved for the gods and demigods of the ages, and one carefully tucked away from the ancient and corrupt deities slumbering inside the earth. They marked me for judgment, I could hear them say so.

Soon my grip on the channeled fury slipped and time resumed its forward march. I felt as though the natural world now regarded me with a mistrust for breaking a sacred and ancient pact.

My enemies, all dead before they hit the ground, fell like the raindrops dripping from the clouds. But for all my effort, it wasn't enough. Four more portals opened, each producing four vampires with two thralls apiece. They walked out from the shadows into Hexed Springs from hellscapes I could never imagine, even in my worst nightmare. All I could see beyond the portals was a flurry of teeth and claws and screams raging inside their unholy realm.

As they rushed forward, yelling and screeching, my vision faded and strength left my body. I guess I shouldn't have been surprised. Opening my sixth sense for a simple duel had nearly killed me. I was surprised I hadn't evaporated on the spot for controlling a power not meant for mortal humans.

I hoped my friends had found safety. I reckoned I'd served as an effective distraction and bought them enough time. Everything I was, who I was, began to slip away. The impressionable child searching for a family. The reckless teenager playing with guns. The aloof young man wandering aimlessly between lives and loves.

And, finally, the coward hiding in No Man's Land.

All in all, I'd tried to be a good guy, in my own way. But there's no such thing as a good guy with a wanted poster, is there?

A wave of comfort wrapped around me like a grandmother's quilt as I shrugged off my regrets, knowing I'd fulfilled my duty as a guardian once again. I chuckled and grinned. I was going out on a good deed, one of the best kinds you can do: laying down your life to save your friends.

I blinked and the world went dark.

NIGHTMARES III

It was morning again and the old shaman promised to meet me at the top of the butte at sunrise. Hiking up rocky slopes isn't an easy task after a night of too much whiskey, not to mention doing it with a heavy fur on your shoulders and two cups of coffee in your hands. But I didn't mind so much, considering the old man and I had wintered together a few times when I was younger. He was his tribe's storyteller, keeper of all the ancient tales passed down from generation to generation, and I'm a sucker for a good story.

Winter's dying breath hung all around us. Usually, the village was alive by now, kids playing in the fountains below, women weaving spells to accomplish the day's tasks, and men coming and leaving on various hunts. But now the pueblos carved into the sides of the crescent-shaped butte sat lonely and still.

Life around here was much more subdued, and not just because of the cold. My former associates at the cavalry, rangers and all, had radically shifted their priorities a couple weeks ago after some law got passed that gave the government the right to forcibly remove extramundane folks from their lands. Called it 'Mortal Preservation,' or something dramatic like that. It didn't sit well with me, so I cut out to hide among the sun elves at their remote home in the Rocky Mountains.

Spring had already sprung, according to the almanacs, and the ability to ride the range again ate away at my patience. Maybe in a day or two I'd get out of here. Get farther away from the marshals and dragoons who surely sought after me for going AWOL and violating my probation. The days would have already turned hot toward the Mexican border. I could head south, lay low, see what no-good schemes came my way.

I reached the top of the butte without spilling a drop of our coffee. It was pretty up here, crisp and bright. Sunshine touched the summit before it reached anything else when it peeked over the horizon. The sun shone deep orange-red this morning, and the sky was painted a cornflower blue. A few wisps of clouds stretched across the wide blue yonder, their tufts crowned in soft pinks and yellows.

The old man wasn't up here yet. He's usually up before I am, performing some sort of ritual. Greeting the dawn and burning sage was 'good medicine,' he said. After spending enough time with me, he added coffee to his list of good medicine.

"Shikoba, you up here? I brought coffee," I called, searching around.

I turned and saw no one behind me, save for a black heron perched on a rusty boulder cradled near the edge of the butte. I greeted it and drank in the splendor of its dark feathers against the majestic backdrop. After a moment, the bird spread its wings wide and turned to look me square in the eyes. It clucked a sharp and hasty warning call, repeating it over and over, getting louder each time. Behind me, a clap of thunder erupted, and I spun to see a storm gather out of nowhere.

When I turned back around, there were no clouds, and there sat the old man, cross-legged against the boulder with a small bundle of sage burning in his hands.

"Morning, old timer," I said, squatting down next to him.

"Calamity, did you bring our coffee?" he asked.

I handed him the hot cup. His aged hands quivered as he accepted it. "How about this sunrise? You ever see anything like it?"

Shikoba gazed toward the heavens but didn't react.

"I have had a vision of the end," he said.

The old man had been sick lately. Time had carved canyons in his face, sapped the black from his braids, and withered the sinews in his muscles right before my eyes.

"Whose end? Yours? Come on, you've got a few more seasons left in you. Besides, you've promised to show me Cheyenne lands, where my grandmother grew up, remember?"

Shikoba shook his head. "You cannot anchor yourself in the past to come to terms with your present. That time has passed. Besides, I've seen the end of my people, Calamity. It may not only be my time to go, but everyone in this land."

A brisk wind cut through me, and I pulled my furs around my shoulders as he spoke. The smoke from the village below blotted out the sun.

"It is not just me who knows it is the end," he said. "I see it in the buffalo, who are sacred to my people. The buffalo sustains us. Hides, bladders, stomachs, the furs that you and I wear on a cold morning, they all come from the buffalo. They are our protectors. But they can protect us no longer."

"I don't understand. What does your vision have to do with our ends?"

"When the white man wants to build a railroad, or he wants to farm cattle, he takes the land and kills the buffalo. Our buffalo resisted for many generations, but now white men have hired many hunters to do nothing but shoot the buffalo. Boys kill the buffalo. Men kill the buffalo. Soldiers kill the buffalo. Then skinners come for the corpses and pile their wagons full, so my people cannot use the buffalo parts. The skulls of the buffalo are piled as high as ten men."

I rubbed the stubble on my chin and sighed. "And now your people are starving."

"Not anymore. My people are saved."

"But not you?"

"No, I have other duties yet," he said. "But I am comforted knowing the buffalo have saved my people again."

"How so?"

"The White Buffalo appeared to me in a vision last night. She took my people to the mountain in Indian Territory. They walked past the soldiers at Fort Sill and camped at Mount Scott for one night. The next morning, the mountain's face opened wide and my people followed the last herd of buffalo inside, where they found a world that was green and fresh. The rivers ran clear, not red. The redbuds were in blossom and wild plums filled the trees. They are safe now and will never have to see this cruel world again."

The old man watched the last of the sage burn up and float away into the sky. He rested his wrinkled hand on my shoulder and squeezed. "Do you know where we are, Calamity?"

I tilted my head, confused. "We're sitting on top of Rusted Butte."

"The day the cavalry murders the desert elves and takes you hostage. The day you are branded a butcher. Why do you think we are here?"

I tried to stammer out an answer, but I didn't have any explanation. "I—I have no idea. Kael'un is dead and the elves are in mourning. Some want to mount for war, but the council forbade it."

Shikoba hummed, eyes focused on the sunrise. "The sun won't rise again here for some time. The kindred's ancestral spirit mourns their loss and curses the land with darkness."

"I didn't know you believed in elven spirits," I said.

"Many spirits governed these lands long before mortals and extramundane appeared. Some were lost to time, but others remain. Every Indian tribe or orc clan or elven kindred believes in their own spirits. Some are the same with different names. With enough belief, though, anything can manifest here, brought into existence from the energy at the Nexus." He turned to face me. "What do you see now?"

I looked down at my boots, which were firmly planted in a puddle of mud. It was nighttime and a pink storm raged overhead. Flames blazed through a massive tree, and the town around me looked like it had been rearranged by a tornado and an earthquake. But nothing moved. All was still and quiet.

"Strayhaven? What's happening?"

"This is the vision of your end, Calamity. The beginning of your end, that is." Shikoba pointed to the ground. A man lay there, sprawled out in the mud. His hands were burned and his revolver glowed red, a crackle of electricity arcing across the barrel. It was me.

I jumped back and grabbed Shikoba's arm. "Am I dead?"

"Yes," he said with a chuckle. "You opened your spirit to too much mana. You allowed yourself to be a conduit to power that did not belong to you, and you were unprepared. Your life force burned away maintaining the magic you wielded. Far too much for a mortal to handle."

I felt the urge to run, to flee this nightmare and get back to the real world. I'd wake up in my bed in my shack in the town of Hexed Springs. I'd be Cal Cooper again and I'd be just fine. I didn't want to be a part of this vision any longer.

A specter appeared out of nowhere and stepped with purpose toward my corpse. Their black cloak fluttered as they drew down their hood to reveal a skeletal visage, a ram's skull with one broken horn. Yellow flames burned within their empty eye sockets. They knelt down and scooped up a dwindling white flame hovering over my body.

The old man cleared his throat. "Wait," he said, holding out a hand. "I have claimed this soul, Death."

My jaw dropped. "Death?"

The specter did not react. A whispering voice echoed from the void before roaring into the air. "You do not claim souls, Watcher. I am the Gatherer. I ferry the dead. You observe the living for the spirit called Grandmother Earth."

Shikoba the Watcher approached the specter and took my flame into his own hands. "This one is mine. I have been watching him as I watch the earth."

"You do not claim souls," the specter said again. "We do not interfere with the actions of living beings. You watch. You observe. We maintain the cycle of life."

Shikoba smiled and rolled the little flame around his palm. He blew on it, stoking it back to a sustainable burn. "This one has violated the cycle of life. He has corrupted time and drank from the forbidden power. I am responsible for him. And, as you can see, he is no longer dying."

The specter again did not react. It regarded the old man with no expression. "You interfere with mortal lives. It is not the way of such things."

Shikoba nodded and placed the flame back inside my heart. I felt unsteady as a jolt surged through my chest. I stumbled and fell to the ground on top of my dead self as the two continued to argue.

"With the seal broken, you know the Eternals will return. I have been watching and I know it is true," Shikoba said.

The specter's yellow eyes slowly turned to him. "They cannot be permitted to return."

Shikoba nodded in agreement. "It is not

the way of such things."

The specter paused and looked down at me as I writhed at the foot of its robe. "But I collect the souls."

"You do, but there is no soul here to collect," the Watcher said, gesturing toward me. "I will take responsibility for this mortal. But stay near, old friend. There will be many souls to collect in this realm soon."

The specter lifted the hood blanketing its skeletal face with the darkness of the void and swept away in silence across the open plains.

"Shikoba, what the hell is going on?" I said from my place in the mud.

"I told you of my people and their journey to the new realm? That was Strayhaven for the elves, many eons ago. A link between the mortal and immortal realms meant to protect the two from each other. But this place was corrupted. And now it is destroyed."

My memories suddenly rushed back. Bolting from the Nexus with Abigail, Clem, and Toussaint. Strickland's deranged face as he died bleeding on the ancient tablet. Clem splitting the Sentinel clean open. Rita, the vamps, and everything in between since the Massacre at Rusted Butte.

"It's all my fault, isn't it?" I asked.

Shikoba nodded. "You may not have known it, but you played your part. The white man's greed shattered this realm, but the Cold Ones, the vampires, they poisoned it in service to the Eternals before humankind came along. The Nexus was the seal that kept the forbidden magics away from us all, severing the bridge between worlds, for fear the evil would return. But now things will never be the same. And neither will you."

I stared up at the sky, still frozen in time. A pink bolt of lightning pierced the clouds and raindrops hung suspended in the air. The lands of Strayhaven and Hexed Springs had blended together, like a deck of cards being shuffled. Nothing belonged where it was.

Shikoba knelt over me, his kind eyes holding mine. I gripped his leathery hand and felt its warmth course through me.

"Why did you save me from Death? Who are you, really?"

"I was the man you knew as Shikoba, yes. My body died three winters ago, the last time I saw you, before you were a government ranger. But one does not serve as Grandmother Earth's favorite shaman without earning a favor or two," he said with a grin. "Now I am a guardian spirit, charged with watching the plains. I am taking a great risk for you, Calamity. I have broken my pledge to never interfere with the natural course of life."

"You'd break supernatural law for me? Much obliged. I'd tip my hat to you, but I can't seem to get up," I said, trying my damnedest to get out of the mud puddle. "What happens now?"

"I will release my hold on time and allow you to cheat fate. With the seal broken, spirit magic flows freely through the world again. Many others can wield the power now. Some will perform miracles, but many will not."

He looked around at the chaos and sighed. "A dark presence looms, Calamity. I need you to be the corporeal guardian that can intervene, since I cannot. Never again."

"I'll do my best, but I don't see what one little mortal can do against some kind of everlasting doomsday spirits."

Shikoba smiled. "You will not be alone. Trust in your friends and embrace your new sorcery. Wild Magic flows through you, but do not indulge as you just have. It is no gift, but a curse. An infection. And one that will claim your life in the end."

This wasn't the first time I'd been sentenced to death. Felt different, though, when the judgment is handed down from the heavens. At first, a panic shot through my heart, then anger. Why me? Why did I deserve such a burden and responsibility? I'd been moaning and groaning for years to have the opportunity to do something legendary, but I didn't expect it to be so … heavy.

"What would you have me do that won't screw things up like I already have?" I asked. "I do not know for certain. But try being a good man and I believe the rest will make itself clear," he said.

I sighed and accepted my fate. It sounded like some of these ethereal beings had an agenda, and breaking the seal at the Nexus was the first of something terrible to come. As I stared up at the cloud, and the pink bolt piercing its underbelly, I saw them. Thousands of unblinking eyes dotted the surrounding darkness. Shikoba noticed them, too.

"I'm afraid it is time for me to leave you, Calamity. I do not know what will happen from here, but I know you will wake again and remember all of this as a very strange dream. You would do well not to forget what you have learned."

The world came roaring back. Rain splashed my face and a blast of thunder shook through me. I could hear the growls of vampires ready to pounce. When I looked back at the old man, he was gone, and a black heron stood in his place.

I watched it take off into the night sky.

Then frigid clawed hands yanked me from the mud.

CHAPTER TWENTY-FIVE

I don't know how long I was out this time. One second, I was falling apart, swarmed by vampires, and the next, I was awake, face down on a cold, dank surface. However long it was, it wasn't enough to soothe my aching body. My throat was on fire and my clothes smelled of blood and vomit, and a throbbing pain pulsed in my skull, thumping in sync with my heartbeat. What did I do this time?

Then I remembered. The vampires, the lightning, and little old me. My mind recalled it as a dream, but my body knew it was real. And it hurt. I'd bitten off way more than I could chew, a god-sized portion of mana that had fried my insides. Then the Watcher, Shikoba, came to me in a vision, said he'd allow me to cheat fate and give me a second chance.

Boy, was I in deep now.

I pushed myself up and looked around. It

took a second for my eyes to register the cage bars in front of me. I waved a hand in front of my face and blinked several times to get my vision tuned, but something was still wrong. When my hand traveled over my left eye, it disappeared into blackness. I slapped my temple and shook my head furiously, but nothing seemed to bring back sight to my left eye. I surrendered my panic once I realized that was something the guardian spirit had mentioned. That my body might never fully recover from my power trip.

I collapsed at the back of the cage and heaved a sigh. I'd been locked behind bars on several occasions. Never stayed more than a few days at most, on account of my posse always breaking me out or bribing the sheriff to 'lose' me during a prison transfer. I didn't know if my two-person posse had made it out alive or if they'd ever be able to find me, wherever I was.

The air was musty and stale, and condensation gathered lightly on the iron bars. A wooden torch sizzled in its sconce, providing the only light in the stone-walled room, which gave me a glimpse of my surroundings. Next to a table displaying a number of hooks, prongs, and needles, an iron maiden stood slightly elevated on a four-legged platform. Underneath it, a wide metal vat had been placed to catch the drippings from the torture victim. I winced at the thought of being trapped inside the horrible device. It appeared to have been used recently.

Next, I examined my cell. It wasn't very big, maybe six feet wide on all sides, and it was part of a line of holding pens, just like inside a prison. There were people in the other cages. Emphasis on the word *were*. I shoved my head between the bars and whispered for my cellmate's attention, only to see a starved and bony man panting on the floor. A thrall.

The Patriarch's guards must have taken me captive and locked me in their dungeon. That was the only place that made sense. Was I going to become a thrall, too? Enslaved to the Montagues as revenge for killing Lucius's clandestine lover? I shuddered at the thought. If that was the case, I'd rather the spirit had left me for dead.

Someone was approaching. The dull stomp of a gentleman's boots grew louder and closer. I shrank back into the shadows of my cage, for all the good it would do me. I had nowhere to run, and it wasn't like they didn't know I was in there.

Lucius Montague burst through the door and searched down the row of pens until he saw me. The vampire didn't look like his usual self. He was worked up into a rage, disheveled hair, messy attire. Despite his emotional state, he appeared to be fully human, and not like the other vampires I'd encountered lately who'd transformed into their predatorial states. As he came closer, an invisible force drew me to the front of the cage and pressed me hard into the bars. I squirmed against the cold metal and looked him in the eyes. He'd been ... crying.

"I knew I shouldn't have trusted you, human. I asked you for your honesty and you lied to my face," he screamed, his voice exploding through the small space. He reached inside the bars and gripped me by the throat, throttling me against the cage three times before dropping me to the floor.

My head rang, but I managed to sit up and face him, despite being dazed. "Lucius, Lord Montague, however you prefer to be addressed, I swear to you I had no idea what I was getting into."

He leaned forward and spit at me. "Save your deference, worm. You killed my true love and abducted my daughter. You will tell me where she is now or I will pull it from your mind, slowly and painfully."

"Strickland's wife, yeah. You were the one she was having the affair with." I wiped his saliva off my cheek. The liquid burned like oil from a chili pepper. "I didn't know she was the girl's mother and, truthfully, I don't know where your girl is."

"Strickland never loved Leah. He only used her to climb rungs of the social ladder," Lucius snapped. "I was her true love. There was nothing duplicitous about it. We were to be wed, damn you." He banged his fist against the bars.

"A vampire marrying a mortal human

woman? Your father would have never allowed it."

"Leah didn't have to be human forever. We'd sworn a blood oath to love each other forever, despite her mundane origins. She willingly asked to become a vampire, so eternity could be ours," he said mournfully.

I came to my feet and shambled up to the cage door. "I saw what you were keeping down there. That was no human or vampire. She was a feral monster. There was no saving her, and you know it. Your daughter was half-dead when I found her, too. You oughta thank me for getting her out of there."

Lucius gripped the bars, rattling them so violently I thought they'd come loose. "You know nothing about the transformation. They both could have turned out fine, if you'd given them until the next full moon."

"So until then, you thought you'd keep her locked up down there? And what if she had stayed feral? Were you going to feed her cattle and miners forever?" I growled back. Our voices boomed through the chamber.

Lucius turned sharply and scoured the room, then, without losing his intensity, lowered his voice. "The cage was for Leah's safety. She was in an uncontrollable fugue state. She had broken loose several times looking for Abigail. I couldn't risk anyone discovering her. Especially not my family. I expected Strickland to raise and protect our daughter, thinking she was his own, until I could find a better solution."

I scoffed. "You know, this is sweet and all, and I'm somewhat sorry for your loss, but you're, what, hundreds of years old? I'm having a hard time believing you fell for some human woman and had it in your demonic heart to become a daddy."

The temperature dropped a few degrees and the light within the room dwindled. "I don't need to justify my decisions, my life, or my love to anyone, let alone mortal filth like you."

Even in the face of Lucius's power, I felt a surge of confidence. The chances of me getting out of here safely were slim. With my back against the wall, literally, I thought up a gamble, a desperate last-ditch effort to save my hide before I went down fighting.

"Look at it this way, neither of us are innocent here. Your decisions killed a few humans, humans I happened to know personally, and mine killed a few vampires close to you. You let me out of here so I can find your daughter, and when I bring her back here we can call it even."

Lucius laughed, a sad, yet grim laugh. "I must decline. For the past two weeks, my men have raided human homes and began removing them from our newly combined realms. It will only be a matter of time before I find Abigail myself. In the meantime, I expect you to remain here and suffer."

My jaw dropped. The past two weeks? I'd been down here longer than I thought. Sounded like humans were getting a taste of their own medicine. After forcing the extramundane from their homes, they've gone and experienced the same thing. Sometimes, two wrongs do, in fact, make a right, but none of this felt good—even if humankind deserved it.

I clenched my fists and ground my teeth. "I won't let you turn me into one of these thralls, if that's what you're thinking."

Lucius took his eyes off me and casually rubbed his forefinger and thumb together. "You should know, I have, personally, never taken a thrall, nor did I support the use of them. I had planned to outlaw the practice when I became Patriarch someday. After careful consideration, I have decided my father was right. There can be no peace as long as humans live unchecked upon the earth. You will serve as a fine species of chattel. That said, I don't wish to ever see your face again. I'll be offering you to my sister as payment of an overdue debt. She'll come to claim you as soon as she finishes galivanting across the world, whenever that may be. Until then, you'll stay here and rot, while I force you to relive your most painful memories, day after day, until I've dominated your spirit completely."

"You didn't happen to count how many of your vampire cronies I blasted away before they brought me in, did you? What makes you so sure

I won't do the same to you?"

Lucius got a real kick out of that. "I'm aware of your newfound abilities to cast magic. Thankful, too, that you dispatched my father's forces so I could capture you for myself. You're not the only mortal to gain the ability to manipulate nature, you know. But, like all other humans, your mortal coil lacks the ability to wield it." He smirked and pointed at my ghostly white eye and charred hands. "I am, frankly, surprised you hadn't killed yourself already."

The vampire called my bluff. And he was right; there was no way I was going to be able to call up any magic in my current state, especially not enough to defeat someone as powerful as him.

I raised my hands in defeat. "Okay, okay. I'll tell you where the girl is. I just need you to do one thing."

A curious look crawled across the vampire's face before it was replaced by a surprised satisfaction. He leaned in toward the cage. "What do I need to do?"

"You need," I said, holding back a snicker, "to go get a tan."

Even Lucius chuckled at my joke. He shook his head before meeting my eyes again. His expression now cold and empty. Without saying anything, he turned and made for the door.

"The next time I see you, ranger, you'll be nothing more than a bag of blood used for feeding my family. That, or my sister's slave. Your choice."

CHAPTER TWENTY-SIX

I woke up in a sweat for the next few days. Nightmares found me much more easily ever since Lucius's threat to make me relive my worst memories. Some nights I could feel a presence in my mind picking and poking around my thoughts. Other nights, not so much. I was so tired. My willpower was slipping. And I stopped caring.

My weariness didn't help ease my claustrophobia. I can't stand being cooped up for long. Winters can be unbearable, if I'm trapped in a cabin for too long. Maybe over the years I became addicted to living on the trail, hopping from one town to another. Or maybe it was the thought of becoming stagnant. What good is life if you're not living it, spitting in the face of people who won't let you be free? If I hadn't got myself caught up in this ancient blood feud, I'd probably have been cutting out of Hexed Springs. Instead of rotting alone in a jail cell.

A pair of thralls came and went, delivering only enough sustenance to keep me alive. I didn't even mind the occasional maggot after the fourth day. Everything tastes good to a starving man. The thralls never listened when I asked for steak and potatoes, nor would they bring me a stiff drink. In fact, they never talked back. They carried out their tasks with blank stares and empty expressions. Made me miss talking to my horse.

My stomach started to twist something awful today. I tried to doze off a few times to make up for the lack of sleep last night, but the pangs were too powerful and wrenched me awake every time. The thralls only provided a small bowl of water a day, and my parched mouth felt like sandpaper.

I was ready to give up. If I was going to end up as some blood bag for a Montague vamp, I may as well get on with it. No one was coming for me down here. Hell, outside of me and the Montagues, I couldn't think of anyone who knew this dungeon existed.

Or so I thought.

Gunfire popped in the hall outside the dungeon door.

Whatever was happening, it was sudden and it was quick. Shouts, grunts, and screams clambered after the ruckus. A thrall dressed in a servant's outfit rushed through the heavy oaken door guarding the holding cells. Before he could bar the door, his abdomen burst open from buckshot fired from the flared barrel of ebony and gold guns. In stepped the fashionable Toussaint, his navy-blue jacket flowing like a duster in a high-noon duel, followed immediately by Clementine, her befeathered hat and trusty rifle gleaming in the torchlight.

"Bonjour, Cal Cooper," Toussaint said. He blew out the smoke puffing from the ends of his pistols while the elaborate tubes and gears coiling around them loaded his next shot.

"Lord above, Cal, you look like hell. What happened to your eye?" Clem asked.

"Good to see you, too, Clem. I'll tell you later. What the hell are you two doing here?"

Clem smashed the lock on my cage. "Rescuing you, dummy. What's it look like?"

The door swung open, and I stretched my arms and legs once again. It hurt like hell. My joints were rusty and my spine was full of knots.

"Got a gun for me?" I asked, rubbing my thighs to force blood into my legs.

"No, but your circus buddy, Oliver, provided us with an outline of this place. There's an armory on our way out. Reckon that's your best bet," Clem said.

I growled in disappointment. I'd felt incomplete without Cloudsplitter at my side. Damn vamps better not have lost it.

"I'm damn glad to see you both," I said. "No offense, but I'm surprised you came, professor. Reckoned you'd had enough taste for adventure after the sky fell around us."

Toussaint shrugged. "Au contraire, mon amie. I was happy to volunteer to fly in the face of danger once more. Even when there was no time to prepare."

Clem laughed. "Actually, I guilted him into it after I told him I was your only friend willing to help. Said as a gentleman he couldn't let me go it alone."

"Well, it's the thought that counts," I said with a smile. "Never thought I'd say it, but I missed that sour attitude of yours."

She feigned a gag. "Time in the joint's made you soft. You can hug us after we escape this hellhole."

Clem led the way, taking us out into a long stretch of corridor lined with dark stones hewn from some faraway mountain. Like the dungeon, it, too, exuded a dank coolness. As we walked, the gloominess eventually transitioned into an elaborate manor hall, accented with the beauty of decor and artifacts afforded by medieval wealth.

"Where are we?" I panted. It took a while for my lungs and legs to get used to moving again.

"In the tunnels beneath the Montague estate," Clem said. "We came in through a chasm created when Strayhaven fused with Hexed Springs. Lucky your pal Oliver found it or else we'd have never found you. We can't go back the way we came from, though."

"Did you consider sneaking in and not

drawing the attention of everything within a mile from here? In my experience, a jailbreak works better when the alarms haven't been raised," I said.

Clem shot a thrall charging up behind us. "In my experience, people say 'thank you' when they're being rescued. And, for your information, we were being stealthy. That is, until the professor here got trigger happy."

Toussaint rolled his eyes and shook his head. A few steps later, he stopped in front of a wooden door with an iron ring pull handle. "I believe this is the armory. Your belongings should be inside. And for the record, I was not trigger happy. I was merely startled during an attempt to collect a biological sample from a thrall that I thought was dead."

"Let the man collect his samples, Clem," I said.

Clem covered the hallway as Toussaint and I stood on either side of the big door. He tossed me one of his fancy pistols. His homemade gun was top heavy, with all its added mechanical bits, but the grip was almost more comfortable than my own revolver's.

Almost.

With a nod, Clem kicked open the door. Three thralls snapped to attention and charged as a unit. Within a heartbeat, they were in firing range. Toussaint and I stood side by side and blasted away. My target fell backwards like he was being yanked down with a rope around his neck. I was surprised at how strong the pistols were and how quickly they reloaded. The gears whirred and clicked another round of buckshot within a second of firing.

Two of the thralls lay dead, both victims of mine, while Toussaint was still firing. He'd clipped one with a few pellets, slowing it down some, but largely missed anything vital to stop it. The last guard leapt over a trunk and fell dead as I finished it for my partner.

"When this is all over, would you be open to shooting lessons?" I asked.

He wagged a finger. "That would be unnecessary. I believe my weapon simply needs calibration. I was hitting all of my targets up until now."

"Sure, sure," I said, nodding. "Now help me search through this mess for my stuff and let's get out of here."

We stepped over the dead thrall and examined the room. Dozens and dozens of dark bottles were stacked inside a rack, specially crafted to handle their shape and size, that ran the length of the leftmost wall. Not only was it an armory, it was also a wine cellar. Perhaps during soirees and fancy shindigs liquor makes a decent weapon in the subtle war of words.

I searched the cabinetry lining the other side of the room. It was loaded full of munitions organized by size, shape, and lethality. These weren't run-of-the-mill weapons; they were state-of-the-art, military-grade armaments and explosives. I scanned some of the more unfamiliar pieces. "They've got enough firepower to actually take on the army in this arsenal."

"Cal, your belongings," Toussaint called.

Clem was getting antsy guarding the door. "Pick up the pace, boys. More could be on the way."

My bandoliers, duster, bandana, satchel, and hat had been casually piled on a table in the corner of the room, while my holster and gun belt were slung over a chair. I grabbed my black bandana first, tying it up like an eyepatch across my left eye. I strapped the rest of my gear on quickly, inspecting each piece as I went. My knife was safe in its sheath, and there were still plenty of bullets in the bandoliers. I picked up the gun belt and took out my Cloudsplitter, still gleaming in all its glory. I jumped when a pop of static electricity zapped my hand. Latent power left over from the collapse of the Nexus pulsed through my grip, and it felt great.

After getting a taste of raw power, perhaps now I'll know just how to wield it and stay within my limits.

"Anyone coming?" I asked Clem.

She lifted her rifle and rested it on her shoulder. "I can't hear anyone. You ready to go?"

"Not yet. I want to know what's going on above ground first."

"We'll tell you later. Now, come on," Clem pleaded.

I crossed my arms and gave her a look. She sighed, knowing I wouldn't leave without an explanation. "It's been a few weeks since the night you disappeared. The vampires have been attacking us almost every night. They claimed to have declared war against humankind. No matter how many we kill, it seems like they just keep coming. Toussaint and I managed to hold them off for a while, given my newfound sharpshooting skill and his knowledge of their weaknesses, but we got overrun a few times and barely escaped with our lives. Not long after, the elves and other extramundane came to our aid. Things are about to stalemate, Cal. But if you could do your thing and melt half a hundred more vamps with your lightning, then maybe we can finish them off for good."

"Afraid that'll never happen again. See my eye? Price I paid to wield that much power. Write that down in your journal, professor. Humans can't just use magic as they please."

To no surprise, Toussaint holstered his gun and produced his notebook, jotting down what I'd said.

"What about the girl? My horse?" I asked.

"Both fine. Buck's safe with the Eriksen girl and her dad, and Abigail's under the care of the elves. That boy, Aldon, convinced them to take her in, even though she's half-vampire."

I breathed a sigh of relief. I felt a burden lift knowing everyone I cared for had made it out safely the night I was captured.

I folded my arms across my chest and looked at Clem. "I've got one more thing to ask of you two. And I don't think you're going to like it."

"Sure, we've come this far. What else can I do for you?" Clem said, sarcastically.

"Even though things may seem to be coming to a stalemate, Lucius Montague isn't going to stop his war against humans. And he'll stop at nothing to see me dead if I escape. I need to kill him first."

Clem groaned. "What's one more vampire? He's only some kind of prince of darkness, but sure, let's knock him off, too."

"You've got the right idea, Clem. I like your attitude," I said with a smirk.

"And just how do you plan on taking him down? Don't imagine plain bullets are gonna do much good. You said yourself you can't wield much magic right now, and I sure as hell don't know what I'm doing with my powers."

Clem and I continued our bickering until Toussaint interrupted us.

"Excuse me," he said. He was holding an open bottle of wine. He swirled it casually, then peered down the neck.

"If you two will listen to me for a moment, I believe I have a plan."

CHAPTER TWENTY-SEVEN

"You know where you're going?" Clem asked as we approached the end of the maze of tunnels we'd spent the last ten minutes running through.

"Not really, but I reckon if you're tracking a prominent philanthropic vampire through his stately manor, you go room by room until you find the most luxurious one," I said.

"Lord above. This plan better work," she said.

We came up to a homely little staircase that looked like it led to a servant's door. We each nodded, checked our gear, and marched up one by one, not sure what was on the other side. I carefully pushed open the door, revealing an elegant ballroom.

I looked back at Clem. "Remember the Hawthorne Bank in Las Cruces?"

"Oh, this is much fancier than that," she said, her eyes all agog over the exquisite decor.

The Montague's grand ballroom was, indeed, far fancier than the Hawthorne Bank. I drank in its extravagance. The vaulted cathedral ceiling was embellished with detailed frescoes depicting ancient histories. Long blood-red drapes hung alongside the dark stained-glass windows that decorated one entire wall of the room. On the opposite wall hung more majestic family portraits and a variety of sculptures. A painting of Nosferatu, an ancient, supreme vampiric demon and the first ancestor of the Montague lineage, stared down from the center of the mantel. His cold eyes followed me as we moved through the room.

Thick marble columns bore the weight of the room, like Atlas holding the world, each bearing a golden plaque featuring the family's crest, a letter 'M' emblazoned upon a pair of rapiers crossing behind a horned skull. There was even a grand piano resting in the corner with its lid propped open, displaying a gilded interior.

At the rear of the room on an elevated dais sat the pièce de résistance—a sinister throne composed of black branches that had been braided together, curling around the riser like ivy. The ominous chair was smooth as driftwood, yet spined with thorns long as my arm.

I'd probably have considered taking more time to enjoy the ballroom's incomparable and unrivaled beauty, if Lucius Montague and his entourage hadn't been standing directly ahead of us.

Their black eyes settled on us as we approached the dais, and each vampire, except Lucius, was practically licking their chops. Lucius was wrapped in a black shroud. Hate simmered in his eyes and his long, black hair tied neatly in a bun on his head. He was backed by four other vampires, each of equally charming looks and monochromatic Gothic attire. They were primed for a fight.

Lucius calmly dropped his outer cloak and removed his dinner jacket, then rolled up his sleeves to elbow length. "Your attempt at escape ends here, ranger. Pity my sister won't be able to enslave your mind, but she'll understand that I needed to put you down. Perhaps I'll eat your friends first and make you watch."

I tipped my hat to the vamps. "Appreciate the offer, gentlemen, but I'm afraid we can't stay for supper. I'm somewhat embarrassed that I did not bring the proper evening attire."

One of Lucius's cronies bared his fangs in a huge grin. "What about that one?" he hissed, pointing to Toussaint. "He knows how to dress, for a human. My lord, I ask for the pleasure of consuming this one for myself."

I took a few steps forward. "Now, hold on, pal. Didn't your vampiric demon spawn of a mother teach you it ain't right to play with your food? We won't leave you empty-handed, though. We were kind enough to bring up a few bottles from your wine cellar for you to enjoy instead."

The vampires scrunched up their faces in confusion.

"What on earth are you talking about?" Lucius asked.

Toussaint unbuckled his jacket and spread it wide like a pair of wings. Using his shoulder holster, he'd strapped two bottles to his chest. He slipped them both out, smoothly uncorked them, and swirled one under his nose. "I must confess, this particular vintage is divine. Very rare to find such a liquid around Hexed Springs. Why don't you have a taste?"

With one swift movement, he chucked both bottles in the air toward the dais.

"Now, Miss Clementine!"

Like tracking a clay target at a firing range, Clem followed the bottles until they were right over the vampires. She fired one shot and shattered both bottles, letting their contents rain down on the monsters below. They shielded their fine garments with their arms. For a moment there, I reckoned they thought they were about to be sprayed with white wine. Shame they were mistaken, though.

The liquid hit all five vamps, Lucius included. Before they could shake any of it off, they screeched and flailed wildly, their skin sizzling and erupting in a burst of steam.

Turns out we hadn't found the wine cellar

after all.

We'd stumbled upon the Montague's hidden supply of holy water meant for their treacherous kin.

One by one, the vampires fell to their knees, writhing in agony as they cursed us in an ancient tongue. Their appendages cracked and folded in the wrong directions. Some of them were trying to save themselves by transforming into their true form, but it didn't matter. They fried like bacon in a hot, greasy skillet.

All of them except Lucius.

Whether he hadn't received a lethal dose of the holy water or was more powerful than we knew, I wasn't really sure. But in between his squelching and coughing, this prince of darkness successfully transformed into something truly horrifying. His tattered clothes ripped at the seams as he grew ten times his size. The pale white flesh disguising his true form fell away, revealing gray, leathery, moist skin underneath. His legs also bent in the wrong direction, something akin to a dog's hind legs, while batlike wings spread to fill the room. A pair of horns pierced through his skull and black ooze dripped from his almond-shaped eyes.

It took my breath away. And not in a good way.

The beast growled and gripped the air, as if he were tearing apart a piece of cloth. As he spread his hands apart, the wall behind him tore open, and a black mist fell at his feet. Four dark tendrils manifested from the dark vapor mist and coiled around the fallen vampires, or, rather, what was left of them. The corpses dissolved into the mist, which enveloped Lucius's demon form, and sprouted forth from his chin as octopus tentacles. The elder vampire roared, glowing with a frightening fel energy.

Clem, Toussaint, and I didn't wait around to watch the full transformation. We each got a few shots off before Lucius bowled toward us. His claws longer were than knife blades. The dark mist swam around us as he clawed at my eyes and chest.

Clem and Toussaint sputtered out coughs as Lucius prepared for a second attack. I froze in panic, trying to think of a way to kill Lucius or get my friends out. All I could think about was watching Rita driving Bartholemew into the flames of her home as it burned to the ground. Which gave me an idea.

Vampires don't like sunlight and can't survive in it with too much exposure. A vast manor like this doesn't *not* have windows, though, right? I bet the lush curtains and tapestries served another purpose besides bringing an air of aristocracy to the place. They blocked the sunlight during the day and were drawn open to allow in moonlight at night.

"Clem, shoot the braziers," I yelled.

Clem pawed at her swollen eyes, but managed to find a clean shot. She nicked the brass bowl at the top of the brazier holding the fire that illuminated the ballroom. The flames spilled out and licked at the curtains. After a few moments, they lit up like campfire tender and sunlight poured across the room, sizzling the demon's scars where the holy water had burned through. Lucius darted back toward the dais, which was still shrouded in darkness. On his way back, he whipped an inky tendril at Toussaint, knocking him into the grand piano. He yelped in pain as the piano let out a discordant tune.

Meanwhile, anger radiated from Clem. Her eyes flashed emerald green and her hair burned like orange flame, just like it had before she destroyed the Sentinel. She threw off her hat and leveled her rifle, aiming at the tentacles dangling from Lucius's chin.

Her rifle boomed, cranking out four shots in rapid succession. Each bullet found its mark, slicing the tendrils right off the demon's face. He roared in pain as they flopped to the ground, wriggling like chickens with their heads cut off. A pair of them rolled down the dais into the sunlight and melted into a bubbling, black ooze. Another coiled itself around the spiked throne, splintering it into pieces.

Lucius rubbed at his injured chin as Clem and I reloaded. His voice boomed through the ballroom. "I can do this for eternity, mortals. With the seal broken, I wield my creator's power.

Your attacks are futile."

"Reckon you say that once this room fills with sunlight," I said, sidling up next to Clem.

Lucius made an unnatural noise like an inverted laugh and raised his hands toward the sunbeams streaming in. He chanted in that ancient tongue again, drawing a finger across the room. As he did, the black mists floated up, coating the walls and ceiling in deep shadow.

"Futile," he repeated.

The knot in my gut told me he was right. Clem's emerald-green eyes faded as she succumbed to fear. I prepared to surrender myself in exchange for my friend's lives. I holstered my gun and raised my hands above my head. Lucius hummed as I stepped forward, allowing me to approach.

Which is when I noticed the professor had scampered out of the piano and was standing behind Lucius's wing. He was clutching a thorn longer than a French baguette.

Hope welled up inside me. I stoked it, allowing it to fill my soul. I took a deep breath, closed my eyes, and watched a brief moment in the future play out in my mind.

I turned to Clem and winked. "Play along."

She stared at me with an empty and hopeless expression, then nodded.

I slowly climbed the steps to the dais, then fell to my knees. I lowered my hands and gave the professor the signal to wait, all while keeping my eyes trained on the demon.

"I submit," I cried. "I submit. Just spare my companions. Please."

Lucius stared at me for a moment. All traces of the handsome vampire had gone now, replaced by something purely evil. The tentacles were growing back, and the black ooze continued to drip from his eyes.

"No," he said.

Then he picked me up and drew me up toward the tentacles. They lashed at me, sticking to my skin and coiling around my body.

"Now," I yelled.

The professor darted out of the shadows and launched the thorn upwards. The thorn spun end over end. I snatched it out of the air just as a tentacle coiled around my throat and I drove the stake into Lucius's heart.

His tentacles went slack and whipped around violently as the darkness spell failed. Sunlight flooded the room again, reactivating the boiling effects of the holy water, and continued stripping away the demon flesh. Clem channeled her fury into bullets, each whizzing above my head, ripping apart Lucius's face. His claws released me as he stumbled backward, but I managed to hang on to the thorn and plant a boot in his chest, giving me the leverage to drive the stake in even further. Almost like drilling for oil, I hit a vein and black blood sprayed across the room like a geyser. I leapt down just as Lucius tripped over the shattered throne and fell to the ground. He flailed and slammed his claws down, again and again, cracking the marble floors.

Clem, Toussaint, and I joined up again, side by side, and pointed our weapons at the unholy beast. Clem's head became wreathed in flame once more. She lowered her silver barrel, and Toussaint extended both his mechanical flintlocks. I aimed Cloudsplitter right between Lucius's eyes.

Buckshot, lightning, and hellfire hit the demon at the same time. His whole body arched as the empowered bullets burst through his skull. He screeched a terrible guttural noise as the tentacles groped at the hole in his head, digging out the black slime dripping out of the wound. The black vapors fluttered and dissipated, unable to mend his wounds.

I plucked another long shard of black thornwood off the marbled dais as I walked up to the panting demon. The black ooze had dried from his eyes, and our gazes met. His eyes were full of terror. I wondered what he saw in mine.

Whatever it was, it was the last thing he ever saw.

I pressed the second thorn into the hole in his skull. His limbs seized up and every last bit of his breath escaped from his body. His pupils faded to white. I stood there for a moment, his black blood pooling around my feet, and watched him die in silence.

Toussaint walked over to me with a slight limp. Clem wrapped an arm under his and helped him along.

"You all right, Cal?" she asked.

"Sure," I said.

"I know that look. You ain't all right."

"It's nothing. Let's get out of here before anybody else shows up."

The ballroom was quiet except for our footsteps. I spied a corridor that led to two very tall doors and motioned for my partners to follow me.

"Consider yourself rescued, mister," Clem said as we hoisted open the giant door. "Professor, you ended up being pretty useful back there. I think it's safe to say you might just fit in with us gunslingers."

Toussaint hobbled up to us and laughed. "Kind of you to say, but I believe I prefer the safety of academic research. I may have had my fill of adventure." He was shaking.

"They all say that, but the thrill never goes away forever. You'll be back at it," Clem said.

"I'll take your word for it, Miss Clementine. Now let us …" Toussaint's eyes became glued to a bookshelf in an unoccupied study near the main entrance. He went over and picked up a handful of thick volumes that had been resting on an ornate pedestal.

"What's that you're stealing?" I asked.

Toussaint hugged the old tomes to his

chest and wrapped his jacket around them. “Something far more valuable than a biological sample.”

Clem jabbed her elbow at me. “Reckon your bad influence is rubbing off on him, don’t you think?”

CHAPTER TWENTY-EIGHT

Three whole days passed by without me thinking about anything that had transpired at the Montague mansion. After we put an end to all the mortal and immortal threats, Toussaint went back to his vardo and read over the books he'd stolen. Said they contained valuable information that he'd share with me soon. Clem made me lunch and then let me sleep in one of her premium rooms for some R&R. I felt like a king after staying in that cramped cage down in the dungeon for so long. After a series of hot baths, a few more good meals, and a couple glasses of whiskey, I was ready to rejoin the post-Collapse city of Hexed Springs.

Clem set a plate of beef and potatoes on the bartop for me when I came downstairs. She even gave me a helping of her famous blackberry crumble, my favorite dessert.

"Let me see that eye of yours," she said,

peeling back the black bandana. She inspected it. "Hmm. Still bone white. Can you see this?"

She snapped her fingers near my blind eye.

"Nope," I said.

"You know how the papers dubbed you 'Deadeye' all those years ago? The nickname really fits now, doesn't it?"

I let out a loud huff. "Har har."

Steam rose off the potatoes and the beef looked tender and juicy. I scooched the plate closer to me and chowed down. After being alone in the dark for weeks, I felt like I needed to practice talking all over again, and Clem was happy to lend an ear. She pulled out a rag and started polishing the bartop as I chatted away, describing how I used mana to harness the power of a thunderstorm, how I cheated death, and anything else we hadn't covered already.

And probably a few things we had, too.

"You know, I noticed a different view out of my window this morning. Is it true everything in town got shuffled around?" I asked.

Clem nodded. "Mmm hmm. Whole town seems rearranged, like somebody shook up a jigsaw puzzle, dumped it out the box, and called it finished. We now live in a sprawling metropolis of mismatched architectural styles from across history."

"Ain't that something," I said. "Gotta learn how to navigate town all over again."

"Strayhaven is no more. It all got shuffled

into Hexed Springs. The parts that survived, that is. We've started calling the new central avenue 'the Dust.' It's handy to orient yourself to it and then work your way out from there. I think it's the only part of that paranormal town that stayed the same after the Nexus blew up. Still has all the same shops and such. The ruins of the temple are there, too."

The layout of the Dust ran through my mind while I chewed on a blackberry seed. The elven quarter with its treetop cottages, the odd cottage called the Elixirium, the little red-light district. Didn't make sense to me how everything could fit together unless Hexed Springs itself grew to three times its original size.

"While I'm thinking about it, have you seen my house? I might have left the door open and I'm hoping all my stuff is still inside."

Clem let out a tense exhale. "Yeah, about that. I found your house. Oddly enough, it got resituated not far from here."

I hopped up from the barstool. "Ain't that something? I can come see you every day, neighbor. Let's go see it."

"No need. It's nothing but a heap of rubble."

I groaned and let my fork fall to the plate with a clang. "Aw, hell. Somebody go and cave in it?"

"Doubtful. Seems to me you've got no one to blame but yourself for building a shoddy old outhouse for a home. Poor thing probably couldn't withstand the earthquake and being jerked across town. Don't worry, I'll keep your room open for you," Clem said.

"But what about my valuables?"

"Cal, the only thing valuable in that place was the painting I gave you all those years ago. Damn fine piece of art. It's a shame it got mangled in the fall. I did find a stuffed fish, though. Hung it up on the wall there. Hope you don't mind."

My prize catch looked good on the wall of the new and improved Howling Beast Saloon & Inn. It really tied the room together, if you ask me. Clem had the place polished up and repaired, complete with brand-new dining room tables with luxurious velvet chairs. Seemed like it would have cost her a pretty penny to fix all that damage.

She interrupted me as soon as I opened my mouth. "Don't say nothing. I know what you're thinking."

"What?"

She slapped the wet rag on the counter and stared me down. "You're gonna ask me how I paid to fix this place up because you've still got your half of the loot on your mind."

I tilted my head and clicked my teeth. "Well, I wasn't going to say anything, but ..."

Clem sighed and reached under the counter. She hauled out a fat stack of cash tied together with a red bow, dropping it on my empty plate.

"I was going to wait until your birthday, but since you're so impatient, I reckon I'll give you your present now."

My eyes grew wide as I thumbed through the money. I lost count after I hit two thousand. It was plenty more than she owed me, plus interest.

"So the natural world really has gone topsy-turvy, huh? You knocking off banks again?"

A sly smile crossed her freckled face. "Yes and no. Turns out Ross Strickland held the lien against my saloon. I reckon that he owed me, seeing how it was his men and machine that tore up the place, and since he died and doesn't need all that money anymore, well ..."

"You paid the bank a visit and the money was just lying there, so you kept it as your own?"

"Something like that," she said with a chuckle. "Cal, you really should see the place for yourself. Rumor has it Strickland's own security forces raided his mansion, his bank, anything that had his name tied to it. It's emptier than a beggar's pantry."

I took a moment to revel in the schadenfreude. "Serves him right. Probably forced all those men to work for him the way he did me. He had it coming if you ask me. Kinda jealous I didn't get in on any of that score."

"And here I was telling you to answer his wanted ads. At least you were the one to put a bullet through him, even if it did sort of lead to a series of apocalyptic events."

"Sure."

I paused longer than I should have to answer her and looked out the window. To anyone unaware of our town's turmoil, it would have appeared to be a perfect summer afternoon.

"Ah, now, there you go again. I slap down a tower of cash in front of you, after you, me, and the professor survive taking down a corrupt tycoon and a super demon, and all you wanna do is mope?"

I knew she was poking fun, but I didn't feel like playing along. Something had been eating at me since I watched those men die. It brought up a lot of questions, ones I'd bottled up inside since I arrived at Hexed Springs.

"Clem, I've been thinking ..."

"Did it hurt?" she said. She cut her laughter short when she saw my blank stare. "I'm sorry, Cal. If you're wanting to talk, let's talk."

I waved her off and sighed. "Nah, it's nothing."

Clem placed her hand over mine and looked me right in the eyes. "Cal. Talk. I'm listening."

I wasn't sure where to begin and, honestly, I wasn't even sure what I really wanted to say. I shifted in my seat, cleared my throat. "Look,

Clem. You know why I came to Hexed Springs."

"Sure, I do," she said. "You stood up to cavalry after they used you to kill those poor elves. That big heart of yours made you do the right thing, and you came looking for help."

"That's not the only reason. I came here to punish myself, to force myself into exile, so I'd stop acting like a fool. After we parted ways, I couldn't stay out of trouble, fighting and robbing folks I had no business messing with. Turns out I was lashing out, angry at losing everyone I'd ever known. Of course, I didn't realize it at the time but I was spiraling, something the law picked up on real quick. Once I got tired of running, I got desperate and joined the army in exchange for my freedom. All the good that did."

"I told you, Cal, gunslingers just don't have a place in the world anymore."

"I don't believe I share the sentiment," I said. I tilted my head and averted my gaze. "If anything, the past few days have shown us there might be plenty of need for gunslingers. Particularly ones with certain magical abilities."

She blew out a breath and paced away, then came back with her hands on her hips, her lips twisted in frustration. "I thought I made it clear that my life was here at this saloon, taking care of my girls and my sweet little Angus. You still expecting me to throw caution to the wind and ride out for vengeance against some ideal we once believed in, all those years ago?"

"Vengeance is an idiot's game, Clem. Just look at Strickland and Lucius. Matter of fact, look at me. Vengeance fools you into thinking you're doing the right thing, when all you're doing is helplessly rolling along like tumbleweed, caught up in greedy schemes that offer nothing but pain and regret." I took a moment and peered out the window again. Across the way, sitting on a barrel of water was a black heron, its long yellow beak tapping at the water's surface. I smiled. "And I reckon it's time to stop fooling myself."

Now it was Clem's turn to let silence fill the conversation. She looked around her fancy new establishment. "Life was good to me after I left you behind. No offense to you, but I had to. Once I'd gone, I finally found my happiness. Took me long enough. Lord knows I traveled down my fair share of dead ends," she said, twirling a finger through her hair. "But now I'm here. And now you're here."

"Yep, now I'm here," I said.

"Cal, I realize now that I tried to manipulate your happiness. I thought what was good for me would be good for you. But truth is, we're not all on the same path, nor is there a miracle cure for all life's ailments."

"Oliver Van Pelt would argue with you there, but go on."

She rolled her eyes. "And for the low, low price of ten dollars, I'm sure he'd let you have a measly ounce. Listen, if you want to leave Hexed

Springs and go your own way, I'd understand. You can ride out and find your own purpose, your own happiness. If that's what you really want."

"I hear what you're saying and it all makes sense. But I reckon Hexed Springs is my home now. It's time for me to stop searching for meaning in the past and start living for right now. Make my own luck again. Besides, I've got business to attend to here. People are counting on me now."

"That's what I like about you, Cal," she said with a smile. "Sure, your methods might need work, but you're always looking to help out. What I'm trying to say is that I know who you are, but maybe you've been feeling confused because the problem is that you don't?"

"Could be. Only time will tell, I suppose. For now, I've got a purpose. There's a little girl orphaned because of me. And I know how hard it is to be one. I might not be the most upstanding citizen, but I'm a better influence than none."

Clem leaned over and gave me a peck on the cheek. "You're a good man, Calamity Cooper."

And in that moment, I was at peace with myself. I liked the feeling. It was better than any feeling I'd ever found in a bottle. I smiled an honest smile, which Clem returned.

Clem clapped her hands together and leaned over the bar. "Why don't we get out of here? Go take a walk around the new town."

I gathered my hat and placed it upon my head. "I'd like to go see Abigail first, if that's possible."

Clem took my arm and escorted me out into the dusty avenue. "I've already arranged a visit for you tomorrow morning. But today, I've got somewhere important for us to be."

* * *

Clem led me down to the meeting hall where an emergency town meeting had been called. I was surprised to find so many non-human folks in the room, new faces packed shoulder to shoulder like a can of sardines. Even grouchy Colin was there, although he stuck to the corner nearest the entrance. I tipped my hat to him from across the room, but he refused to return my greeting. I noticed Mr. Eriksen and Astrid, one of the few people I recognized, as I scanned for more familiar faces.

"Oh, and that reminds me," Clem said, "I took Buck over to the livery. Those two have been looking after her."

"She's in good hands, then. I should go see her. Want me to take you along? Properly introduce you?" I asked.

"To your horse?"

"No, dummy, the attractive gal who takes care of her."

Clem stuttered, then waved a flustered hand at the suggestion. "What? Don't be silly."

"When's the last time you had a date? You've been too busy running this joint to pursue the affairs of the heart," I said with a sly grin.

Her face flushed red and she flashed me a playful look. "Calamity Cooper, I swear. It is none of your business, mister." I could tell she was thinking about it. After a moment, she cleared her throat. "But if you wanted me to accompany you, just for a brief chat, I reckon I wouldn't say no. I like barnyard animals. And strong metal-working gals. But that'll have to wait."

Clem winked at me and pushed me deeper into the crowd. I reluctantly snaked my way through as folks made way for Clem. She climbed the steps to a platform, where a lectern was placed square in the middle. I found my own corner of the room and leaned up against the wall. All this public speaking stuff wasn't my thing. As Clem got ready to speak, Toussaint wandered over to me and clapped a hand on my shoulder. We exchanged smiles.

Clem knocked on the speaker's podium and said in a commanding voice, "All right, let's get this over with." The room went quiet as everyone gave her their full attention. "It's been a month since our little town, or towns, I guess, got smushed together. I don't know much in the way of magic, but something tells me things ain't ever going back to the way they were. So here we are, mortals and immortals, sharing the same space."

A murmur rippled through the crowd. A man raised his hand and began to complain, but Clem cut him off. "I don't care how you feel about the extramundane, Rufus. Right now we're going to get along and make this work for everyone, understood? Anyone else have a problem with that?"

Nobody said anything other than "no, ma'am."

"All right, then. Who wants to give us an update on the state of the community? Professor DuBois, why don't you go first?"

Toussaint's presence elevated the IQ of the room, not to mention his outfit classed up the place. He sported a purple jacket with gold buttons and flared sleeves. The crisp upturned collar of his undershirt stood tall around his neck. A vial of raw mana was suspended from a silver chain around his neck. He'd come dressed to impress, like it was some kind of formal affair. Although, I reckon that's just how he dresses on Wednesdays.

"My friends, I have good news and bad news. The good news: I was recently the recipient of a substantial gift and research grant from the Order of Odd Fellows, an organization dedicated to studying the occult mysteries and histories of our world. A trunk full of translated copies of Merlin's archives, saved from the ruins of the Library of Alexandria, I might add, were delivered before the Collapse." He stood there proudly, waiting for applause I reckon.

Nobody in the room reacted.

"The complete archive of all supernatural knowledge? A prestigious organization of the occult funding my research? Is this not impressive?"

"I think it's mighty impressive, sweetheart."

My heart leapt as a familiar voice cut through the crowd and a woman stepped forward. She stood tall and proud among the others, despite still nursing substantial burn wounds.

"Now how about the bad news?" Rita said.

Toussaint sighed. I patted his shoulder and whispered, "I'd be interested in those books later, mon amie." He smiled then continued.

"The bad news is I've postponed my research into the Nexus ruins. I hope to continue my research there someday, but right now my skills as a physician are in dire need. Many mortals have developed supernatural powers, some which have caused them injury. I am happy to report, though, most patients seem to be adapting well to the increased presence of mana. I haven't lost a soul in two weeks."

"What about the extramundane? Any word on dangerous spell-slingers we should know about?" Clem asked.

An elven elder rose to speak. I hadn't met

him, but he looked like a fighter, someone who'd dealt with dangerous and powerful foes for a living. "I have performed a thorough audit of the roster of inmates sentenced to the Underkeep. There are, indeed, missing detainees, many of whom pose a significant threat to defenseless mortals."

Right on cue, Oliver Van Pelt pushed himself up on a thin black cane, sensing a business opportunity. It had a jewel-encrusted skull on top that matched the brooch on the velvet vest under his usual black-and-white striped suit.

"The Elixirium is happy to supply its patented potions to assist the magicless humans within Hexed Springs. My wagon is parked outside in the town square where I will demonstrate its effectiveness after this meeting concludes. Bulk pricing is available," he said with a flourish.

A few folks with desperate, worried eyes dug into their pockets for cash.

"Save your solicitations for after the meeting, please. This goes for everybody," Clem said, exasperated.

Oliver bowed his head. "Apologies, Miss Clementine. In that case, may I provide an update?"

Clem nodded in a way that meant 'make it quick.'

"Trade has been disrupted for some time now. As some of you are aware, no posts or telegrams have arrived since the Convergence either.

After an independent investigation conducted by yours truly, I've found that the telegraph lines were snapped. Even more curious, the maps I used to navigate the region are no longer accurate." He removed his top hat for dramatic effect. "It appears we are cut off from the outside world, for the time being."

"That's just dandy," Clem said. "I propose we ration supplies until someone can get the area mapped again and update the trade routes."

"I can do that," Rita volunteered. "I know this land better than anybody. I can untangle these paths and fix them on a map in no time."

"I'll go, too," a new voice said. The tall woman wore a ten-gallon cowboy hat and hawk feathers for earrings. I recognized the scars on her leather vest. They were markings accrued through lots of hard work and exposure to the elements.

"Name's Ruby Dunne and I deliver post for the Pony Express," she said. "That is, I did, until me and my fellow Freedmen and Freedwomen found our town mysteriously relocated a few miles from yours. I've got a stagecoach and a quick horse, and I'm pretty good with a rifle. Never been robbed, neither. I'll help get this territory explored. But y'all are gonna have to help us out, too." She shot a hard glance over to Amos and his Confederate uniform. "Starting with removing any reminders of the failed Confederacy and the enslavement of my people."

Everyone turned to Amos, who sat still, lost in a daydream. He snapped out of it after Ruby cleared her throat.

"Oh, these old threads? Found 'em in an open grave a few years back," he said.

"Will somebody clothe Mr. Martin in something less offensive? I mean that in both smell and symbol," Clem said, burying her face in her hand. She looked up at the ceiling and whispered a curse, then turned back to Ruby. "We're happy to help, Miss Dunne. Now who else?"

Mr. Eriksen shot up an eager hand. "My daughter, the master blacksmith, has performed a miracle. I don't know who knows this, but I reassembled our family forge, stone by stone, after we journeyed from our homeland across the Atlantic. After the Collapse, the ancient runes glow once more, and my daughter can forge weapons and armors with mystical properties, just like our Viking ancestors once did."

My ears perked up. With my newfound disposable income, I'd have to look into her services.

People murmured amongst themselves, waiting for someone else to speak. Clem rapped her knuckles on the podium.

"If there's no one else, I reckon we oughta talk about the elephant in the room." Everyone seemed to know exactly what she meant, and dread fell upon the crowd. "Fighting between the vamps and mortals has stopped. Can't help but feel a storm brewing between us, though.

For now, I urge everyone to lay down your arms against your extramundane neighbors, but stay vigilant for the vampire threat."

Oliver twisted in his seat before interjecting. "My contacts say that despite the death of Lucius Montague, the old Families still retain most of their influence within the paranormal hegemony. But there are rumors of a developing power vacuum that we must be aware of."

"Care to elaborate, mister?" someone said from the back door. I unfolded my arms and stood to attention.

Amos turned and bowed down low in his goofy, overly polite manner. "Excuse me, miss. Why don't you come in and have a seat? You can take mine."

I cursed under my breath. I never travel anywhere without Cloudsplitter, but given the trauma of the past few days, I must have left it behind in my room at Clem's. I prayed I wouldn't need it as I stared down the vampiress standing in the doorway, one Amos had just invited inside.

Her eyes sparkled as she accepted the invitation. Amos offered his hand, which she accepted, squeezing his fingers as he led her to a chair. Her black leather boots tapped with authority across the wooden floor. She released him from her grip as she sat, flashing her fanged smile, which made Amos titter and stumble like he'd just finished off six pints of beer. She had on a black leather vest with gold trim and a red necktie, with tight pants to match. She relished having all eyes on her.

"I don't suppose you'd mind a paranormal representative of the old Families on your little city council, would you?" she asked, blinking doe eyes at Clem.

Oliver stood up and removed his hat. "For those of you who don't know, this is Miss Lilith Montague." He spun around to face her, his deference—or ass-kissing, as I like to call it—on full display. "Of course we would welcome your esteemed presence, as well as your valuable input. I simply meant there are others that would seek to create an imbalance of power with your family during its state of mourning."

Lilith threw up a hand. Her black nails peeked through fingerless gloves. "My father, the Patriarch of House Montague, mourns my brother's death, true, but has decreed there will be no ill will for killing my brother. His leadership had, sadly, become a detriment to our family. In Lucius's stead, my father has given me his full support as his successor and primary heir. At my behest, the family is fully prepared to assimilate with the mortals and continue our philanthropic efforts in order to make Hexed Springs a peaceful home for everyone."

Somehow, I didn't believe all that. I looked at Clem, who was already looking at me. Her stare told me she was thinking the same thing. Maybe my distrust of wealth and authority was rubbing off on her. I don't think Rita was fond of Lilith either. She stared at her with visible disgust.

"I reckon we'd be grateful for the support," Clem said, arching an eyebrow.

"Good," Lilith said. "Now, I'd like to discuss the fate of the Strickland girl, Abigail. What is her status?"

Toussaint leaned forward and addressed the vampiress. His pupils dilated as he locked eyes with her. "She was very ill, afflicted with both the symptoms of pneumonia and vampirism. I discovered she was actually half-vampire, half-human, which complicated her treatment. I believe her immune system was compromised as another vampire had tried to re-infect her with vampirism."

"Interesting," the vampiress purred. "My brother very much wanted her to become a member of the Montague family, but that view was not shared by our Patriarch. We wish the girl to remain in human custody."

A shocked murmur went around the room. A woman pointed at the vampiress, tears welling up in her eyes. "Do you know how many of us your kind has killed over the past month? How many children were orphaned or murdered?" Her anguished voice spoke aloud what I'm sure many folks were thinking.

Lilith folded her hands over her lap and hung her head. "I am truly ashamed and disgusted by what happened. On behalf of my family, I apologize profusely for what my brother's retinue did to your people. Rest assured, everyone who served under Lucius and fought in the chaos will be tried and executed as a show of good faith."

Another man rose. "To hell with all that! You and all your kind will rot in hell. Just who do you expect to take care of Strickland's girl?"

Lilith ignored the comment. Her professionalism didn't waver at all, but she seemed aware of the townsfolk ready to tear her to pieces. "Her welfare is of mortal concern. However, the family will make a financial donation to whoever aids in her transition."

Oliver seized upon the opportunity to turn this into a business deal. He said, "And I would be thrilled to utilize those funds in order to create a home for the newly displaced and orphaned normal and paranormal children across town." He drew a rainbow shape in the air with his hands as if painting words on an imaginary sign. "I'll call it the Orphanarium."

Several folks groaned and sprang to their feet, flinging curses left and right. Things were starting to get out of hand. Before blows could be exchanged, I wandered out of my corner and divided the crowd. People shut up real quick as I raised my hands. They looked upon me with a hint of respect, something I wasn't used to.

"I'll take her. And I don't want your family's money. I'll care for her on my own," I said.

The room stayed quiet. Lilith's fangs poked into her lip as she smiled in smug satisfaction. "Very well. I think everyone here should not forget that you killed dozens of my kind the night of the Collapse. I believe we should celebrate this diplomatic offer as an olive branch between our kinds."

"We'll see," I said, coolly, as I leaned back against the wall.

Lilith rose to her feet. "I appreciate the invitation to have a voice in mortal affairs. Again, I hope you'll allow me the opportunity to prove to you that I am truly in favor of rebuilding this place with peace and prosperity in mind, along with providing reparations for the horrible atrocities committed by my brother's retinue."

Most folks, extramundane and human alike, avoided her eyes and grumbled amongst themselves. After a sufficiently awkward pause, Lilith took it as her cue to leave, bowing before us all and walking out of the meeting hall. She quickly escaped from the sun and climbed into a black, windowless stagecoach waiting for her outside.

After she'd gone, Clem looked out on the crowd who watched her, waiting for her to lead. She looked at me for a moment, pleased as punch, yet serious about the reality of the situation.

"I know I'm not alone in the opinion that

we need a form of protection from the vampires. We can't trust their peace offering without having some kind of armed assurance of our own. Any ideas?"

Rita glanced over at me then stood up. "I think we should pool together our resources and hire a marshal."

Clem nodded. "Since we live on unincorporated land, our marshal won't have any real legal authority beyond what we bestow upon them. But, as a former outlaw living in a territory known for its banditry, I propose we avoid the term 'marshal' and hire something more akin to a guardian, like the rangers of old."

"That's a great idea, hun," Rita said. "I nominate Cal Cooper as the new guardian and ranger."

I jerked my head to the platform. Clem stood there, smiling. Part of me wanted to flee and never look back; I was done being a ranger.

"I second the nomination," Toussaint said. "My friend Cal Cooper is an accomplished gunslinger and budding wizard. I'll volunteer my research and manuals into spellcasting to train him until a proper sorcerer can make him an apprentice."

"I don't know, y'all," I said.

Before I could say anything more, Oliver held his hands high and agreed with performative joy. "Marvelous idea, all! Cal Cooper, the man who released us from the iron grip of debt and who destroyed the Montague threat. The legendary gunslinger and reformed outlaw. He's a perfect fit. Hear, hear!"

"Hear, hear," the crowd roared back in agreement.

I was stunned by the show of support. Something told me Clem and company had planned this all along.

Clem gestured a hand at the crowd. "You're the best guardian we've got, and not a bad one to boot. Your closest friends all vouch for you. What do you say, Cal?"

I stood silent for a moment as every eye in the place stared me down in anticipation. I had spent my whole life thus far sticking it to Uncle Sam and his lawmen. I was used to being a social bandit of the frontier, a romanticized rebel of the wilderness, and a ruffian who had ridden off into the sunset against his own wishes. It didn't matter if the Watcher was right. Even if I was only a man at the wrong place and the wrong time, it was high time for me to stay put and handle the responsibility being thrust upon me. I chuckled at the irony.

"Mighty kind words, everyone. I reckon if this is what y'all want, I'll be happy to oblige."

I eyed my companions and smirked.

"But I'm gonna need a posse to do it."

EPILOGUE

That night I sat alone in my room, ruminating on my many thoughts, as I watched my candlestick burn down to the quick. The drinking parlor below was silent and empty; Clem's hired hands had closed up for the night. Renovations and preparations for a formal grand re-opening were nearly complete.

Angus pushed open my door and trotted inside. The dog made himself comfortable on my pillow, but I honestly didn't mind. I stroked his old, gruff head as he dozed off to sleep.

I touched my blind eye. So much had happened.

Our little world had changed here in No Man's Land. Paranormals and normals thrust together like never before, living on top of each other. In some instances, quite literally. It would only be natural for conflict to bubble up. And now I was the first and only line of defense, in case the Montagues broke the peace agreement or some other supernatural monstrosity paid us a visit.

Once again, I'd found myself thrust in the spotlight. At least this time, it was for something a little more honorable.

Things were about to get weird in Hexed Springs, I could feel it. Trouble was brewing, no doubt in my mind of that. There were rumors that powerful and dangerous extramundane—the ones who'd escaped the Underkeep—had been seen around the city. And those were just the local problems we knew about. It was only a matter of time before Marney, the cavalry, and the whole US government caught wind of our situation. A seemingly endless magical resource and a population to exploit? The feds would be drooling like a hog dreaming of dinnertime.

For all my disdain for law and order, I was confident in my decision. This town needed a guardian, someone who could ward off evil magics and protect the populace from threats, internal and external.

I ran my hand over Cloudsplitter and caught my reflection in its polished metal. It was time to turn over a new leaf, become a new man and brave another frontier, one more personal and vulnerable, not to mention dangerous. I was finally going to redefine what it meant to be a ranger and a peacekeeper. And the first person I was going to help was a little girl, who I was excited to actually meet in the morning.

And so, after years of robbing, shooting,

looting, thieving, lying, cheating, and generally riding in defiance of the law, I'd finally crossed a line and done something that I never would have imagined in a thousand years.

I, Calamity Cooper, newly minted wizard gunslinger, became Hexed Spring's first supernatural sheriff.

Cal Cooper will ride again.

NO MAN'S LAND: PLAIN SIGHT
COMING 2022

ABOUT THE AUTHOR

Luke Atkinson

Luke is an award-winning writer and communications professional. Born in Oklahoma in what was once No Man's Land, he was immersed in Wild West mythology and tall tales while growing up on the Great Plains. Luke graduated from the University of Oklahoma with a professional writing degree in journalism. Today, he lives in Chicago with his wife, son, and two big dogs.

www.ingramcontent.com/pod-product-compliance
Lightning Source LLC
LaVergne TN
LVHW020518100826
845148LV00010B/1272

9780578309057